Sweet Rivalries

Aurora Delaney

Published by Aurora Delaney, 2024.

SWEET RIVALRIES

First edition. October 8, 2024.

Copyright © 2024 Aurora Delaney.

ISBN: 979-8227127457

Written by Aurora Delaney.

Chapter 1: Whispers of the Past

The moment I stepped inside, it felt like the world outside faded away, replaced by the warm, inviting glow of the chocolatier shop. Max looked up, his expression transforming from concentration to delight as he caught sight of me. "Well, if it isn't the prodigal daughter," he exclaimed, wiping his hands on his apron. "Back from the big city to grace us with your presence?"

I rolled my eyes, but the smile tugging at the corners of my mouth betrayed my amusement. "I wouldn't say 'grace' is the right word, but here I am, in all my unglamorous glory." The shop was just as I remembered, its walls lined with jars of colorful confections, and the display case teeming with truffles that glistened like jewels. Each one seemed to whisper secrets from our childhood, secrets we had shared over countless afternoons spent concocting chocolate-covered dreams.

Max leaned against the counter, his dark curls falling into his eyes, and there was an undeniable warmth in his gaze. "You look good, Clara. New York hasn't chewed you up and spat you out just yet?" He leaned in closer, lowering his voice as if sharing a precious secret. "Or did you finally figure out how to survive in that jungle?"

"Barely," I confessed, running a hand through my hair, a gesture that was starting to become habitual. "It turns out surviving is much easier when you have a safety net, like a small town filled with chocolate and old friends." I took a step closer, feeling a twinge of nostalgia as I watched him expertly roll a truffle in cocoa powder.

"Ah, yes. Safety nets and chocolate. The twin pillars of a well-balanced life," he quipped, his laughter ringing through the air. For a moment, I let myself bask in the comfort of his presence, the familiarity of his teasing bringing back memories of lazy summer days spent on the porch, concocting grand plans of escape.

"Speaking of safety nets," I said, my tone shifting slightly as I leaned against the counter, "what's become of this place? I half expected it to be gone, replaced by some trendy brunch spot where avocado toast reigns supreme."

Max's expression turned serious for a moment. "Well, you know how it is. The town has changed a lot since you left. Some shops have closed, and new ones have opened, but this place? It's still holding on, thanks to your mom and her secret recipes." His eyes sparkled with mischief. "And my questionable ability to keep up with demand."

I chuckled, imagining the chaos of busy afternoons, customers eagerly waiting for their chocolate fix. My mom had poured her heart and soul into this shop, using her talents to create something beautiful. It was more than just a business; it was a legacy.

"Your mom's still here?" I asked, my voice softening at the thought of her familiar embrace. The warmth of our memories flooded back, of afternoons spent in the kitchen with her, learning the delicate art of tempering chocolate.

"Of course! She's practically glued to the shop," he replied, gesturing to the back room where the soft clattering of pans could be heard. "She'll be thrilled to see you."

Just then, the bell chimed again, and the door swung open, letting in a gust of autumn air that carried with it the rich scents of cinnamon and nutmeg. A couple entered, hand in hand, laughter spilling into the shop as they scanned the display case. I took a step back, allowing myself to blend into the background for a moment, content to watch Max in his element.

"Two truffles, please," the woman said, her voice bright and cheerful. I could see the way Max's eyes lit up as he engaged with them, his charm effortlessly disarming.

As they chatted, I felt a pang of longing. It was strange how easily I slipped into the role of a bystander in my own life. Here I was, back in my hometown, yet I felt more like a ghost haunting the spaces of my past.

Once the couple left with their sweet treasures, Max turned back to me, wiping his hands on his apron again. "So, what's the plan? Are you here to stay, or just passing through?"

I hesitated, the question hitting closer to home than I expected. The truth was, I didn't know. My life in New York had been a whirlwind of ambition and exhaustion, filled with the bright lights of opportunity but shadowed by the relentless pace that left little room for anything real. "I... I'm not sure. I thought I'd take some time to figure things out, maybe help out here for a bit," I admitted, feeling the weight of uncertainty settling in my stomach.

Max raised an eyebrow, his expression playful yet probing. "Help out? You mean I'll get a break from your sarcasm while you dive into the world of chocolate? This is a surprising twist."

I couldn't help but laugh. "Hey, it's a skill I've honed over the years. I can provide comic relief while also covering for you during rush hours. A win-win."

He stepped closer, crossing his arms with a mock-seriousness. "You realize it's not just a job, right? This place has its own rhythm. If you jump back in, you might find more than just chocolate waiting for you."

A sudden chill ran down my spine, the weight of his words sinking in. Did I really want to face the ghosts of my past? The lingering memories of old loves and unfinished business? Yet, something about the idea of rekindling the bonds that once defined me felt both terrifying and exhilarating.

"Well, I can handle a little chaos," I replied, forcing a smile as I shifted my gaze to the colorful jars lining the shelves. "After all, what's life without a little sweetness mixed with chaos?"

Max's grin returned, and I could see the approval in his eyes. "Then welcome back to the chocolate kingdom, my friend. Just be warned—once you step in, it might be hard to leave."

His words hung in the air, a tantalizing promise mingling with uncertainty. As I inhaled the rich scent of chocolate and sugar, I felt a spark of hope igniting within me. Maybe, just maybe, this return could be the beginning of something beautiful, something worth savoring.

As I settled into the rhythm of the shop, the vibrant hum of customers filled the air. Laughter mingled with the clinking of china and the soft sound of music playing in the background. The walls were adorned with whimsical artwork of chocolate creations, each piece telling a story of indulgence and nostalgia. I moved around, reacquainting myself with the familiar chaos that felt strangely comforting.

"Can you believe how busy it is?" Max called out, deftly stacking boxes of chocolates with a speed that made my head spin. "It's like the entire town decided to come out for a chocolate emergency today."

I grabbed a few truffles from the display, the smooth chocolate melting in my mouth. "It's a good thing you're the hero of this story, then. What would they do without your culinary wizardry?"

"Probably buy subpar chocolate from that new place across the street," he replied, rolling his eyes dramatically. "You know the one—the one with the overly pretentious name? 'Cocoa Nirvana' or something like that? As if chocolate needs to be elevated to spiritual levels."

I chuckled, imagining the hipster vibe of that shop. "Next, they'll be selling organic, ethically sourced, gluten-free chocolate bars with quinoa. The horror!"

Max snorted, but the sound quickly turned into a mock-serious expression. "I'd rather stick with your mom's family recipes and let the rest of the world figure out its chocolate identity crisis. Who needs spiritual enlightenment when you have dark chocolate with sea salt?"

I watched as he expertly decorated a cake with a flourish, each swirl of frosting a testament to the artistry he had perfected over the years. It was inspiring to see him thrive in this environment, and I felt a pang of jealousy mixed with admiration. Here was a man who had turned his passion into something tangible, while I was still fumbling in the shadows of my own ambition.

"Do you ever think about expanding?" I asked, genuinely curious. "You could have a bakery-café combo! Chocolate croissants, rich mocha lattes, the works."

Max raised an eyebrow, an amused smirk creeping onto his lips. "And you'd be my secret weapon? The prodigal daughter turned barista? That's a plot twist I didn't see coming."

"Hey, I'm all about multitasking! I can serve coffee and throw in witty repartee to elevate the experience. You'd have a hit on your hands," I said, leaning against the counter, embracing the lightness of our banter.

"True," he said, "but what if you discover you're allergic to caffeine? Then we'd have a real crisis on our hands."

"Fine, I'll stick to chocolate then. But seriously, Max, you've created something special here. It deserves to be shared with more people. Just think of all the chocolate lovers out there who are missing out."

He paused, contemplating my words as he arranged a batch of truffles into a box with meticulous care. "You know, Clara, sometimes I think about it. I just don't know if I'm ready to take that leap. It's one thing to manage this place; it's another to expand and risk everything."

"I get it," I said softly. "But sometimes, taking risks is how we grow. Look at me—I took the leap to New York, and I'm still trying to figure out what that even means."

"Speaking of risks," he began, his tone shifting slightly. "What about you? Are you just going to stay here and work in the shop? Or do you have some grand plans up your sleeve?"

I opened my mouth to reply, but the words caught in my throat. The truth was, I was still figuring it out. The idea of returning to New York seemed daunting, and yet the thought of sticking around in this familiar place felt suffocating. "I guess I'm just... exploring my options," I finally said, forcing a smile.

Max raised an eyebrow, clearly unconvinced. "Exploring, huh? So, you mean wallowing in nostalgia while trying not to face the music? Classic Clara."

"Is that what you think?" I shot back, feigning indignation. "I'm simply embracing my roots!"

"Embracing your roots while avoiding reality? Sounds poetic," he quipped, leaning in closer with a teasing grin.

The banter felt like a lifeline, grounding me in a moment where everything else felt uncertain. "Alright, Mr. Chocolate Wisdom. I'll take your critique under advisement."

We shared a laugh just as the bell chimed again, and a familiar face stepped inside. My heart did a little flip. Emily, my high school nemesis turned college friend, stood at the entrance, a look of surprise washing over her features as she spotted me.

"Clara Hart? Is that really you?" she exclaimed, her voice a blend of disbelief and delight.

"Emily! What a surprise!" I stepped forward, a mix of emotions bubbling to the surface. We had once been so close, but life had a way of tossing people apart.

"I heard you were back in town, but I didn't believe it until now. How long has it been?" she asked, her eyes sparkling with genuine curiosity.

"Too long," I replied, attempting to summon the camaraderie of our past. "I just needed a little break from the city chaos."

Emily nodded, glancing at Max as if processing the scene. "And it looks like you're fitting right back in," she said, her tone laced with intrigue.

"Trying to," I replied, feeling a twinge of vulnerability. "Max was just reminding me how much I've missed this place."

"Ah, yes. The sweet siren call of chocolate and nostalgia," she mused, her smile wide and bright. "So, are you staying for good or just dipping your toes back in?"

Max jumped in, his playful demeanor returning. "She's considering becoming my right-hand woman here in the chocolate kingdom. I'm trying to convince her that it's a brilliant plan."

Emily's eyebrows shot up. "Really? Clara, that could be a game-changer for you! What do you think?"

I hesitated, suddenly aware of the spotlight on me. Here, in the chocolate shop where I had spent countless hours, surrounded by laughter and comfort, was the possibility of a new beginning. Yet, it felt as if I was standing at a crossroads, the weight of decision pressing heavily upon my shoulders.

"I think it could be fun," I said slowly, measuring my words. "But I also need to figure out what I really want."

Emily tilted her head, studying me with an intensity that made me feel exposed. "You don't have to have it all figured out right now. Just take one step at a time."

Her sincerity wrapped around me like a warm blanket, urging me to confront my fears. Maybe this unexpected reunion was exactly what I needed to reignite my passion. As the laughter and chatter of the shop enveloped us, I felt a flicker of excitement. The future was unwritten, and perhaps it was time to embrace the chaos and sweetness of life again, one truffle at a time.

The chatter in the shop was vibrant, weaving a tapestry of voices that melded with the clinking of utensils and the comforting sound of chocolate being tempered. I watched as Max expertly maneuvered through the chaos, every motion fluid and confident. It was impressive how he transformed the madness of a busy afternoon into a dance of creativity and joy. I felt a rush of warmth, a realization that maybe I had been missing out on more than just the chocolate; I had missed the connection, the laughter, the sense of belonging that came with sharing life's simple pleasures.

Emily leaned against the counter, her arms crossed, an amused smile playing on her lips as she observed Max. "So, what's your secret, Max? Is there a hidden stash of cocoa beans in the back that keeps you this energetic?"

Max flashed a grin, wiping his brow with the back of his hand. "You caught me! I'm actually fueled by pure chocolate and a sprinkling of delusion."

"You'd think you'd be more humble," she replied, rolling her eyes, and I couldn't help but laugh at their playful banter.

As they exchanged quips, I couldn't shake the nagging feeling that I was at a pivotal moment, teetering on the edge of a decision that could change everything. A sudden rush of confidence surged within me, and I turned to Max. "Alright, I'll take the plunge. I'll help out, but I demand a fair salary: unlimited chocolate and the title of 'Chocolatier-in-Training.'"

Max feigned deep thought, scratching his chin dramatically. "Hmm, I'll have to consult my board of directors. But I think we can negotiate some kind of arrangement."

I rolled my eyes but felt a surge of excitement bubble up inside me. "Fine, but I want to learn how to make those lavender-infused truffles. They always seemed so fancy, like something out of a Parisian café."

"Deal," Max said, sealing our agreement with a mock salute. "Prepare yourself for a culinary journey that will involve a lot of mess, more laughter, and probably a few too many chocolate-covered disasters."

Emily chimed in, her eyes sparkling with mischief. "Oh, this is going to be a social media sensation! 'Clara's Chocolate Catastrophes' could be your brand."

"Or 'Clara's Confections Gone Wrong.' That has a nice ring to it," I shot back, unable to suppress a smile.

As the afternoon wore on, I settled into my new role with unexpected ease. I found joy in wrapping truffles, packaging them with care, and writing cheeky labels. Max guided me through the intricacies of chocolate-making, his enthusiasm contagious. The shop became a whirlwind of creativity, our laughter mingling with the clinking of dishes and the rhythmic sound of chocolate being poured into molds.

Just as I was getting into the groove, the bell chimed again, and a gust of cool air swept through the shop, drawing my attention to the doorway. A figure entered, tall and striking, with tousled hair that framed a chiseled jaw. My heart skipped a beat as I recognized him—Jake, the boy who had once been the center of my teenage universe, now a man who somehow managed to look even better than I remembered.

"Clara?" he said, his voice warm and familiar.

"Jake," I breathed, caught between surprise and a wave of emotions I hadn't anticipated.

"What are you doing back here?" he asked, his eyes flickering with curiosity as they roamed the shop before landing back on me.

"I just moved back," I replied, my heart racing. "I'm helping out at the chocolatier shop."

"Ah, the sweet life," he said, grinning as he glanced around. "Looks like some things never change."

"Like your knack for showing up at the most inconvenient times?" I teased, my voice sharper than I intended.

He laughed, an easy sound that wrapped around me, making me feel uncharacteristically warm. "You have no idea. I was just passing through town when I caught a whiff of something divine. I had to investigate."

Max, ever the opportunist, jumped in. "Well, if you're looking for divine, you've come to the right place. Clara here is officially on board to help make our chocolate dreams come true."

Jake's eyebrows shot up, a playful glint in his eyes. "So, the city girl has come back to her roots? That's interesting."

"Don't make it sound so ominous," I replied, unable to shake the feeling that this was a test I hadn't studied for.

"Just curious," he said, his expression shifting slightly as he leaned against the counter. "What made you come back after all this time?"

I hesitated, the truth sitting heavy on my chest. "Just... needed a change," I managed, focusing instead on the truffles I was wrapping.

"Ah, the classic escape. Don't worry, I won't pry." He studied me for a moment, and I felt the weight of his gaze. "But it's good to see you. Really."

"Thanks," I replied, wishing I could summon the courage to tell him how much I had missed this place—and him.

The air between us crackled with unspoken words, and as Max tried to steer the conversation toward chocolate flavors, I felt the tension shift. Jake was here, and the memories rushed back like a tide, drowning me in the sweetness of our past.

"I was actually going to ask if you wanted to join us for dinner tonight," Jake said, his tone casual but the glint in his eyes suggesting there was more beneath the surface.

"Dinner?" I echoed, caught off guard. "With you?"

"Why not? It's been ages since we caught up. We can reminisce about the good old days and laugh about how naive we were."

I opened my mouth to refuse, the instinct to protect myself bubbling up, but the idea of sitting across from him, sharing stories and laughter, felt tantalizingly tempting. "Okay, why not?" I said, surprising even myself.

"Great! I'll pick you up at seven?"

"Sure." I smiled, feeling both exhilarated and terrified.

As he turned to leave, my heart raced. The moment felt charged, electric, as if the past was colliding with the present, opening the door to possibilities I had never considered.

"Clara!" Max called, bringing me back to reality. "Are you ready to make those lavender truffles?"

"Absolutely," I said, shaking off the whirlwind of emotions.

But just as we began to gather the ingredients, the door swung open again, and a rush of cool air swept through the shop. A figure stepped inside, their silhouette casting a shadow that made my heart drop.

It was Kate, my childhood rival, who had made it her life's mission to one-up me at every turn. I hadn't seen her since high school, and the last thing I expected was to find her here, in the place that had once been my refuge.

"Clara Hart," she said, a smirk forming on her lips as she surveyed the shop. "Back to play chocolatier? How quaint."

I swallowed hard, feeling the tension in the air shift once more. "What do you want, Kate?"

Her smile widened, the glint in her eyes sharp. "Oh, just wanted to see how the competition is doing."

My heart raced, the sweet anticipation of dinner with Jake fading into the background as I braced myself for whatever was coming next.

Chapter 2: Melting Hearts

The warm glow of the shop enveloped me like a cozy blanket, filled with the rich aroma of dark chocolate and the sweet notes of vanilla wafting through the air. I stood at the counter, my hands dusted with cocoa powder, rolling chocolate ganache into perfectly rounded truffles. Max was nearby, his laughter echoing like music as he dipped fresh strawberries into a bubbling cauldron of chocolate. Each fruit emerged with a glossy coat, shimmering under the soft lights that hung like stars from the ceiling. It was a scene straight out of a fairytale, and I couldn't help but feel a sense of enchantment wrap around me, pulling me back from the shadows that had lingered since my departure from the city.

"Careful there," he teased, flicking a drop of melted chocolate in my direction. "That's a one-way ticket to a sticky situation."

I chuckled, dodging the chocolate splash with a feigned gasp. "You think you're clever, don't you? Just wait until I show you my secret ganache recipe. Your little games won't stand a chance."

Max feigned horror, his eyes widening comically. "Not the secret recipe! Anything but that!" He clutched his heart, dramatically stumbling back against the counter.

We both laughed, the sound weaving through the air, bright and carefree. Each shared moment seemed to stitch together the fabric of our friendship, pulling it tighter and more vibrant. As I watched him work, the way his brow furrowed in concentration and the playful smirk that danced on his lips, I felt a warmth bloom in my chest. This was home—filled with laughter, creativity, and the delightful mess of our shared passion.

But as I mixed ingredients, a small voice in the back of my mind whispered doubts. How could I reclaim this joy when my heart still carried the weight of my past mistakes? My heart thudded against my ribcage, a steady reminder that I was still the girl who had left the city in a whirlwind of chaos, leaving behind shattered dreams and unfulfilled promises. I bit my lip, pushing the thoughts aside as I watched Max expertly twirl a strawberry, coating it in the velvety chocolate with a flourish.

"You're getting better," I remarked, nudging him with my elbow. "Pretty soon, you'll be a professional chocolatier."

"Ha! You say that like I'm not already a professional," he replied, his tone mock-serious as he expertly raised an eyebrow. "I mean, look at me. I'm practically the Picasso of chocolate."

"More like the Picasso of chaos." I smirked, watching him stumble over a bowl of nuts that had rolled off the counter.

"Hey! I meant to do that," he shot back, grinning as he knelt to pick up the mess. "It's an abstract representation of the art of chocolate-making. Very avant-garde."

I couldn't help but shake my head, my heart swelling with affection for this man who brought such lightness into my life. In those moments, as laughter echoed off the walls and the air shimmered with the scent of chocolate, I found solace. Maybe it was possible to carve out a new beginning, one truffle at a time.

The hours slipped away, and soon the sun began to dip below the horizon, painting the sky in soft hues of lavender and rose. Max stepped back from the counter, admiring our work—a stunning array of chocolates and confections, each one a tiny masterpiece.

"Not too shabby, right?" he said, crossing his arms with a satisfied grin.

"Not too shabby at all," I agreed, feeling a swell of pride. "We make a pretty good team."

As we began to clean up, I noticed a change in the air, a tension that lingered just beneath the surface. When our eyes met, the playful banter faded into a silence that felt charged, electric. It was as if a thousand unspoken words danced between us, waiting for the right moment to break free. My heart quickened, pounding against my chest like a caged bird, eager to escape.

"Hey," he said softly, his voice low and serious, breaking the momentary stillness. "Can I ask you something?"

"Sure," I replied, feeling a flutter of anticipation mixed with trepidation.

"Why did you really leave the city?" His gaze held mine, searching, as if he could see through the layers I'd wrapped around my heart.

The question hung in the air, heavy with implication. I opened my mouth, but the words faltered, caught in a web of hesitation. I had rehearsed this moment a million times, preparing for the inevitable confrontation with my past, but now, standing in the cozy warmth of the chocolate shop, the weight of my truth felt unbearable.

"Max, I..." I began, feeling the heat rise in my cheeks. "It's complicated."

"Complicated is good. Complicated means you're human." He stepped closer, his eyes unwavering. "I just want to understand you better. You don't have to share everything, but I want you to know I'm here, whatever it is."

The sincerity in his voice melted some of the ice surrounding my heart, and I felt a flicker of hope stir within me. Maybe it was time to unburden myself, to let someone in. I took a deep breath, summoning the courage I had so long buried.

"Okay," I whispered, my voice barely audible. "I'll try."

His smile returned, warm and inviting, as if he had just cracked open a door to a world of possibilities. With each passing second, I felt the distance between us close, the weight of my fears lifting just a little. The moment stretched, taut with anticipation, as we stood on the precipice of something new—something that felt both terrifying and exhilarating.

The realization washed over me like a wave, invigorating yet daunting. For the first time, I felt ready to explore the depths of our connection, even as shadows of my past lurked nearby, reminding me that the road ahead wouldn't be easy. Yet, standing in that little chocolate shop with Max, I knew I wasn't alone anymore. And perhaps, just perhaps, it was worth the risk.

The evening air was thick with the sweet scent of chocolate, curling around us like a warm embrace as I gathered the remnants of our late-night escapade. The shop, usually filled with customers buzzing about their sweet cravings, was now a tranquil sanctuary, lit softly by the glow of fairy lights that flickered above us. Each twinkle cast a soft glow on the glossy confections we had painstakingly crafted together, turning our work into an art exhibit of decadent treats.

Max wiped his hands on a flour-dusted apron, the fabric stretched across his broad shoulders, making him look even more enticing in the dim light. "So, what's next on our chocolate odyssey? Are we going to revolutionize the way people eat candy?"

I grinned, tossing a stray piece of chocolate at him, which he dodged effortlessly. "Only if you promise to wear that ridiculous apron while doing it. I can see the headlines now: 'Local Chocolatier and His Saucy Sidekick Transform Treats with Apron Flair!'"

He burst out laughing, the sound rich and hearty, filling the corners of the shop with a warmth that pushed away the evening's chill. "Please. The world isn't ready for that level of sartorial elegance. But if we're aiming for world domination, we should definitely add 'with style' to our resume."

"World domination through chocolate and comedy—now that's a legacy I can get behind." I couldn't help but revel in the ease of our exchange, each playful jab and lighthearted tease drawing me closer to him. I felt lighter, as if the burdens I had carried were dissolving like sugar in warm water.

As we cleaned up, the conversation shifted from our chocolate empire to our pasts. Max leaned against the counter, crossing his arms. "You know, you've mentioned your time in the city, but you've never really told me why you left."

There it was again—the question that lingered just out of reach, teasing the edges of my resolve. I took a deep breath, the words swirling in my mind like the melting chocolate we had been molding all evening. "It's a long story," I said cautiously, trying to gauge his reaction.

"Long stories are my favorite. They usually come with the best twists and turns," he replied, a lopsided grin tugging at his lips. "And I promise not to roll my eyes at any plot holes."

His playful tone made me laugh, a sound that seemed to lift the weight from my chest, if only for a moment. "Alright, here goes nothing." I leaned against the counter, gathering my thoughts. "I had this grand vision of city life—brimming with opportunity, excitement, and maybe a sprinkle of chaos. I moved there with a heart full of ambition and a head filled with dreams."

Max's eyes sparkled with interest, urging me on. "And then?"

I hesitated, the memories flooding back like a tide I hadn't prepared for. "And then I got caught up in the hustle. I took a job at a high-powered marketing firm, where my creativity felt like it was slowly being suffocated beneath spreadsheets and deadlines. The city was alive, and yet I felt like I was drowning."

"Wow, that sounds intense," he said, his expression shifting to one of empathy. "But everyone has to feel that at some point, right? The weight of their dreams pressing down on them?"

"Exactly," I replied, my voice barely above a whisper. "But I didn't just feel it; I lost sight of who I was. The ambition that had fueled me turned into a blind race, and I ended up compromising my happiness. I thought I could handle it, but in the end, I couldn't. I burned out, and it took leaving everything behind to realize I needed to rediscover what truly mattered."

Max nodded, the corners of his mouth turned down in sympathy. "So, you just packed up and came here? To this little chocolate shop in the middle of nowhere?"

"Not quite that simple," I chuckled, feeling the bittersweet truth seep through. "I drove for hours, letting the road guide me. It was only when I stumbled upon this place that I felt a spark of hope again. I could breathe here—like the weight had lifted, even if just a little."

"Honestly, it sounds like you were brave," he said, his tone shifting to something deeper, more sincere. "Many people would've kept pushing through. But you chose yourself."

"I didn't feel brave. It felt more like running away," I admitted, biting my lip. "But maybe it was a necessary escape, a chance to piece together my life again. It's just that... I still carry the remnants of my past with me."

His gaze bore into mine, intense yet gentle. "That's completely normal. You can't just turn off feelings like a switch."

I nodded, the flicker of connection between us flaring hotter. "But sometimes, I wish I could. Like now—here with you, it feels easy, but I still fear what happens when I confront the ghosts of my past."

Max stepped closer, his voice dropping to a whisper. "You don't have to face those ghosts alone. I mean, look at us—we've created this little bubble of laughter and chocolate. You can take your time, and when you're ready, I'll be right here."

The sincerity in his words sent warmth flooding through me, mingling with the sweet aroma of chocolate in the air. For the first time, I felt a flicker of hope blossom within me—a belief that maybe I could build something beautiful again, and perhaps with him by my side.

Just then, the door swung open with a tinkling chime, shattering the moment. A gust of cool air rushed in, sending a chill through the cozy shop. An older woman, her silver hair tucked into a neat bun, stepped inside. Her eyes widened as she surveyed the chocolate-laden counter, delight spreading across her face.

"Good evening! Oh, my stars, it smells heavenly in here! Are you two the masterminds behind this confectionery wonderland?" she exclaimed, her voice rich with warmth and enthusiasm.

Max straightened, flashing his charismatic smile. "That would be us! Welcome! Would you like to sample some of our latest creations?"

The woman beamed, her face lighting up like a Christmas tree. "Oh, I'd love to! You have no idea how long I've waited to find a place like this. My granddaughter has been begging for chocolate-covered strawberries, and I think I just stumbled upon the answer to her prayers!"

As Max engaged the woman in conversation, I felt a pang of disappointment at the interruption. Yet, I also recognized the serendipity of the moment—this was the joy I craved, the laughter and connection I had missed.

I watched as Max expertly led her through our offerings, his charm flowing as easily as the chocolate we had poured earlier. There was something magical about witnessing him in his element, making people smile with a simple treat. Perhaps this was what I needed—a reminder that life was still beautiful, filled with sweetness even amidst the mess.

And as the laughter bubbled between us, I felt the shadows recede just a bit further. Maybe, just maybe, the path ahead held more than just echoes of my past; it offered the promise of something new, waiting to unfold like a delicate chocolate shell, ready to reveal its heart.

The woman lingered at the counter, her enthusiasm contagious as she sampled our chocolates, each taste accompanied by an exaggerated gasp of delight. "Oh, this is exquisite! You truly have a gift, young man," she declared, her eyes shining like those of a child in a candy store. "I'll take a dozen of these, please! And, oh, those strawberries! You simply must sell them by the dozen!"

As Max enthusiastically packaged her order, I found myself lost in the moment, a warm sensation wrapping around me. Here, in the midst of laughter and chocolate, I felt lighter, as if the weight of my past had started to dissolve into the sweet air. The more I observed Max, the more I realized how naturally he embraced this world—the connection with customers, the joy of creation. It was intoxicating.

"Do you have a name for this delightful establishment?" the woman asked, her hands busy placing the chocolates into a decorative box.

"We've been considering 'Hearts & Chocolates,' but it's still a work in progress," he replied with a wink, glancing at me as if inviting my input.

I raised an eyebrow, crossing my arms. "It's charming, but it sounds like we're catering to a very specific demographic. What about something that captures the mess and magic of chocolate?"

Max nodded thoughtfully, his eyes sparkling with mischief. "What about 'Cocoa Chaos'? It has a ring to it!"

"Chaos? Oh dear, I don't want my granddaughter thinking she's stepping into a circus," the woman chuckled, shaking her head. "But I do like the idea of something that hints at the delightful messiness of making chocolates. You two have a great chemistry. It's like watching an artist at work!"

My cheeks flushed at the compliment, a mixture of embarrassment and joy bubbling up inside me. Max caught my eye, a knowing smile spreading across his lips. "We're just getting started. Wait until you see our new chocolate creations next week!"

"Chocolate creations?" I echoed, caught off guard by his enthusiasm. "What are you cooking up now?"

"Oh, just a little something inspired by your stories of city life," he teased, leaning in conspiratorially. "I thought we could create a 'Cityscape Truffle'—something sophisticated yet playful."

"Like what?" I challenged, eager to play along.

"How about layers of dark chocolate ganache with a hint of espresso and a sprinkle of sea salt?" he proposed, his eyes glinting with excitement.

"Are you just going to whip that up right now, or do you actually have a plan?" I laughed, crossing my arms again.

He feigned deep contemplation. "Well, I have a plan—sort of. I'll definitely need your expert hands for the ganache and, of course, your keen sense of taste to critique my... genius."

"Genius? Careful with that word; it comes with expectations." I rolled my eyes playfully, the ease between us settling comfortably once more.

The older woman, now entirely captivated by our banter, clapped her hands together, cutting in. "Oh, I'd love to see that! You two should make a whole line of city-inspired chocolates—imagine the tourists! 'Taste the city in every bite!'"

I smiled at her enthusiasm, but a small part of me felt an ache of uncertainty. Could I really commit to this? Would I still be a part of this joyous endeavor once the dust of my past settled around me again?

"Alright, it's settled then!" Max exclaimed, his voice bright. "We'll create our own cityscape right here in the shop. One truffle at a time!"

As he finished packing the woman's order, I caught a glimpse of the clock ticking on the wall. The time slipped away so easily in this whimsical space, but reality was never far behind. Just as the woman paid, her smile radiant as she gathered her box of chocolates, the door opened again.

A gust of wind rushed in, bringing with it the scent of rain and the sound of thunder rumbling in the distance. A tall figure stepped inside, soaking wet, with dark hair plastered to his forehead. He shook himself off like a dog fresh from a swim, and my breath caught in my throat as I recognized him.

"James," I breathed, my heart thudding in an odd mix of surprise and dread.

"Mind if I join the chocolate party?" he said, his voice low and slightly teasing, yet laced with a hint of irritation.

"James!" The woman exclaimed, her eyes darting between us. "Do you know these two?"

"Unfortunately, yes." He stepped further inside, shaking the water from his hair, and I couldn't help but notice how he seemed to take up space, imposing yet strangely magnetic. "What are you doing here?"

"I work here now," I replied, my voice steady despite the fluttering in my stomach.

"Oh? So, the city didn't swallow you whole after all?" His tone was lighter than I expected, a teasing lilt that belied the tension swirling beneath the surface.

I swallowed hard, the memories of our time together flashing before my eyes. "No, I came back. This place... it's different."

"Different, huh?" he said, arching an eyebrow, his gaze sharp. "I can see that."

Max, sensing the shift in energy, stepped closer to me, his posture defensive yet reassuring. "You here for some chocolate, or just to stir up trouble?"

James smirked, glancing around at the confections, his expression unreadable. "Maybe a little of both. You know I can never resist good chocolate." His eyes settled on me, and for a moment, the rest of the world faded away, leaving only the unresolved tension between us.

As the rain started to pour outside, I felt a storm brewing within me, caught between the past and the present, the comfort of chocolate and the chaos of my emotions. This was the moment where everything could tip, where choices would unravel and shape what came next.

"Why don't you join us?" Max suggested, his voice steady, trying to diffuse the tension that crackled like static in the air. "We were just about to come up with a new truffle flavor."

"Oh, I'm sure I can think of a few ideas," James replied, his gaze lingering on me, a challenge evident in his eyes.

I felt my heart race, caught between laughter and tension, a tightrope strung high above the uncertainty below. Just as I opened my mouth to respond, the lights flickered, momentarily dimming, and I heard a crack of thunder loud enough to rattle the windows.

"Okay, maybe I'll stick around to see how this turns out," he said, his tone shifting to something more serious as the storm outside began to rage.

The door swung shut behind him, sealing us inside the shop, and I felt a pulse of anxiety mixed with excitement. With the wind howling outside and the rain drumming against the roof, the atmosphere in the chocolate shop became charged, a precarious balance of sweetness and unpredictability.

As we stood together, the three of us surrounded by chocolate and the brewing storm, I sensed that everything was about to change. A choice loomed ahead of me, one that could shatter the delicate peace I had only just begun to cultivate. And before I could fully grasp the implications, the lights flickered again, plunging us into an unexpected darkness, and all I could hear was the relentless pounding of the rain outside, echoing the tumult within my heart.

Chapter 3: Unexpected Rivals

The bell above the door jingled with a familiar chime, the sound wrapping around me like a warm blanket on a chilly evening. I glanced up from my spot at the counter, where I was trying to focus on the latest delivery of artisanal chocolates. The rich, velvety scent wafted through the shop, mingling with the earthy aroma of freshly brewed coffee. It was a sanctuary, a space that belonged to me now, filled with eclectic decorations that reflected the essence of the place: a mismatched collection of vintage coffee mugs, an old record player softly crooning classics, and shelves overflowing with a curated selection of local goods. Each item told a story, but today, the story was interrupted by the entrance of Oliver.

He strolled in, exuding confidence as if he owned the very ground we stood on. The moment he stepped through the threshold, it was as if someone had switched the air conditioning to high, sending a chill that had nothing to do with the temperature. His tailored suit, an unforgiving shade of charcoal, accentuated his lean frame, and his smile—oh, that smile—was too perfect to be genuine. It was the kind of smile that could charm the coins out of your pocket, and I immediately braced myself for the onslaught of his charm.

"Good morning, ladies," he said, his voice smooth as silk, dripping with a charm that made my skin crawl. He turned to me, his gaze sharp and assessing. "I hope you don't mind me barging in like this. I've heard wonderful things about this little slice of heaven."

Max, who had been behind the espresso machine, froze mid-brew, his brow furrowing. "What do you want?" His tone was clipped, his posture tense, the easygoing vibe of the shop suddenly taut with unspoken tension.

"Relax, my friend. Just here for a friendly chat," Oliver said, flashing a smile that could have easily melted the heart of a glacier.

"I'm Oliver Sinclair. I hear you're the one who runs this charming establishment." He extended a hand toward Max, who eyed it like it was a venomous snake.

"Yes, and I run it just fine without help from someone like you," Max shot back, a defiance in his voice that felt like a shield around him.

I glanced between the two men, a feeling of unease settling in the pit of my stomach. This wasn't just an encounter; it was a collision of worlds. Oliver was the type of man who could turn a quaint coffee shop into a sleek corporate chain, and I could already envision the local charm being stripped away piece by piece. It wasn't just a business to me; it was home.

"Isn't that the beauty of entrepreneurship?" Oliver continued, seemingly unfazed by Max's hostility. "We all want to grow, expand our horizons. Imagine a few more shops just like this, spreading joy and caffeine to more people. You'd be a part of something bigger."

Max's jaw clenched, his eyes narrowing. "And lose the heart of what we've built here? This place is special because it's unique, not because it fits into some corporate cookie-cutter mold."

I felt my heart race, a tumult of emotions swirling within me. I wanted to scream at Oliver, to tell him that he didn't belong here, that he couldn't just waltz in and threaten everything I held dear. But I also felt the weight of Max's words, how he poured his soul into every cup served, every laugh shared. I had found solace here, and it was under threat from a man who viewed it as merely a lucrative opportunity.

"Come on, Max," Oliver said, his voice turning almost coaxing, yet there was an undercurrent of condescension. "You know I can help you reach heights you never imagined. Don't you want to be able to serve your amazing coffee to even more people?"

I couldn't help but chime in, my voice sharp with conviction. "It's not about numbers, Oliver. It's about the experience, the connection.

This place is a refuge for those who need it, not just a stop on someone's coffee tour." The words felt bold and cathartic, but Oliver simply raised an eyebrow, amused.

"Ah, the idealism of youth," he replied, his tone mocking yet oddly intrigued. "You have a good heart, but you'll soon learn that passion doesn't pay the bills."

The tension escalated, and as their words volleyed back and forth, I could feel my loyalties fraying at the edges. I was drawn to Max's fervor, the way he breathed life into the shop, but Oliver's charisma had a magnetic pull that was hard to ignore. I caught Max's gaze, a fleeting moment of connection that sent a jolt of energy through me, but then it was gone, replaced by the sharpness of Oliver's words.

"Just think about it," Oliver said, his eyes glinting with an opportunistic glimmer. "A partnership. I could bring the resources you need to thrive without sacrificing what makes this place special. It's a win-win."

Max scoffed, turning his back to Oliver as he resumed making coffee, the steam curling upward like a fragile dream dissipating in the air. I could sense the frustration radiating off him, the way his hands moved with a little too much vigor, as if he were trying to crush the very idea of Oliver's proposal.

As the door swung closed behind Oliver, I felt the weight of the moment settle in the silence that followed. The air felt heavier, the room tinged with unresolved tension, the aftermath of a battle that had only just begun. My heart raced with uncertainty, caught in a web of emerging feelings for Max and a growing animosity toward Oliver.

"What a piece of work," Max muttered, his voice low and bitter. He didn't turn to me, but I could see the tension in his shoulders, the way he tried to shake off the remnants of their encounter. I wanted to comfort him, to assure him that I was on his side, but the knot in my throat held me back.

"Do you think he really wants to buy the shop?" I ventured cautiously, my curiosity battling against the protective instinct to shield Max from any more hurt.

"Of course he does," Max snapped, turning to face me, his frustration palpable. "He sees a gold mine where I see a home. I won't let him take that from us."

His fierce declaration ignited a spark within me, a desire to stand beside him in this fight. The shop was more than just a business; it was our refuge, our little haven against the chaos outside. And if I had to go to war with charm and passion against Oliver's cold, calculating ambition, I'd do it, no matter the cost.

The days that followed felt charged, each one a precarious balancing act as I tiptoed through the minefield of emotions erupting between Max and Oliver. The shop had become a stage, where every interaction between the three of us played out like a carefully choreographed dance, complete with unexpected missteps and moments that left my heart racing. Max was fierce in his resistance, throwing himself into his work with a fervor that was as admirable as it was exhausting. I watched him, the way his brow furrowed with concentration, the way his hands deftly moved, as though he could craft a shield of caffeine and pastries against Oliver's encroachment.

I found solace in the early mornings, the golden light spilling through the window as I set up for the day. The soft glow bathed the shop in a warmth that felt comforting, almost magical. I could hear the familiar sounds of the coffee grinder, the gentle hiss of the espresso machine, and the soft chatter of regulars who wandered in, their smiles like familiar bookends to my day. It was in these moments that I felt truly at home, surrounded by the aromas of cinnamon and freshly baked scones.

But each morning, just as the warmth enveloped me, Oliver would stroll in, sharply dressed and disarmingly charming. He always managed to find me, flashing that infuriatingly perfect smile as he leaned against the counter. "You really should consider a career in real estate, you know," he teased one morning, his tone light, but his eyes betraying a deeper intent. "With your knack for creating such inviting spaces, you could sell anything."

I rolled my eyes, trying to ignore the way his words both amused and annoyed me. "I'm far too busy for that nonsense," I shot back, crossing my arms. "I have a shop to save."

"Ah, the shop," he replied, feigning a sigh of mock concern. "What a noble endeavor. But tell me, what happens when you realize the coffee shop is just a coffee shop? Don't you want more?"

His question hung in the air, an unwanted echo that lingered even after he'd left. Did I want more? I found myself pondering the question late into the night, nestled in my bed, the soft glow of my bedside lamp illuminating the pages of a book I couldn't focus on. My thoughts drifted to Max, the way he poured his soul into each cup, the laughter we shared in the quiet moments between the rush of customers. He was my anchor, my refuge, and yet Oliver's presence had stirred something inside me, a flicker of curiosity about what lay beyond our little haven.

The tension escalated with each passing day. Max was relentless in his determination to defend the shop, often losing himself in late-night meetings with our small team, sketching out plans to improve the shop's offerings, to create an experience that was undeniably us. He had introduced a weekend brunch menu that was a roaring success, packed with regulars who seemed to adore the vibrant atmosphere we cultivated.

But even in these moments of triumph, I could feel Oliver looming like a dark cloud on the horizon. He began visiting more frequently, slipping in during peak hours, effortlessly charming the customers, making casual observations about the business that sounded almost like strategic scouting. I could see Max's jaw clench at every compliment Oliver offered, the way he forced a smile through gritted teeth while still managing to serve up lattes with the grace of a barista who had grown tired of the show.

One evening, as we were closing up, the tension hit a breaking point. The last customer had left, the gentle hum of the coffee machine finally quieted, leaving only the sounds of our ragged breaths in the aftermath of a long day. I was wiping down the counter when Max suddenly spoke, his voice low and taut. "You should have seen the way he was looking at the espresso machine today. Like he could take it apart and turn it into some kind of franchise."

I paused, my cloth suspended in mid-air. "Max, it's not just about him. It's about you. This place is special because of what you put into it."

"Special?" he scoffed, turning away, the intensity of his frustration palpable. "It's a liability, a quaint little corner that's about to be swallowed whole. You don't get it, do you?"

"No, I do!" I retorted, my voice rising in the dim light. "I'm here, aren't I? I chose to be here. And I'm not going to let him take that from us without a fight."

Max whipped around, surprise flickering in his eyes. "You think you can just wade into this mess and pick sides? This isn't a game, and it's certainly not a fair fight. He has resources. He's like a shark circling the wounded."

A silence enveloped us, heavy with the weight of unspoken truths. I felt my heart pounding, each beat echoing against the walls. "And what about you? What do you plan to do? Just give up?" The words slipped from my mouth before I could catch them, charged with a raw honesty that shocked even me.

His gaze softened for a moment, vulnerability flashing across his face before the mask slipped back on. "I can't lose this place. Not to him."

"Then let's not let it come to that," I urged, stepping closer, my fingers brushing against the cool counter. "We can come up with a plan, something that showcases everything this shop represents. Show Oliver he's underestimating us."

For a moment, the heat between us crackled, a silent acknowledgment of our shared goal, but then the tension twisted again, the prospect of facing Oliver igniting something fierce in both of us. "I don't want to drag you into this. It's messy, and I can't guarantee you won't get hurt."

"I'm already in it, Max," I insisted, my voice steady now, fueled by determination. "You might not see it, but this place is as much a part of me as it is of you. If we're going to fight, let's do it together."

He studied me, the conflict etched across his face, a mix of gratitude and reluctance. And then, as if the weight of the world had shifted slightly, he nodded. "Okay, together then."

As we stood there, a fragile alliance forming in the fading light, the door swung open with a jingle, and Oliver stepped back into our lives with that infuriating grin plastered on his face. "Am I interrupting something?" he asked, feigning innocence, but the glint in his eye told a different story. I felt the air crackle with tension again, the two worlds colliding once more.

"Just discussing the future of this little haven," Max replied, his tone a mix of defiance and resolve. The shift was palpable, like the moment before a storm breaks. I stood beside him, ready to face whatever came next, my heart racing with the thrill of the unknown.

The air crackled with unspoken tension as Oliver stepped inside, his presence instantly shifting the atmosphere of the shop. I could almost hear the uninvited drama he brought with him, a scent more cloying than the rich coffee beans that permeated the room. I shot a quick glance at Max, who straightened his posture, an unmistakable air of defiance in his demeanor. Whatever tentative alliance we had forged moments earlier was now a thin veil, threatened by Oliver's casual arrogance.

"Good to see you both," Oliver said, leaning casually against the doorframe. "I couldn't help but overhear your little planning session. It sounds so... spirited."

Max's eyes narrowed, the muscles in his jaw tightening. "What do you want, Oliver?" His voice was steady, but the fire behind it was unmistakable.

Oliver feigned an innocent shrug, the corners of his mouth curling into that maddeningly charming smile. "I'm just here to check on my favorite coffee shop. I wouldn't want to miss out on the latest brew," he quipped, stepping further into the space, his polished shoes echoing against the wooden floor. "Besides, I thought it was time for a friendly chat about the future."

"Friendly? You don't strike me as the type who does anything for free," I retorted, crossing my arms and trying to muster the bravado that seemed to elude me when faced with his relentless charm.

He chuckled, a sound like tinkling bells that felt completely out of place in our little refuge. "Touché. But let's be real, shall we? I'm not here to put a damper on things. I just want to help you see the bigger picture." He gestured to the rows of artisanal pastries and the vibrant array of locally sourced goods lining the shelves, as if he were assessing a stock portfolio. "This shop has potential—potential that I can help you unlock."

Max stepped forward, his voice rising slightly. "And what would that cost us, Oliver? Our identity? Our soul?"

I could feel the weight of the moment hanging in the air, heavy with stakes that felt impossibly high. It was a delicate balance—on one side, the familiar warmth of the shop that had become my sanctuary, and on the other, the possibility of change, of growth, wrapped in Oliver's slick assurances. I was beginning to feel like a pawn in a game I had never intended to join.

"Come now, Max," Oliver replied, his tone condescending yet annoyingly smooth. "I'm offering a partnership, not a takeover. Think of all the lives you could touch if you opened a few more locations. Imagine your coffee and scones bringing joy to more people than just your regulars."

Max scoffed, shaking his head as he moved behind the counter. "You don't get it. This place isn't just about profit margins and expansion. It's about connection, community. That's what keeps people coming back, not some cookie-cutter marketing plan."

I watched as Oliver's expression shifted slightly, his charming facade cracking just enough for me to catch a glimpse of frustration lurking beneath. "You're making this harder than it needs to be," he said, his voice lowering, almost pleading. "I can help you succeed, Max. You're talented, but you're swimming against the current here. Let me guide you."

"You mean let you lead me to the slaughter," Max shot back, the heat in his voice palpable.

I sensed a shift in the room, the air becoming thick with unresolved tension. "Max, we need to consider the possibilities," I interjected, stepping between them. "What if there's a way to grow without losing everything that makes this place special?"

Max looked at me, his expression a tumult of emotions. I could see the weight of his frustration and the flicker of hope that maybe there was a middle ground. "And if we fail? If we lose everything trying to be something we're not?"

Oliver stepped forward, his gaze intent as he focused on me. "I think you're underestimating your own power. You have a spark, both of you. Together, you could light up the entire neighborhood. Don't you want to be more than just a coffee shop?"

I hesitated, the words swirling around in my mind, fighting against each other. The thought of failure was daunting, but what if Max and I could hold onto our integrity while also expanding our reach? What if we could introduce more people to the warmth of our little haven without diluting its essence?

"What if we do this on our terms?" I suggested, my voice steady as I locked eyes with Max. "What if we collaborate with you, but keep the heart of this place intact? We could build something amazing."

Max's gaze softened, a flicker of understanding sparking in his eyes. But before he could respond, Oliver's face brightened, the flicker of triumph shining through. "Now you're speaking my language," he said, an unsettling grin spreading across his face. "Let's discuss this further, shall we?"

The air hummed with tension, the possibility of a partnership hanging precariously in the balance. But just as we were beginning to find common ground, the door swung open with a crash, the bell jingling wildly as a gust of wind followed the new arrival into the shop. It was a local news reporter, her camera crew trailing behind her, bright lights illuminating the space and instantly shifting the atmosphere once more.

"Good evening, everyone! I hope I'm not interrupting," she exclaimed, her enthusiasm infectious, but the vibe in the room shifted dramatically. I caught Oliver's gaze darting to the camera, the glint of opportunity lighting up his features.

"Perfect timing!" he announced, his voice booming as he turned toward the reporter. "We were just discussing the exciting future of this beloved coffee shop!"

I felt a rush of panic as Max's expression morphed from disbelief to anger. "This isn't what we agreed to," he muttered under his breath, his frustration palpable.

The reporter, oblivious to the tension, moved closer, her microphone poised. "I've heard rumors about changes coming to this establishment, and I'd love to get the inside scoop. How are you planning to revolutionize the local coffee scene?"

Before I could process what was happening, Oliver stepped into the spotlight, a smooth grin plastered on his face. "I'm here to help Max grow his business, to bring the taste of his exceptional coffee to a wider audience. Together, we're going to create something extraordinary."

I felt the color drain from my face as the reporter's camera zoomed in, capturing every moment. Max's eyes widened, the anger giving way to a mixture of panic and betrayal. "You can't do this," he hissed, but Oliver merely smiled, a shark circling its prey.

"This is just the beginning," Oliver said, his tone dripping with self-assurance. "Buckle up, folks. The best is yet to come."

The camera focused on Max, the tension radiating from him like an electric current. My heart raced as I took a step back, the implications of Oliver's words crashing over me. Just when we were finding our footing, the ground felt like it was crumbling beneath us.

As the reporter began to ask more questions, I knew we were on the precipice of something monumental, something that could either save our sanctuary or destroy it completely. Max's jaw clenched, the weight of the world resting on his shoulders, and I could see the storm brewing in his eyes.

And then, just as Oliver began to answer another question, my phone buzzed in my pocket. The vibration felt like a warning, an urgent call to attention. I fished it out, my heart leaping as I glanced at the screen. The message was from a number I didn't recognize, but the words sent a chill through me: "I know what's really happening at the shop. Meet me tonight. It's urgent."

The world around me faded into a blur as I stared at the screen, the gravity of the situation anchoring me in place. I looked up just in time to see Max's gaze meet mine, confusion and worry etched on his face. In that moment, I knew that everything was about to change—again—and we were teetering on the edge of something both thrilling and terrifying. The air was thick with uncertainty, and I couldn't shake the feeling that the real battle was just beginning.

Chapter 4: Heartbeats in the Rain

The rain pelted the windows like a thousand tiny drummers rehearsing for a grand performance, their rhythmic chaos creating a symphony that drowned out the world beyond. I could hardly remember the last time I'd felt this cozy, curled up on a battered couch in the back of the shop, a thick blanket wrapped around my shoulders like a protective cocoon. Max sat across from me, a mug in hand, steam rising like soft whispers into the dim light. He'd always had this knack for making the ordinary feel extraordinary, and on this particularly tempestuous afternoon, it was no different.

"Ever think about how rain is like nature's way of saying it's okay to be a little messy?" he asked, his eyes sparkling with mischief.

I chuckled, my heart fluttering at the sight of his boyish grin. "You mean to tell me that every time it rains, I can throw caution to the wind and leave my house a disaster zone? I might have to plan a rain-themed party just to celebrate that revelation."

"Absolutely. The messier, the better. Just think of the artistic possibilities." He swept an arm theatrically, as if envisioning the chaos of splattered paint and unmade beds.

I took a sip of my hot chocolate, the rich warmth spreading through me, and leaned back, settling into the moment. It was these stolen afternoons that made the struggle of running the shop worthwhile—the laughter, the playful banter, the way he always seemed to know when I needed a little light.

But that light was dimmed by the ever-looming shadow of Oliver. My thoughts skittered like rain on pavement. He had been distant lately, lost in his own world, a reality filled with threats that felt all too real. The shop, our sanctuary, was at risk, and with every passing day, it felt as if the walls were closing in. Yet here, in this moment with Max, the troubles of the outside world felt like a distant storm, the kind you could hear but not see.

"You're quiet," Max said, his gaze piercing through my pretenses. "What's brewing behind those lovely hazel eyes?"

I hesitated, not wanting to dampen the mood. "Just thinking about how lucky we are to have this place. It feels like a fortress, you know? Like no matter what's out there, we can create our own little bubble."

His expression shifted slightly, the corners of his mouth still turned up but his eyes reflecting a deeper understanding. "And bubbles can burst, right?"

I nodded, the weight of his words anchoring me. "Yeah, but until they do, we should enjoy it. I mean, who knows what tomorrow will bring?"

"I prefer to think of it as creating our own adventures, bubble or no bubble." He grinned, and my heart swelled with an inexplicable affection for him.

We fell into a comfortable silence, the kind that didn't require words. Instead, we shared smiles that spoke volumes, a language crafted from countless moments just like this. But as the rain lashed against the glass, a sudden crack of thunder jolted me back to reality, a stark reminder that nothing lasts forever.

"What if we closed early today?" Max suggested, breaking the silence. "I mean, we're not exactly bustling with customers."

"Not exactly," I replied, an idea blooming in my mind like a sudden ray of sunshine breaking through clouds. "But what if we took that time to do something completely different? Something reckless?"

"Reckless, huh?" He raised an eyebrow, leaning in as if I'd just suggested we rob a bank. "Like what?"

"Let's play a game of creating ridiculous drink recipes," I proposed, the thrill of spontaneity dancing in my veins. "We can concoct the most absurd combinations and see if they actually taste good. If they don't, we can always drown our sorrows in more hot chocolate."

"I like it," he replied, a playful smirk curling his lips. "But I'm warning you now, I'm a genius in the kitchen. Prepare for greatness."

As he gathered the ingredients from our eclectic shelves—everything from cocoa powder to a dubious-looking jar of lavender—I couldn't shake the feeling of foreboding creeping back in. It was as if the storm outside mirrored my internal tempest. Each time I laughed at his ridiculous concoctions, I felt the tension ease, yet doubt hovered just beyond the warm glow of our makeshift paradise.

"Okay, here's my masterpiece." Max grinned, presenting a frothy green drink that looked like something straight out of a witch's cauldron. "Behold, the 'Cucumber Cloud.' A refreshing blend of cucumber, mint, and maybe a touch of disaster."

I giggled, taking a cautious sip. "Oh, God. It's... interesting." I tried to mask my horror. "Definitely a... unique blend."

"Interesting is just a euphemism for 'I'll never drink this again,'" he teased, leaning closer as if sharing a secret. "Your turn."

I rummaged through the ingredients, my mind racing. "Alright, get ready for 'Choco-Matcha Meltdown.' It's chocolate, matcha, and a sprinkle of desperation."

His laughter filled the small space, bright and infectious. I carefully mixed the ingredients, the vivid green swirling together with rich chocolate until it formed a mesmerizing whirlpool of colors.

As we continued to concoct ridiculous drinks, the atmosphere shifted from one of playful banter to something electric. Our eyes caught each other, lingering a beat longer, charged with a chemistry that felt palpable. It was then that everything around us faded—the rain, the storm, even Oliver's shadow in the back of my mind—and all that existed was this moment, suspended in time.

With a sudden urge, I leaned closer, brushing my lips against his in a tentative, almost hesitant kiss. It was soft and sweet, a collision of everything I'd been yearning for. A warmth surged through me, pushing away the lingering doubts, if only for a moment. But as swiftly as it began, the kiss melted into uncertainty, a delicate dance of what could be and what was. I pulled back, breathless, the world outside rushing back in, a reminder that our sanctuary was under threat.

"What was that?" he asked, his voice a blend of surprise and curiosity, his gaze searching mine.

"Just a moment," I whispered, but my heart pounded with a heaviness I couldn't shake. As much as I wanted to dive deeper into this unexpected connection, the shadow of uncertainty loomed, reminding me that every kiss has its consequences, especially when the storm outside was nothing compared to the one brewing in my life.

A flicker of uncertainty danced in the space between us as I pulled away, the warmth of his breath lingering like a ghost. The rain drummed steadily on the roof, the sound almost like an echo of my racing heartbeat. I had crossed a line, or perhaps I had merely wobbled on its edge, teetering between the intoxicating thrill of desire and the grounding weight of reality. Max's brow furrowed, his eyes searching mine as if trying to decipher a puzzle that had suddenly become far more complicated.

"Did I miss the part where you said we were playing spin-the-bottle?" he quipped, attempting to mask his own surprise with humor, but I could hear the tremor beneath his words.

"Let's call it an impromptu experiment in chemistry," I replied, my voice steadier than I felt. The playful edge in my tone was a shield, a way to deflect the rawness of what had just happened.

"Chemistry, huh?" He leaned back slightly, a grin breaking through the uncertainty. "So we're talking about lab rats and beakers now?"

"More like beakers and hot chocolate," I said, waving my mug in the air. "And the occasional emotional explosion."

We shared a laugh, but beneath the surface, the unspoken tension still simmered. I could sense it in the way his gaze lingered on my lips, and in the way the world around us dimmed into a soft blur. The warmth of the cocoa began to fade, leaving behind a cool reminder of the very real challenges looming outside our bubble.

"Do you think it's too late to put up a 'Closed for Emotional Distress' sign?" he asked, his voice teasing yet sincere.

"Maybe just a 'Caution: Flammable Emotions Ahead' sign instead," I shot back, feeling the corners of my mouth twitch upward despite the weight of the moment.

The playful banter acted as a temporary bandage for the gnawing anxiety creeping in at the edges. I didn't want to spoil our stolen afternoon by delving into the darker clouds gathering in my mind, but the more I pushed the thought away, the heavier it felt. The shop was in trouble. Oliver was barely speaking to me, his frustrations brewing like the tempest outside, and I was still trying to figure out how to reconcile my feelings for Max with the uncertainty of what lay ahead.

"Want to make a pact?" Max asked, breaking through my thoughts. "No doom and gloom until the last drops of hot chocolate are gone."

"Deal." I smiled, but the grin faltered as I took another sip, savoring the taste as I tried to push the weight of reality further away. "But I'm warning you, I might have to throw in some sarcasm to balance things out."

"Sounds like a fair trade. I'm all about fair trades." He leaned in, the playful glint in his eyes sparking a warmth that chased the chill from my mind. "Speaking of fair trades, what about your ridiculously amazing drink? I'm ready for the next round."

"Oh, I was thinking more along the lines of a marshmallow volcano," I said, excitement creeping back in as I imagined fluffy peaks topped with melted chocolate. "It's basically a sugar explosion waiting to happen."

He raised an eyebrow, feigning skepticism. "Are you sure we can handle a volcano? I mean, the last thing we need is to add fire to this emotional chaos."

"Fire adds flair, Max," I retorted, a grin spreading across my face. "It's all about the showmanship."

"Alright, showgirl, let's make this volcano happen," he replied, rolling up his sleeves like a master chef preparing for battle.

As we rummaged through the supplies, the storm outside continued to rage, but inside our little sanctuary, it felt like we were conjuring magic. The kitchen became our laboratory of whimsy, where we could escape the storm swirling in our lives and lose ourselves in the sweetness of imagination. With each gooey marshmallow I tossed into the melting pot of chocolate, I felt a bit of my anxiety dissolve, like sugar melting into hot water.

"Okay, but if this volcano erupts, you have to take full responsibility," I warned, stirring the mixture as it bubbled and popped.

"Responsibility? Me? I'd prefer to think of myself as an adventurous co-conspirator." He leaned in closer, inspecting the bubbling concoction with exaggerated seriousness. "I take no blame for the outcome of this experiment."

We both laughed, the sound mingling with the symphony of raindrops, and for a moment, I was able to forget the troubles waiting outside the door. The marshmallow volcano took shape, towering high, a testament to our reckless abandon.

"Behold!" I announced dramatically, presenting our creation like a trophy. "The 'Volcano of Sweets and Chaos!'"

"May it never erupt," he declared, raising his mug in a toast. "To sweet escapes and reckless decisions."

"To sweet escapes!" I echoed, clinking my mug against his with a sense of camaraderie that felt rare and precious.

But as we took our first bite, savoring the explosion of flavors and textures, the delightful chaos of melted chocolate and marshmallow enveloping us, a shadow slipped through my mind. I had pushed it away before, but Oliver's presence lingered like a distant storm on the horizon, and the laughter began to feel bittersweet.

"What if this is the last time we get to do something like this?" I blurted out, the words slipping past my lips before I could stop them.

Max's smile faltered, the weight of reality crashing back in like a rogue wave. "What do you mean?"

"Just...everything," I said, the words tumbling from my mouth like the rain outside. "With the shop, with Oliver, everything feels so uncertain."

"Hey," he said gently, his hand reaching across the table, fingers brushing against mine. "We're going to figure this out. You don't have to carry this alone."

His touch sent a jolt through me, a reminder of the warmth that filled the room, but the worry still curled around my heart. "I just don't want to lose this," I confessed, my voice a whisper. "I don't want to lose us."

Max leaned closer, his expression serious now, the playful banter replaced with a depth that made my heart race. "You're not going to lose me. No matter what happens outside these walls, we're still here. Together."

But even as he spoke those reassuring words, I could feel the clouds gathering. Oliver had been my anchor, my confidant, and now he seemed adrift in a sea of resentment and misunderstanding.

The bond between Max and me felt like a fragile thread, beautiful but precarious. I wanted to believe in his words, but the weight of my worries threatened to pull me under.

As the rain lashed against the windows, I resolved to enjoy this moment, even as the storm within and outside raged on. I would savor the sweetness of our shared laughter and the warmth of his touch, knowing that whatever awaited us beyond the door could wait just a little longer. The chaos of life might be relentless, but in this moment, as we shared our marshmallow volcano and lost ourselves in the magic of the afternoon, I felt a flicker of hope—a spark that maybe, just maybe, we could weather the storm together.

The sweet, chaotic concoction of our marshmallow volcano lingered in the air, a reminder of the moment we had carved out for ourselves amid the storm. Max's fingers brushed mine as he leaned back, his expression shifting from playful to contemplative. I could see the gears turning in his mind, wrestling with the weight of the world pressing down on both of us.

"Do you ever think about running away?" he asked, breaking the spell of our previous levity, his voice low and earnest.

"Like, to a tropical island? Or just to the next town over?" I shot back, attempting to infuse some levity into the moment. "Because I hear the weather's pretty nice there."

"Is that what you want?" he asked, his gaze piercing through my lighthearted facade. "To escape?"

I took a moment, contemplating the weight of his question. "It's not so much about escaping as it is about finding a place where I don't have to worry about everything falling apart," I admitted, a heaviness creeping into my chest. "With Oliver and the shop—sometimes it feels like I'm in a never-ending game of Jenga, and I'm just waiting for the next piece to tumble."

Max shifted closer, the seriousness of our conversation cloaking the room in an intensity I hadn't anticipated. "You know, I get that.

Sometimes, I think about moving on, too, like we're in this... this limbo. It's frustrating."

"Then why don't we just—" I began, the words tumbling out before I could filter them, "Why don't we just do something crazy? Go on an adventure. Just us. No plans, no responsibilities."

The idea hung between us, vibrant and wild, igniting a spark of mischief in his eyes. "Are you suggesting we throw caution to the wind and become nomads? Because I'm not sure I packed my survival kit."

"Fine, let's just start small. A road trip. We could explore the coast or find some little café tucked away somewhere. We can escape to anywhere that isn't here, even if it's just for a weekend."

His smile returned, a glimmer of excitement dancing in his eyes. "You're on to something there. A spontaneous adventure sounds... dangerously fun."

The prospect of hitting the road ignited a flicker of hope within me, but as quickly as it sparked, I felt a heaviness settle in. What about Oliver? Would I be running away or merely delaying the inevitable? "But what about Oliver? He's got enough on his plate without me just disappearing."

"Yeah, but you need to take care of yourself first," Max replied gently. "You can't save the shop or Oliver if you're drowning in worry. A little adventure might just give you the clarity you need."

I pondered his words, the duality of my feelings clashing like storm clouds. Part of me longed for the freedom of the open road, the chance to escape into spontaneity, while another part anchored me in the present, tethered to the messiness of reality. "You really think a road trip could help?"

"I do," he said with conviction, a smile breaking across his face. "And if nothing else, it'll be a great excuse to spend more time together."

"Okay, let's do it," I declared, surprising even myself with the confidence in my voice. The adrenaline of making a decision pushed my worries aside, if only for a moment. "We'll leave this weekend. I can set things up at the shop so it's covered."

"Deal. And if you're really going to set things up, then I might need you to whip up another batch of that volcanic hot chocolate first." His teasing tone cut through the seriousness, and I felt the laughter bubble back up, a welcome release.

"Only if you promise not to burn the shop down while I'm gone," I shot back, my smile genuine this time.

But as the evening wore on and the rain continued to pour, the underlying tension returned, a reminder that no matter how lighthearted we tried to be, reality lurked just beyond our laughter. The door to the shop creaked open, the sound slicing through our cozy bubble, and I froze mid-laugh, my heart skipping as I glanced toward the entrance.

"Could it be a customer?" Max asked, his voice a blend of curiosity and concern.

"Not likely," I replied, a knot tightening in my stomach. "It's way too late for anyone to be browsing for books."

And then I saw him—Oliver. He stood in the doorway, drenched from the rain, his expression unreadable, shadowed by the storm outside. My heart sank.

"Oliver," I breathed, the word a mixture of surprise and dread. I had hoped to avoid this confrontation for a bit longer. "What are you doing here?"

He stepped inside, shaking off the rain like a disgruntled dog, his eyes narrowing at the sight of Max and the chaos of our kitchen. "I came to talk," he said, his voice steady but edged with frustration.

"Now? In the middle of a storm?" I asked, trying to keep my tone light, but the weight of his presence felt like an anchor pulling me down.

"Yeah, well, I didn't exactly have a choice." He looked from me to Max, a silent challenge hanging in the air, thick with unspoken accusations. "I'm not leaving until we sort this out."

Max shifted uncomfortably beside me, a tension building that felt as palpable as the storm outside. "Oliver, maybe now isn't the best time—"

"No, it's the perfect time," he interrupted, stepping further into the shop, his eyes locking onto mine. "I need to know where we stand. I can't keep pretending everything is fine while you're off playing house with...him."

The air thickened, and for a moment, it felt as if the storm outside had seeped into our little bubble, filling it with static and uncertainty. I glanced at Max, who met my gaze with a mix of concern and determination, and then back at Oliver, whose expression was one of hurt layered with anger.

"I was just trying to have a moment of—"

"Of what?" Oliver cut in, the frustration spilling over. "Of pretending we're not in crisis? Of playing with cocoa and marshmallows while the shop is falling apart? You think I don't see that?"

My stomach twisted at the accusation, his words cutting deeper than I'd expected. "I'm not ignoring anything, Oliver. I just needed a break. We both did."

"A break?" He scoffed, incredulous. "Is that what you call it? You're ready to run off on some road trip with him while I'm here trying to keep everything from crumbling?"

"It's not like that," I protested, my heart racing. The storm outside mirrored the tempest inside me, each raindrop echoing the conflict brewing in this cramped space. "I just wanted to clear my head."

"By abandoning ship?" Oliver pressed, his voice rising, anger and hurt mingling in the air.

"Maybe I need to find out what I want," I replied, my voice steadier than I felt. "And it doesn't mean I'm abandoning anything. I'm just trying to figure it out."

Oliver took a step closer, his brow furrowed in frustration. "And what about me? What about this place? You can't just run away from everything."

"I'm not running away!" I shouted, the emotions spilling out of me in a flood. "I'm trying to save myself. To save us."

In that moment, the storm outside erupted in a violent crack of thunder, shaking the windows as if nature itself echoed our turmoil. Max glanced nervously at the door, the tension crackling like static in the air.

Oliver opened his mouth to respond, but before he could speak, a loud crash resonated from the front of the shop, the sound of something heavy hitting the ground. The door swung open wider, rain spilling inside, and the world outside came rushing in.

"What was that?" Max asked, his voice barely rising above the chaos.

I held my breath, dread pooling in my stomach as I stepped toward the door, my heart pounding in my chest. "I don't know."

As I peered into the downpour, a figure emerged, silhouetted against the storm, drenched and panting. The air felt charged, thick with tension and unanswered questions, a palpable cliffhanger hanging over us like the storm clouds outside. Just as I thought the tension couldn't escalate further, the figure stepped into the light, revealing a familiar face—a face I never expected to see again.

"Surprise!" came a voice that sent chills down my spine, an unwelcome blast from the past shattering the fragile moment we had tried so hard to preserve.

Chapter 5: Cracks in the Foundation

The sweet, intoxicating scent of melting chocolate hung in the air, wrapping around me like a warm embrace as I stood in the kitchen, my fingers expertly tempering dark chocolate. It was a ritual I cherished, each swirl of the spatula and every gentle flick of my wrist merging into a rhythm that calmed my racing heart. But today, the familiar cadence felt strained, almost foreign. Max's absence gnawed at me like a persistent itch I couldn't scratch, leaving a bitter aftertaste in the otherwise saccharine atmosphere.

Every sound echoed with the weight of our unspoken words. The whir of the mixer, the soft thud of chocolate slabs being placed on the counter, the distant chatter from the front of the shop—it all melded into a cacophony that highlighted his distance. My heart fluttered with a mixture of hope and dread as I recalled that kiss, a moment suspended in time, yet somehow irretrievably altered by the tension that followed. It was as if a fragile glass ornament had shattered, scattering shards of uncertainty across the floor.

The days rolled by, each one blending seamlessly into the next, yet feeling achingly different. I immersed myself in the craft, experimenting with wild flavors that danced on the edge of whimsy: lavender-infused ganache, chili chocolate bites that promised a slow burn, and the surprisingly delightful pairing of grapefruit with bittersweet chocolate. I poured every ounce of my creativity into the shop, hoping it would pull Max back into the warmth of our shared passion. But as I observed him from the kitchen, engaged in intense discussions with Oliver, the air between us crackled with unspoken words, each glance he threw Oliver's way like an arrow aimed at my heart.

"Do you really think we can take the shop to the next level with this plan?" Oliver's voice drifted back to me, thick with ambition and a hint of skepticism. My stomach twisted at the thought, an unsettling reminder of how his presence shifted the dynamic I once felt secure in. I had watched Max light up while discussing growth strategies, his enthusiasm palpable, yet my own spirit dimmed with each passing moment. The shop was our dream, yet here was Oliver, a tempting offer dangling like a golden carrot, making me wonder if Max saw me as a hindrance rather than a partner.

I wiped my hands on my apron, taking a deep breath as I gathered the courage to confront him. My heart raced, each beat echoing the weight of what I was about to say. The kitchen door swung open, and there he was, his brow furrowed in concentration, his fingers brushing through his hair in that way that always made my heart skip. "Hey, I thought I'd find you here," he said, his voice warm yet distant, as if he were speaking from across a chasm rather than just a few feet away.

"Max, we need to talk," I said, forcing the words through a throat tight with unshed tears. The moment hung heavy in the air, and I could see the flicker of surprise in his eyes, swiftly replaced by that familiar guardedness.

"About what?" He leaned against the counter, arms crossed, a posture that screamed both nonchalance and defensiveness. The walls I had built around my heart began to crumble under the weight of his indifference.

"About this—about us." I stepped closer, my hands trembling slightly as I gestured between us. "I feel like you're slipping away, and I don't want to lose you. Not now, when everything we've built is at stake."

Max's gaze darted to the floor, and I could see the tension coiling in his jaw, a visible battle raging within him. "Losing the shop is a real possibility, Lena. I'm just trying to find a way to save it. You know how much this means to me."

I nodded, the lump in my throat growing larger as his words cut deeper than I had anticipated. "But what about us? You and me?

Is this just business for you now?" My voice cracked, a tremor of vulnerability breaking through the bravado I had clung to.

"It's not just business," he snapped, and the sharpness in his tone felt like a slap. "But I can't think about anything else right now."

The silence that followed was suffocating, and in that moment, the distance between us felt insurmountable. I took a step back, retreating from the intensity of his gaze. "I get it, but I can't be your second thought. I refuse to be. This shop isn't just a dream; it's our dream. If you're more focused on Oliver and his proposal, then maybe I'm not the right partner for you."

The words tumbled out before I could catch them, each syllable weighted with fear and desperation. Max looked up, a mix of confusion and hurt flickering in his eyes. "Lena, don't say that. You know how much you mean to me."

I laughed, though it was a hollow sound. "Do I? Because right now, it feels like I'm just another ingredient in your recipe for success."

The words hung in the air, suspended in an awkward silence. I could feel the heat rising in my cheeks, the sting of tears threatening to spill over. "I don't want to lose the shop, Max. I can't—"

"Stop," he interrupted, stepping forward, his voice softening. "You're not losing anything. I just... I need to figure this out."

"Then figure it out with me." My heart ached as I spoke, the vulnerability of the moment pressing against my chest like an invisible weight. "I'm scared, Max. Scared that when the dust settles, you won't want me anymore."

Max opened his mouth, a flicker of something—understanding, maybe?—crossing his features. "You're not just my business partner, Lena. You're..."

"Am I?" I challenged, crossing my arms, suddenly feeling small and exposed. "Then why does it feel like I'm fighting for scraps of your attention?"

"I don't want you to feel that way," he said, frustration lacing his tone. "But Oliver's making it difficult to focus on anything else. I don't know what I want right now."

As his confession lingered in the air, I felt a bittersweet pang in my chest. "Then let me help you find it. Don't shut me out, please." My voice trembled, each word a plea, an offering wrapped in a bow of hope.

He ran a hand through his hair, the gesture somehow both endearing and infuriating, as if he were trying to untangle the chaos inside his head. "Okay," he finally said, his voice barely above a whisper. "Let's figure it out together."

And just like that, in the simmering tension of that cramped kitchen, with the sweet aroma of chocolate enveloping us, I felt a flicker of warmth, a promise that perhaps we could rebuild what had been shattered. The air was still thick with unresolved tension, but for the first time in days, it felt like a step toward something more solid, something that could withstand the trials ahead.

The next few days felt like a tangled skein of yarn, each thread a different shade of anxiety and unspoken words, knotting together in ways I could hardly untangle. I threw myself into the kitchen, enveloped in the comforting embrace of cocoa powder and sugar, determined to craft something spectacular to reignite the spark between us. But each batch of truffles, each decadent layer of chocolate cake, came with an undercurrent of tension that seemed to shadow every moment we shared.

Max was a ghost of himself, his laughter muted, his eyes often lost in the distance, contemplating Oliver's vision for the shop, a vision that felt more like a takeover. I noticed how he leaned in closer to Oliver, engaged in conversations that buzzed with business jargon and potential profits, while I stood on the sidelines like a forgotten garnish on an extravagant plate. "Maybe I should just wear a sign that says 'chocolate girl' instead of a name tag," I muttered to myself one afternoon, trying to joke my way through the palpable distance. The absurdity of it made me chuckle, but the laughter quickly turned into a sigh.

One evening, the kitchen bathed in a soft, golden glow from the overhead lights, I felt the walls closing in. My fingers, dusted with flour, trembled slightly as I shaped the dough for a new pastry. The recipe was an ambitious mix of sweet and savory—a nod to the whimsical side of my culinary spirit. But the warmth of the oven did little to thaw the cold knot in my stomach, the anxiety swirling tighter with every second I spent without clarity.

"Hey, Lena, do you think we could use more raspberry in this?" Max's voice broke into my thoughts as he peered over my shoulder. I turned, startled, and met his gaze. His blue eyes were filled with a mix of concern and a hint of that familiar mischief that used to make my heart race.

"Is this where you tell me to stop experimenting and stick to what sells?" I quipped, not bothering to hide the bite in my tone. The irritation bubbled up, uninvited.

"I mean, if you want to make all our customers diabetic, who am I to stop you?" he shot back, a grin creeping onto his face. The moment felt like a tightrope walk—one slip away from disaster.

"Very funny, but last I checked, chocolate shops thrive on sweetness, not sarcasm." I rolled my eyes, trying to soften the sharp edges of my words.

"Touché. But seriously, this looks incredible." He leaned closer, his shoulder brushing against mine. The warmth radiating from him was a stark contrast to the chill of the unresolved tension hanging between us.

I took a deep breath, the scent of butter and sugar swirling around us, trying to capture a sense of calm. "I just want to remind you of what we're about, Max. Not just the business side of things."

He shifted, the weight of my words visibly settling on him. "I know, I know. But this is complicated."

"Complicated? Or just a mess we need to clean up?" My frustration bubbled over, and before I could stop myself, I added, "Maybe it's not just the shop that needs fixing."

Max's expression hardened, the playful light in his eyes dimming. "This again? I'm doing what I think is best for us, Lena."

"By pushing me away?" I shot back, my voice rising slightly. "You think shutting me out while you plan with Oliver is what's best? Do you even hear yourself?"

He opened his mouth, but the words seemed to evaporate, lost in the tension between us. "You don't understand how much is at stake," he finally said, frustration etching deep lines across his forehead. "We need to be strategic about this."

"And what strategy involves ignoring your partner?" I folded my arms, the gesture meant to protect myself but instead only making me feel more exposed.

Max exhaled sharply, running a hand through his hair, his frustration palpable. "It's not about you; it's about the business."

"Right, and here I thought I was part of that business," I retorted, feeling the anger rise within me.

"Of course you are!" His voice rose to match mine, the kitchen atmosphere thickening with our emotions. "But I can't think of everything all at once!"

"Then let's tackle it together!" The desperation in my voice made me wince, but I pressed on, willing to lay it all on the table. "I'm scared, Max. Scared that this will all fall apart, and we'll lose everything we've built. Including us."

There was a pause, an awkward silence that felt heavy, charged with all the unspoken fears and desires. His gaze softened, and I could see the conflict playing out behind his eyes. "Lena…"

"Just say it," I urged, desperation creeping into my tone. "If you don't want this anymore, if you don't want me, just say it."

His expression shifted, the vulnerability breaking through his tough exterior. "I never said that."

"Then what are we doing?" I stepped closer, the distance between us feeling like an insurmountable chasm. "We can't keep pretending that everything is fine when it's not."

"I want this," he said, his voice lower now, almost a whisper. "I want you. But I'm scared, too. I can't lose you, but I also can't lose the shop."

The words hung in the air, a fragile thread woven between us. "Then let's figure it out. Together," I implored, my heart pounding with the weight of my hope.

He nodded slowly, the fight in him wavering as he took a step toward me. "Okay, together. But we have to be honest with each other."

"Agreed." I exhaled, the tension easing just a little, like a crack of light breaking through a stormy sky. "Let's promise to communicate. No more shutting down."

Max's lips curled into a tentative smile, the familiar warmth returning to his eyes. "No more shutting down," he echoed, his voice steadier now. "And maybe a little more experimenting with pastries, because if this shop is going to survive, we need to be on our A-game."

I laughed, the sound echoing through the kitchen like a melody. "Okay, fine. But you better be ready for some weird combinations. How do you feel about chocolate avocado mousse?"

His eyes widened, a playful glint sparkling. "That sounds like a crime against humanity, but I'm game if you are."

The laughter danced between us, bridging the gap that had felt insurmountable moments before. As we worked side by side, creating and joking, I could feel the foundation beneath us beginning to solidify. Maybe we were still standing on shaky ground, but at least we were facing it together, armed with a renewed commitment to not just our business, but to each other.

The tension hung in the air like the rich scent of cocoa, both intoxicating and suffocating. The kitchen felt alive around us, bustling with the whir of mixers and the gentle crackle of caramel bubbling on the stove. Yet amid the clatter and clang, my heart raced, and my thoughts swirled in a storm of confusion and hope. Max and I had cracked open the door to honest communication, but I still sensed the fragile balance between us, teetering on the edge of something that could either bind us closer or push us apart.

I watched him move, graceful yet pensive, as he measured out ingredients with precision, each scoop and pour a reminder of our shared history. We had always worked well together, our collaboration a dance that seamlessly intertwined our individual strengths. But now, it felt like a delicate choreography where one misstep could send us spiraling into chaos. The laughter we had shared earlier in the week seemed like a distant memory, replaced by the gravity of what lay ahead.

"What do you think of this?" I asked, breaking the silence, my voice carrying an undertone of vulnerability. I held out a tray of mini tarts, each delicately filled with a swirl of chocolate mousse and topped with a candied orange slice. "Too much flair, or just enough pizzazz?"

Max paused, his brow furrowed in concentration. "They look stunning, but we need to be careful about how extravagant we get. Our regulars love the classics."

"A little flair never hurt anyone," I countered playfully, though the truth felt heavy in my chest. "Besides, who says we can't be a little daring? That's what sets us apart."

"True," he said, offering me a soft smile that made my heart flutter, despite the lingering tension. "But daring doesn't always mean extravagant. Sometimes, it's about how we present the familiar."

"Mr. Businessman," I teased, rolling my eyes. "Isn't that just a fancy way of saying we should play it safe?"

"Not safe—strategic," he replied, his tone lightening as we fell back into our rhythm. "There's a difference."

I opened my mouth to argue, but the sound of the bell above the shop door jingled, interrupting our banter. I turned to see Oliver striding in, all confident charm, his presence instantly altering the atmosphere. The playful warmth that had momentarily cocooned us evaporated, leaving behind an icy tension that crawled up my spine.

"Hey, team!" he called out, his voice dripping with enthusiasm. "I've got some exciting news!"

Max's posture stiffened, his expression turning cautious. "What's up?"

Oliver grinned, seemingly oblivious to the unease radiating from us. "I've been thinking about some marketing strategies, and I believe we should launch a pop-up event. It'll not only attract new customers but also get our loyal fans buzzing."

"Sounds intriguing," I said, attempting to mask my apprehension. "But what's the plan?"

"Picture this: a chocolate festival right here in our shop, featuring tasting stations, workshops, and maybe even a few surprise guests," he explained, his eyes sparkling with excitement. "We can showcase our unique flavors and bring in the community!"

Max exchanged a glance with me, a flicker of concern passing between us. "That's a lot to take on, Oliver. We're already stretched thin," he cautioned, his protective instincts kicking in.

"Exactly!" Oliver replied, undeterred. "But it's a chance to elevate the shop's profile. We can't afford to sit back while the competition heats up. We need to strike while the iron is hot."

"Hot iron or not, we still have to be practical," I interjected, feeling my pulse quicken. "We need to make sure this event aligns with our vision."

"Of course, Lena. But think about the exposure," Oliver countered smoothly. "Imagine the social media buzz, the new clientele! We can make this place the talk of the town."

Max rubbed the back of his neck, visibly torn. "It sounds great in theory, but we need to think about logistics. We don't have the resources to pull off something of this scale without careful planning."

Oliver's smile faltered for a split second, but he quickly masked it with charm. "You two worry too much. We can manage this! I'll take care of the marketing. Just trust me."

Trust was a fragile commodity in our trio, and I could see the doubt flickering in Max's eyes. "Let's discuss it more before we make any commitments," he said slowly, the weight of leadership resting heavily on his shoulders.

As Oliver nodded, I felt a surge of resolve bubbling within me. "How about we brainstorm ideas together?" I suggested, looking at Max with a determined smile. "We could incorporate some of the experimental flavors I've been working on. If we're going to do this, let's make it memorable."

Max's expression softened, a glimmer of pride breaking through his uncertainty. "That could work. If we're going to take a risk, let's do it our way."

Oliver raised an eyebrow, his excitement bubbling back to the surface. "Now that's the spirit! I knew I could count on you two."

As we began tossing ideas back and forth, the initial tension began to dissolve, and the kitchen buzzed with creativity. I felt invigorated, my mind racing with possibilities: a "chocolate and wine" pairing station, chocolate-dipping demonstrations, and even a quirky contest to see who could create the most outlandish chocolate dessert. Laughter erupted between us, and I could feel a flicker of hope igniting. Maybe this could be the push we needed to rally our spirits and bring the community together.

Just as the momentum built, my phone buzzed on the counter, breaking the flow of our discussion. I glanced down to see a message from my mom: "We need to talk. Important news." The tone was urgent, and a knot formed in my stomach as unease settled in.

"Everything okay?" Max asked, catching my change in demeanor.

"Uh, yeah, just my mom," I stammered, my voice betraying the sudden chill that had spread through me.

"Do you need to take it?" He looked concerned, his eyes searching mine.

"Just a minute," I said, stepping away to answer the message. "What's up?"

"Lena, it's about your dad..."

The rest of her words blurred together, a whirlwind of panic that left me reeling. I blinked, the warmth of the kitchen fading as reality crashed over me. My heart pounded in my chest, and I felt a sudden urgency to grasp hold of something solid. "What do you mean?" I whispered, my breath hitching.

"Things aren't great. He's been in and out of the hospital."

A weight pressed down on me, heavy and suffocating. I could feel the world spinning off its axis, the kitchen fading into a mere backdrop of chaos. I was about to reply when I heard Oliver's laughter drift over, a sound so innocent and carefree. But now, in stark contrast, the news from my mom felt like a punch to the gut, uprooting everything I had fought to build.

"Hey, is everything alright?" Max's voice broke through my haze, but all I could do was nod, the words caught in my throat.

"Yeah, just... family stuff," I managed, my heart racing with a fear that gnawed at my insides.

But the moment felt heavy, like a dam about to break. As I turned back to join them, my eyes landed on Max, his brow furrowed with concern, and Oliver, full of enthusiasm, blissfully unaware of the storm brewing just beneath the surface. And in that instant, I realized I was standing on the precipice of two worlds, the foundations of my life shifting beneath my feet.

"Can we talk?" I blurted out, urgency lacing my tone, my heart pounding.

Max nodded, but the flicker of anxiety in his eyes mirrored my own, as Oliver looked back, curiosity dancing across his features. Just as the words hung in the air, my phone buzzed again. I glanced down and saw another message, one that sent a chill racing up my spine: "We'll be in town tomorrow. You need to be there."

"Tomorrow?" I breathed, my heart racing as panic flooded my senses.

Max's gaze sharpened, and for a moment, time stood still, the air thick with unspoken words and a future that felt uncertain. Just then, a crash echoed from the back of the kitchen, sending my heart into overdrive.

"Did you hear that?" I asked, eyes wide, dread creeping in.

Before Max could respond, the door swung open, and chaos erupted, plunging us all into a whirlwind of confusion and fear.

Chapter 6: Sweet Sacrifices

The air inside the chocolatier's shop buzzed with the heady aroma of melted chocolate, a scent so rich it could wrap around you like a warm blanket on a cold winter night. I stood behind the counter, nervously smoothing my apron as I surveyed the scene unfolding before me. Local faces lit up with curiosity and delight as they mingled, their laughter echoing against the walls adorned with vibrant paintings of cocoa trees and swirling patterns that seemed to dance in time with the upbeat music spilling from the small speakers in the corner. Each truffle I had painstakingly crafted sat temptingly on the display, an array of colors and flavors begging to be sampled.

"Okay, everyone! Gather around!" I called out, my voice cracking just slightly. The room quieted, and all eyes turned toward me. This was it—the moment I had been working toward for weeks. My heart raced as I glanced down at the assortment of confections, each a little piece of my soul wrapped in delicate chocolate. I took a deep breath, trying to ground myself in the present, away from the anxiety that had been gnawing at me since the idea for this tasting event had sprung to life.

"Welcome to our first community tasting! We're thrilled to share our new creations with you all today. Each piece tells a story, a blend of flavors inspired by our wonderful neighborhood." I motioned toward the truffles, my hands trembling slightly. "Feel free to try as many as you like, and please, let me know what you think!"

The crowd began to shift closer, their enthusiasm palpable as they picked up the first samples. I watched their faces transform from curiosity to sheer bliss as they tasted the chocolate. A small boy, probably no older than eight, took a cautious nibble of a raspberry ganache and then his eyes widened, his mouth full. "This is the best thing I've ever eaten!" he exclaimed, and my heart soared.

Amidst the joy, however, a shadow crept through the doorway, sliding in with the grace of a panther. Oliver. His presence was magnetic, pulling the attention of nearly everyone in the room as he made his way toward me. I could see the effortless charm radiating from him, like sunlight glinting off a polished surface, and my stomach twisted in knots. Just last week, I had poured my heart into a particularly delectable espresso truffle, imagining it would bring people together, only for Oliver to swoop in like a ravenous crow, ready to pick apart my creation, my dreams.

"Fancy seeing you here, Clara," he said, his voice smooth as melted chocolate, a grin spreading across his face. "I didn't know you were such an aspiring chocolatier." His dark eyes sparkled with mischief, and for a moment, I could feel the weight of my insecurities pressing down on me like a heavy cloak.

"Thanks, Oliver. I didn't know you were a critic." I shot back, a little more sass creeping into my voice than I intended. "What brings you to our humble little tasting? Looking for something to critique?" I managed to keep my tone light, but inside I was fuming, a swirling tempest of emotions threatening to spill over.

"Actually, I came to see how you're faring after the rumors. I mean, people love a good chocolate scandal, don't they?" He leaned against the counter, casually inspecting a coconut cream truffle as if it were a jewel in a display case.

I gritted my teeth, forcing a smile. "Well, I appreciate your concern, but we're just fine. The community is rallying around us. Isn't that what really matters?"

"Touché," he replied, his gaze locking onto mine with an intensity that made my heart race and my breath hitch. "But are you really fine, or are you just playing the part?"

I didn't have an answer. Every moment I spent in his orbit felt like walking a tightrope, the ground below me teetering on the edge of collapse. The evening unfolded around us, laughter and conversation weaving a tapestry of community spirit, while tension simmered just beneath the surface. As people continued to sample the truffles, I struggled to keep my composure, focusing on the joyous feedback rather than the smirk on Oliver's face.

"Hey, what do you say we do a little taste test?" he suggested, his playful grin broadening. "I'll choose a truffle, and you can guess the flavor."

"Fine," I said, rolling my eyes, trying to mask my growing annoyance. "But if you choose the caramel sea salt, I'm officially declaring it a personal victory."

Oliver laughed, his laughter like the ringing of chimes, a sound that both irritated and intrigued me. "Oh, you're on. Let's make it interesting. Winner gets to decide the next community event."

"Deal," I said, the words slipping out before I could consider the implications. The stakes were suddenly high, but I had an advantage. After weeks of experimenting, I knew my creations inside and out.

With that, the playful rivalry shifted the energy in the room, drawing others in. I watched as he picked a dark chocolate truffle, expertly crafted with a hint of chili. My heart raced as I tasted it, the unexpected heat igniting a spark on my tongue.

"You've got guts," I admitted, trying to maintain my bravado as I swallowed. "But it won't be enough to beat me."

As the event rolled on, I felt the warmth of community washing over me, soothing my worries. Laughter bubbled around me like the effervescence of champagne, a stark contrast to the icy tension that Oliver brought. With each smile and compliment from the attendees, I reclaimed a piece of myself that I had feared lost. Yet, just as I began to feel the joy of the evening, I caught a glimpse of Oliver's gaze drifting toward the door, and my heart sank.

The momentary reprieve shattered as the door swung open, and a figure appeared, their silhouette casting a long shadow that crept across the floor like an ominous omen. I didn't recognize the newcomer, but the energy shifted instantly. Conversations halted, eyes darted between me and the figure, and I felt the laughter die in my throat, replaced by a cold knot of dread.

In that moment, I understood that the sweet sacrifices I had made to keep the chocolatier alive were only the beginning.

The tension in the room escalated, coiling tightly like a spring ready to snap. I watched as the newcomer, a striking figure dressed in a tailored coat that seemed to shimmer with an unspoken confidence, stepped fully inside the shop. Her dark hair fell in smooth waves around her shoulders, framing a face that held both beauty and a hint of mischief. As she swept her gaze across the crowd, it was as if she were taking inventory of their reactions, measuring their excitement and delight against her own inscrutable intentions.

"Is this a party or a funeral?" she quipped, her voice melodic yet sharp, cutting through the murmur of surprise that rippled through the room. The crowd responded with a mix of laughter and confusion, a wave of curiosity washing over the initial tension.

"Welcome!" I managed to call out, pushing through the sudden anxiety tightening my chest. "We're just showcasing our latest creations. Feel free to join us!" I forced a smile, hoping to project an aura of calm amidst the storm swirling just beneath the surface.

She approached with a confident stride, her heels clicking against the wooden floor, a sound that commanded attention. "I see you're trying to make a name for yourself, little chocolatier," she said, leaning casually against the counter. "What's your secret?"

"Passion, mostly. And a bit of sleepless nights," I replied, my voice steadier than I felt. "It's all about infusing love into each truffle. Care to try?" I offered her a plate, my heart racing.

"Only if you're prepared for the critique," she challenged, a playful glint in her eye.

The challenge hung in the air between us, thick with anticipation. I watched her pick up a lavender-infused dark chocolate truffle, examining it as if it were a rare artifact. "Lavender, huh? A bold choice. Do you think people are ready for something that... unconventional?"

"Why not?" I replied, a smirk tugging at my lips. "It's either that or the plain old caramel, which I assure you I can whip up in my sleep."

"Ah, but the plain old caramel is what people expect," she countered, popping the truffle into her mouth. "Expectations are such a bore, don't you think?" Her eyes widened in delight as the flavors danced on her palate, and for a moment, I felt a flicker of camaraderie.

"Exactly! I'm all about breaking molds here. Who wants to be just another face in the crowd?" I leaned in closer, the atmosphere around us charged with a spark of competitive spirit. "Besides, if everyone played it safe, we wouldn't have chocolate bacon truffles now, would we?"

She chuckled, her laughter light and infectious, and I could feel the ice between us thawing. "Touché. You might just have a point. What's your name, little chocolatier?"

"Clara," I replied, lifting my chin slightly. "And you are...?"

"Vivienne," she said with a theatrical flourish, as if her name alone held the weight of a grand title. "And I must say, I'm intrigued. It's rare to find someone willing to challenge the status quo, especially in a place as quaint as this."

"Quaint?" I echoed, feigning indignation. "I prefer 'charmingly rustic.'"

Just as Vivienne was about to respond, Oliver cleared his throat, his earlier charm morphing into something sharper. "Ah, Vivienne, I didn't expect to see you here," he said, his tone dripping with false cordiality. "What brings you to our little tasting?"

"Just curious to see what all the fuss was about," she replied, casting a sideways glance at me, her expression unreadable. "You know how it is, Oliver. Can't let all these ordinary folks get too comfortable."

Oliver's smile faltered for a split second, and I seized the moment. "Well, we're glad you could join us. If you have any suggestions or critiques, I'm all ears. This shop thrives on feedback." I shot Oliver a pointed look, daring him to challenge my resolve.

Vivienne's interest seemed piqued. "Now that's the spirit! But do you really think you can handle the truth? You might be running a quaint little chocolate shop, but I've seen my fair share of failures masquerading as 'art.'"

"I'm not afraid of criticism," I replied, crossing my arms defiantly. "I'd rather fail spectacularly than blend in with the background."

"Now that's refreshing." Vivienne's eyes sparkled as she leaned closer. "Let's see how deep your conviction runs. What's next on the tasting agenda?"

"Next?" I glanced back at the display, trying to remember my carefully organized lineup. "How about the chili chocolate? A little spice to kick things up a notch?"

"Spice?" she echoed, her eyebrow arching in playful challenge. "Or desperation? Let's find out!"

I served her a sample, my heart racing as I watched her bite into the rich dark chocolate, the faint heat of chili mingling with the sweetness. A moment stretched as the flavors melded, the crowd around us holding their breath. Finally, she closed her eyes, a soft sigh escaping her lips. "Now that is impressive. The heat is subtle but bold, and the chocolate is velvety smooth."

My chest swelled with pride at her words. "Thank you! I've been experimenting with that one. It's meant to surprise."

"Surprise, indeed. I could get used to this," she admitted, a grin spreading across her face. "What else do you have hidden in that magic cabinet of yours?"

As I continued to showcase more of my creations, the mood in the shop shifted. Laughter and chatter filled the air, with people eagerly sampling the truffles and sharing their thoughts. I reveled in the moment, the community around me buzzing with energy, my heart buoyed by the growing excitement.

Oliver, however, hovered at the edges, his smile turning into a mask, his eyes watching me with a mix of admiration and annoyance. I could feel the weight of his gaze like a storm cloud looming overhead, threatening to spill at any moment.

"Looks like you've found your muse," he commented dryly as Vivienne moved on to another truffle. "Just hope she doesn't lead you astray."

"Or perhaps she'll help me soar," I shot back, a playful smile on my lips. "I'm not one to shy away from a little adventure, Oliver."

Vivienne laughed, and her presence felt electric, the kind of spark I had longed for since this journey began. But as I glanced back at Oliver, the tension in the air shifted again, a foreboding feeling creeping into my mind.

The evening continued with laughter and banter, and for a moment, I forgot about the stakes that hung over my head, losing myself in the joy of connection. But deep down, I knew that every chocolate truffle I shared was a step deeper into an unknown territory, where not just my business, but my heart, was at stake.

The room thrummed with energy, a lively blend of conversations and laughter weaving through the air like strands of delicate chocolate. I moved among the tables, my heart lightening with every compliment tossed my way. Each praise felt like a reassuring pat on the back, soothing the worries that had gnawed at me since the event's inception. The chocolate creations gleamed under the warm glow of fairy lights strung across the ceiling, and as Vivienne sauntered through the crowd, she radiated confidence, her charm drawing people in like bees to honey.

"Clara!" she called, her voice lilting with enthusiasm. "Have you tried the chocolate stout truffles yet? They're a revelation!"

I looked over, catching sight of a group gathered around a platter adorned with rich, dark treats. "You're not just buttering me up, are you?" I teased, moving to her side. "I might just put you to work here if you keep this up."

"Only if I get to wear one of those adorable aprons," she shot back with a playful wink, her eyes dancing. "But seriously, these truffles are what you'd call 'life-changing.'"

"That's the goal," I replied, my chest swelling with pride. "To change lives, one truffle at a time."

"Good plan! But I must admit," she said, leaning in conspiratorially, "I'm a bit worried about Oliver lurking in the background. What's his deal, anyway?"

I shrugged, the warmth of her camaraderie battling with the tension his presence instilled. "He's... complicated. He's a smooth talker, and he knows how to play the crowd. I wouldn't be surprised if he has ulterior motives."

"Ah, the classic bad boy with a heart of chocolate. Intriguing," Vivienne mused, glancing toward Oliver, who had taken a seat in the corner, observing us with a smirk that sent a shiver down my spine. "Are you sure you're up for this? It feels like a romantic comedy waiting to happen, and I'm not sure if you're the heroine or the sidekick."

"Definitely the heroine," I shot back with a laugh, my confidence buoyed by her playful banter. "But this isn't a movie; it's my life. I have to take charge and make things happen, right?"

"Right!" she agreed, raising her glass of sparkling cider in a toast. "To making things happen!"

As the crowd mingled, I started to notice the conversations shifting. Whispers began to ripple through the room, conversations hushed, and heads turned toward Oliver. He was telling a story, his voice low and smooth, and I could see the way the crowd hung on his every word, their eyes sparkling with intrigue.

"Seems he's got them eating out of his hand," I muttered, my smile faltering as I watched him. "I can't let him take the spotlight away from the shop."

Vivienne caught my arm, her grip steadying me. "Hey, you're the one who put in the work. Don't let him overshadow you. Shine like the chocolate you are."

I took a breath, steadying myself as I stepped away from Vivienne, determination coursing through my veins. I moved toward the crowd, ready to reclaim the narrative. "Ladies and gentlemen!" I called, raising my voice above the chatter. "Thank you for being here tonight! It means the world to us. I want to introduce you to my personal favorite: the chili chocolate truffle!"

The crowd turned to me, their attention shifting from Oliver's suave storytelling back to my vibrant enthusiasm. I quickly launched into an explanation of the truffle's creation, the marriage of spice and sweetness, how it represented my vision for the shop. I could see the excitement building as I handed out samples, laughter echoing in the space as they bit into the unexpected heat.

As the evening wore on, I felt the weight of the crowd's approval. Oliver, however, seemed to revel in his role as the undercurrent to my sweet overture. He waited until I was least expecting it, then approached, an insufferable grin plastered across his face. "Impressive speech, Clara. But let's see if your truffles can actually hold up to a real taste test."

I raised an eyebrow. "Oh? Is that a challenge I hear?"

He nodded, feigning innocence. "I wouldn't dream of challenging the great chocolatier, but I think a little friendly competition could be fun. How about we have a taste-off? Your best against mine. Winner gets to dictate the future of this little shop."

I clenched my jaw, irritation flaring. "And you think you can just waltz in here and dictate anything? This shop is my heart, Oliver."

"Exactly, which is why it's important to know who's best." He leaned closer, lowering his voice just enough for only me to hear. "Besides, I'm curious to see how much you're willing to sacrifice to keep it afloat."

The crowd began to murmur, excitement coursing through them. I looked around at the eager faces, and despite the frustration bubbling inside me, I knew that I couldn't back down now. "Fine. Let's make it interesting. We'll each choose a truffle, and the winner gets to choose the next community event, as well as—" I paused, thinking quickly, "—the other's secret recipe."

A collective gasp spread through the crowd, a ripple of anticipation. I could practically feel the stakes rise, the air thickening with tension. Oliver's grin widened, a predatory glint in his eyes. "Now we're talking. I accept your challenge, Clara."

As we both prepared our creations, a hush fell over the crowd. I took my time, crafting a decadent mocha truffle infused with a hint of cinnamon, determined to showcase not just my skill but my heart. With each delicate swirl of chocolate, I poured everything I had into it, knowing that failure wasn't an option.

Oliver worked with his usual flair, flashing a smile at the audience as he presented a visually stunning raspberry and champagne truffle. "An elegant choice for an elegant shop," he quipped, and the crowd oohed and aahed in response.

When it was time for the taste test, the anticipation was electric. The first bite was met with silence, and then the crowd erupted into chatter, trying to discern the subtle flavors. My heart raced as I watched their reactions, the balance of anxiety and excitement swirling within me.

Vivienne, standing at the forefront of the crowd, took a bite of my truffle and closed her eyes in bliss. "Oh, Clara, this is divine!"

I let out a breath I hadn't realized I was holding, hope bubbling within me like the finest melted chocolate. But just as I felt the tide turning in my favor, a commotion erupted at the door. The sound of glass shattering echoed through the shop, and I turned, my stomach dropping.

A figure burst through the entrance, breathless and wild-eyed. "Clara! You need to come quick. There's a—"

Before she could finish her thought, the lights flickered ominously, plunging the shop into darkness for a heartbeat, and when they flickered back on, the crowd was buzzing with confusion. Oliver's smirk faltered, and I felt a chill creep up my spine.

"What's going on?" I demanded, trying to make sense of the chaos unfolding.

The newcomer stepped closer, her eyes wide and frantic. "There's a fire at the back of the shop! We need to evacuate!"

My heart raced as panic clawed at my chest, and I glanced at Oliver, who looked equally startled. In a heartbeat, the sweetness of the evening had turned bitter, and as I turned to face the crowd, the reality of our situation began to sink in. The community I had brought together was now a whirlwind of fear and uncertainty, and I knew, with every fiber of my being, that this was only the beginning.

Chapter 7: Shattered Dreams

The aroma of rich chocolate wafted through the air, clinging to my clothes like an uninvited guest. Each bite-sized truffle I handed to eager guests felt like a piece of my heart, meticulously crafted but now vulnerable under the scrutiny of their sweet-toothed enthusiasm. I smiled wide, plastering on a façade of enthusiasm, while inside, a storm brewed. The tasting event, meant to be our moment—a spotlight shining on our little chocolatier—had turned into a chaotic whirlwind, swirling with doubt and discontent.

I glanced over at Oliver, who was effortlessly charming the crowd, his voice a melodic lure drawing in curious patrons. His laughter danced above the clinking glasses and animated chatter, a siren song that drew attention like moths to a flame. The sheer magnetism of his presence felt like a dagger twisting in my gut. Oliver, my partner in both business and life, had transformed from the sweet boy who shared chocolate secrets with me into a force I struggled to reckon with.

Each time he flashed that disarming grin, it felt like he was not only selling chocolates but also a vision of grandeur I hadn't been included in. His plans to host a larger event—one that could potentially overshadow my efforts—clanged in my mind like a church bell tolling at a funeral. It was as if the bright dreams we had spun together were unraveling before my eyes, thread by delicate thread, revealing an uncomfortable truth: I was no longer the center of his universe.

With a shaky breath, I poured a cup of rich hot cocoa for a guest, my hands trembling slightly. The crowd continued to swell, but I felt like I was sinking. I could hear snippets of Oliver's chatter, his voice resonating with warmth and confidence. "Imagine this place filled to the brim with people, all tasting the finest chocolates!" he exclaimed, his eyes sparkling with excitement. The applause and laughter that followed stung more than I cared to admit.

I forced myself to focus on the task at hand, arranging an assortment of chocolate-covered strawberries on a silver platter, their glossy sheen making them look almost too perfect to eat. A few patrons approached, their eyes lighting up as they reached for the plump berries, and I greeted them with my best customer service smile. "These are freshly dipped. You won't regret it!"

But my mind was elsewhere, wrestling with the creeping feelings of anger and disappointment. Each compliment hurled at Oliver was another reminder of how I had unknowingly stepped into the shadows of his ambition. I thought of Max, my steadfast partner, and how our shared dreams for this chocolatier now felt less like a vibrant painting and more like a rough sketch, the details muddied and uncertain.

Our eyes met across the room, his gaze a calm harbor amidst the tumult. Max had a knack for finding clarity in chaos; I admired that about him. He approached me as the event began to fizzle, the crowd gradually thinning as patrons drifted off into the night, chocolate buzz fading into the crisp evening air. "You good?" he asked, his brow furrowing with concern.

"I'm peachy," I replied, perhaps a bit too brightly, and he raised an eyebrow, unconvinced. I couldn't burden him with my swirling thoughts, the bitterness pooling like stagnant water within me. But the look in his eyes told me he knew me too well, and he wasn't buying my forced cheerfulness.

"Let's take a breather," he suggested, his voice low and soothing, cutting through the disarray of my thoughts. I nodded, grateful for the escape. We slipped away from the remnants of our gathering, retreating to the back of the shop where the faint hum of conversation was replaced by the comforting silence of our kitchen.

The space was a comforting blend of chaos and order, with the remnants of our passion scattered about—flour dust lingering in the air and empty molds waiting for the next round of creations. I leaned against the counter, the cool marble offering solace, as Max began tidying up the clutter left behind. His movements were methodical, each action a testament to his patience.

"What's really going on?" he asked gently, never one to shy away from the heart of the matter. I bit my lip, the weight of unspoken words heavy on my tongue. "I don't know, Max. I just..." The words were stuck, tangled in a mess of insecurities and fears. "I thought we were in this together, you know? Building something special. But now it feels like I'm just... here. In the background."

He paused, his hands stilling as he turned to face me, concern etched across his features. "You're not in the background. This is our shop, our dream. Just because Oliver has ideas doesn't mean he's pushing you aside." His voice was steady, a lifebuoy in my turbulent sea of emotions, but the truth felt more complicated.

"I know, but it doesn't feel that way. I want to be part of that vision too, but it's like he's aiming for a star, and I'm just trying to keep my feet on the ground." My voice wavered, raw and honest, and for a fleeting moment, I felt vulnerable, exposed in a way I hadn't allowed myself to be before.

Max stepped closer, his presence a grounding force. "Then tell him. If you want a seat at the table, you have to pull up a chair." His words wrapped around me, a reminder that I was not alone in this. But deep down, I feared that pulling up a chair meant exposing my insecurities to the very person I felt betrayed by.

"Easier said than done," I muttered, casting my gaze to the floor, the tiles suddenly much more interesting than the conversation. A soft sigh escaped Max's lips.

"Life's not meant to be easy, especially when it comes to chasing dreams. But if you don't speak up, you'll always be left wondering what could have been."

His words hung in the air, heavy with truth. My heart raced as I weighed my options, knowing that confronting Oliver could either mend our fraying ties or further unravel the dreams we had nurtured together. But as I stood there, the reality washed over me like a tidal wave—our dreams were intertwined, and I had to be brave enough to chart my own course.

The kitchen was an oasis of calm, a stark contrast to the whirlwind outside. As the last of the guests filtered out, the weight of my unresolved feelings hung heavily in the air. I watched Max busy himself with the remnants of our event, a reassuring rhythm in the clatter of pans and the hum of the fridge. The scent of cocoa lingered, intoxicating and bittersweet, a reminder of everything we had built and everything now at stake.

"I guess I'll clean up," I said, attempting to ease the silence with a touch of humor. "It's not like the chocolate will wash itself away." Max chuckled, his laughter like a soothing balm.

"True, but if it did, I'd be investing in a chocolate-washing robot right now," he replied, his eyes sparkling with mischief. "Who wouldn't want a machine that can scrub the floors while tasting truffles?"

The playful banter momentarily lifted the heaviness, but I could still feel the shadow of Oliver's announcement looming over us. I grabbed a sponge, letting the warm water envelop my hands as I began scrubbing the sticky remnants of our event from the countertop. "You really think I should talk to Oliver?" I asked, testing the waters, my voice wavering slightly.

Max paused, his brow furrowed. "You don't just think—you know. If you want to keep your dreams alive, you need to make your voice heard. Otherwise, it'll be his show, and you'll just be a supporting character in a play you didn't even audition for."

"Great, so I'm stuck playing the role of the confused best friend who serves chocolate but secretly dreams of stardom," I sighed, shaking my head. "Do you think I'm being ridiculous?"

He turned to me, his expression softening. "Ridiculous? No. Passionate? Absolutely. There's nothing wrong with wanting to be seen and heard, especially when it comes to something you've poured your heart into."

As I rinsed the sponge, the cool water cascaded down my fingers, sending shivers up my arm. His words struck a chord deep within me, a reminder that this chocolatier was not just a business; it was a piece of my soul laid bare for the world to savor. I wiped down the last surface, the finality of my actions echoing in the quiet room.

"Okay, I'll do it," I declared, the resolve settling in my chest like molten chocolate solidifying into something tangible. "I'll talk to him."

Max's smile was warm, a beacon of support. "That's the spirit. Just remember, you're not alone in this. You've got me."

His reassurance was like the comforting embrace of a favorite blanket, a reminder that I had someone who believed in my dreams as much as I did. As I gathered the last of the dirty plates, I felt the gears in my mind start to turn. Maybe it wouldn't be so bad after all.

As night descended, I stepped outside, the cool air wrapping around me like a soft scarf. The streetlamps flickered, casting a warm glow over the cobblestone path, the quaint little town coming alive under the blanket of stars. I inhaled deeply, the sweet scent of chocolate still dancing on the breeze. My heart raced at the thought of what lay ahead, and I could feel a twinge of excitement mingling with my anxiety.

The next day unfolded in a swirl of anticipation, the sun casting a warm glow over our little shop as I prepared for the busy morning rush. Each chocolate I crafted felt like a step closer to my impending confrontation with Oliver. I meticulously arranged the truffles, their glossy surfaces glimmering under the bright lights. My hands moved with a confidence I hadn't felt in days, a flicker of hope igniting within me.

As the door chimed, signaling the arrival of customers, I greeted them with a genuine smile. The warmth of their appreciation reminded me of why I had embarked on this journey in the first place. I handed a box of assorted chocolates to a young couple, their eyes sparkling with delight. "You two will love these! Each one has a little surprise inside," I teased, watching as they exchanged excited glances.

Just as I lost myself in the rhythm of my work, the familiar jingle of the door announced Oliver's arrival. My heart sank slightly at the sight of him, the vibrant energy he exuded contrasting sharply with the turmoil brewing inside me. He sauntered in, a casual air of confidence radiating from him like the scent of freshly baked cookies.

"Morning, sunshine!" he exclaimed, his eyes gleaming with enthusiasm. "I've been brainstorming more ideas for the big event. It's going to be epic!"

His excitement was palpable, a glittering thread woven into the fabric of our shop, but beneath that enthusiasm, I felt my resolve starting to waver. "Right. The big event," I replied, trying to keep my tone light despite the heaviness in my chest.

He approached the counter, leaning on it with an easy grace. "I think we should hire a photographer. Get some stunning shots to promote it."

"Oliver, can we talk for a second?" The words spilled from my lips before I could second-guess myself. The lightheartedness in his eyes dimmed just a fraction, the shift in atmosphere palpable.

"Sure, what's up?" He straightened, the playful demeanor giving way to genuine curiosity. I glanced around, the shop buzzing with customers but somehow feeling isolating in that moment.

"Maybe we can step outside?" I suggested, my pulse quickening as I led him through the door and into the fresh air. The sunlight bathed us in a warm glow, but my stomach churned with uncertainty.

"Is everything okay?" he asked, concern flickering across his face. I took a breath, the cool air filling my lungs, gathering my thoughts like a painter preparing to start a new canvas.

"I just feel like I'm not being heard in this partnership," I blurted, the honesty spilling forth like melted chocolate. "You're moving ahead with this bigger event, and I feel... sidelined. It's like I'm not even part of the picture anymore."

He looked taken aback, the playful facade fading as he processed my words. "I didn't mean to make you feel that way. I thought we were in this together. I wanted to expand, to showcase what we've built."

"I know," I interrupted, urgency lacing my tone. "But it feels like you're doing it all on your own. I want to be part of this, too. This shop, these chocolates—they're as much mine as they are yours."

Silence enveloped us, thick and heavy, as he searched my face for understanding. "I thought I was including you in my plans," he said finally, his voice low. "I didn't realize how much I was overshadowing you."

My heart softened at his honesty, the vulnerability in his eyes pulling me back from the precipice of my frustration. "I need to feel like we're building this together, not just you leading the charge while I hold the fort down."

His expression shifted, understanding washing over him. "You're right. I got caught up in my vision without considering yours. Let's fix this."

Relief surged through me like the first taste of a favorite dessert after a long day. "So, what do we do now?" I asked, allowing a hint of hope to creep into my voice.

He grinned, that infectious charm returning. "How about we blend our ideas? You bring your magic, and we'll create an event that showcases both of our strengths. Together."

As we stood there, the weight of unspoken words lifting, I felt a renewed sense of purpose blossoming within me. This was our chocolatier, a canvas awaiting our collaborative masterpiece.

The tension hung in the air like the rich aroma of melting chocolate, a palpable reminder that the journey ahead would require careful navigation. As Oliver and I began to sketch out plans for the event, his enthusiasm ignited a spark within me that I hadn't expected. There was a thrill in collaboration, a dance of ideas blending into something greater. Yet, beneath that excitement lay an undercurrent of unease, a flicker of doubt that lingered like the bittersweet aftertaste of dark chocolate.

"Okay, so what do you envision?" I asked, leaning against the counter, my heart still thrumming with the adrenaline of our earlier conversation. The sunlight poured through the shop's large front window, illuminating the dust motes swirling in the air, and I felt the warmth seep into my bones.

"I'm thinking a theme that really showcases our story," Oliver suggested, his eyes alight with creativity. "Something that connects the community to the heart of our chocolatier. We can have local vendors, live music—maybe even a chocolate fountain!"

The idea of a chocolate fountain made my heart flutter with delight. The very image of guests laughing, their hands dipping fresh fruit into a cascade of melted chocolate, brought a smile to my face. "A chocolate fountain could be a showstopper," I agreed, imagining the whimsical scene. "But we also need to keep our focus on the truffles. That's what makes us unique."

Oliver nodded, his brow furrowed in thought. "Absolutely. We'll create a signature truffle for the event—something that tells our story, our journey together." The sincerity in his eyes made my stomach flutter, a combination of hope and fear. What if this event was the turning point for both our business and our relationship?

Just then, Max stepped into the room, a few chocolate molds in hand. "Did someone say signature truffle? Count me in! I have a few ideas that could blow everyone's taste buds away."

I grinned at him, appreciating his infectious enthusiasm. "I was just telling Oliver we should create a signature truffle for the event."

Max's eyes sparkled with mischief. "How about a truffle infused with hints of lavender? It'll be like a tiny piece of a garden in every bite!"

"Or what about chili pepper?" I interjected, my creative juices flowing. "A little kick to surprise everyone!"

Oliver chuckled, shaking his head. "Looks like we're off to a good start. Let's aim for a balance—something sweet with a hint of surprise. After all, we want them to remember us for more than just the chocolate."

As we bounced ideas off one another, laughter echoed through the kitchen, the earlier heaviness lifting as our shared vision began to take shape. Yet, even amidst the joy, a nagging feeling tugged at the back of my mind. I wondered if we were merely painting over cracks in a foundation that still needed work.

Later that evening, as the sun dipped below the horizon, casting a warm orange glow through the shop, I took a moment to breathe. The excitement of our plans thrummed through my veins, yet a subtle tension still lingered. I glanced out the window, watching as the world outside transitioned from day to night, the streetlights flickering on one by one.

"Hey," Oliver said, breaking my reverie as he stepped beside me. "What's on your mind?"

I hesitated, unsure if I should share the turmoil that still churned within me. "Just thinking about how we're shaping this event. It's a big step for us."

"True, but it's also an exciting one. We're building something here." He nudged me playfully. "It's a team effort. Just remember, I can't do this without you."

His sincerity warmed me, but a deeper fear lurked in the shadows. What if my voice got lost again amid his ambitions? "You promise we'll stay balanced?" I asked, looking him in the eye, searching for that unwavering commitment I craved.

"Of course. I'd never dream of sidelining you again," he assured me, his expression earnest.

"Good. Because I'm all in," I replied, determination solidifying my resolve.

That night, I tossed and turned in bed, my mind racing with the details of the upcoming event. Thoughts of our signature truffle danced through my head, each flavor playing out like a vivid dream. Yet, with every potential combination, the anxiety of the future gnawed at me. What if the event didn't turn out as we envisioned? What if it pushed us further apart instead of bringing us together?

The following days flew by in a flurry of chocolate-making sessions and brainstorming meetings, the excitement contagious as our ideas transformed into tangible plans. I relished every moment spent creating unique flavors and designing a space that would welcome guests with open arms.

Just as I felt we were gaining momentum, a message from Oliver sent a jolt of panic through me. "We need to talk. Important news."

I stared at the screen, my heart racing. What could be so urgent? Was he pulling the rug out from under us again? I felt a wave of nausea wash over me as I quickly typed a response, trying to keep my emotions in check. "When? I'm at the shop."

"Give me ten minutes."

The seconds dragged on, each tick of the clock echoing like a drumroll in my ears. Finally, he arrived, his expression serious as he stepped through the door.

"Hey, everything okay?" I asked, a hint of worry creeping into my voice.

He took a deep breath, his gaze flickering around the shop, as if gathering his thoughts. "So, I got a call from a local magazine. They want to feature us in their next issue."

Excitement bubbled within me, but I could see the tension in his posture. "That's amazing! Right?"

"Yeah, but... they want to do an in-depth interview. And they're interested in the event we're planning."

"That's fantastic, Oliver!" I exclaimed, my heart soaring. "We'll get so much exposure!"

He rubbed the back of his neck, a nervous habit of his. "There's a catch, though. They're pushing for a more upscale image—think fine dining, exclusive vibes."

I furrowed my brow, the rush of exhilaration dampening. "But that's not really who we are, is it?"

"I know, but it could bring in a lot of business." His eyes bore into mine, a mix of hope and anxiety swirling within them. "What do you think?"

The pressure of his question hung heavy, twisting my insides into knots. "I think we need to be true to ourselves. We can't change our identity for anyone."

Oliver sighed, the lines around his eyes deepening. "I get that. But what if this opportunity doesn't come around again? What if we miss out?"

"Then we create our own opportunities," I replied firmly, a fire igniting within me. "We can find a way to showcase our charm without losing what makes us unique."

He nodded slowly, but uncertainty lingered in his expression. "Okay. Let's stay true to our vision, then. We'll just have to work even harder to make it appealing."

As we stood there, the weight of our conversation heavy in the air, the atmosphere shifted. The door swung open with a jingle, and in walked a figure I hadn't expected: a woman in a tailored suit, her expression poised and determined.

"Excuse me," she interrupted, her gaze sweeping over us. "I'm Chloe from 'Taste & Style.' I'd like to discuss your feature."

My heart sank as I exchanged a quick glance with Oliver, the tension palpable. I felt like we were caught in a delicate web, one wrong move could send us tumbling down. "Uh, we were just discussing—"

Chloe cut me off, her voice smooth yet authoritative. "I'm thrilled to be here. But I need to know if you're prepared to elevate your brand. This is a prime opportunity, and I'd hate to see it wasted."

A knot tightened in my stomach as Oliver's face registered a mix of eagerness and uncertainty. I could feel the stakes rising, and I knew we were at a crossroads. "We're ready for the challenge," he said, but his eyes darted to me, searching for validation.

My heart raced as I faced this unexpected twist. "We're committed to showcasing our true essence," I replied, the conviction in my voice unshakeable.

Chloe's lips curled into a smile, a glimmer of interest in her eyes. "That's good to hear. But let's see if your passion translates into what we need. Show me what you've got."

The air crackled with tension, a potent mix of excitement and dread. As Chloe stepped further into our world, I couldn't shake the feeling that everything was about to change.

Chapter 8: Breaking Barriers

The scent of chocolate lingered in the air, thick and intoxicating, as I paced the small back room of Max's shop, my heart drumming like a heavy bass line against the walls. I could almost taste the bittersweet aroma on my tongue, but it was overshadowed by a growing tempest within me. The early afternoon sun streamed through the window, casting stripes of light and shadow across the wooden floor, illuminating the chaos of unwrapped candy and half-finished confections scattered about. It felt as if the room itself was a reflection of my mind—disorderly yet somehow magical, like a scene from a whimsical storybook.

"Max," I said, my voice rising above the low hum of the cooling machines, "we need to stop pretending everything is fine!" The words burst forth, raw and unfiltered, propelled by the wave of frustration that had been building for weeks. Each syllable hung in the air like a bitter promise, threatening to shatter the fragile veneer of our easy camaraderie. I was surprised to see the way his shoulders tensed at my outburst, the muscle beneath his t-shirt rippling with unspoken tension.

Max turned to face me, his expression a mix of shock and something softer, a hint of understanding that seemed to flicker in his eyes like a candle's flame. "You think I'm pretending?" he asked, his tone sharp, yet there was a vulnerability beneath it that I hadn't noticed before. It was as if my words had peeled back a layer of armor he'd worn for far too long.

"Yes!" I replied, stepping closer, the space between us charged with unvoiced fears and dreams. "You've been acting like this is just another day in the shop, but it's not. We're on the brink of losing everything." The stark reality of our situation seeped into my voice, heavy and palpable.

A heavy silence enveloped us, broken only by the distant sound of customers laughing and chatting outside, oblivious to the turmoil brewing within the chocolate walls of the shop. Finally, he sighed, the sound escaping him like a released breath, heavy with the weight of his own fears. "You think I don't feel it?" His words hung between us like a thick fog, and I could see the struggle etched into his features. "Every day, I wake up with this knot in my stomach, terrified that the next round of bills will be the ones that push us over the edge."

I watched as the facade he'd worn like a shield crumbled before me. Max was not just the quirky chocolatier with the tousled hair and the twinkle in his eye; he was a man, laden with responsibility and dreams that stretched far beyond the confectionery counters. In that moment, our shared vulnerability bridged the distance between us, binding us with threads of honesty and unacknowledged longing.

"I thought it was just me," I admitted, my voice softer now. "I thought I was the only one feeling lost." The confession tasted bitter yet liberating, like dark chocolate melting on my tongue. "When I came back here, I wanted to help, but I didn't know how."

A flicker of surprise crossed Max's face, and his eyes softened, the tension in his brow easing as he moved closer, closing the distance that had felt insurmountable just moments ago. "I never wanted to burden you with all this," he said quietly, his vulnerability lending a gentleness to his demeanor. "But I need you, Claire. More than I can say."

The sincerity in his voice sent a shiver through me, igniting a spark of hope in the pit of my stomach. It was more than just an admission of his struggles; it was an invitation, a call to arms in the battle for our dreams. "Then let's fight for it," I urged, stepping forward, my resolve solidifying. "Let's fight for the shop. For us."

His eyes widened, a mix of surprise and something else—a flicker of desire that sent my heart racing. "You're serious?" he asked, searching my gaze as if trying to discern the depth of my commitment.

"I am," I replied, feeling the weight of our shared fears lift slightly as a new determination filled the air around us. "We've both got dreams we haven't even begun to chase. Let's not let this shop, our childhood dreams, slip away because of fear."

Tears pricked at the corners of my eyes, blurring the world momentarily, and I could see that they mirrored his own. "You know what I wanted to be when I grew up?" I continued, unable to keep the memories at bay. "A chocolatier. I wanted to create sweets that made people smile. I still want that."

Max nodded, his expression earnest and encouraging. "Me too. I remember telling you about my plans to open this place, the visions I had of it filled with laughter and the scent of chocolate. It's just... it feels like the weight of the world is pressing down on me, and I'm afraid I'll fail."

In that moment, a pact formed between us, invisible yet solid, strengthened by the tears we shared and the fears we confronted. We stood together in the heart of the shop that had become our sanctuary and our battleground, ready to take on whatever the world threw at us. I took a deep breath, the scent of cocoa wrapping around me like a warm embrace, and smiled at him. "We're in this together, right? We'll tackle the debts, the marketing, everything. You won't have to shoulder this alone."

His smile broke free, bright and genuine, illuminating the shadows that had crept into his features. "Together," he echoed, a hint of relief washing over him as if I had just lifted a boulder off his chest.

The warmth of our shared resolve ignited a fire within me, and for the first time in weeks, I felt alive, the intoxicating blend of hope and determination fueling my spirit. I took his hand, squeezing it tightly, and for a fleeting moment, the world outside faded away, leaving just the two of us and the dreams we were ready to reclaim.

The next morning dawned with a gentle haze, the kind that cloaked the town in soft whispers of promise and potential. I stood in the kitchen of the chocolatier, the faint sound of the bell above the door chiming softly as customers trickled in. The air was still thick with the warmth of yesterday's revelations, a potent mix of anxiety and excitement swirling like steam from the chocolate fountain in the corner. It felt as though we were on the precipice of something monumental, and I could barely contain the buzzing energy coursing through me.

Max was already at work, meticulously arranging a display of truffles in hues of dark chocolate and raspberry pink, a labor of love. I watched him for a moment, the way his brow furrowed in concentration, a slight curl of a smile tugging at the corners of his lips whenever he turned to glance at me. "You know," I said, leaning against the counter, "if we keep this up, we might just have a miniature art gallery on our hands. Should we start charging admission?"

He chuckled, his laughter warm and inviting, and it wrapped around me like a favorite sweater on a chilly day. "Maybe we should. But you might scare away the customers with your terrible jokes," he teased, his eyes glinting with mischief. I feigned offense, crossing my arms dramatically.

"Terrible? I'll have you know my jokes are finely aged, like a good wine or...well, an aged chocolate," I countered, a smirk breaking through my playful pout.

"Ah, so you're suggesting you're like an exquisite vintage?" he quipped, arching an eyebrow. "I'd argue you're more of a new release, full of freshness and unpredictability. Just like your humor."

I laughed, feeling the tension from the day before begin to melt away. It was astonishing how easily we fell into this rhythm, bantering as if no time had passed, as if yesterday's fears had not loomed over us like dark clouds.

"Speaking of unpredictability," I said, brushing a stray hair behind my ear, "we need to talk about the chocolate festival coming up next month. We can't just show up and hope for the best. If we're going to make a statement, we have to plan."

Max's face shifted from amusement to contemplation. "You're right. It's our chance to really showcase what we can do. We need something bold, something that will turn heads and—"

"Make people swoon," I finished for him, the thought sending a thrill through me. "We should create a signature piece. Something that embodies everything we stand for."

He leaned back, his eyes sparkling with ideas. "What about a chocolate sculpture? Something that represents our journey—how we've overcome challenges and found our way back to this place."

I felt a rush of inspiration. "Yes! We could craft a heart, but with an intricate design that symbolizes strength—like vines wrapping around it or something."

"Vines that could represent how we've grown and tangled together," he added, his gaze steady on mine. "I like it."

And just like that, our creative juices began to flow, ideas bursting forth in a flurry of laughter and enthusiasm. We spent the morning sketching designs on paper, occasionally breaking into fits of laughter as we imagined the reaction of the townsfolk. "What if we made it life-size?" I suggested, my eyes widening at the thought. "We could put it in the center of the festival and offer a selfie station! Who wouldn't want to take a picture with a giant heart made of chocolate?"

Max's expression turned contemplative. "Or we could make smaller hearts and have them filled with different flavors. Everyone loves a good surprise."

"Now you're talking," I replied, feeling buoyed by the excitement of our collaboration. As the clock ticked on, the shop filled with the scents of melting chocolate and freshly baked pastries, each aroma weaving its way into our shared vision.

The day passed in a whirl of activity, the laughter echoing off the walls as we gathered supplies, mixed ingredients, and crafted our plans. For the first time in ages, it felt like we were moving forward, like we were part of something bigger than ourselves. I noticed the way Max's demeanor shifted; the weight that had pressed on him seemed to lift, revealing a spark of youthful enthusiasm I hadn't seen in a while.

When the evening approached and the last customers trickled out, I glanced at Max, who was wiping down the counters, his face illuminated by the soft glow of the overhead lights. "You know," I said, "I don't think we would have come this far without that little outburst yesterday. It was like tearing down a wall we didn't even know existed."

He paused, leaning against the counter, his expression serious. "It's funny how things shift when you allow yourself to be vulnerable. I've spent so much time trying to maintain control, but you were right; pretending only makes everything worse."

"Right?" I agreed, stepping closer, our previous tension replaced by a shared understanding. "It's liberating to share the burden. I think it makes us stronger."

His gaze softened, and for a moment, it felt like the world outside ceased to exist, as if we were cocooned in our own universe where nothing else mattered.

But then the door swung open, and a familiar voice pierced the air. "Max! Claire! What are you two lovebirds plotting?"

It was Sophie, the ever-enthusiastic owner of the café down the street. Her entrance felt like a splash of cold water, jolting us from our moment. I exchanged a glance with Max, the flush of surprise rising to my cheeks, while he shot me a playful look, as if to say, "Do we dare to engage?"

"Just some ideas for the festival!" I called back, my heart racing as I fought to maintain my composure. "No lovebirds here, just a lot of chocolate and maybe some wild dreams."

Sophie stepped inside, her laughter infectious, bouncing off the walls. "Well, I hope those wild dreams include a lot of chocolate because I came to borrow some for my special mocha tomorrow. You know, the one that'll make the entire town fall in love."

"Of course," Max said, regaining his footing. "We've got plenty. Take your pick!"

As Sophie wandered deeper into the shop, I couldn't help but feel a pang of disappointment at the interruption. Yet, amid the flurry of chatter and laughter, I realized how vital this was. Our plans for the festival were blossoming, but the real magic lay in the connections we were forming—not just with each other, but with the community around us.

With Sophie's enthusiasm filling the space, I felt a sense of camaraderie blossom, threading us all together in a web of dreams and ambitions. Even in the midst of uncertainty, we were finding our way, one chocolate heart at a time.

The following day unfurled like a fresh canvas, vibrant and full of possibility, and I found myself standing at the shop's entrance, the bell jingling cheerfully as I pushed the door open. The early sunlight streamed through the windows, illuminating the rich, dark wood of the counters and the meticulously arranged displays of chocolates. The heart-shaped truffles we had brainstormed the night before seemed to beckon from their pedestal, promising sweet rewards for anyone daring enough to taste them.

Max was already behind the counter, his hair slightly tousled as he worked on the latest batch of ganache. I took a moment to simply watch him, to appreciate the way his hands moved with precision, each motion deliberate and confident. It was as if the worries of the world melted away in the warm glow of the kitchen, leaving behind only the intoxicating aroma of melting chocolate. I couldn't help but think how far we'd come since that raw conversation, how our pact felt like a living thing, growing and evolving with every idea exchanged.

"Hey there, maestro," I called out, leaning against the counter with a playful smirk. "How's the ganache? Ready to turn our festival dreams into reality?"

Max looked up, a playful smile breaking across his face. "Only if you promise not to critique my technique. I'm still getting over the last time you called my whisking 'an act of desperation.'"

I chuckled, holding up my hands in mock surrender. "Okay, okay, I'll try to keep my criticisms to a minimum. But no promises if you set the kitchen on fire again."

"Noted. No fire today. Just chocolate and glorious creations," he replied, his eyes sparkling with mischief. "Speaking of which, I was thinking we could add a twist to the heart truffles. Maybe a hint of chili for a surprising kick?"

"Chili?" I echoed, my eyebrows shooting up. "Are we trying to make love and war at the same time? I'm not sure I'm ready for that kind of heat."

He laughed, shaking his head. "Imagine the reaction! It'll be unforgettable."

The banter continued, each quip drawing us closer together, filling the space with laughter and creativity. As we worked, we crafted ideas not just for chocolates, but for the festival itself, building plans like layers of rich, velvety ganache. We spoke of decorating the shop in vibrant colors, turning it into a haven of joy where chocolate lovers could escape the mundane and embrace the extraordinary.

As the day wore on, the phone rang, cutting through our laughter. I glanced at Max, who sighed as he reached for it. "Chocolatier's shop, Max speaking."

I watched him closely, noting the way his demeanor shifted from lighthearted to serious. His brow furrowed as he listened, and I couldn't help but wonder what was brewing on the other end of the line. The playful atmosphere evaporated, replaced by an air of tension that coiled around us like a dark cloud.

"Really?" he said slowly, his voice low. "You're sure about that? Alright, I'll... I'll talk to you soon."

When he hung up, I felt a knot form in my stomach, a feeling that something was amiss. "What was that about?" I asked, stepping closer, searching his face for clues.

"Just... a business inquiry," he replied, avoiding my gaze. "Nothing to worry about."

But I could see the worry etched in the lines of his forehead, the way his fingers gripped the edge of the counter as if it was the only thing anchoring him to this moment. "Max," I pressed gently, "you know you can talk to me. What is it?"

He hesitated, his eyes darting away, and for a heartbeat, I feared he might retreat back behind his carefully constructed walls. But then he met my gaze, and I saw the storm brewing behind his eyes, the uncertainty swirling in the depths. "It's about the shop," he finally admitted, his voice barely above a whisper. "They're looking to increase the rent again. This time, it's steep—too steep."

A chill ran through me, settling heavily in my chest. "Wait, what? But we just started to turn things around! This can't be happening now."

"I know," he replied, running a hand through his hair, frustration etched on his features. "But if we can't make the numbers work, it's going to be a problem. And if we can't find a way to stay afloat—"

"Don't say that," I interrupted, my heart racing. "We can't let this stop us. We've come too far. We just need to get creative."

He nodded, though doubt still clouded his eyes. "That's the plan, but we need a solid strategy. I can't keep pouring everything I have into this place if it's just going to slip away."

His words hung between us, a heavy reminder of the reality we faced. The laughter and playful banter from earlier felt like a distant memory, swept away by the stark reality of impending loss. "Let's sit down tonight and brainstorm some ideas," I suggested, trying to project an air of optimism I wasn't sure I felt. "We can think of promotions, maybe a fundraising event to generate some buzz. There has to be something we can do."

Max's expression softened slightly, a flicker of hope igniting in his eyes. "You're right. We'll figure this out together."

But just as we were beginning to regain our momentum, the door swung open once more, and a figure stepped inside. It was someone I hadn't expected—a man in a tailored suit, his demeanor polished yet intimidating, like he had just walked out of a corporate boardroom. The moment he entered, the air in the shop shifted, the warmth and familiarity giving way to an unsettling chill.

"Max," the man said, his voice smooth yet commanding. "We need to talk about your lease."

Max's expression turned guarded as he stepped forward. "What are you doing here, Victor?"

The name hung heavy in the air, and I could see Max stiffen, his posture tightening like a drawn bowstring. I exchanged a worried glance with him, sensing the undercurrent of tension that crackled between them.

Victor moved closer, his gaze sharp, as if appraising every detail of the shop, of us. "I'm here to discuss your options. You have until the end of the month to comply with the new terms."

"What new terms?" I interjected, my heart racing. "What gives you the right to make demands here?"

Victor turned to me, an amused smile flickering on his lips. "I'm merely here to ensure that this establishment remains profitable. You understand how business works, don't you?"

Max shot me a glance, a warning hidden behind his frustration. "We'll figure it out, Victor. This shop means a lot to us."

Victor smirked, unfazed. "And I'm sure you'll find a way to keep it—if you're willing to do what it takes."

The tension thickened, and I could feel the weight of uncertainty bearing down on us like an approaching storm. Max's face was a mask of determination and worry, and I realized in that moment how precarious our situation truly was.

"Let's discuss this further," Max said, his voice steady but edged with tension. "But I won't let you bully us into a corner."

Victor shrugged, a practiced ease settling over him. "Just remember, the clock is ticking. Make your move, or you might find yourself out of business before the festival even begins."

With that, he turned and walked out, leaving the door swinging in his wake, the bell chiming a dissonant note that echoed the anxiety rising in my chest.

I turned to Max, my heart racing. "What just happened? We have to fight back!"

He nodded, determination igniting in his gaze. "We will. But we need a plan, and fast."

The stakes had never been higher, and as we stood there, the world around us fading, I felt the thrill of both fear and resolve. Together, we would face whatever Victor and the world threw our way, but I knew that in this battle for our dreams, everything hinged on what we were willing to risk.

As the sun dipped below the horizon, casting long shadows through the shop, a new wave of determination surged within me.

We were in this together, but I could feel the weight of uncertainty looming like a dark cloud, and I couldn't shake the feeling that our fight was only just beginning.

Chapter 9: New Beginnings

The aroma of melting chocolate and baked vanilla wafted through the air, wrapping around me like a warm, inviting blanket. The kitchen was alive, an orchestra of whirring mixers, clattering pans, and the low hum of our shared laughter, punctuating the sweet scent that clung to our skin. Max was in his element, effortlessly sprinkling crushed pistachios atop a freshly frosted cupcake, his brow furrowed in concentration, yet a playful grin danced at the corners of his mouth. I was grateful for this unexpected partnership, the way our shared determination transformed the chaotic atmosphere into something almost magical.

"Careful!" I teased, pretending to gasp as he nearly tipped a cup of rich ganache too close to the edge of the counter. "We're trying to create art here, not a chocolate tsunami."

He shot me a mock glare, his eyes sparkling with mischief. "A chocolate tsunami could be a new marketing idea. 'Drown in our decadence'—I can see it now."

We both burst into laughter, the sound echoing off the tiled walls. It was moments like this that made the grind of saving the chocolatier seem less like an uphill battle and more like an adventure. As we worked, I couldn't help but admire how he embraced the chaos of our project with such enthusiasm. He had a way of turning even the simplest task into a delightful challenge, and I found myself drawn not just to his talent, but to his unwavering spirit.

We were a mismatched duo: I, the dreamer with a head full of recipes and schemes, and Max, the realist who kept us grounded with his practicality. It was as if we were two pieces of a puzzle that didn't quite fit but somehow created a picture worth looking at. Each brainstorming session turned into late-night talks where we shared our dreams, fears, and the occasional silly anecdote from our pasts. I could hardly remember a time when I'd felt so at ease with someone, the way our laughter mingled like the scent of sugar and spice filling the room.

In the quiet moments between tasks, I would steal glances at him, marveling at the way his hands moved with purpose, shaping our vision into reality. I had expected working together would be fraught with tension, yet there was a rhythm to our collaboration that felt effortless. He was methodical, while I tended to get swept up in wild ideas. We balanced each other, and I found comfort in that equilibrium. It was in those soft exchanges that my feelings for him began to shift, unfurling like petals of a flower awakening to the sun.

As I sprinkled edible glitter atop our latest creation—a decadent chocolate cupcake crowned with a swirl of caramel frosting—I caught myself lost in thought. Max was explaining his vision for the shop's social media, but my mind was adrift on the tide of emotions he stirred within me. "What if we host a 'Chocolate Lovers Night'? People could come in for tastings and bring their favorite chocolates to share," he suggested, pulling me back to the present.

"Or we could have a 'Choco-Challenge,'" I replied, my excitement bubbling over. "Like, who can create the most outrageous cupcake using our chocolates. We can judge them ourselves!"

Max laughed, the sound rich and genuine. "I love it! You've got this crazy energy about you that makes even my most boring ideas seem brilliant."

I flushed at the compliment, momentarily losing my train of thought. The challenge ahead felt daunting, but in that moment, with flour dust dancing in the sunbeams filtering through the window and the golden glow of evening settling in, I felt something shift inside me. I looked at him—really looked—and noticed the way his lips curled slightly when he was genuinely happy, or the way he occasionally brushed a stray lock of hair from his forehead, a simple gesture that made my heart race.

The challenges we faced seemed to grow lighter, our shared laughter defying the heaviness of uncertainty. It was becoming clearer to me: this chocolatier wasn't just a shop—it was a reflection of us. Every cupcake we decorated, every idea we batted back and forth, was a piece of our hearts poured into the delicate molds of chocolate. This venture, our dream, could thrive if we nurtured it as we were nurturing our bond.

As the night deepened and the stars began to twinkle outside, we found ourselves in a bubble of creativity. I was placing the final touches on a batch of gourmet truffles when he casually asked, "Do you ever think about what this all means?"

"Like, the chocolatier or us?" I replied, holding my breath, hoping he meant the latter.

"Both, I guess." He paused, turning serious for a moment, his gaze steady on mine. "I mean, we're putting everything we have into this. It's not just about saving the shop—it's about what it represents for us."

His words struck a chord, resonating within me like a soft chime. "You're right. It's about finding our place in the world, isn't it? This is our chance to create something meaningful."

Max nodded, his eyes searching mine as if he were looking for something deeper, something unspoken. In that charged moment, the air between us thickened, ripe with possibilities. I could feel my heart racing, a thrilling mixture of excitement and fear. What if we were not just building a chocolatier but also crafting the beginnings of something even more profound? I swallowed hard, wondering if I dared to entertain the idea that we were becoming something more than just partners in chocolate.

Just as I was about to voice that thought, the sound of glass shattering echoed through the shop, pulling me abruptly from my reverie. The moment shattered like the fragile sugar sculpture I had spent hours perfecting. We both spun around, the warmth of our connection momentarily forgotten, replaced by the cold weight of unexpected tension.

The sound of shattering glass jolted me back to reality, my heart racing as I turned toward the noise. Max's expression shifted from amused concentration to wide-eyed concern. We both rushed to the source, a tall window that offered a picturesque view of the bustling street outside, now marred by a cascade of broken glass. A startled pigeon, evidently more adventurous than prudent, fluttered in a panic, its wings flapping chaotically as it struggled to find its way out.

"Great, just what we needed—an avian intruder," I muttered, trying to lighten the moment as I surveyed the mess. But the nervous energy coiling in my stomach hinted that it wasn't just the bird that had unsettled me.

"Is it still there?" Max asked, his voice laced with equal parts worry and amusement. He stepped cautiously toward the window, eyes narrowed as he surveyed the scene. "It looks like it's auditioning for a role in a bad comedy."

With a deep breath, I joined him, half-expecting the bird to suddenly turn and dive bomb us like a feathered torpedo. "Maybe it's just trying to find a way to join our cupcake decorating committee."

Max chuckled softly, but the smile faded as we took in the shards of glass glinting dangerously on the floor. "We should clean this up before someone steps on it. I don't need the liability."

I grabbed a broom from the corner and began sweeping up the mess, the soft rasp of bristles against the floor somehow soothing amid the chaos. "It's a little too early for our first injury, don't you think?"

"Definitely too early," he replied, a grin creeping back onto his face. "We haven't even finished planning our grand reopening yet."

As we worked together, the tension of the moment slowly faded, replaced by our familiar banter. I would occasionally glance at him, the soft glow of the overhead lights catching the flecks of chocolate smudged on his cheeks, and I couldn't help but smile. It felt like we were building not just a business but a life crafted from the sweet moments in between.

Once the glass was cleared, I leaned against the counter, wiping my hands on my apron. "So, how are we going to keep this place afloat? Because I refuse to let this be a pigeon-riddled disaster."

Max paused, a thoughtful look crossing his face. "What if we tap into the local community? Host events, workshops—get people involved beyond just selling them chocolate. We want them to feel part of something special."

I nodded, invigorated by the idea. "Like a 'Chocolatier's Apprentice' class? Teach people how to make their own confections?"

His eyes lit up. "Exactly! We could do themed nights—like truffle-making for date nights. It's romantic and educational. Maybe even a 'DIY Chocolate Bar' event where customers can create their own flavor combinations."

"Now you're speaking my language." I grinned, imagining couples laughing together, experimenting with flavors, and even more, the camaraderie of sharing their creations. "And we can document everything for social media! Show the messy behind-the-scenes moments—people love that."

"Like your epic frosting fail last week?" He raised an eyebrow, a teasing smile forming on his lips. "The one where the frosting decided to revolt and cover half of your face?"

I laughed, recalling the incident with fondness. "Okay, maybe not that, but you have to admit, it was a great flavor!"

"Who knew chocolate-coconut-lavender would be such a... unique combination?" he said, winking. "We'll just make sure that one doesn't end up on the menu."

The playful banter made the air between us lighter, and I found myself lost in his gaze, the moment stretching longer than it should. Just as the warmth of our shared laughter settled in, the bell above the door jingled, drawing our attention to the entrance.

A woman stepped inside, her vibrant scarf swirling around her neck, accentuating her bright smile. "I heard you were open! Is this the famed chocolatier I've been reading about?"

"Only the best in town!" I replied, stepping forward with my most charming grin. "What can I get for you?"

Max joined me at the counter, his demeanor shifting from casual partner to enthusiastic salesman. "We have fresh truffles, gourmet cupcakes, and our special dark chocolate bars. Everything is made with love."

"Love and a touch of chaos, apparently," I chimed in, shooting him a playful smirk.

"Chaos builds character," he quipped, leaning against the counter as if it were his throne.

The woman laughed, the sound brightening the room. "I love it! I'll take a dozen truffles. Surprise me!"

As I began assembling her order, I felt a rush of excitement. There was something invigorating about being in the thick of it, creating connections and witnessing the joy that chocolate could bring. Each truffle, carefully crafted, was not just a treat but a small piece of art—a tangible representation of our efforts to breathe life into this place.

While I worked, Max kept the conversation flowing, chatting with her about her favorite flavors and encouraging her to try something new. Watching him in action, I realized how effortlessly he engaged people, his charisma adding another layer to our partnership. He had a way of making even the simplest of exchanges feel special.

Once her order was packed, she grinned widely, handing me a few bills. "You two are a breath of fresh air. I can't wait to tell everyone about this place!"

"Thank you!" I said, the warmth of her words wrapping around me like a hug.

As she left, I turned to Max, an excited buzz thrumming through me. "This is it. We're building something real, something that matters."

He nodded, his expression serious yet bright. "And we're doing it together. That's what makes it worth it."

The moment hung between us, electric and full of promise. But just as I felt a rush of connection, the weight of reality crashed down again as I recalled the challenges that loomed ahead. The looming financial crisis, the mounting pressure to succeed, and the uncertainty of whether our efforts would be enough to save the chocolatier.

"What's next?" I asked, the momentary lightness fading.

Max's gaze turned thoughtful. "We keep pushing forward. We'll create those classes, hit the social media hard, and maybe even partner with local businesses. We need to bring the community in, make them feel invested."

"Right," I replied, forcing a smile to mask the nervous flutter in my chest. "Together, we can tackle anything."

With that resolve echoing in my mind, we turned back to the work ahead, the weight of uncertainty hanging in the air. But despite the tension, I knew one thing for certain: I would fight for this chocolatier, and I would fight for whatever it was blooming between us. The taste of something sweeter lingered on the horizon, and I was determined to savor every moment, no matter how messy or chaotic.

The evening wore on, thick with the sweet scent of cocoa and the promise of something more. As we prepped for the next day's special events, I felt a surge of energy coursing through me. The laughter and playful banter with Max had invigorated my spirit, but the reality of our situation loomed like a shadow just outside the soft glow of our little chocolatier.

"Let's tackle this head-on," I declared, rolling up my sleeves and grabbing a bowl of ganache, the thick, glossy mixture practically shimmering under the fluorescent lights. "What's the plan for tomorrow? We need to make a splash."

Max leaned against the counter, arms crossed, the light from the window framing him like a scene from a romantic film. "How about we do a flash sale on social media? 'Tomorrow only: half-price truffles!' That'll draw people in."

"A brilliant idea, but we have to make sure we can handle the demand," I replied, smirking. "I don't want a repeat of last week when we ran out of cupcakes before noon."

"Ah, yes, the Great Cupcake Crisis. It was like watching a feeding frenzy at a buffet. I think I saw someone almost dive over the counter."

We both chuckled, the memory weaving a lightness through the air, but my heart still trembled with the weight of our plans. The fear of failure nagged at me, a persistent whisper beneath the laughter. Yet, as I glanced at him, all that chaos felt worth it. The chemistry between us crackled, and I couldn't help but wonder how far it would stretch before it snapped.

"I can't help but think about what happens if this doesn't work," I said, my voice suddenly quieter, tinged with apprehension. "What if we don't pull enough customers? What if we lose the shop?"

Max's expression shifted, the playful glint in his eyes replaced by a serious resolve. "Then we figure it out together. This isn't just about the chocolates; it's about building something that reflects who we are. And if we don't succeed, we'll find another way. We always do."

I appreciated his steadfastness, the way he faced uncertainty with courage. "What if we ran a contest? 'Win a Year's Supply of Chocolates'—that should draw attention."

He nodded, his enthusiasm reigniting. "That's brilliant! It creates buzz, gets people talking, and who doesn't want free chocolate?"

"Right? Plus, we can use their entries to build an email list for future events," I added, my excitement bubbling back to the surface. "It's like giving them a taste of the sweetness we offer."

We spent the next hour brainstorming details for the contest while mixing batches of truffles. The kitchen felt alive, a sanctuary of creativity amid the outside world's worries. Yet, a nagging thought loomed in the back of my mind—what if this was all just a sugar-coated distraction from the harsh realities we faced?

As I dipped a fresh batch of strawberries into melted chocolate, the door swung open again, and in walked the local journalist I recognized from the town's website. Sarah, with her camera slung around her neck and a notebook in hand, brought an air of excitement that immediately filled the room.

"Just in time to catch the chaos!" I joked, wiping my hands on my apron. "We're hosting a 'Chocolatier Challenge' contest, if you'd like to join in."

She grinned, snapping photos of our antics as if she could already see the story coming together. "I heard about the reopening. Thought I'd swing by and see what the buzz is all about. Mind if I ask a few questions?"

"Not at all!" Max exclaimed, enthusiasm written across his face. "We'd love to show you what we're cooking up!"

I felt my heart lift as we started explaining our plans, our voices rising with excitement. Sarah's eyes sparkled with curiosity, and every so often, she jotted down notes or snapped a photo, capturing the energy that crackled in the air. The idea of being featured in an article filled me with both pride and a hint of anxiety. This could be the exposure we needed—or it could be another reminder of our precarious situation.

"Can I get a picture of you two? The dynamic duo saving the chocolatier?" she asked, her voice bright.

Max exchanged a look with me, a mix of mischief and eagerness. "Let's do it! Just don't catch me with chocolate on my face, alright?"

"Too late for that," I shot back, pointing at the smudge of frosting on his cheek.

"Hey! It's called 'chocolate chic,'" he shot back, feigning indignation. "I'm starting a trend."

As Sarah snapped the photo, a sudden crash echoed from the back room. My heart dropped as I exchanged worried glances with Max, our playful moment shattering in an instant.

"What was that?" I asked, my heart racing.

"I don't know. Let's check it out." Max gestured for me to follow, and we both hurried toward the sound, our earlier excitement replaced by concern.

We pushed open the door to the back room, and the sight that greeted us made my stomach drop. Flour bags lay scattered across the floor, and the industrial mixer was tipped over, wires hanging like limp spaghetti. A small figure huddled next to it, a shadow in the dim light.

"Lucy!" I gasped, recognizing our friend's little sister, who had been a frequent visitor since we opened. "What happened?"

She looked up at us, her eyes wide with shock and a hint of guilt. "I was trying to help. I thought I could make the cookies by myself."

Max knelt beside her, concern etched on his face. "It's okay, Lucy. Accidents happen. Let's get this cleaned up, alright?"

As we began to tidy the chaos, I couldn't shake the feeling that this mishap was more than just a playful mistake. It felt like a sign—a warning that something else was coming. The chaos was growing around us, and the chocolatier, our dream, was hanging by a thread.

Just then, the door swung open again, and in strode a figure I didn't expect—Mr. Collins, the landlord, his face stormy and serious. "We need to talk," he said, his voice low and urgent.

My heart sank as I looked at Max, who met my gaze with equal concern. What now? I could sense the tension in the air, a heaviness that promised more than just a discussion about rent or repairs.

"Is it about the lease?" I asked, trying to keep my voice steady.

He nodded, a grim look settling on his face. "We have a situation."

As the words hung heavily in the air, a chill crept down my spine. My gut twisted with dread, and I felt the weight of the chocolatier's future hanging in the balance, like a delicate chocolate creation about to crumble under the pressure of a careless hand. The world around us shifted, and suddenly, all the work we'd done, all the laughter, felt precarious, teetering on the edge of uncertainty.

I braced myself for whatever was coming, knowing that nothing would ever be the same again.

Chapter 10: Sweet Surprises

The evening unfolded like a sweet serenade, the notes of laughter and conversation weaving through the air, punctuated by the occasional pop of a champagne cork. The chocolatier, with its once-ordinary walls, had transformed into a dazzling sanctuary of cocoa delights. I stood amidst towers of truffles, each glistening like a tiny jewel, and inhaled the rich aroma that swirled around me—dark chocolate mingling with hints of vanilla and caramel. It was intoxicating, almost euphoric, and my heart swelled as I observed the vibrant tapestry of people around me.

The fairy lights twinkled like stars trapped in the intimacy of our shop, casting soft shadows over the colorful displays. I had spent hours crafting the perfect arrangement of our signature chocolates, each piece carefully chosen not just for its flavor, but for its story. There were the sea salt caramels, a nod to my childhood trips to the beach, and the raspberry ganaches, inspired by lazy summer afternoons spent picking fruit with my grandmother. Tonight, those memories hung in the air like the sweet notes of a well-loved song.

"Did you ever think we'd be here?" Max leaned closer, his breath warm against my ear, sending a shiver down my spine. He was wearing that navy apron, the one I loved so much, his sleeves rolled up to reveal his forearms dusted with cocoa powder. There was something about him in this moment—his eyes sparkling with mischief, his hair tousled just right—that made my heart race. I turned to meet his gaze, and a smile broke across my face like the dawn breaking over the horizon.

"Not a chance," I replied, laughter bubbling up, both in disbelief and sheer delight. "Last month, we were just trying to figure out how to keep the chocolate from burning." The memory of us huddled over a pot of bubbling fudge, frantically stirring as if our lives depended on it, made me chuckle. "Now look at us. We're practically the chocolate royalty of Charleston."

Max laughed, a rich, warm sound that wrapped around me like a cozy blanket. "Royalty, huh? So does that mean I get to wear a crown made of chocolate?" He gestured to the towering chocolate fountain we had set up, the warm, gooey stream cascading down like a sweet waterfall.

"Only if I get to wear a cape," I shot back, my eyes sparkling with playful challenge. "Chocolate is best served with flair, after all."

Just then, a group of our friends approached, their eyes wide with excitement. "This place is incredible!" Emma exclaimed, her voice rising above the ambient chatter. She reached for a sample, popping a piece of orange-infused dark chocolate into her mouth. "Oh my god, you have to try this!"

The contagious energy ignited a series of conversations, each one more animated than the last, and I felt myself riding the wave of their enthusiasm. We toasted with sparkling cider, and I watched as the night unfolded—a celebration of not just our chocolate, but of community, of hard work, of resilience.

I caught sight of Max as he expertly maneuvered through the crowd, a chocolate-covered plate in hand. He was in his element, effortlessly charming everyone he spoke to. There was something undeniably magnetic about him; it was like he exuded warmth, pulling people into his orbit. My heart swelled with pride at the thought of building this dream together.

As the evening progressed, I noticed a shift in the atmosphere, a subtle undercurrent of tension that was hard to pinpoint. The laughter continued, but whispers floated through the crowd, stealing some of the spotlight. I caught snippets of conversation—people speculating about a rival chocolatier, rumors swirling like the chocolate we served. I furrowed my brow, the warmth of the evening starting to fade, replaced by an unsettling chill.

"Max!" I called out, weaving through the crowd until I reached him. "Did you hear that? There are rumors going around about the new chocolatier opening downtown. They're saying they're going to take us down." I searched his eyes for reassurance, but found only a flicker of uncertainty that mirrored my own.

"Let them talk," he said, his voice steady but laced with a tension that made my stomach twist. "We've worked too hard to let anyone take away our joy tonight. Besides, our chocolates speak for themselves." He gestured to the vibrant displays, a look of determination replacing the initial flicker of doubt.

"True," I replied, a smile creeping back onto my face as I recalled the countless hours we had spent perfecting our recipes. "But it's still annoying, isn't it? The nerve of them, coming into our territory. It's like a bad rom-com plot twist."

"Or a classic case of jealousy," he added, chuckling softly. The warmth of his laughter soothed the tension in my chest, but the underlying worries remained, gnawing at the edges of my mind.

As I turned to survey the bustling crowd once more, I spotted a familiar face in the throng—Clara, my former mentor, standing at the edge of the chocolate fountain, an enigmatic smile playing on her lips. She had been an unexpected presence in my life, a blend of encouragement and challenge that had shaped my journey in ways I still didn't fully comprehend. The last time I saw her, we had parted ways on less-than-stellar terms, her abrupt departure leaving a bitter taste in my mouth, much like dark chocolate when it's not balanced with something sweet.

I watched as she whispered something to a guest before glancing over at me, her expression inscrutable. The tension in my chest flared anew, mixing with confusion and an odd sense of anticipation. Was she here to support us or to sabotage? The evening felt charged with unanswered questions, and I couldn't shake the feeling that Clara's presence heralded a storm I wasn't prepared for.

"Hey," I said, my voice barely rising above the din, "I think I need to go talk to her."

"Wait," Max caught my wrist, his eyes searching mine. "What if she's here to stir things up? You don't need that drama tonight."

I hesitated, the pull of curiosity battling the instinct to avoid conflict. But there was an undeniable urge to confront the past, to unravel the threads that had led us to this moment.

"Just for a second," I said, determination creeping into my tone. "I need to know why she's here."

With that, I made my way toward Clara, the tension coiling within me, ready to snap. This was my chance to face the unexpected twists that seemed intent on testing everything I had built with Max.

Clara stood at the edge of the chocolate fountain, her presence both magnetic and unnerving. I could see her perfectly manicured nails tapping lightly against the edge of the table, an unconscious habit that betrayed her simmering thoughts. The laughter of our friends faded into a distant hum as I approached, my heart racing in a rhythm that felt alarmingly out of sync with the joyous atmosphere around us. The evening shimmered with light and laughter, yet here, it felt like a shadow had slipped in, threatening to cloud everything I had fought to build.

"Clara," I greeted, forcing a smile that didn't quite reach my eyes. "Interesting to see you here."

She turned, her expression shifting between surprise and amusement, as if I had just thrown a curveball in a game she thought she had mastered. "Isn't it? I thought I'd check out the competition," she replied, her voice smooth like the chocolate we so painstakingly crafted. "I must say, you've done an impressive job. The place looks fantastic."

"Thanks," I replied, the word tasting bittersweet on my tongue. The memory of her abrupt exit from my life—like a dark chocolate

truffle that had been left too long in the sun—lingered. "Are you...
back in town for long?"

"Oh, just visiting," she said, dismissing the question with a wave
of her hand. "But I couldn't resist the invitation. I had to see how my
protégé was doing."

Her words dripped with a mixture of pride and condescension,
as if she were inspecting a project she had abandoned but still felt
ownership over. I couldn't help but wonder if her presence here was
a part of some grand design, or if it was simply a coincidence.

"Your protégé has been busy," I replied, the sharpness of my tone
surprising even myself. "Building a business takes a lot of work, you
know."

"Ah, I can imagine." She leaned closer, her eyes glinting with
something I couldn't quite place—was it envy, or was it genuine
curiosity? "Tell me, how's the chocolate-making going? Any new
flavors on the horizon?"

"We have a few tricks up our sleeves," I said, crossing my arms
defensively. "But you know how it is—some things are better left to
those who actually put in the effort."

Clara's lips curled into a smirk, and I couldn't shake the feeling
that she relished this little verbal sparring match. "You always did
have a way with words. But I suppose you've had to grow thicker skin
in this business."

I could sense the weight of her words, heavy and laced with the
remnants of our past mentorship, but I refused to let her pull me into
the undertow of doubt. "Thicker skin? Sure. But I prefer to think of
it as just knowing my worth. Something I hope you've found too."

For a moment, her expression faltered, and I caught a glimpse of
something raw beneath her composed exterior. "You're sharper than
I remember. But let's not pretend this is only about chocolate, shall
we?"

I paused, the air around us thickening as the tension escalated. "Then what is it about, Clara? Are you here to critique my chocolate, or to critique me?"

"Can't it be both?" she quipped, her smile returning, but it didn't reach her eyes. "Your chocolates are lovely, truly. But I can't help but wonder how long this little venture of yours can last in the fickle world of culinary arts."

Her words cut deeper than I wanted to admit, and I felt a wave of heat rise in my cheeks. "Well, at least we're not just sitting on the sidelines, waiting for the next big thing to come along," I shot back, my voice steadier than I felt. "We're in the game, and we're making our mark."

"Touché," she replied, her tone shifting to something more contemplative. "But you have to understand, the industry can be brutal. There are those who'll do whatever it takes to knock you down."

"And you'd know all about that, wouldn't you?" I shot back, regretting the sharpness even as the words left my mouth. "I mean, you left without a word, didn't you?"

For a moment, the vibrant sounds of the party dulled, and I could see the flash of hurt in her eyes before it was quickly masked by her practiced indifference. "I had my reasons, but let's not dwell on the past. You've made your choice, and I respect that."

The soft sounds of clinking glasses and chatter began to seep back into the space around us, but the emotional current between us crackled like static electricity. I was beginning to wonder if confronting her had been a mistake when Max suddenly appeared at my side, his presence like a soothing balm against the tension.

"Hey, I was looking for you," he said, glancing between Clara and me, eyebrows furrowing slightly. "Everything okay?"

"Just catching up," I replied, forcing a casual tone that felt foreign against the backdrop of my swirling thoughts. "Clara was just sharing some... wisdom about the industry."

"Always the teacher, aren't you?" Max said, the warmth in his voice breaking through the chill in the air. "I think we've got it covered for now."

Clara's eyes narrowed slightly, and I couldn't help but feel a rush of appreciation for Max's protective nature. "Wise choice," she replied, a hint of mockery in her tone. "You two make quite the team. I suppose the chocolaty love story will sell well, too."

"Don't you think chocolate is romantic?" Max replied, a playful grin spreading across his face. "It's rich, complex, and sometimes it even melts in your mouth."

"Aw, look at you," Clara said, her voice dripping with sarcasm. "A regular poet. Just remember that sweetness can sometimes mask bitterness."

I felt a pang of unease at her words, the underlying message echoing in my mind. As she sauntered away, her figure merging with the throng of guests, I couldn't shake the sense of foreboding that clung to me like a lingering aftertaste.

"Are you okay?" Max asked softly, his eyes searching mine for any signs of discomfort.

"Just peachy," I replied, though the weariness in my tone gave me away. "I guess I just didn't expect her to show up tonight."

"It's not a problem. You're doing great. We're doing great," he said, his hand finding mine, grounding me amidst the storm of emotions swirling inside. "And I know we can handle anything that comes our way."

I nodded, squeezing his hand in silent gratitude, but I couldn't shake the feeling that Clara's return marked the beginning of a new chapter—one filled with challenges I hadn't anticipated. As the evening wore on, I watched the people around me revel in the chocolate delights we had created, and for a fleeting moment, I felt a swell of hope. Maybe we could navigate this new storm together. But deep down, I knew that Clara's presence was only the beginning, and the real test of our resolve was yet to come.

As the evening stretched on, the energy inside the chocolatier oscillated between vibrant and electric, a beautiful chaos of sound and sight. The lingering aroma of chocolate mixed with the fresh scent of summer, as if the very air we breathed was infused with sweetness. I watched our patrons savor our creations, their eyes lighting up with every bite, and felt a swell of pride that could rival the chocolate fountain's impressive cascade.

"Can you believe this?" Max leaned in close, his breath warm and inviting. "Look at how happy everyone is."

"I know, right? This is what we dreamed of," I replied, my voice barely rising above the jubilant din. I was momentarily swept away by the sheer joy radiating from the crowd, but then, as if a storm cloud had passed overhead, Clara's words echoed in my mind: "Sweetness can sometimes mask bitterness."

"Hey," Max said, his brow furrowing as he studied my face. "You're not still thinking about her, are you?"

"I—" I hesitated, caught between the happiness of the moment and the lingering tension Clara had left in her wake. "No, it's just... she has a knack for showing up at the worst times."

"True," he replied, his tone shifting to something softer, more serious. "But we're here now, and it's all about us. Nothing else matters tonight."

"Right," I said, forcing a smile, though my heart felt heavy with unspoken worries.

The laughter around us erupted again, and a few friends wandered over, clutching their chocolate-dipped spoons as if they were trophies. Emma, ever the instigator, leaned in with a conspiratorial whisper. "So, when do we get to see you two officially announce your chocolate romance? I mean, the chemistry is practically oozing off the truffles!"

I laughed, shaking my head. "Oh, please. It's not like we have a planned press release for that."

Max's eyes danced with mischief as he interjected, "I think the chocolate does the talking for us. Nothing says 'couple goals' like hand-crafted confections."

"Seriously," Emma continued, grinning like a Cheshire cat. "All this chocolate and the undeniable chemistry? You two should get a reality show. I can see it now: 'Love & Chocolate: The Sweetest Adventure.'"

"Okay, stop!" I exclaimed, cheeks burning with embarrassment. "You're going to make me lose my appetite. I can't think about reality TV when there are perfectly good bonbons to be savored."

Max chimed in, pretending to be serious. "But the world needs to see the genius behind 'Chocolate Romance.'"

I rolled my eyes, but the playful banter made me forget Clara for just a moment. As laughter enveloped us again, I couldn't help but steal glances at Max. Each smile he sent my way felt like a little spark of joy, igniting a warmth deep within. I was grateful for this night and the people surrounding us, but I couldn't shake the unease that still lingered like a hint of dark chocolate on my palate.

Then I spotted Clara again, lurking near the entrance, her eyes scanning the room as if searching for something—or someone. A pit formed in my stomach as I turned back to Max, my voice dropping to a whisper. "I think she's up to something. I can feel it."

"Let's not let her ruin our night," he replied firmly, his gaze steady. "We're better than that."

"Easier said than done," I muttered, feeling a sudden chill in the air, as if her presence was siphoning away the warmth and light of our event. I forced myself to focus on our guests, their laughter becoming a balm against the creeping worry that threatened to overshadow the evening.

But Clara had a way of weaving herself into the fabric of every room she entered. It was as if she were a dark thread in a brightly colored tapestry, impossible to ignore. Suddenly, the music shifted to a slower, more romantic tune, the atmosphere morphing into something softer and more intimate. Couples began to sway, and I felt an urge to pull Max closer.

"Dance with me?" I asked, my heart racing at the thought of being enveloped in his arms.

He smiled, and I could see the warmth in his eyes. "Always."

As we moved together, the world around us blurred, the worries of the night fading into the background. The warmth of his body against mine sent a shiver of joy through me, every note of the music wrapping us in a cocoon of comfort. We swayed slowly, and I rested my head on his shoulder, my heart finally finding a moment of peace.

But peace is often a fleeting thing. Just as I began to relax, I felt Clara's presence loom over us. My instincts kicked in, and I glanced over Max's shoulder to find her standing a few feet away, arms crossed, an inscrutable expression plastered on her face.

"Interesting dance moves," she called out, her voice a mixture of mockery and intrigue.

I pulled back slightly, ready to defend the moment, but Max stepped in front of me, the protector I knew he could be. "What do you want, Clara? This isn't the time or place for whatever you're planning."

"Oh, don't worry," she replied, her voice dripping with faux sweetness. "I'm just here to enjoy the show. But it's fascinating how easily you've forgotten the realities of this business. You think a night like this guarantees success?"

Max opened his mouth to respond, but I cut in, feeling a surge of defiance. "We're not just in this for one night, Clara. We've built something real here."

"Real? Or a sweet illusion?" she shot back, the challenge hanging between us like a taut string, ready to snap. "You'll find out soon enough that the world of chocolate—and love—is far more complicated than it seems."

Her words hit me like a cold wave, and I could feel Max stiffen beside me. "What do you mean by that?" he demanded, his voice low but firm.

Clara smiled, a chilling expression that sent shivers down my spine. "Just a little reminder that the sweet can turn sour in an instant. You should keep your friends close and your enemies even closer."

Before I could respond, she turned on her heel and slipped back into the crowd, leaving behind a silence thick with tension. I felt my heart race, the celebratory atmosphere transforming into a storm cloud hovering above us.

"What was that about?" Max asked, his voice taut with concern.

"I have no idea," I replied, but the unease curled in my stomach like a serpent ready to strike.

Just then, the door swung open, and the night air rushed in, carrying with it an unfamiliar energy. A figure stepped inside, their silhouette framed against the warm glow of our chocolatier, but it was the gleam of recognition that stopped my heart cold.

My breath caught as the newcomer stepped into the light, revealing a familiar face that sent my world spiraling. Clara's earlier words echoed in my mind, the warning ringing louder than ever. The night that had begun with sweetness now hung heavy with uncertainty, a cliffhanger suspended in time, leaving everything hanging in the balance.

Chapter 11: Fragile Foundations

The day had started with a glimmer of promise, sunlight dancing through the kitchen windows, catching flecks of cocoa dust and the shimmer of tempered chocolate. My heart fluttered with the kind of optimism that felt foreign but welcomed, especially after weeks of relentless worry about the chocolatier. The small shop, with its walls lined with dark wood and shelves burdened with whimsical confections, had become more than just a business to me. It was a canvas where I poured my soul, my hopes, and an occasional bit of heartbreak.

But just as I poured my first batch of hazelnut pralines, imagining how their rich, nutty aroma would waft through the air, Oliver breezed back into our lives like a summer storm, disrupting the fragile calm I had begun to cultivate. His presence was magnetic, a blend of charisma and ambition that had always made me uneasy, like a beautiful mirage that threatened to dissolve upon closer inspection. He entered the shop with the confidence of someone who believed the universe bent to his will, his tailored suit sharply contrasting the warm, cozy aesthetic of our chocolatier.

"Emma!" he called, his voice slicing through the rich scent of melted chocolate. "You won't believe the opportunity I've unearthed. I can't wait to share it with you and Max!"

I could already feel my stomach churn at the prospect. It was as if he could smell the remnants of my determination fading, and he was here to capitalize on it. Max, my partner and the heart of this venture, was drawn to Oliver's glimmering promises like a moth to a flame. His excitement was palpable, his eyes lighting up with each of Oliver's words. "What's the plan?" Max asked, practically bouncing on his heels.

Oliver's smile widened, revealing a dimple that had a tendency to disarm. "A partnership! Imagine it—your artisanal chocolates showcased in high-end stores across the city. With my connections, we could elevate your brand to the heights it deserves!"

I could almost hear the faint sound of alarm bells ringing in the back of my mind. "And at what cost?" I murmured, more to myself than to them, the words catching in my throat like a stubborn chocolate truffle.

But before I could voice my doubts, Oliver continued, "We could turn this charming little shop into a household name! All I need is a small stake in the business."

"A stake?" I repeated, the term hanging in the air like a thundercloud. My fingers clenched around the whisk as I fought against the bitter taste of unease creeping into my chocolate ganache.

Max's enthusiasm danced in the air, sweet and sticky like the syrup I used for my caramels. "Emma, this could be the break we need! Just think of it! More resources, better equipment, we could—"

"Lose control," I interjected, my voice sharper than intended. The realization hit me like a sudden chill, and I took a breath, steadying myself against the rising tide of emotion. "This is our dream, Max. I don't want to share it with someone who doesn't see it as we do."

But Oliver, unyielding as ever, leaned closer, his voice softening as if he were unveiling a secret. "It's not about losing control. It's about expanding your horizons. Sometimes you have to take a leap to soar higher."

"Or you can fall flat on your face," I shot back, my heart racing.

"Emma, you're being unreasonable," Max replied, the words coming out in a rush as if he were trying to stem the flow of an impending flood. "This is a great opportunity! You're just scared of change."

"Maybe I am," I admitted, my voice dropping. "But what's the price of that change, Max? You know how Oliver operates. He's charming, but he's also calculating. I can feel it."

Oliver raised an eyebrow, the glint of challenge in his eyes. "I promise you, I have your best interests at heart. I wouldn't dream of taking over. I just want to help."

But his words felt like sugar coating over a bitter pill, and I found myself yearning for the simple days when the only challenges we faced were melting chocolate and temperamental tempera paints. I missed the clarity that had once defined our vision—just the three of us: me, Max, and our devoted chocolatier. Now, it felt as if we were standing at the edge of a precipice, the unknown stretching out before us like a vast, dark ocean.

"You don't get it, do you?" I challenged, my voice wavering slightly. "This isn't just about business; it's about us. About our dreams. I can't just sit back and watch someone else steer the ship."

Max stepped back, frustration knitting his brow. "It feels like you don't trust me—or us. I thought we were in this together."

With those words, the air thickened with tension, the weight of unspoken fears and desires pressing down like the heavy velvet drapes that adorned the shop's windows. My heart ached at the thought of losing what we had built together, but was I really being unreasonable? Or was I merely protecting our fragile foundation?

As the silence deepened, the clattering of spoons and the hum of the chocolate machine faded into the background, replaced by a rising storm of emotions. I caught a glimpse of Oliver, his posture relaxed yet predatory, and for a moment, I felt a flash of something akin to dread mixed with determination.

"Let's take some time to think this through," I suggested, my tone more measured. "We owe it to ourselves to consider all sides."

Max sighed, running a hand through his hair in that familiar gesture of frustration. "Fine, but this could be the best thing that ever happened to us, Emma."

As he turned away, I could see the flicker of disappointment in his posture, a stark reminder that the balance of our relationship hung delicately in the air, threatening to crack under the weight of unvoiced feelings and competing ambitions. With Oliver lurking in the background, promising everything while concealing the cost, I felt the familiar sting of doubt.

In that moment, as I melted chocolate for our signature truffles, the bittersweet blend mirrored the turmoil within me. I was torn between ambition and loyalty, a tension that twisted in my gut. I had to navigate this labyrinth of emotions, where trust and desire clashed like two titans, and I was left standing in the rubble, hoping that our fragile foundations wouldn't crumble beneath the weight of it all.

The days that followed Oliver's proposal felt like a tightrope act performed in a windstorm, each step I took balanced precariously between ambition and trepidation. The chocolatier, once a sanctuary of creativity, became a battleground for unspoken worries and simmering tension. The sweet aroma of chocolate that used to wrap around me like a comforting embrace now felt like a bittersweet reminder of everything I stood to lose.

Max was buoyant, almost giddy with enthusiasm, every new idea Oliver proposed met with an eagerness that was both infectious and alarming. I found myself drowning in his excitement, wondering how one man could wield such charm while simultaneously threatening the delicate ecosystem we had cultivated. "Emma, just think about it!" he would say, eyes bright as he bounced around the shop, his arms waving like a conductor guiding an unseen orchestra. "More foot traffic, more exposure! We could even expand the menu to include pastries!"

I forced a smile, the kind that didn't quite reach my eyes. "And lose our soul in the process?" I would counter, trying to steer the conversation back to safer waters. "Remember why we started this? It was about passion, not profit."

But Max's gaze would flicker, caught between the idealism we once shared and the undeniable allure of Oliver's propositions. "This isn't just about money. It's about growth! We can still be us while becoming something bigger."

Bigger. The word echoed in my mind like an ominous drumbeat, amplifying my fears. What if bigger meant losing the intimacy that had made our chocolatier special? What if Oliver's ambitions turned our carefully curated world into a soulless production line, with numbers and metrics overshadowing creativity?

One particularly brisk morning, as the leaves outside danced in a fiery display of autumn hues, I found myself alone in the shop, the hum of machinery my only companion. I stood in front of the display case, gazing at the carefully arranged confections—golden caramel-filled bonbons, dark chocolate ganaches, and vibrant raspberry tarts—all testaments to our hard work and love. I could almost hear their stories, each bite a memory of laughter, late-night brainstorming sessions, and the smell of fresh bread wafting through the air.

Just then, the bell above the door jingled, and I looked up to find Oliver sauntering in, his presence enveloping the room like the scent of vanilla. "Morning, Emma!" he called out, his tone laced with an enthusiasm that felt almost disarming. "I've been thinking about our partnership, and I've got some new ideas to discuss."

"Fantastic," I said, my voice barely concealing the tension simmering beneath the surface. "What's on your mind?"

He leaned against the counter, a casual posture that belied the seriousness of our situation. "Let's consider a marketing campaign that really showcases what you do here. You know, bring in influencers, maybe even a launch event—something extravagant! We can make this place the talk of the town."

The idea sounded dazzling on the surface, but beneath it lay a tangle of worry. "And when the dust settles, what will we have left? A flashy facade, perhaps, but at what cost?"

"Emma, you're thinking too small," Oliver replied, a hint of impatience creeping into his voice. "This is a chance to make a mark. Don't you want to be known as the chocolatier that redefined the game?"

"Redefined the game? Or sold out?" I shot back, my heart racing at the confrontation I hadn't intended to instigate.

His expression shifted, and I caught a glimpse of the underlying frustration that lurked just beneath his polished exterior. "You need to trust me," he said, the intensity of his gaze locking onto mine. "This is what you've wanted all along, isn't it? To create something that lasts?"

The air between us crackled with unspoken tension, the weight of his expectations pressing down on my shoulders. I wanted to scream, to shake him and say, "You don't understand!" Instead, I took a breath, struggling to gather my thoughts. "What I want is to make chocolates that speak to people. I want every truffle to tell a story, not just sit pretty on a shelf for the sake of Instagram."

"And that's exactly what I'm trying to help you do! But you can't stick your head in the sand and ignore the realities of this world." His voice was low now, almost coaxing, as if he were trying to peel away the layers of my resistance. "This is the modern age, Emma. Social media isn't going away. You can either ride the wave or get washed away."

With every word he spoke, the dream I had held so tightly began to feel like a fragile bubble, about to burst at any moment. "What if riding the wave means losing myself?" I asked, my voice quivering. "What if we end up becoming everything we never wanted?"

The room fell silent, our breaths mingling in the stillness, each heartbeat echoing the weight of our decisions. Oliver shifted slightly, breaking eye contact for the first time, and I sensed a crack forming in his carefully curated facade. "I get it," he finally said, his tone softer, more genuine. "Change is scary. But what's scarier is standing still while the world passes you by."

That phrase, 'standing still,' struck me with the force of a thunderclap. Was that what I feared? Being stagnant? Watching as others moved forward while I remained anchored to the past? But then again, was moving forward worth it if it meant compromising everything I believed in?

Just as I was about to respond, the door jingled again, and in walked Max, his face flushed with excitement, eyes alight with hope. "You won't believe the call I just had!" he exclaimed, oblivious to the charged atmosphere. "A local magazine wants to feature us in their next issue! Can you imagine? All those new customers!"

As I looked between Max and Oliver, the gears of my mind began to churn. The intoxicating prospect of publicity swirled with the nagging sense of unease. "That's great, Max! But—"

"No buts!" he interrupted, grinning wide. "This is our moment! We can't let it slip through our fingers."

I felt the weight of his optimism press against my chest, but alongside it, a gut feeling gnawed at me. As Oliver leaned back, arms crossed, his smirk hinted at a victory, the stakes of our budding partnership became clearer. This was more than just business; it was about trust, ambition, and the fragile threads connecting us.

"Let's celebrate!" Max declared, grabbing two mugs of hot chocolate from the counter and pouring them with an enthusiasm I couldn't help but admire. "Here's to new beginnings!"

But as I raised my mug to clink against theirs, the bittersweet taste of cocoa mingled with the uncertainty curling in my stomach. The future felt like a wobbly tower of stacked truffles, precarious yet promising. With every passing moment, I could feel the foundations we had built trembling beneath the weight of choices unmade, a fragile dance of loyalty and ambition, threatening to spin out of control.

The evening air in the chocolatier was thick with the scent of melting chocolate, the flickering candlelight casting dancing shadows across the walls. It felt both cozy and suffocating, an odd blend that mirrored my internal turmoil. Max and Oliver were deep in conversation, their laughter echoing against the backdrop of clinking mugs and the gentle hum of the espresso machine. Each sound served as a reminder of how precariously my heart balanced between wanting to belong and fearing the changes creeping into our little sanctuary.

"Emma, come join us!" Max called, his exuberance infectious. He gestured for me to sit with them at the small, round table where Oliver had taken up residence, sprawling comfortably in his chair as if he owned the place. "We're just discussing the magazine feature and how we can leverage it!"

I approached cautiously, a smile plastered on my face that felt more like a mask than a reflection of my true feelings. "Leverage it how?" I asked, taking a seat across from Oliver, who regarded me with an expression that danced between amusement and challenge.

"Well, we could invite some local influencers," Oliver suggested, his voice smooth as melted chocolate. "Host a tasting event. Get people talking, get the buzz going. We'll turn this little shop into the hottest spot in town!"

"And then what?" I replied, my tone sharper than I intended. "We become just another trendy place that people visit for a photo op and not because they genuinely love what we create?"

"Come on, Emma," Max chimed in, his enthusiasm unwavering. "This is our chance! We could reach a whole new audience and—"

"Lose our essence in the process," I finished, crossing my arms. "We can't forget why we started this. It's not just about the numbers or the trends."

Oliver leaned forward, his expression shifting, perhaps sensing the urgency in my tone. "It's about evolution, Emma. Every successful brand adapts to the market. You have to think big to stay relevant."

"Relevant?" I scoffed, the bitterness seeping into my voice. "You make it sound so simple. But you're not the one pouring your heart into each chocolate, are you? Each piece is a reflection of us, not a product to be marketed."

A flicker of tension sparked in Oliver's eyes, and for a brief moment, I could see past his charming facade to something sharper, something more ruthless. "Then let's ensure our heart beats louder than the rest," he retorted, a smirk returning to his lips. "We can do both."

I felt my chest tighten, the realization dawning that Oliver's vision for us and mine were on wildly different trajectories. Max seemed caught in the crossfire, his gaze shifting between us, the excitement draining slightly from his face. "Look, let's not fight about this," he finally interjected, rubbing the back of his neck. "We need to find common ground. This feature could put us on the map."

"Or it could erase everything we've worked for," I shot back, my frustration spilling over.

Oliver waved a hand dismissively, his nonchalance grating on my nerves. "You're being dramatic, Emma. All I'm suggesting is we embrace this opportunity."

"I'm not being dramatic," I said, rising from my seat. "I'm being realistic. You see potential, but I see strings attached." I couldn't believe I was standing up to him like this, but something deep within me urged me to take a stand.

Max's face tightened, the conflict brewing in his eyes. "Emma, please. Let's not turn this into a war zone. We need to make decisions together, not push each other away."

"Together, yes," I agreed, my tone softening. "But we also need to be honest about what we want. We can't compromise our values."

Oliver leaned back, crossing his arms, the amusement slipping from his face. "If you're not ready for growth, that's one thing. But I will not let your fears hold us back."

The tension hung heavy in the air, each breath feeling like a plunge into icy water. I wanted to scream, to shake both of them and plead for them to see my side. But what was I really fighting for? My vision? Or the fragile bond that held us together?

"I can't be a part of something that doesn't feel right," I finally said, the words tumbling from my mouth with a weight that surprised even me. "If that means stepping back, then maybe that's what I need to do."

Max's eyes widened, and for a moment, it felt as though the world around us paused. "Emma, don't say that," he whispered, fear creeping into his voice. "We can work this out."

"Can we?" I challenged, my heart racing. "Or are we just going to keep burying our heads in the sand, pretending that Oliver's grand plans won't change everything?"

"I just want to help," Oliver interjected, a defensive edge creeping into his tone. "But if you're not on board, maybe we should reconsider everything."

His words felt like a slap, igniting a fire of panic in my chest. I shot a glance at Max, who looked lost, caught in a storm of conflicting loyalties. "You really think this is how we grow?" I asked, my voice trembling. "By bringing in someone who doesn't share our vision?"

"Maybe it's time to accept that change is necessary," Oliver replied, his voice cool and composed. "You can't live in a bubble forever."

A silence enveloped us, thick and suffocating, as my heart raced against the fear of what came next. I glanced at the window, watching as the evening light faded, casting long shadows that mirrored the uncertainty brewing within me.

Just as I was about to respond, a loud crash interrupted the moment, causing us all to jump. The sound came from the back of the shop, where the kitchen lay. My stomach dropped as I rushed toward the sound, fear twisting in my gut.

"What was that?" Max called, following closely behind.

Oliver's smirk faded, replaced by genuine concern as we hurried toward the source of the noise. My mind raced, conjuring images of shattered glass and ruined chocolate. As we turned the corner into the kitchen, the sight before us froze me in my tracks.

There, among the scattered shards of what used to be our precious display of chocolate sculptures, stood a figure cloaked in darkness, their face obscured by the shadows. A gust of wind from the open window sent a chill racing down my spine as I took a cautious step forward.

"Who are you?" I demanded, my voice trembling, but strong enough to mask the fear clawing at my insides.

The figure remained still, then slowly raised a hand, revealing something glinting ominously in the dim light. My heart raced, the air thick with an unspoken threat, and as I took another step closer, my world tilted on its axis, the fragility of everything I held dear suddenly laid bare before me.

Chapter 12: Torn Allegiances

The scent of warm sugar and freshly baked pastries wafted through the air as I stepped into the shop, wrapping around me like a comforting blanket. Sunlight filtered through the windows, casting golden patches on the wooden floor, and the sound of laughter tinkled like chimes in the background. Max stood at the counter, his hands animatedly gesturing as he spoke to Oliver, the weight of their conversation pulling my heart into a knot. It felt like I was watching an intimate performance where I was both the audience and the unwilling star. My chest tightened as Oliver's laughter echoed, bright and sharp, cutting through the syrupy atmosphere of the bakery.

I shook off the momentary pang of jealousy, reminding myself that Oliver was a friend, an ally even, and certainly not the enemy. But there was something about the ease with which they interacted, the way Oliver leaned forward, clearly enthralled by whatever Max was saying, that sent a ripple of unease through me. I couldn't stand there and let it fester. My grandmother's words echoed in my mind, urging me to listen to my heart, even if it led me to an uncertain conclusion.

"Hey, you two!" I called out, forcing my voice to break through the cheerful din of the shop. The two men turned, their expressions morphing from surprise to warmth as they acknowledged me. Max's smile, the one that always felt like home, washed over me, momentarily banishing the shadows of doubt. But it was fleeting. "What are we discussing? I hope it's not too serious without me," I added with a playful lilt, trying to infuse some levity into the tension brewing within.

"Just a little bit of shop talk," Max replied, his voice light, but I could see the flicker of something unspoken in his eyes. "Oliver was just sharing some ideas for the upcoming festival. Apparently, he has a vision for a dessert that could steal the show."

"Is that so?" I raised an eyebrow, crossing my arms over my chest, feigning nonchalance. "And what exactly does this dessert entail? Chocolate-infused mystery, or perhaps an avant-garde take on traditional favorites?" The banter flowed easily, yet beneath my jest lay a current of irritation. Oliver's gaze shifted to me, a hint of challenge sparkling in his eyes.

"Oh, it's definitely more than just chocolate. Imagine a layered cake, each tier representing a different flavor of the season. It would be the talk of the festival," he replied, his enthusiasm spilling over. The way he described it, his hands carving shapes in the air, made it sound nearly enchanting.

Max jumped in, his excitement matching Oliver's. "And we could set up a tasting booth, with samples of each layer. Just think about the foot traffic we could draw!"

As they enthused over this shared vision, my mind wandered, contemplating the weight of my own decisions. This was what I'd always wanted—to be part of something that felt bigger than myself, to contribute to a community that was vibrant and alive. But now, standing on the sidelines while two of my closest companions plotted this delightful spectacle, the anxiety simmered just below the surface.

I cleared my throat, ready to voice my reservations, when a sudden voice pierced through my thoughts. "Are you sure you're up for this, Max? I mean, things have been hectic, and it's a big undertaking," I said, not fully intending to divert the conversation, but finding it a necessary pivot.

Max's gaze darted to me, surprise mingling with concern. "What do you mean?"

"Just that—" I hesitated, searching for the right words, "I don't want you to burn out trying to make everything perfect. We're already juggling so much."

He studied me for a moment, his brow furrowed as he processed my words. "I appreciate your concern, really. But I thrive on this kind of chaos. It's invigorating!"

"Maybe," I pressed on, "but even the most skilled jugglers drop a ball now and then."

"Are you implying I'm not skilled?" he teased, a smirk creeping onto his lips, but the lightness didn't reach his eyes.

I bit back a retort, my heart racing with the implications of what I was really trying to say. There was more at stake than just desserts and festivals; there was a fracture forming beneath the surface of our friendship, and I was terrified of what it might mean.

"Okay, let's say I'm not skilled," I replied, matching his playfulness with a smirk of my own. "What then? You just keep throwing ideas at me until I either agree to one or throw flour in your face?"

The laughter that bubbled up from him was like a balm, easing the tension as it wrapped around us. But as the lightness settled, the reality loomed larger. I needed to confront Max—not just about the festival but about everything that had been stirring inside me.

"Max," I began, my voice softer now, almost hesitant. "Can we talk? Just the two of us?"

His expression shifted, the laughter evaporating as he nodded, concern etching lines on his forehead. "Sure. Let's step outside."

As we moved toward the back of the shop, the world beyond felt bright and unyielding, just as my heart felt in that moment. I knew we were standing at a precipice, and the decision that loomed ahead could change everything.

The moment we stepped outside, the warm sun washed over us like a comforting embrace, but my nerves felt anything but warm. I could hear the distant sounds of laughter and the clinking of glasses from the nearby café, yet they seemed to belong to another world, one where I could remain blissfully unaware of the chaos stirring within my heart. Max leaned against the cool brick wall of the bakery, arms crossed, his posture relaxed but his expression uncertain.

"Okay, what's on your mind?" he asked, tilting his head slightly as he studied me, a playful smile dancing on his lips but failing to reach his eyes. I knew he could sense the shift in the atmosphere, the tension crackling like static before a storm.

I took a deep breath, fighting against the urge to backpedal, to fill the air with lighthearted chatter about the day or the latest pastry experiment gone awry. "It's about us," I finally said, and his smile faltered, replaced by something more serious. "And Oliver."

"Oliver? What about him?"

My pulse quickened as I felt the weight of his gaze pressing into me, urging me to reveal the truth tangled within my heart. "He proposed a big idea for the festival," I began, my voice trembling slightly, "and I can't help but feel like it's more than just about the festival for you two. It feels... personal."

"Of course it's personal! This is about our bakery and the community. I thought you'd be excited about it!" His frustration bubbled just beneath the surface, like the batter we often whipped together, waiting for the right moment to rise.

"It is exciting! It's just—" I paused, my words getting lost in a whirlwind of uncertainty. "I'm worried that the closer we get to him, the further we drift from what we had."

Max straightened, running a hand through his tousled hair, his eyes narrowing as he considered my words. "What do you mean by 'what we had'? Are you saying there's something between us?"

The question hung in the air, heavy and charged, and I could feel the heat of embarrassment creeping up my cheeks. "Yes, no, maybe. I don't know, Max! I just feel torn."

"Torn?" He echoed, a hint of incredulity lacing his tone. "You're torn because of Oliver? You do realize he's not the one you're going home with at the end of the day, right?"

His words were like a splash of cold water, awakening me to the undeniable truth. I was standing here, teetering on the edge of something precarious, caught between my feelings for Max and the confusing allure of what Oliver represented.

"I know! But it's not just Oliver. It's this whole thing we've built together, and I feel like I'm standing in the middle of a tug-of-war."

"Why do you think I'm here with you now? I want to figure this out too. I just didn't know you were feeling so... conflicted." He stepped closer, the warmth of his body radiating against the crisp afternoon air. "You've always been my constant. Why would you let someone else mess with that?"

I swallowed hard, emotions swirling like whipped cream in a mixing bowl. "Because you're planning a future with Oliver, and I can't ignore that!" The words spilled out before I could reel them back in, each syllable a raw testament to my fears.

"Wait, what? Planning a future? No, you've got it all wrong. Oliver and I are just brainstorming ideas for the festival. It's not a life plan."

"Then what is it? Because it feels like he's moving in while I'm still trying to figure out if I even have a place." My voice cracked, revealing the vulnerable edges I had tried so hard to conceal.

"Are you serious? You think Oliver has any claim over me? You're the one I care about," he said, taking a step forward, closing the distance between us until the warmth of his body brushed against mine. "It's always been you, and I thought we were on the same page."

My heart raced as I took in the intensity of his gaze, the sincerity reflected there. It was in moments like these that the world around us faded, leaving just the two of us suspended in time. "But you're so wrapped up in this vision with him, Max. I don't want to be the one holding you back if that's what you want."

He shook his head, frustration written across his features. "You think I want to spend every waking moment planning dessert with him? It's like trying to chase the sun with a bowl of pudding—messy and utterly impossible. I want us to create something together."

"Then why don't we?" The question lingered in the air, a challenge wrapped in hope.

"What do you mean?" His brow furrowed in confusion, the lines on his forehead deepening as he searched my face for clarity.

"I mean we could plan for the festival too! Together! The three of us, if you think Oliver is so vital, but I want us to be a team."

Max blinked, the gears visibly turning in his mind as he contemplated my proposal. "You want to work alongside Oliver? Like, share ideas, collaborate? You know he has this... charisma. It can be intimidating."

"Intimidating? Please, I've spent years watching you bake alongside your grandmother. You have more charisma in your pinky than Oliver has in his entire body. This isn't about competition; it's about collaboration."

"Fine, but if he tries to take the lead, I won't hesitate to remind him who really runs this bakery." There was a playful challenge in his eyes, and despite the tension, I couldn't help but smile.

"Oh, so now you're feeling territorial?" I teased, feigning a look of surprise. "What happened to that guy who was all zen about sharing the spotlight?"

"Maybe he's realizing that the spotlight looks better when you're not sharing it with someone who's determined to outshine you."

"Touché," I laughed, the sound bubbling up from a place of genuine relief. "So we're agreed? We'll work together on this festival, but it's still us at the center?"

"Always," he affirmed, the warmth of his voice igniting a flicker of hope within me. But just as the moment felt right, an unexpected cloud drifted in—Oliver's laughter echoed from the shop, slicing through our intimate bubble like a knife, reminding me of the uncertainty still lurking just beneath the surface.

"Right, but that doesn't mean I won't keep my eyes peeled," I said, the weight of my words hanging between us, knowing full well that navigating our tangled relationships would require more than just good intentions.

"Then let's make a pact," Max proposed, a playful spark lighting up his eyes. "If it gets messy, we'll throw flour at each other. Deal?"

"Deal," I replied, a grin spreading across my face as I felt the tension ease ever so slightly. But as the laughter faded and the shadows lengthened around us, I couldn't shake the feeling that this was just the beginning of something much larger than any festival or cake could ever capture.

The air was thick with the scent of vanilla and the lingering warmth from the oven as we re-entered the bakery, the vibrant atmosphere a stark contrast to the storm of emotions swirling within me. Max's laughter drifted alongside the chatter of customers, yet I couldn't shake the sense that we were standing on shaky ground. I tried to focus on the task at hand—brainstorming for the festival—but the shadow of uncertainty loomed over us, darkening what should have been a joyous collaboration.

"Okay, so what's our first move?" I asked, attempting to inject some lightness into our conversation. I leaned against the counter, arms crossed, hoping to channel my energy into something productive. Max took a moment, eyes scanning the room before locking onto me with a newfound determination.

"How about we do a taste test first? We can whip up some samples and see what resonates with people. It'll give us a feel for the crowd," he suggested, a spark igniting in his voice. I could see the gears of his mind turning, the creative juices flowing, and it felt like the first step toward rebuilding the connection that had felt so fragile moments before.

"Great idea! We could do a cupcake version of your layered cake. Everyone loves a mini treat, and it allows for a range of flavors," I chimed in, relief washing over me as I felt the familiar thrill of collaborating with him. Together, we dove into discussions about ingredients and flavors, tossing ideas back and forth with a rhythm that felt almost effortless.

"Chocolate raspberry, lemon basil, and maybe a salted caramel twist for good measure?" Max suggested, raising an eyebrow playfully. "What do you think? Too adventurous for our sleepy town?"

I grinned, leaning in conspiratorially. "I think adventurous is our middle name. Or at least it should be. Why not have a bit of fun while we're at it?"

With each idea we tossed around, I felt the weight of my earlier fears start to lift, only to be momentarily stalled by the sharp clang of the bell above the door. I turned, watching as Oliver entered the bakery, his presence sweeping through like a gust of wind. My heart sank a little, but I quickly masked it with a smile.

"Look who it is!" Max said, enthusiasm bubbling back into his voice. "Just in time for the brainstorming session. Join us?"

"Absolutely," Oliver replied, his voice smooth and confident as he approached the counter. "I've been thinking about what we discussed earlier. I have a few more ideas that might really elevate our booth at the festival."

As he leaned against the counter, the way he interacted with Max felt intimate, as if they shared a language I wasn't part of. I swallowed down the bubbling jealousy, focusing instead on the task at hand. "Great! Let's hear them," I encouraged, trying to sound genuinely interested while my insides twisted like a pretzel.

Oliver launched into his proposals, his words flowing as easily as the syrup we used in our desserts. I watched the way Max's face lit up at Oliver's suggestions, his passion evident, and I felt a pang of something that resembled longing. It was as if I were watching my two best friends conspire to build something beautiful, while I stood on the sidelines, unsure of my place in it all.

"Let's not forget about presentation," Oliver continued, leaning in closer to Max, who was now scribbling notes with fervor. "We need something that draws people in visually. Something unforgettable."

"Unforgettable, huh? Are we aiming for a Michelin star or just a good old-fashioned county fair?" I quipped, attempting to inject some humor into the moment, but my words felt lost in the air, hanging heavy between us.

Max chuckled lightly, but Oliver didn't seem to catch my drift. "Both? Why not?" he replied, flashing a charming smile that only fueled the turmoil in my stomach.

I watched as the two of them began to plot and plan, drawing sketches on paper and brainstorming names. It was like they were building a castle, and I was relegated to the role of a mere brick. I could feel the tension creeping back in, so I decided to step away from the counter, taking a moment to breathe.

As I wandered toward the back of the shop, I found solace in the rhythm of the ovens humming softly, the gentle clatter of pans providing a backdrop for my spiraling thoughts. I wasn't just a brick—I was a pillar. I had to remind myself of my worth and the contributions I could make to this budding partnership.

Max soon followed, his footsteps steady and purposeful. "Hey, you okay?" His voice was laced with concern, cutting through the haze of my spiraling thoughts.

"Yeah, just... taking it all in, you know? It's a lot," I said, attempting to sound more nonchalant than I felt.

He studied me for a moment, then sighed, running a hand through his hair in that way I found endearing. "I know it's a lot, but I want you to know that you're not just a part of this; you're essential to it. We need your creativity, your input. Don't hold back."

"Right, but it feels like I'm just the extra when you two are so in sync."

"That's not true!" he replied, his voice firm yet kind. "Oliver and I have our thing, sure, but that doesn't diminish what we have. If anything, you elevate it. You're the secret ingredient."

His words warmed me, a soothing balm for my wounded pride. "Okay, I'll take the compliment, but I'll also need you to remember that this is about all three of us. I won't let myself be pushed aside."

"Trust me, you won't be," he said, his expression serious. "We're in this together."

Just then, Oliver sauntered into the back room, a smirk plastered across his face. "What's this? A secret meeting without me?"

I exchanged a glance with Max, our silent communication unbroken even as Oliver interrupted. I felt the familiar tension return, but I shook it off, determined to maintain my focus.

"Just discussing how we can conquer the festival," Max replied, a playful edge creeping into his tone.

"Well, I like the sound of that," Oliver said, crossing his arms, his smile widening. "Why don't we get to work then? I've got some ideas that might just blow your minds."

We returned to the counter, and as Oliver outlined his vision, I forced myself to engage, to contribute. Yet, as the conversation flowed, I couldn't shake the feeling of being adrift, like a boat tossed in a storm. The dynamic between Max and Oliver felt charged, and every time their eyes met, I felt an unexplainable knot tighten in my chest.

Hours passed in a whirlwind of ideas, laughter, and the occasional sweet treat taste test. Yet, despite the camaraderie that filled the bakery, a gnawing apprehension settled in my gut. I could see the potential for something beautiful taking shape, but there was a darkness lurking beneath the surface that refused to be ignored.

"Alright, team," I said, attempting to lighten the mood as the afternoon wore on. "How about we make a pact to never let dessert ruin our friendship?"

"Agreed," Max replied, a twinkle in his eye. "Dessert is life, and life is messy. We just have to deal with the aftermath together."

Suddenly, the door swung open, and a gust of wind rushed in, causing papers to scatter across the counter. I turned to see a figure silhouetted in the doorway—my heart skipped a beat. It was Claire, my former co-worker, her face pale, eyes wide.

"Guys, you need to listen to me," she panted, taking a step forward, breathless and frantic. "There's something you need to know about Oliver."

The air shifted, tension crackling as we all turned to face her, and I felt the ground shift beneath me. What could she possibly reveal that would change everything?

Chapter 13: Hidden Cravings

The evening air was heavy with the scent of melting chocolate, a rich, velvety aroma that seemed to swirl through the cozy corners of the shop. The soft glow of overhead lights bathed the space in a warm embrace, illuminating jars filled with vibrant confections and the gleaming surface of the marble counter where I often danced with creativity. I lost myself in the rhythm of the evening, my fingers dusted with cocoa powder, instinctively shaping truffles as if they were extensions of my own thoughts.

It was during one of these playful moments, a time when the world outside faded into a mere whisper, that I stumbled upon it—an old, leather-bound recipe book, its spine cracked and the pages exuding a sense of history that drew me in like a moth to a flame. I pulled it from the shelf, brushing off a layer of dust that had settled like an uninvited guest. As I flipped through the yellowed pages, I felt an electric thrill run through me. Handwritten notes scrawled in elegant cursive danced alongside faded photographs of confections that seemed to tell stories of their own. Each recipe was a testament to the artistry of the chocolatier who had come before me, a legacy waiting to be reborn.

"Max! Come here!" I called, unable to contain my excitement.

Max, my loyal sidekick and partner in chocolate mischief, emerged from the back room, wiping his hands on a flour-dusted apron. His curiosity piqued, he leaned over my shoulder to glimpse the contents of the book. "What have you found?" he asked, eyes wide, a playful smirk already forming on his lips.

"It's a treasure trove of recipes," I declared, my voice brimming with enthusiasm. "Look at this one—Cinnamon-Cayenne Chocolate! Can you even imagine the flavor explosion?"

He laughed, leaning closer, his shoulder brushing against mine. "Only if we can use a touch of sea salt. You know I can't resist the sweet and savory combo."

With a spark igniting between us, we began to sift through the pages, each recipe invoking a wild flurry of ideas. It felt as if the book had been waiting for us, whispering secrets of sweetness and spice. The night unfurled like a delicate ribbon, our laughter bouncing off the walls, mingling with the sound of melting chocolate as we experimented with new flavors. The air crackled with the thrill of creation, each concoction a burst of joy that filled the shop, but beneath it all, a flicker of doubt lingered—a reminder of Oliver's proposition that had started to loom larger in my mind like an ominous cloud.

As I whisked melted chocolate with a flourish, I glanced at Max, his face alight with mischief. "What if we add a splash of whiskey to the ganache?" he suggested, waggling his eyebrows suggestively.

"Max, you're trying to turn our truffles into a late-night bar special," I teased, but the idea tickled my fancy.

"Okay, hear me out," he said, leaning closer, conspiratorial. "Just imagine: Bourbon-Infused Salted Caramel Chocolates. They'll knock people's socks off."

"Only if they don't knock me over in the process," I shot back, but the thought lingered, inviting and dangerous, like a secret waiting to be discovered.

Hours melted away as we continued to blend flavors, our creativity spiraling in delightful directions. Max's laughter was infectious, wrapping around me like a warm blanket on a chilly evening. We filled molds with our creations, an array of flavors shimmering like jewels beneath the shop's soft lights.

Yet, even as the warmth of our camaraderie enveloped me, a flicker of unease lingered in the back of my mind. Oliver's offer hadn't just been an invitation; it was a potential turning point in my life, an opportunity that could pull me away from the only world I truly loved—the world of chocolate, of laughter, of late-night experiments with Max. Would the allure of a larger business and the promise of stability overshadow the simple joys that had fueled my passion?

I could see Oliver in my mind, his earnest expression as he laid out his grand vision, the way he believed in the future we could build together. But what was that future built on? I loved my little shop, the way the soft clinks of truffle molds and the gentle hum of the mixer became a symphony of comfort. Could I really trade that for the sterile, structured world of corporate chocolate?

"What's on your mind?" Max's voice broke through my reverie, pulling me back to the present.

"Just thinking about how much I love this," I said, gesturing to the scattered ingredients, the chaotic beauty of our workspace. "How I never want it to change."

"Change isn't always bad," he said, leaning against the counter, arms crossed, a teasing smile playing on his lips. "But I get it. You're like a chocolate squirrel hoarding nuts for the winter. What are you saving for? A perfect truffle?"

His quip made me chuckle, the tension in my chest easing slightly. "Maybe I am. Or maybe I just want to savor every moment of this—us."

He cocked his head, that knowing look settling in his eyes. "You know, we can find a way to make both happen. Who says you can't grow without losing your heart?"

The earnestness in his tone tugged at something deep within me. As the last of the evening light faded, leaving only the glow of our shop, I realized that my fear of change wasn't rooted in the fear of losing everything I loved but rather in the uncertainty of what I could gain. And perhaps, just perhaps, that gain could include new flavors, new recipes, and the sweet thrill of a future where both Oliver's ambitions and my chocolate dreams could coexist.

With newfound resolve, I took a deep breath, and let the soft rhythm of laughter and creativity wash over me, ready to face the questions that awaited.

The sun dipped below the horizon, casting a warm golden glow that painted the shop in shades of amber. I watched as the last rays of light filtered through the window, illuminating the fine dust motes that danced like tiny fairies in the air. Max and I had lost ourselves in the world of flavor, and the chocolate-covered chaos around us was the only proof of our late-night escapades. We had pushed the boundaries of tradition, daring to create concoctions that whispered of the past while shouting into the future.

"Okay, how about a lavender-infused dark chocolate?" I suggested, my mind racing with the possibilities. "I read somewhere that it's supposed to evoke calmness."

Max raised an eyebrow, a playful smirk dancing on his lips. "Calmness? I'm not sure that's what people are looking for when they're knee-deep in chocolate." He plucked a lavender sprig from the small herb pot by the window, twirling it between his fingers as if it were a magic wand. "But let's see if we can turn calm into decadent chaos."

With the lavender as our muse, we set to work. The scent of dried flowers mingled with the rich aroma of melting chocolate, creating a fragrant symphony that wrapped around us like a cozy scarf. I found myself humming along to an imaginary tune, the rhythm of our creative frenzy lifting my spirits. Max caught my eye, and without missing a beat, he began to dance, twirling around the counter as if he were auditioning for a culinary ballet.

"What are you doing?" I laughed, trying to focus on melting the chocolate without being swept away by his antics.

"Just trying to channel my inner chocolatier," he quipped, striking a pose that would have made any pastry chef proud. "What do you think? Too much drama?"

"Just the right amount!" I shot back, playfully nudging him with my elbow. The laughter bubbled between us, light and airy, momentarily pushing aside the heaviness that had settled in my heart.

As I poured the lavender essence into the glossy chocolate, a sudden thought struck me. "What if we make a heart-shaped mold for these? A limited edition for Valentine's Day!"

Max paused, his eyes gleaming with mischief. "Heart-shaped? You mean to tell me you're not a fan of love-themed chocolates?"

"I think they're sweet, but you know how people can be. It's like they expect a fairy tale in every bite." I rolled my eyes, remembering the pressure that accompanied such expectations, the cloying sweetness that sometimes masked the complexities of life.

Max leaned closer, mischief sparkling in his eyes. "Well, let's give them a twist then! How about we add a hint of chili? You know, spice things up a bit?"

I grinned, the idea igniting a spark of inspiration. "Yes! Let's create the 'Love with a Kick' truffle. Because nothing says romance like a little fire in your belly!"

As we poured the lavender-chocolate mixture into the molds, I felt the excitement of discovery wash over me. This wasn't just about creating chocolates; it was about crafting experiences, memories, and perhaps even a little mischief that would linger long after the last bite.

Max and I continued to play with flavors, giggling like kids in a candy store as we bounced ideas off each other. The concoctions grew more outrageous, from raspberry and basil truffles to honey and rosemary caramels. Each time we unveiled a new flavor, it felt like we were opening a treasure chest, discovering gems hidden beneath the surface.

Just as we were about to try our latest creation, the bell above the door jingled, and I looked up to see Oliver stepping inside. He was a sight for sore eyes, with his warm smile and tousled hair. The moment he walked in, a hush fell over the shop, as if the air shifted in his presence. I felt an odd mix of comfort and tension—my heart fluttering like a startled bird.

"Hey, you two!" he called, his voice like a soothing balm against the backdrop of our playful chaos. "What's cooking in here? Smells incredible!"

Max, ever the charmer, flashed a grin. "Only the finest chocolate, Oliver! Care to join our little experiment?"

"Absolutely," Oliver replied, his gaze flitting between us, assessing the scene. "What are we making?"

I felt my heart race, knowing that revealing our wild concoctions might lead to some eyebrow-raising reactions. "We're calling it 'Love with a Kick,'" I said, trying to sound nonchalant as I held up the heart-shaped molds.

Oliver chuckled, his expression a mix of amusement and intrigue. "That's quite the name. Are you sure it's not going to backfire?"

"Backfire? More like ignite passion!" Max interjected, pretending to fan himself dramatically. "Imagine giving these to a crush and suddenly feeling all hot and bothered. It's a culinary game-changer."

I rolled my eyes but couldn't suppress a smile. "Only if the crush has good taste, right?"

Oliver laughed, a genuine sound that filled the room with warmth. "Well, it sounds like you're both having too much fun. Mind if I steal a moment of your time?"

"Sure," I replied, though I felt a twinge of anxiety creep in, like a shadow lurking at the edge of my happiness. "What's up?"

He stepped closer, his expression turning serious. "I've been thinking a lot about our conversation the other day." The air shifted, and I could feel my stomach twist in knots. "I know I threw a lot at you, but I really believe that we could make a fantastic team."

"Right, the whole corporate takeover thing," I said lightly, trying to mask the anxiety that fluttered inside me. "What do you have in mind?"

Oliver hesitated, his gaze steady and intense. "I want to help you expand, but I don't want to change the essence of what you've built. Your shop, your creations—everything about it is special. I just think we could reach a wider audience, share your magic beyond these walls."

Max leaned against the counter, watching the exchange with a keen eye. "That sounds like a dream come true, doesn't it?"

I opened my mouth, ready to counter, to deflect, but found myself momentarily speechless. The truth was, his vision was enticing, like a forbidden fruit hanging just out of reach. Would the allure of a broader platform overshadow the intimate connection I had with each truffle I crafted? The prospect felt like standing at the edge of a precipice, a dizzying mix of exhilaration and fear washing over me.

"I appreciate that," I finally said, my voice steadier than I felt. "But I'm also really protective of this place. It's more than just a business to me."

"I get it," he replied, his expression softening. "I wouldn't want to take that away from you. I just want to help you grow, to take that passion and turn it into something that resonates with even more people."

In that moment, I felt the weight of his words sink in. It was an invitation, but also a challenge. What if this was the opportunity I had been waiting for? What if I could find a way to keep the heart of my shop while exploring new horizons?

Max's voice cut through the tension like a breath of fresh air. "Well, while you two debate the fate of the chocolate empire, I suggest we try out this 'Love with a Kick' truffle. It's the real test of whether passion and chocolate really do mix!"

Oliver chuckled, the tension easing slightly, and I felt the warmth of camaraderie wrap around us again. With a quick nod, I decided to embrace the moment, to savor this unexpected twist, and maybe—just maybe—find a way to reconcile my fears with the sweetness of possibility.

With a laugh, I watched as Max took a tentative bite of our "Love with a Kick" truffle. His eyes widened in surprise, the chocolate melting into a symphony of flavors on his tongue, and I could practically see the gears turning in his head as he processed the spicy bite that followed the initial sweetness.

"Oh, wow," he exclaimed, wiping his mouth dramatically. "This is not just a truffle. It's a love letter to the taste buds! The sweet flirting with the spicy? Who knew they'd get along so well?"

I couldn't help but chuckle, feeling the warmth of our camaraderie wrapping around me like a favorite blanket. "I guess you could say it's a match made in heaven," I replied, feeling my heart flutter at the thought of our creations finding their way into the hands of eager customers.

Oliver leaned against the counter, arms crossed, a soft smile on his lips as he watched our banter unfold. "You both have a gift for turning the ordinary into something extraordinary," he said, a hint of admiration coloring his tone. "This is what I want to help amplify—your passion. Imagine turning this little shop into a destination."

"Destination? Sounds fancy," Max interjected, his tone teasing. "What do we do, put up a neon sign that says 'Chocolate Paradise'?"

"Or 'Chocolatopia'!" I added, feeling a wave of excitement wash over me at the thought. "The place where dreams are dipped in chocolate!"

Oliver laughed, but then his expression shifted, the lightheartedness giving way to a more serious undertone. "I'm serious, you know. With the right marketing, the right partnerships, we could attract tourists and chocolate lovers from all over."

I felt the weight of his words, the dizzying prospect swirling in my mind. "And what happens to the cozy feel of the shop?" I challenged, my voice tinged with protectiveness. "What about the personal touch? I don't want it to feel like a factory."

"Why can't it be both?" Oliver countered, his gaze steady. "You can expand without losing what makes this place special. You can bring your heart into everything you do. Just look at the truffles you've created tonight!"

"Yeah, but they're a little... unexpected," I replied, glancing at the heart-shaped molds. "What if people don't get it? What if they don't want a 'kick' with their romance?"

Max shrugged, taking another bite of the truffle as he pondered. "Or what if they love it? What if this is the beginning of something amazing?"

There it was again, the idea that hung in the air like the sweet scent of chocolate, tantalizing and impossible to ignore. I felt a tug-of-war within me, the yearning for growth battling with my desire for familiarity. "I need time to think," I said finally, my voice low but resolute. "This is a big decision, and I can't rush into it."

"Of course," Oliver replied, nodding in understanding. "Take your time. I'm here whenever you want to discuss it further."

Just then, the bell above the door jingled again, and my heart leaped as I turned to see Sarah, one of our regulars, enter the shop. She was a whirlwind of energy, her dark hair bouncing as she rushed in, the chill of the evening air swirling around her like an exuberant child.

"Hey, you guys! I couldn't wait to see what new magic you've conjured up!" she exclaimed, her eyes lighting up as they landed on the counter, where our latest creations awaited. "I could smell the chocolate from two blocks away! What is happening here?"

"Only the most exciting thing," Max said, his voice dripping with drama. "Prepare yourself for an explosion of love!"

Sarah's eyes darted to the heart-shaped molds. "Are those what I think they are? Please tell me they're not just ordinary chocolates."

"Not even close," I replied, unable to suppress my smile. "Meet our 'Love with a Kick' truffles."

Her eyes widened as she picked one up, turning it over in her hands like it was a precious gem. "Okay, I'm in. Hit me with the flavor!"

With a playful grin, I watched as she took a bite, her expression shifting from delight to surprise and then pure exhilaration. "Oh my God! This is incredible! It's like...wow! It's sweet and then BAM! There's the heat! You guys are geniuses!"

"Don't let it go to our heads," Max chuckled, but I felt a rush of pride at her reaction.

"It's so good, I might just start a petition to make it the official chocolate of love!" Sarah declared, tossing her hair back with dramatic flair. "I mean, if it can handle all that heat, it deserves the title."

As we shared in the laughter and excitement, I felt the walls of uncertainty around me begin to crumble. Perhaps Oliver was right; maybe this was the time to embrace change. But as the energy in the shop grew more vibrant, my heart still tugged in the opposite direction, a voice whispering that the essence of what I loved most could slip away.

Suddenly, my phone buzzed on the counter, the sharp vibration cutting through the laughter. I picked it up, glancing at the screen, my heart racing as I saw a familiar name. It was a message from my mother, a simple text that sent a shiver down my spine: "We need to talk. It's about the shop."

The air thickened with tension, my heart pounding as I felt a swell of anxiety rise within me. Sarah's laughter faded into the background, and I could hear the pounding of my pulse in my ears as I read and reread the message.

"What's up?" Max asked, his brows knitting together in concern as he noticed my sudden stillness.

I shook my head, trying to brush off the worry. "Just family stuff," I said, forcing a smile that felt more like a mask.

"Family stuff? That sounds suspiciously vague," he teased lightly, but his eyes bore into mine, searching for the truth.

"Yeah, well, it can wait," I replied, my voice unsteady as I slipped the phone back into my pocket. The last thing I wanted was to unload my family drama on the two people who had made this evening so special. But the weight of that text loomed large, hovering over me like a storm cloud, threatening to pour down when I least expected it.

Just then, Oliver leaned in, his eyes catching mine, an unspoken understanding passing between us. "Whatever it is, we're here for you," he said softly, his tone sincere.

"Yeah," Max added, offering a reassuring smile. "We can handle anything together."

The warmth of their support wrapped around me, but as I looked around the shop, filled with laughter and the sweet aroma of our chocolate creations, I couldn't shake the feeling that something was about to change. Just as I opened my mouth to respond, the bell above the door jingled again, and in walked a figure I hadn't seen in ages.

My breath caught in my throat as I recognized the familiar silhouette. It was Jenna, my childhood best friend, the one person who had once shared in my chocolate dreams before life had led us down separate paths.

Her eyes met mine, and in that instant, the shop became silent, the weight of unspoken words hanging between us like a fragile thread waiting to snap. I felt my heart race, confusion and nostalgia battling for dominance as I stood frozen in place, the tension thickening in the air.

What did she want? Why now? And more importantly, what would this mean for the world I had built so carefully around me?

Chapter 14: Bitter Truths

The next day unfolded like a piece of fine chocolate—rich, textured, and deceptively simple, masking the complexities simmering beneath the surface. The moment I stepped into the shop, the familiar scent of warm cocoa enveloped me, wrapping around my shoulders like a beloved shawl. The morning sunlight streamed through the large windows, casting a golden glow over our latest creation: a dark chocolate infused with subtle chili notes, finished with a delicate sprinkle of sea salt. It was a confection meant to tantalize and surprise, much like the emotions brewing in the pit of my stomach.

Max stood at the counter, his brow slightly furrowed as he examined the glossy chocolate bars with the kind of focus usually reserved for a master craftsman on the verge of a breakthrough. His dark hair fell into his eyes, and I felt a twinge of affection—how could I not? Max was passionate, dedicated, and at times maddeningly optimistic. It was the optimism that made my heart both swell and constrict, especially now, in this moment charged with anticipation. "This is incredible," he said, lifting one of the bars to his lips, the corners of his mouth twitching into a grin that could melt even the most bitter chocolate.

But just as the sweetness of the moment began to seep into my veins, Oliver sauntered in with his usual swagger, all energy and charm, like a walking sparkler ready to light up our carefully crafted world. "We need to talk about the tasting event," he declared, and I felt the warmth in the room dissipate like sugar dissolving in hot water.

I swallowed hard, my stomach twisting into a knot that felt less like anticipation and more like dread. "What tasting event?" I asked, attempting to maintain an air of nonchalance, though my heart was pounding like a jackhammer against my ribs.

Oliver shot me a quizzical look, one eyebrow arched in that infuriatingly knowing way of his. "The one that could put us on the map! We're showcasing the shop to potential investors next week. It's going to be huge!"

My pulse quickened, and the sweet atmosphere transformed into something sharp and sour. "I don't want to lose what we've built together," I blurted, my voice shaky as if I were standing on the edge of a precipice, looking down into a churning sea of uncertainty. "This shop, our creations—everything we've done—feels so fragile. What if they change everything?"

Max's expression hardened, caught in the crossfire between my fears and Oliver's boundless enthusiasm. "It could be a great opportunity, though. We've been struggling to keep up with bills. This might be what we need," he offered gently, but his words felt like a double-edged sword.

"I know, but I can't help but think about how much we've poured into this place," I shot back, my voice rising. The conflict felt insurmountable, as though the walls of our sanctuary were closing in around us. The sunlight that had felt so warm moments ago now felt like an unwelcome spotlight, illuminating all the cracks in our perfect little bubble.

"Look, I understand your hesitation," Max said, his tone soothing, but there was an undercurrent of tension in his words. "But we need investors if we want to expand. This is our chance to take the next step. Think of what we could do with the right backing."

"Maybe we don't need to take the next step. Maybe we just need to keep doing what we're doing," I argued, desperation clawing at the back of my throat. "I love this place. I love us, the way we create together."

"You make it sound like we're doing something wrong," Oliver interjected, his voice rising to match my own. "What's so wrong about wanting to grow?"

"Nothing," I retorted, my hands balling into fists at my sides. "But growing doesn't have to mean losing our identity. We're not just a brand; we're a family."

Silence descended in the shop, thick and uncomfortable. I could feel the tension like a living thing, curling around us and squeezing. Max's gaze drifted to the window, as if seeking solace from the world outside, while Oliver rubbed the back of his neck, visibly frustrated.

"I just want to make sure we don't end up like those soulless chain shops," I continued, my heart racing. "You know, the ones where everything is standardized and nothing is made with love?"

Max turned back to me, his expression softening. "I get it, I really do. But what if this is the path that lets us keep doing what we love? What if we can bring that soul with us?"

I shook my head, a knot tightening in my chest. "What if it changes everything? What if they don't care about the soul? What if we end up just another storefront on a crowded street?"

"I guess we'll find out," Oliver said, an edge of frustration creeping into his tone. "But right now, we're standing on the edge of something big. We can't let fear hold us back."

There it was—the crux of the matter, laid bare like an open wound. I took a deep breath, letting the words hang in the air between us, heavy and suffocating. My heart ached with the weight of what felt like an impending fracture in our carefully constructed reality, a reality that had been built on laughter, late nights, and a shared dream of creating something beautiful.

As I turned away, the weight of unspoken emotions suffocating me, I felt the sting of unshed tears prick at my eyes. This was not just about chocolate; it was about everything we had forged together. The warmth of the shop felt like a distant memory, replaced by an icy dread that settled deep in my bones. What was I willing to risk for the future, and at what cost?

The tension in the shop clung to me like melted chocolate on my fingers, sticky and oppressive. As Oliver walked over to the tasting table, I noticed the way he flitted around, full of uncontainable energy, his hands gesturing as he spoke with a fervor that bordered on fanaticism. Each word dripped with the promise of expansion and success, but beneath his excitement, I sensed an unyielding current that threatened to sweep us all away. Max stood at his side, his eyes gleaming with the thrill of ambition, and I felt a pang of betrayal—was I the only one who recognized the fragile nature of what we had built?

"Okay, imagine this," Oliver said, a wide grin stretching across his face, "we host the event, impress the investors, and suddenly we have enough funding to not only revamp the shop but also to start distributing to local cafes. We could be everywhere!"

My heart sank deeper into my chest. "And then what? We become just another name on a shelf, another faceless brand?" I shot back, frustration seeping into my tone. "What's the point of growth if we lose what makes us special?"

"Growth doesn't mean losing identity," Max chimed in, trying to balance the scales. "It means evolving. We can still be us, just—better."

I crossed my arms, feeling the familiar stir of defiance. "Better for who, Max? For us or for them?"

Oliver rolled his eyes, that charmingly exasperated look etched on his face. "This isn't just about chocolate bars; it's about building a legacy. Do you want to be known as the little shop that could have made it but didn't?"

A heavy silence fell. I glanced at Max, who seemed lost in thought, his brow furrowed as he weighed my emotions against the gleaming allure of potential fame. The flickering overhead lights cast shadows that danced across the walls, each movement echoing the turmoil within me. My chest tightened as I considered the years we'd poured into this venture, the countless late nights spent refining recipes, the laughter shared over burned batches, and the fierce pride I felt whenever a customer left with a satisfied smile.

"What if the legacy we're building is meant to be small, intimate?" I asked, my voice softening. "What if that's where the heart of our shop lies?"

Max opened his mouth to respond, but Oliver cut him off, determination etched into his features. "And what if our hearts can reach further than we ever imagined? You're thinking too small, and it's holding us back. Think about it—a community of people who love our chocolate, who can taste our passion! That's a dream worth fighting for!"

I was silent, grappling with the wave of doubt that threatened to drown my resolve. The aroma of cocoa wafted through the air, and I inhaled deeply, reminding myself of the warmth it brought—the memories of our shared laughter, the way we had poured ourselves into every bite of chocolate, crafting something more than just a product.

"Look," I finally said, my tone firm yet vulnerable, "I get that we need to make money, but I'm terrified we'll lose what makes us unique. If we're in it just for the money, then what's the point? I don't want to wake up one day and feel like I've sold my soul for a storefront."

"Is that what you think we're doing?" Max asked, his eyes searching mine. "That we're not serious about the craft?"

"No, that's not it!" I protested, exasperated. "But I don't want to compromise on the very thing that brought us together in the first place."

Oliver crossed his arms, his expression shifting from enthusiasm to something colder, sharper. "You know, for someone who claims to care about this shop, you sure seem resistant to the idea of making it better."

Max shot him a look that silenced the air between us. "That's enough, Oliver. We all care. That's why we're having this conversation."

The room felt charged, as if the very walls were echoing our unspoken fears. I stood there, heart racing, as the reality of our situation loomed like a specter over us. I thought about the countless hours spent in the back kitchen, where the hum of the mixer became a kind of music, the joy in crafting something exquisite—a piece of our hearts wrapped in chocolate. Could I really stand by while it all changed?

"Maybe it's not just about chocolate," I said finally, lowering my voice to a whisper. "Maybe it's about us."

Silence fell again, a heavy, pregnant pause. Max's gaze softened, but Oliver's face tightened as he struggled with the implications of my words. "What are you saying?" he asked, the challenge evident in his voice.

"I'm saying that this shop is a piece of us," I replied, my pulse quickening. "It's our dreams, our fears. It's not just a business; it's a part of who we are. I want to make sure we don't lose that in the shuffle of investors and tasting events."

Oliver ran a hand through his hair, clearly torn. "But it could change everything for the better. Why can't we have both? Why can't we keep our identity and grow?"

I wanted to scream, to shake him until he understood, but the heat of the moment cooled as I realized I had to tread carefully. "What if we take a step back? We can host the event, but let's do it on our terms. We showcase what makes us unique—the stories behind our recipes, the love that goes into every piece of chocolate."

Max's eyes lit up, and I could feel the energy shift slightly as he began to nod. "That's a brilliant idea," he said, a spark igniting in his expression. "We can create an experience, not just a tasting. We can share our story, our journey, and connect with the investors on a deeper level."

Oliver stared at us, the realization washing over him like a wave. "Okay, I see where you're coming from," he said slowly, the edges of his conviction softening. "But let's not lose sight of the bigger picture. We have to appeal to them without losing ourselves in the process."

Relief surged through me, but I knew this wasn't a complete resolution. It was merely a reprieve, a momentary halt in a conversation that would undoubtedly circle back around. The stakes were high, but as I glanced at Max, I felt a flicker of hope. Maybe, just maybe, we could find a way to keep our heart intact while also reaching for the stars. The uncertainty still lingered, but it felt a little lighter now, like a dusting of powdered sugar on a delicate truffle.

"Let's plan it together, then," I said, a smile breaking through the heaviness of the moment. "Let's make it a celebration of who we are."

As we brainstormed ideas, laughter filled the air once more, and I felt the warmth of camaraderie wrap around us, bright and vibrant like the golden hues of melted caramel. Maybe the bitter truths could lead us to something sweeter than we'd ever imagined.

The meeting transformed into an impromptu brainstorming session, the air around us crackling with a mix of excitement and apprehension. We gathered around the small wooden table, its surface littered with cocoa dust and sketches of potential designs for the tasting event. Ideas flowed freely, each one infused with a splash of our collective passion. As we mapped out the details, the earlier tension began to dissipate, replaced by an energy that hummed like the espresso machine in the corner.

"What if we created a chocolate passport for each guest?" I suggested, my fingers tracing the outline of a cocoa bean on the table.

"They could collect stamps from different tasting stations, each one representing a flavor or a story from our journey."

Oliver leaned back in his chair, a thoughtful expression on his face. "That could work. It adds an interactive element, makes them feel part of something. Plus, it could be a great way to showcase our unique flavors, like that chili chocolate."

"Right! And we could have little tasting notes with each stamp," Max chimed in, his eyes brightening. "Guests could write their thoughts down as they go. It's personal, it's engaging. It feels like we're inviting them into our world."

I felt my heart swell at the thought of sharing our passion so intimately. "Exactly! It's not just about tasting chocolate; it's about tasting our story."

A grin spread across Oliver's face, and he leaned forward, enthusiasm radiating from him. "Now we're cooking! What about some live demonstrations? We could have a mini workshop where people can watch us craft the chocolates."

Max chuckled. "You mean we'd be giving away our secrets? What's next, a guided tour of my secret stash of emergency chocolate hidden behind the counter?"

"Hey, we can't let them know all our tricks!" I joked, but the idea of showcasing our process excited me. We were creators, after all, and sharing that part of ourselves felt like a step toward genuine connection.

As we continued to brainstorm, the shop transformed into a whirlwind of creativity. Laughter bounced off the walls, and I could almost taste the sweet air charged with possibility. We poured over every detail: the decor, the music, the layout. It was exhilarating, the world outside fading as we plunged deeper into our vision.

Hours slipped away, and just as I thought we were finally gaining momentum, a familiar sound cut through the warm atmosphere—the bell above the door chimed, signaling the arrival of a customer. I looked up, expecting to see a regular, perhaps one of our loyal patrons, but my stomach twisted at the sight of the last person I wanted to see.

Diana stood in the doorway, arms crossed, her demeanor radiating disapproval. She was dressed impeccably, as always, in a tailored blazer and sleek heels that clicked against the floor as she strode toward us. The vibrant energy in the room dampened as she approached, her presence an unwelcome storm cloud.

"Ah, if it isn't the chocolate trio," she said, her voice dripping with sarcasm. "What are you concocting today? Another misguided attempt to make your little shop a success?"

Oliver opened his mouth, ready to retort, but I shot him a look, signaling for restraint. This was not a battle I wanted to escalate. "Diana," I said, forcing a smile, "we're actually working on an event to showcase our chocolates. We're really excited about it."

"Excited?" she echoed, a scoff escaping her lips. "You're really going to pull the wool over everyone's eyes with this little tasting party? It's cute, but it's not going to cut it in this market. You need more than just good intentions to impress investors."

Max, who had been trying to stay neutral, finally snapped. "And what would you suggest, Diana? Toss aside our passion for a cookie-cutter corporate strategy?"

"Exactly! You need to think bigger!" she shot back, the fire in her eyes unmistakable. "Investors want numbers, projections, a solid plan. Not 'chocolate passports' and 'live demonstrations.' That's not how the world works. This isn't some high school science fair."

Frustration bubbled within me, an urge to defend our vision rising like the molten chocolate we'd poured hours earlier. "We're not trying to fit into some mold. This is about connection—about sharing what makes us unique."

Diana rolled her eyes, her expression that of a condescending teacher faced with misbehaving students. "Connections don't pay the bills. Don't you understand? It's time to grow up and play the game."

I took a deep breath, fighting the urge to lash out. "And what if we don't want to play that game?" I asked, my voice steady. "What if we'd rather stand firm in our identity and build something that lasts?"

"Lasts?" she scoffed, her laughter harsh. "Do you really think what you're doing will last? You're romanticizing a dying industry. The world is moving on, and if you can't keep up, you'll get left behind."

The words hit me like a blow to the gut, and I struggled to maintain my composure. I glanced at Max and Oliver, who both looked equally unsettled. Was this what it came down to? A battle between our heartfelt vision and the cold, hard reality of a marketplace that cared little for sentiment?

Suddenly, Oliver leaned forward, his voice low but firm. "You may be right about the market, but we refuse to compromise on our values. We're not going to abandon our integrity for a quick buck."

Diana smirked, clearly unfazed. "Integrity doesn't pay rent, boys. You'll find that out soon enough." With a dismissive wave, she turned on her heel and strutted out of the shop, the bell ringing ominously behind her.

A heavy silence settled over us, thick with unease. I felt the weight of her words like a shadow creeping over our optimism. "What if she's right?" I murmured, mostly to myself.

"Don't you dare say that," Max replied sharply, his gaze intense. "She's just trying to rattle us. We can't let her poison our vision."

I nodded, but the seed of doubt had been planted, and I could feel it taking root. "What if we don't succeed?" I whispered, feeling a lump form in my throat.

"Then we'll figure it out together," Oliver said, his voice steadier than I felt. "We'll adapt and innovate. We're not alone in this."

But as we resumed our planning, the enthusiasm felt muted, overshadowed by Diana's harsh reality check. The air crackled with unspoken fears, and my mind raced with possibilities. We had a week to pull this off, to convince investors that we were worth their time and money. What if we failed?

Just as the heaviness settled in, the door swung open again, and in walked a figure I hadn't expected to see. My heart leaped into my throat as I recognized him—a potential investor from one of the exclusive culinary circles we had been hoping to attract. His presence sent an electric jolt through the shop, the weight of my uncertainty surging to the forefront.

"Good afternoon," he said, his voice smooth as dark chocolate, his gaze sweeping over our creations. "I heard there's an event in the works. Mind if I get a taste of what you're offering?"

The room froze, a collective breath held in anticipation. This was our chance—a chance to prove that our passion could be our ticket to success. But as I caught Max's eye, I could see the fear mirrored there. Was this moment a blessing, or was it simply the calm before the storm?

With my heart pounding, I stepped forward, ready to embrace this unexpected opportunity, unaware of how deeply it would impact our future and what choices lay ahead. Would we seize this moment, or would it slip through our fingers like so many grains of cocoa?

Chapter 15: Escaping Shadows

The moment my toes sank into the cool, damp sand, I felt the tension in my shoulders begin to dissipate. The beach, bathed in the fading glow of the setting sun, transformed into a canvas of oranges and pinks that danced across the horizon. I closed my eyes, allowing the rhythmic pulse of the ocean to wash over me, each wave a gentle reminder that life, like the tide, ebbed and flowed. The salty air tangled with my hair, a free-spirited whisper urging me to let go of my worries, even if just for a moment.

As I wandered further along the shoreline, I spotted the elderly couple. Their hands intertwined, they ambled slowly, laughter bubbling between them like champagne. It struck me how their joy was contagious, a warm glow amidst the cool evening. The way they looked at each other—a softness in their eyes, a comfort in their shared silence—reminded me of the fleeting moments I craved with Max. My heart ached with a mix of longing and determination. The love I felt for him wasn't some ephemeral crush; it was a fierce, roaring flame, one that begged to be nurtured despite the shadows lurking in the corners of our relationship.

With each step, the beach transformed around me. Seagulls squawked above, their silhouettes darting across the dying light, while the waves lapped playfully at the shore, teasing the grains of sand. I could taste the salt on my lips, an echo of the freedom I sought. The ocean had always been my escape, a reminder of life's vastness beyond the tangled web of daily woes. But tonight, it felt different—like the water itself was urging me to dive deeper, to confront what lay beneath the surface.

I stopped to pick up a shell, its pearly surface glistening in the twilight. I turned it over in my palm, marveling at the intricate patterns. It was a small treasure, a reminder that beauty often lay hidden, waiting for someone willing to look closely. As I pondered this, a wave of realization washed over me: I had to approach my relationship with Max the same way. Beneath the chaos, beneath the misunderstandings and distance, there was something precious worth protecting. I couldn't let fear or past mistakes tarnish the potential of what we could create together.

Just then, the couple approached, still chuckling over some inside joke. I could feel their warmth radiating toward me as they neared. The woman, with her wild silver curls framing a face full of laughter lines, caught my eye. "Mind if we join you?" she asked, her voice like a gentle melody.

I nodded, feeling a spark of connection. "Of course! The more, the merrier."

"I'm Eliza," she said, her eyes crinkling at the corners. "And this is Harold." He gave a gracious nod, his gaze warm and inviting.

As we began walking together, their stories unfolded like petals in bloom. They spoke of their travels, the little adventures that had colored their years together. Each tale was punctuated by laughter, a testament to the joy they found in life's simple pleasures. I listened, hanging onto every word, envious of the way their love seemed effortlessly intertwined with their existence.

"I swear, the best part of our journey was getting lost in Paris," Eliza declared, her voice animated. "We stumbled upon this tiny café, and while we couldn't understand a word the waiter said, we ended up with the most delectable pastries. Turns out, they had a 'mystery dessert' option—just a gamble, you know? It was glorious!"

Harold chuckled, shaking his head. "I still maintain that our pastry adventure was more memorable than our trip to the Eiffel Tower."

As they spoke, I felt an aching warmth settle in my chest. This was what I wanted with Max—shared moments of spontaneity, laughter over mundane experiences, an unspoken bond that transcended words. I realized then that I needed to stop worrying about what could go wrong and start focusing on what could go right.

"Are you two on vacation?" I asked, curious about their journey.

"We wish!" Eliza replied, her laughter ringing out. "We're here for a family reunion—our grandchildren, you know? But it's good to steal a moment or two away from the chaos." She winked, a playful glint in her eye. "What about you, dear? Is this a break from the grind?"

"Something like that," I admitted, my smile faltering slightly as thoughts of Charleston slipped back in. "Just trying to find a bit of clarity."

Eliza studied me for a moment, her eyes sharp yet kind. "Ah, clarity can be elusive, can't it? Like a shadow that dances just beyond your reach." She turned her gaze to the horizon, where the sun kissed the ocean goodnight. "But sometimes, you just need to let it come to you. Don't chase the light—become it."

Her words struck me deeply, an unexpected gift hidden in the gentleness of her wisdom. I felt a rush of hope—a flicker of what was possible if I dared to embrace the uncertainties. I could fight for my love with Max, not from a place of desperation, but from a wellspring of passion and purpose.

As the last sliver of sun disappeared below the horizon, the sky transformed into a blanket of stars. Each twinkle seemed to echo the possibilities that lay ahead. In that moment, surrounded by laughter and warmth, I realized I was no longer alone in my quest. I had a newfound resolve to reach for what I wanted, to weave my own narrative amidst the chaos. The beach was alive with promise, and so was I.

The air grew cooler as twilight deepened, wrapping around me like a soft shawl. The couple, Eliza and Harold, seemed oblivious to the shifting shadows as they shared more stories, their laughter punctuating the gentle roar of the waves. I had expected a brief encounter on the beach, a passing moment that would soon fade like the last light of day. Instead, I found myself entranced by their warmth and the magic of their connection, as if they were illuminating the very essence of love itself.

"Do you know what the secret to a long marriage is?" Eliza asked, her eyes sparkling with mischief. "It's simple: never stop dating. Just the other day, I told Harold we should recreate our first date. He looked at me like I'd suggested skydiving!"

Harold chuckled, shaking his head. "I'm still recovering from that unfortunate choice of a restaurant, thank you very much."

"Hey now, it was charming!" Eliza retorted playfully. "If by 'charming' you mean a place where the menu consisted entirely of canned soup."

"Your taste was questionable, dear," he replied, grinning. "But I will admit, the conversation was fantastic."

Their banter made my heart swell. I caught myself wondering if Max and I could ever reach that level of comfort, where jokes about past mistakes became a form of endearment rather than a source of tension. The notion felt both thrilling and terrifying. I could picture us, years down the line, laughing over our own culinary disasters or misadventures in the kitchen, but first, we had to navigate the storm brewing in our relationship.

"Do you two have a love story?" I asked, my curiosity getting the better of me.

"Oh, darling, our love story is an epic saga!" Eliza exclaimed, clutching her chest dramatically. "Picture this: a shy girl from a small town, meeting a dashing city boy at a dance hall. He stepped on my toes and I nearly kicked him in the shins!"

Harold pretended to wince, an exaggerated look of hurt on his face. "I swear, I was trying to impress you! How was I to know you'd be the fiercest dancer this side of the Mississippi?"

Eliza leaned into him, a knowing smile playing on her lips. "And yet, here we are, decades later, still stepping on each other's toes in the dance of life."

As they spoke, the ocean swirled around my feet, pulling me back to the present. I glanced at them, warmth blooming within me. Maybe love didn't have to be perfect; maybe it was all about navigating the missteps together. With that thought anchoring my resolve, I decided I would reach out to Max. He and I had danced around our feelings for too long, both fearful of stepping on each other's toes in the messy choreography of love.

Eliza caught my contemplative look. "What about you, dear? Is there someone you're trying to win over?" Her eyes twinkled with mischief, as if she could see right through my worries.

"I—I'm trying to figure that out," I admitted, my heart racing at the thought of Max. "We've had our fair share of ups and downs. Right now, it feels like we're doing a terrible tango."

Harold nodded sagely. "The best relationships have a few missteps. It's how you recover that counts."

His words wrapped around me like a warm hug, instilling a sense of comfort. I could feel the weight of the decisions ahead pressing down on me, but now, for the first time, it felt manageable. Maybe I could stumble, but that didn't mean I had to fall.

The trio continued walking along the shore, the sound of laughter mingling with the waves. A slight breeze rustled the palm trees lining the beach, whispering secrets of old, tales of lovers who had walked this very path long before us. Each gentle gust of wind felt like a nudge, urging me to take the leap I had been so afraid to consider.

As we neared a rocky outcrop, I caught sight of a lone figure silhouetted against the horizon, standing at the water's edge. The person looked lost in thought, their frame still and contemplative, a stark contrast to the lively exchange between Eliza and Harold. My heart skipped a beat as recognition hit. It was Max.

I hadn't expected to see him here, miles from the shop and the chaos of our lives. He stood with his back to me, hands stuffed in his pockets, shoulders hunched against the encroaching night. The sight of him stirred a whirlwind of emotions within me—relief, confusion, and an inexplicable urge to run to him.

"Is that someone you know?" Eliza asked, her voice a quiet murmur, noticing my sudden stillness.

"Yeah," I replied, my heart racing. "That's Max."

"Shall we join him?" Harold suggested, his voice warm and encouraging.

My stomach twisted into knots, part excitement and part fear. I hesitated, torn between the comfort of the moment with Eliza and Harold and the looming confrontation with my feelings. But as I watched Max standing there, alone and seemingly burdened, I knew I couldn't just walk away.

"Yeah, let's," I said, my voice steady despite the fluttering in my chest.

As we approached, I could see Max's profile clearer—his brow furrowed, the lines of worry etched deeply into his features. There was a heaviness in his stance that spoke volumes, a silent testament to the conflict we had both been avoiding. I cleared my throat, suddenly acutely aware of the weight of our shared past.

"Hey," I called out, trying to keep my voice light, even as the tide of anxiety rolled in. "What brings you to my beach?"

He turned, and the moment our eyes met, a spark ignited between us—an undeniable connection that pulled at the edges of my resolve. The air around us crackled, charged with unspoken words and unresolved tension.

"I needed some air," he replied, his voice low, almost a whisper. "Things have felt too heavy lately."

Eliza and Harold shared a knowing glance before stepping back, allowing us our space. I took a deep breath, gathering my courage, feeling the weight of their supportive presence behind me.

"I get that," I said, my heart pounding. "Can we talk?"

He nodded slowly, stepping toward me, the space between us shrinking with each tentative movement. As the waves crashed nearby, I could hear the whispers of the ocean, echoing the hopes and fears that swirled within me. This was our moment to step forward, to confront the tangled mess of emotions that had kept us apart. And for the first time in a long while, I felt ready to dive in.

The moment I stood before Max, the world around us faded, each crashing wave becoming a distant murmur. His dark hair tousled by the wind, he looked so vulnerable and lost, as if he were grappling with some invisible weight. I could sense his hesitation, the way he stood there, torn between reaching out and retreating. It felt as if we were suspended in time, the horizon stretching endlessly behind us, mirroring the vastness of our unspoken feelings.

"Can we talk?" I repeated, my voice firmer now. It was more of a plea than a question, a silent invitation to unravel everything we had left unsaid.

Max nodded, shoving his hands deeper into his pockets. "Yeah, I think we should."

As we walked side by side, I could feel the intensity of the moment crackling like static in the air. I stole glances at him, trying to read his expression, but the shadows cloaked his emotions. The silence stretched between us, heavy and ripe with possibilities. Each grain of sand felt like a reminder of the distance we'd allowed to grow.

"Are you okay?" I ventured, the words slipping out before I could edit my thoughts. I needed to know if he was alright, even as I wrestled with my own swirling feelings.

He sighed, a sound that seemed to carry the weight of a thousand burdens. "I've been better," he admitted, glancing at the water as it glimmered under the soft glow of the stars. "Everything's just... complicated."

Complicated. It was an apt word for our situation, a nice little catchall for the mess we'd created. "Complicated seems to be our default setting lately," I replied, trying to keep the mood light, even as a pang of sadness tugged at my heart.

Max chuckled softly, but there was a strain in it, like a guitar string about to snap. "Yeah, I didn't sign up for this level of emotional gymnastics." He looked at me, and for a moment, I could see the flicker of vulnerability in his eyes. "I thought I could handle it, but... I don't know."

"I thought I could handle it too," I confessed, biting my lip. "I thought I was strong enough to push through everything without feeling overwhelmed. But it's exhausting, isn't it? Trying to keep everything together when it feels like it's all falling apart."

The weight of our shared experiences hung in the air, thickening the atmosphere. I could see the uncertainty swirling in his gaze, like dark clouds threatening a storm. "We've been avoiding this, haven't we? Talking about what's really going on between us?"

I took a deep breath, my heart racing. "Yes. I think we need to face it. Whatever it is, we have to confront it."

Max nodded slowly, the resolve in his eyes mixing with fear. "I've been scared, you know? Scared of messing everything up even more. I can't afford to lose you."

His admission struck me, resonating deep within. The realization that we were both navigating this maze of emotions with the same fear made me feel a little less alone. "You won't lose me," I said, my voice softer now. "But we can't keep pretending everything is fine when it's not. We need to talk about our future."

He shifted, the tension radiating off him like heat from the sand. "What if our future is just... too complicated? What if we're not meant to figure this out?"

"Maybe it's complicated because we haven't tried hard enough." I stepped closer, searching his face for a glimmer of understanding. "We can't just give up. I refuse to believe that love should be this difficult."

A flicker of hope ignited in his eyes, but just as quickly, it dimmed. "It's hard to fight when everything feels like it's against us. The expectations, the pressures, the... the past."

"Yeah, the past," I echoed, the words heavy on my tongue. "But maybe it's time to let go of what has been holding us back. We can't let those shadows dictate our future."

Just then, a sharp cry pierced the night, a sound that didn't belong to the rhythm of the waves. We both turned, startled, as a figure emerged from the shadows on the beach. It was a man, disheveled and wild-eyed, his clothes torn and dirty. The way he stumbled toward us sent a chill down my spine.

"Help! Please!" he gasped, desperation etched across his face. "You have to help me! They're coming!"

I glanced at Max, confusion and concern mingling in his expression. "Who's coming?" he asked, his tone cautious.

The man took a few shaky steps closer, glancing over his shoulder as if expecting something to leap from the shadows. "They know I'm here! You have to hide me!" His voice was frantic, each word laced with panic.

I felt the chill of unease ripple through the air, the weight of our earlier conversation evaporating in an instant. "What do you mean?" I asked, instinctively stepping back. "Who's after you?"

"I don't know how much time I have!" he shouted, his eyes wide with fear. "They're after me for what I know! You have to believe me!"

Max and I exchanged a glance, the moment of connection we'd just shared fraying at the edges. The beach, once a sanctuary, now felt like a stage for a drama neither of us had signed up for.

"Wait," I said, holding up my hands. "You need to calm down and explain what's happening. We can help, but you need to tell us everything."

He took a deep breath, trying to steady himself, but the panic still clung to him like a shadow. "I can't stay here. They'll find me." His voice dropped to a whisper, conspiratorial. "You don't understand what I've stumbled into. I've seen things... things I shouldn't have."

Just as he finished speaking, a distant sound echoed through the night—heavy footsteps, growing louder, unmistakably drawing nearer. I could feel my heart racing, the previous tension replaced with an overwhelming urgency.

"Max, we need to get out of here," I said, instinctively moving closer to him.

The man's eyes darted around, and I saw panic morph into sheer terror. "You don't have time! You need to trust me! They'll be here any second!"

In that moment, the weight of the world shifted again. Our personal turmoil, our fragile connection, now seemed like a distant concern compared to the storm brewing on the horizon. I could see the fear mirrored in Max's eyes as we realized the gravity of the situation.

As the footsteps approached, the night air buzzed with an electric tension. What had we just stumbled into? The thought danced like a flame in the back of my mind, both thrilling and terrifying. I gripped Max's arm, and together, we took a step back, ready to face whatever emerged from the shadows.

The adrenaline surged, filling the space between us, a potent reminder that sometimes, the unknown could pull you deeper into a web of unexpected dangers. I turned to the man, desperate for answers as the ominous sounds closed in. "What do we do?"

But before he could respond, the darkness erupted around us, and I knew our lives would never be the same.

Chapter 16: The Taste of Reconciliation

The clatter of utensils echoed softly in the small café, mingling with the faint aroma of freshly brewed coffee and the lingering scent of baked pastries. I stepped inside, the doorbell tinkling like a cheerful herald announcing my arrival. It was a familiar sanctuary, one I had often sought solace in during turbulent times. The walls, painted in hues of soft teal, were adorned with whimsical artwork that seemed to tell stories of love, loss, and the inexplicable magic of small moments. But tonight, the atmosphere felt charged, electric, as if the universe itself held its breath, waiting for something monumental to unfold.

Max sat at the far end of the counter, surrounded by an array of mugs, each one a tiny vessel of hope and comfort. His brow furrowed in concentration as he meticulously crafted what I assumed was a new concoction. He looked up just as I approached, his expression shifting from focused to startled, and then settling into something more guarded. "Hey," he said, his voice a mixture of surprise and wariness. It was a tone I recognized all too well—the space between us brimming with unsaid words and unresolved tension.

"Can we talk?" The urgency in my voice cut through the gentle hum of the café, sending ripples of awareness through the air. I didn't want to prolong the inevitable; we were standing at the precipice of something, and I could feel it in the very marrow of my bones. Max hesitated for a moment, his eyes flicking to the clock as if measuring the weight of the moment against the demands of his work.

"Sure. I just—" he gestured to the array of coffee beans spread out like a colorful map of his creative process, "I'm almost done here."

I nodded, forcing a smile that felt more like a mask than a reflection of my true emotions. As he busied himself, I scanned the café, taking in the sight of flickering candles casting soft shadows on the walls. Each tiny flame danced to its own rhythm, and I wished I could be as carefree, as unburdened by the gravity of our situation.

Finally, he set down the last cup and leaned against the counter, arms crossed, his posture a barrier between us. "What's on your mind?"

My heart thudded, a chaotic drum echoing in my chest. "It's about us. About Oliver." The name hung in the air like a dark cloud, a weight pressing down on the fragile thread of connection we had been desperately trying to mend.

Max's jaw tightened, the flicker of understanding I had hoped to see dimming as a wall seemed to rise between us once again. "Can't we just—"

"Can't we just what?" I interrupted, frustration bubbling just beneath the surface. "Pretend everything is fine? Because it's not. I feel like I'm walking on eggshells, and I can't do this anymore."

The silence that followed was thick, the kind that makes your ears ring. I could see the gears turning in Max's mind, wrestling with his own demons as he searched for the right words. "Look, I know it's hard. But Oliver..."

"Is always there," I finished for him, the bitterness of truth stinging my tongue. "He's always in the room with us, like an unwelcome guest refusing to leave." I took a deep breath, grounding myself. "We can't keep avoiding it. We need to face this head-on."

Max's expression softened, his arms uncrossing as if he was finally allowing me in. "You're right. I just—I don't want to hurt you."

His honesty was a balm to my frayed nerves, and I felt a flicker of warmth blooming in my chest. "You're not going to hurt me by being honest. You might even help us."

For a moment, we stood in the quiet of the café, the world outside fading into a soft blur as we focused on each other. The intimacy of the moment felt tangible, wrapping around us like a comforting blanket. I stepped closer, my hand resting on the counter between us, a silent invitation.

"Tell me how you really feel about him. About us."

He sighed, the weight of his thoughts visible in the lines etched on his forehead. "I feel like I'm caught in the middle. Oliver has this way of... I don't know, casting a shadow over everything. But you and I have something real, something worth fighting for."

My pulse quickened at his words, a glimmer of hope igniting. "Then let's fight for it. Together."

With that, I reached out, my hand brushing against his. The contact sent a jolt of electricity through me, igniting a spark of connection that I had thought lost forever. "I don't want to lose you, Max," I admitted, the vulnerability in my voice raw and exposed.

He looked down at our hands, a mixture of surprise and longing flickering in his eyes. "You won't lose me. I promise."

The moment felt monumental, the kind of pivotal juncture where paths diverge and destinies are rewritten. I could sense the shift in our dynamic, the way the air crackled with unspoken possibilities. We were teetering on the edge of something beautiful and terrifying, and I knew we had to leap together.

"Can we start over?" I asked, my heart racing as I met his gaze. "No more hiding, no more dancing around the truth."

Max nodded, his expression earnest. "I'd like that. I really would."

As we stood there, hand in hand, I could feel the distance between us shrinking, the walls of uncertainty crumbling like ancient ruins in the face of new beginnings. It was a fragile moment, yet undeniably potent, filled with the promise of what could be if we dared to embrace the chaos together.

Outside, the first stars began to twinkle against the deepening twilight, tiny beacons of hope in the vastness of the night. In that dimly lit café, amidst the comforting chaos of the world, I felt a renewed sense of purpose swell within me. Perhaps reconciliation was not a destination but a journey—one I was ready to embark on with Max by my side.

The warmth of the café began to wrap around us like a favorite old sweater, the kind you wear when the world outside feels too daunting. Our conversation wove in and out like the gentle steam curling from Max's coffee machine, each shared vulnerability a drop of warmth pooling in the small space between us. I felt lighter, like a balloon released into the sky, buoyed by the honest exchange.

Max cleared his throat, breaking the comfortable silence that enveloped us. "So, what's next? We can't just sit here and pretend everything is fine after that conversation." His voice carried a hint of teasing, a reminder of the playful banter we had shared in better times.

I laughed softly, shaking my head. "I guess we have to figure that out together. But first, how about we start with something simple? Maybe you can show me that new drink you were working on?"

A smile spread across his face, the kind that made my heart flutter. "Oh, you mean the secret elixir of life? I thought you'd never ask." He winked, turning away to rummage through the shelves, and the familiar motion warmed my chest with nostalgia.

Watching him work was like witnessing a magician conjuring up spells. His hands moved deftly, measuring ingredients with the precision of an artist painting a masterpiece. The rhythmic clinking of glass against glass was a sweet melody that filled the air as he began to combine flavors. I leaned against the counter, my heart still racing, but now from excitement instead of anxiety.

"So, tell me," I began, my curiosity piqued, "what's the secret ingredient? Something exotic, perhaps? Like unicorn tears or dragon fruit?"

Max chuckled, glancing over his shoulder. "If I told you, I'd have to charge you double. But seriously, it's just a mix of espresso, a hint of cardamom, and a splash of vanilla. It's a little adventurous but familiar enough not to scare you off."

"Adventurous, yet familiar—sounds like us." I couldn't help the way my heart skipped at the thought, the implications of his words sending a thrill through me.

He poured the steaming liquid into a bright turquoise mug, its color reminding me of the vibrant walls that cradled our secrets. "Well, here's to us, then," he said, lifting the mug with a grin. "May we always be a little unpredictable, but not so much that we start a fire or anything."

I raised my own mug in response, the heat radiating through my fingers. "To unpredictability, and to not setting anything on fire—yet."

As I took a sip, the flavors burst on my tongue, each note harmonizing into something entirely unique. "Wow, Max, this is incredible!" I exclaimed, genuinely impressed. "How is it that you can make something so complex taste so... perfect?"

He leaned back against the counter, a hint of pride lighting his eyes. "It's all about balance, really. Just like life. Too much of one thing, and it all goes sideways."

His words resonated deeply, an echo of the conversation we'd just had. We needed balance, a way to integrate the shadows of our past with the bright potential of our future. I set my mug down, feeling a surge of determination. "Okay, so let's talk balance. How do we find it with Oliver in the picture?"

Max's expression shifted, the easygoing banter slipping away as he considered my question. "Honestly? I think we need to define our boundaries. You need to feel secure in this—whatever this is—and I can't be a part-time boyfriend or a consolation prize."

His candor struck a chord deep within me. "You're right. I don't want you to feel like you're competing with a ghost. And honestly, the last thing I want is for you to be stuck in the shadow of someone who doesn't deserve you."

A heavy silence fell between us, punctuated only by the soft whir of the coffee grinder in the background. I knew Oliver had cast a long shadow, and yet here we were, willing to confront it, to reclaim our story. I couldn't help but admire Max's strength, how he was willing to tackle the complexity of our situation head-on.

Suddenly, the door swung open, letting in a rush of chilly air and a tall figure who strolled in with an air of self-assuredness that was unmistakable. My stomach dropped as I recognized Oliver, his presence as disruptive as a loud siren in a quiet night. He glanced around, spotting us at the counter, and a bemused smile spread across his face.

"Fancy seeing you two together," he called out, his tone light but edged with something sharper. "I was just in the neighborhood."

Max's jaw tightened, and I could sense the tension radiating off him like heat from a flame. "You could have called," he replied, his voice steady, yet the undercurrent of challenge was unmistakable.

Oliver approached, a casual swagger to his movements, like he owned the place—or the moment, for that matter. "I didn't think it would be necessary. But hey, don't let me interrupt your little rendezvous. I'm sure you're sharing all kinds of secrets."

I felt the familiar tug of conflict rise within me, the duality of wanting to protect my relationship with Max while grappling with the history I shared with Oliver. "What do you want, Oliver?" I managed to ask, my voice steadier than I felt.

"Just wanted to check in, see how you're doing," he said, a disarming smile plastered on his face. But I wasn't fooled. There was something deeper beneath the surface, a tension I couldn't quite place.

Max stepped forward, his presence anchoring me. "She's doing just fine. Better than she has in a while."

Oliver's eyes narrowed slightly, a glimmer of annoyance flashing across his face. "Is that so? I guess we'll see about that."

The air between us thickened, charged with unspoken words and unresolved feelings. I could feel the battle lines being drawn, and I knew I had to step in before this escalated. "Look, Oliver, this isn't the time or the place."

He leaned against the counter, feigning casualness, but I could see the tightness in his jaw, the way his fingers drummed against the surface as if counting down the seconds until he would lose control. "Oh, I think it's exactly the right time. You're here with him, aren't you? What does that say about our so-called history?"

Max shifted slightly, the protective energy radiating off him palpable. "It says she's choosing not to be tied to the past. Maybe it's time you did the same."

I held my breath, the room swirling with the weight of our shared history and the fierce desire to carve out a new future. I could feel the shift in the atmosphere, the tension so thick you could cut it with a knife. Would this be the moment everything changed, or would we be swept back into the currents of the past, unable to break free?

The air in the café turned electric as Oliver leaned against the counter, a relaxed smile on his face that belied the tension crackling beneath the surface. "So, what's the plan here? You two seem awfully cozy." His casual tone felt like a dagger in the air, and I could sense Max's muscles tense beside me.

"Cozy?" I echoed, my voice a mixture of disbelief and irritation. "You're the one who waltzed in here, uninvited."

Oliver shrugged, his demeanor unfazed. "Just checking in on an old friend. Is that a crime now?"

"An old friend?" Max interjected, his tone sharp. "That's a generous way to describe someone who ghosted for weeks."

I felt a flush creeping up my neck, the history between us wrapped tightly in unspoken words. "Maybe we're all due for a little honesty tonight," I suggested, my heart racing. "But let's keep it civil." Oliver smirked, his eyes dancing with mischief. "Civil? You're asking for a lot, especially considering the history we share." He stepped closer, a confidence that felt dangerously familiar hanging in the air. "What's your plan, really? Just pretend I don't exist?"

Max stepped in front of me, a barrier of strength and resolve. "She's not pretending anything. And if you think she's going to keep letting you play games, you're mistaken."

I admired Max's fierce loyalty, the way he stood protectively, his presence like a shield against the chaos that Oliver brought with him. I took a deep breath, feeling the tension in the room reach a boiling point. "Oliver, I'm not asking you to disappear from my life, but you need to understand that things have changed. I'm not the same person I was when we... when we were together."

"Right, you're with Mr. Coffee over here now," Oliver replied, a hint of bitterness creeping into his voice. "What's next? Are you going to serve him my favorite pastries too?"

I opened my mouth to respond, the hurtful jab cutting deeper than I expected. "This isn't about replacing you, Oliver. It's about moving forward."

"Moving forward? With him?" His incredulous laughter echoed through the café, and I could see the hurt beneath the bravado. "You really think he can give you what you need? He doesn't even know what you want."

Max shot me a glance, a mixture of concern and determination etched on his face. "You know what she wants? She wants honesty, respect, and the freedom to choose who she spends her time with."

"Respect? Oh please, you both are making me laugh," Oliver scoffed, crossing his arms. "And what about my respect? I thought we had something real. It feels like you both are trying to erase me from the picture."

I could feel the weight of Oliver's words pressing down, each syllable stirring a mixture of guilt and anger within me. "No one is trying to erase you," I said, struggling to keep my voice steady. "But I'm not going to let you control the narrative anymore. I deserve to choose who I want to be with."

"Choose?" Oliver echoed, his voice lowering, his expression shifting from indignation to something more vulnerable. "What if I told you I'm not the only one who wants you back?"

A sudden stillness enveloped us, the bustling café fading into a muted backdrop as the implications of his words hung in the air. My heart raced, a mixture of hope and dread swirling within me. "What do you mean?" I asked, my voice barely above a whisper.

He stepped closer, the challenge in his eyes softening. "You know I've always cared about you. You think that just goes away? I can't help but feel like I'm losing something that meant everything."

Max opened his mouth to speak, but I held up a hand, caught in the undertow of Oliver's emotions. "What are you saying, Oliver? Are you really suggesting you want to try again?"

"I don't know," he admitted, running a hand through his hair, frustration evident in his gesture. "But seeing you with him, it's like... like I'm watching a part of my life slip away. It hurts."

The vulnerability in his admission cut through the noise of our earlier tension. I could see the cracks forming in his facade, the bravado melting away to reveal a man grappling with his own fears. "And you think that coming here, throwing accusations, is going to change anything?"

Oliver paused, looking between Max and me, as if weighing the options on a scale of desperation. "I just want a chance to talk about us. About what went wrong."

Max scoffed, arms crossed defiantly. "And what about her chance to talk about what's going right? You can't just waltz back in and expect her to ignore the work we've put in."

"Work?" Oliver challenged, his voice rising. "This isn't a job. It's a relationship."

"And relationships require effort," I interjected, my heart racing as I tried to steer the conversation back to clarity. "They require honesty and the ability to listen. It's not just about one person's feelings."

There was a moment of silence, the tension between the three of us palpable. I could feel my chest tightening as I tried to process everything, the gravity of the choices before me weighing heavily.

Max stepped forward again, his gaze unwavering. "If you're here to throw a wrench in things just because you're feeling nostalgic, then maybe it's best if you leave."

Oliver's eyes narrowed, a flicker of anger crossing his features. "Nostalgic? Don't mistake my feelings for some kind of whim."

The fight in the room was like a wildfire, spreading and consuming every ounce of calm. I felt like I was standing in the eye of a storm, uncertainty swirling around me as I struggled to find my footing.

"Maybe we need to take a step back," I suggested, my voice rising to a decisive tone. "We can't keep going around in circles like this. It's exhausting."

Oliver took a breath, his expression shifting. "What do you want, then? What do you really want?"

The question hung in the air, heavy with meaning, and my heart raced as I realized the truth that lay beneath it. It was a question I had danced around for too long, a truth that had been simmering just below the surface.

"I want to figure this out without the past haunting us," I said, my voice trembling slightly. "I want a future where I can choose freely."

Just as I finished speaking, the door swung open again, this time with an urgency that startled us all. A newcomer stepped in, his presence commanding as he surveyed the scene. It took me a moment to register who it was, but when I did, my heart dropped into my stomach.

"Sorry I'm late!" he exclaimed, breathless as he took in the charged atmosphere. "I had to—"

And just like that, the tension shattered into a million pieces, replaced by the shock of his arrival. The café, the conversations, and the futures we were attempting to piece together hung in the balance, suspended in uncertainty as the weight of unspoken words crashed around us.

Chapter 17: Brewing Storms

The storm swept in like an uninvited guest, crashing through Charleston with a ferocity that turned the streets into rivers and the quaint buildings into shaky sentinels against nature's wrath. Rain hammered against the roof of our chocolatier shop, each droplet a tiny drummer beating out a frantic symphony of chaos. The air was thick with the smell of wet earth and chocolate, the latter being a cruel irony considering we had recently restocked our supplies in preparation for the upcoming festival. Now, those meticulously crafted bonbons sat in their glass cases like forgotten dreams, overshadowed by the frantic dance of the storm outside.

Max stood beside me, his brow furrowed as he peered up at the ceiling, where ominous droplets began to form, glistening like little jewels before splattering onto the wooden floorboards. "We might need to grab some buckets," he suggested, his voice a low rumble amidst the sound of the tempest. I could see the hint of a smile creeping onto his lips, even as the storm raged around us. It was this kind of resilience that endeared him to the community and, if I was being honest with myself, to me as well.

"I'll get the buckets," I replied, feigning confidence, but I couldn't suppress the tremor in my voice. It wasn't just the storm causing it. Oliver's recent visits had been unsettling, filled with cryptic conversations and undercurrents of unspoken tension. I shook my head to dispel the thought, focusing instead on the immediate task. "And some towels too. We'll need to dry off the chocolate before it turns into fondue."

Together, we dashed through the shop, laughter escaping our lips in fits as we dodged the increasingly chaotic torrents. The sound of the rain against the windows was almost comforting, a reminder that we were alive and together, even in the face of disaster. We gathered supplies and quickly set to work, our small team of loyal employees and a handful of determined locals arriving one by one, rain-soaked but willing to fight against the storm's destruction. The camaraderie blossomed in unexpected ways, as if the storm had forged an unbreakable bond among us all.

"Is this a chocolate shop or a water park?" someone joked, tossing a towel my way, its edges soaked through. I caught it with a laugh, grateful for the distraction. The chaos outside became a backdrop to our frantic yet joyful effort, with everyone pitching in, their faces lit with determination and resolve. The warmth of shared laughter and purpose wrapped around us, providing a welcome shelter from the storm, both literal and metaphorical.

Max and I fell into a rhythm as we moved from one task to another, his strong hands steadying me as I climbed on a stool to reach a particularly stubborn leak. "Careful up there," he said, his voice laced with playful admonishment. "I wouldn't want to have to rescue you like some sort of chocolate damsel in distress."

"Please, I can save myself. Besides, you'd only make it worse by trying to swoop in," I shot back, my tone teasing yet underlined with an unintentional warmth that surprised me. The air between us crackled with an electricity that had nothing to do with the storm outside, yet I couldn't fully acknowledge it, not with the weight of Oliver's presence looming over my heart like dark clouds.

As we worked, I caught glimpses of familiar faces, each embodying the spirit of our small town. Mrs. Hargrove, with her neon pink raincoat and a smile that could light up the gloomiest of days, handed out chocolate-covered pretzels like they were lifelines. "You're going to need these for energy!" she chirped, and I couldn't help but chuckle. Her laughter mingled with the rain, a melody that momentarily softened the impending dread gnawing at my insides.

Yet, even amidst the storm's fury and our determined efforts, the thoughts of Oliver persisted. Each time I glanced at the door, half expecting him to waltz in with that infuriatingly charming smile, my stomach twisted in knots. I had thought we were done with the uncertainty he brought, but something about this storm felt like a prelude, a warning. What was he planning? And why did it feel like it involved more than just his typical mischief?

Once the storm began to wane, the power flickered in and out, casting eerie shadows around the shop. The dim glow of our emergency lights flickered overhead, barely illuminating our efforts. We were drenched but triumphant, the puddles slowly receding as we tidied up the chaos the storm had left behind. I glanced at Max, his hair slicked back and eyes alight with that same determination that had drawn me to him in the first place. The world felt heavy and electric, yet somehow, standing beside him made the burden easier to bear.

The last echoes of thunder rumbled in the distance, a reminder that the worst had passed, but the storm had left its mark. "We did it," I breathed, looking around at the nearly restored shop, still reeking of wet wood and chocolate. My heart swelled with gratitude for our community, our family forged in sugar and shared laughter.

"Yeah, we did," Max agreed, his smile radiant despite the exhaustion etched on his face. "We should do this more often—just not in the middle of a hurricane next time."

Our laughter broke through the remnants of tension, but as I looked out the window, watching the rain finally cease, I felt that old anxiety stir again. Something was coming, and I was painfully aware that storms didn't always have to be meteorological to wreak havoc.

The morning after the storm, Charleston emerged from its cocoon of rain with a shimmery sheen that transformed the ordinary into something almost ethereal. Sunlight poured through the windows of the chocolatier like liquid gold, illuminating the dust particles dancing in the air. I stood behind the counter, inhaling deeply, allowing the rich aroma of chocolate to wash over me, blending seamlessly with the crisp scent of fresh air. It felt like a rebirth of sorts, an opportunity to start anew, but even in the brightness, shadows lurked, reminding me of the storm's aftermath.

Max arrived early, a giant steaming mug of coffee in hand, looking uncharacteristically rumpled yet charming in his own right. "You know," he said, his voice slightly muffled by the cup, "I think I may have a new business idea. It's called 'Chocolates in a Rainstorm.' Guaranteed chaos and a side of soggy bonbons."

I chuckled, shaking my head as I took the mug from him, cradling it in my palms. "If we put that on the menu, I fear we might become the only chocolatier in town known for soggy chocolate. Not quite the reputation we're aiming for."

He leaned against the counter, his eyes glinting with mischief. "Well, every shop needs its signature dish. Besides, 'soggy' might be the next big thing in culinary trends. Just wait until the hipsters catch wind of it."

There was an ease between us, a rhythm we had developed through shared laughter and the comfort of knowing we were in this together. As I sipped the warm coffee, the rich flavor enveloped my senses, banishing the remnants of anxiety clinging to me like wet clothes. But then, just as the sun warmed my skin, the door swung open with a creak, sending a chill down my spine. Oliver stepped inside, his presence as unwelcome as a thunderclap in an otherwise serene day.

"Good morning, chocolate enthusiasts!" he called out, his tone deceptively cheerful as he sauntered in, shaking droplets from his hair like a dog fresh from the bath. "How's the recovery effort? I hear it was quite the soirée last night."

"An 'intimate gathering' is more like it," I replied, my tone steely as I wiped my hands on a towel, trying to mask the tension that spiked in the air. "We did what we could to save the shop, but I'm sure you're well aware of how storms can shake things up."

His eyes sparkled with a mix of charm and mischief as he leaned against the doorframe, casually inspecting the mess we had yet to tackle. "You know, I could help out. I have a knack for clean-up. Plus, I've got connections to some contractors who could fix that roof up in no time."

The offer hung in the air like a delicate thread, and I felt Max tense beside me. "Thanks, but we've got it covered," Max interjected, his voice firm. "We'll handle it ourselves."

"Of course," Oliver replied, unperturbed, waving a dismissive hand as if to brush off the tension. "But you two are going to need more than just elbow grease. Sometimes you've got to call in the pros, you know? Especially when it involves structural integrity."

I shot Max a glance, searching for reassurance in the depths of his gaze. It was a small reminder that we were allies against Oliver's unwarranted charm. "We appreciate the concern, Oliver," I said, forcing a smile that felt brittle on my lips. "But we really are fine. Just a bit of paint, some buckets, and we'll be back to normal."

"Normal, huh?" He laughed, a sound that made my stomach twist with annoyance. "That's a good one. I'll bet you're not considering how deep the damage could go." His eyes danced over the shop, scanning for weakness. "You should be careful. A tiny leak could lead to a flood in more ways than one."

"Are you always this dramatic?" I shot back, unable to suppress the sharpness in my tone. "It's just a bit of rainwater, Oliver. We'll fix it."

"Dramatic?" he repeated, feigning offense. "I prefer to think of it as... realistic. But then again, you always were the optimist."

Max's presence beside me felt like a warm anchor, a shield against Oliver's unsettling energy. "We'll figure it out," he said, a confident edge to his voice. "And if you're done checking in, we really need to get back to work."

Oliver held up his hands in mock surrender, a grin still plastered across his face. "Alright, alright. I'll let you get back to your soggy bonbons. Just remember, I'm always a phone call away." He turned on his heel, his presence leaving an unsettling echo in the air, like an unwelcome breeze.

As the door swung closed behind him, I exhaled sharply, the tension evaporating into the sunlight streaming through the windows. "Ugh, that guy," I muttered, frustration bubbling beneath my skin. "Why does he always have to make everything feel like a catastrophe?"

Max let out a soft laugh, shaking his head. "Honestly, he thrives on chaos. It's like his second language. But hey, we've got this. We're a team, and we've survived worse than a little bad weather."

"True," I admitted, my heart swelling at the thought of all we had accomplished together. "And speaking of teams, we still have quite a bit to do before the festival."

We dove into the tasks at hand, organizing shelves, dusting counters, and salvaging what we could from the remnants of the storm. The atmosphere shifted back to lightheartedness as we worked side by side, our banter dancing through the air like the sweet scent of melting chocolate.

"Hey," I said suddenly, a thought striking me as I lifted a box of chocolates to the counter. "What if we hosted a mini 'thank you' event for the community once everything's back to normal? Just to celebrate the fact that we survived the storm, and maybe we could raise some funds for repairs?"

Max's eyes lit up with excitement. "I love it! We could showcase new flavors, get the locals involved. It could be the perfect way to boost morale and show them we're not just about sweet treats; we're about community."

The idea blossomed between us, filled with possibilities and optimism. For the first time since Oliver's arrival, the anxiety that had settled in my stomach began to dissipate, replaced by the warm glow of hope and determination. Perhaps we could weather the storm after all—both the literal one that had passed and the metaphorical one that lingered in the form of Oliver's shadow over our lives. With Max by my side, I felt invincible, ready to take on whatever else might come our way.

The sun climbed higher in the sky, banishing the remnants of the storm with a radiance that felt almost too good to be true. I stood in the chocolatier, my hands sticky with melted chocolate as I prepared samples for our upcoming community event. Max was busy arranging the tables outside, a task that seemed deceptively simple but involved far more coordination than I anticipated. He was a whirlwind of energy, his laughter ringing out like a bell every time he struggled with a wobbly leg or misaligned tablecloth.

"Hey, Miss Chocolatier Extraordinaire!" he called, glancing back at me with a grin that made my heart flutter. "If this event flops, I'm blaming you for overestimating the charm of soggy bonbons."

"Just wait until you taste my new creation," I shot back, carefully dipping a spoon into a bowl of luscious chocolate ganache, the glossy surface glimmering like a polished gem. "I think I've finally perfected the raspberry-infused truffle. It's basically a hug in chocolate form."

"Now that sounds promising. I'll just make sure to keep a bucket nearby for the inevitable sugar crash," he teased, his eyes twinkling with playful mischief. "Wouldn't want you to take me down with you."

The warmth of our banter filled the shop, pushing aside the shadows of doubt that lingered from Oliver's earlier visit. As I rolled the ganache into delicate balls and dusted them with cocoa powder, the rhythmic motion soothed my nerves. I imagined the faces of our loyal customers, their smiles as sweet as the treats we offered. This was what we were building toward: a community gathering where joy could outweigh the chaos.

Just as I was about to pour melted chocolate over a fresh batch of pretzels, the bell above the door jingled. I looked up to see Mrs. Hargrove waddling in, her signature pink raincoat replaced by a vibrant floral dress that could only be described as "sunshine in fabric form."

"Good morning, darlings!" she exclaimed, her voice ringing with infectious enthusiasm. "I brought you a little something for the event." She fished around in her oversized handbag and produced a tin of her famous lemon bars, the tangy aroma wafting through the air.

"Mrs. Hargrove, you are a lifesaver!" I beamed, accepting the tin with gratitude. "These will be the perfect addition to our spread."

"Just remember," she warned, wagging a finger at me, "a touch of zest is essential for a successful gathering. You don't want the event to be as bland as a dry cracker!"

Max, who had just emerged from the chaos of rearranging tables, grinned at Mrs. Hargrove. "Don't worry. With our chocolate treats and your lemon bars, we'll be serving up a feast fit for royalty."

"Ah, you two are so sweet, I'm surprised I don't have cavities just from standing here," she chuckled, shaking her head.

As we chatted, the atmosphere in the shop lightened further, the storm clouds of the past few days replaced by the buoyant anticipation of the event ahead. Laughter echoed off the walls as we set up, the camaraderie weaving a tapestry of shared purpose that enveloped us. Yet, despite the festive spirit, an unsettling feeling simmered beneath the surface. Every time I spotted Oliver's name on my phone, my heart raced, a mix of apprehension and curiosity coiling within me.

"Do you think Oliver will come?" I asked, half-joking as I watched Max arrange a display of chocolate-covered strawberries.

"Honestly? Who knows?" he replied, pausing to give me a skeptical look. "He thrives on drama, and a community event sounds like the perfect stage for his theatrics."

"Or he could surprise us and be genuinely supportive," I countered, even as the doubt gnawed at me. "Maybe he's turned over a new leaf."

Max raised an eyebrow, a smirk playing on his lips. "Yeah, sure. Maybe he'll wear a 'Team Chocolatier' shirt and bring confetti. Or—"

A loud crash interrupted us, the sound reverberating through the shop like a warning bell. We exchanged startled glances, our hearts racing as we dashed toward the source of the noise. The front door swung open wildly, and in stepped Oliver, looking disheveled and a bit out of breath. His eyes were wild, and for a moment, I wondered if he had just survived another storm.

"Oliver!" I exclaimed, my heart skipping a beat as I noticed the blood trickling down his arm, bright against his pale skin. "What happened?"

"Nothing I couldn't handle!" he replied, waving off my concern with a grin that was far too bright for someone bleeding. "But you won't believe what I just saw."

"Maybe you should focus on stopping the bleeding first," Max shot back, worry etched on his features.

"Oh, this? Just a scratch! Now, listen! I was out getting supplies when I stumbled upon something... unusual."

The tension in the room shifted, a palpable curiosity weaving its way through the air. I glanced at Max, who was still eyeing Oliver with a mix of skepticism and concern. "What do you mean 'unusual'?" I pressed, trying to maintain a lightness in my tone that didn't quite land.

"I'm serious!" Oliver insisted, stepping further inside as he pushed back the damp hair clinging to his forehead. "You know that old house on the corner, the one everyone whispers about? There's something going on in there—something big. And I think it could affect all of us."

"Great. Another one of your wild theories," Max said, crossing his arms, but I could see the flicker of interest in his eyes.

"I'm telling you, it's not just a theory! There's something about the renovations—they're not just cosmetic. I overheard some workers talking about it." He leaned closer, his voice dropping to a conspiratorial whisper. "Something about a hidden basement. And trust me, whatever is down there is tied to the history of this town."

A chill crept up my spine, and I felt the room shift as if the very walls were holding their breath. "What do you mean 'tied to the history'?" I asked, my pulse quickening.

"Ghosts, buried secrets, perhaps even treasure," he declared dramatically, though the underlying tension in his voice made me think he wasn't entirely joking. "I thought I'd share before your lovely event, considering you two are so invested in the community. This could change everything!"

My heart raced, both with excitement and apprehension. The thought of hidden secrets lurking beneath our beloved town was enough to spark my curiosity. But Oliver's penchant for embellishment loomed large in my mind. "You're serious?"

"Dead serious," he insisted, his gaze intense. "I suggest you both take a look, especially if you want to know what kind of storm is brewing just beneath the surface."

As he spoke, I glanced at Max, who appeared torn between disbelief and intrigue. A whisper of danger danced in the air, and the urge to uncover the truth felt almost palpable. I took a deep breath, my heart pounding with anticipation. "Let's go. I need to see this for myself."

The determination in my voice seemed to ignite something within Oliver, his eyes gleaming with that familiar spark of mischief. "Now you're talking! Let's dive into the mystery of Charleston."

But as we turned to leave the shop, ready to chase after whatever revelation awaited us, a shadow loomed at the edge of my consciousness—an awareness that whatever we were about to uncover could unravel the very fabric of our community and the fragile peace we had fought so hard to build.

Chapter 18: Sweet Endings and Sour Beginnings

The scent of melted chocolate danced through the air, a sweet balm for the wounds the storm had left behind. Each whiff drew me deeper into the warmth of the shop, wrapping around me like a well-worn blanket, its familiarity almost dizzying. The sun had set, casting a golden hue over the assembled community, where laughter mingled with the clinking of glasses, a celebration of resilience and camaraderie. I was surrounded by artisans, each stall adorned with colorful displays of handmade jewelry, intricate pottery, and vibrant paintings that spilled over with color. The walls of the chocolatier were lined with these creations, their vivid hues contrasting sharply with the rich browns and creams of the chocolate creations that glistened under the soft lights.

As I wandered through the crowd, my heart swelled with pride. My shop had become a haven, a gathering place for creativity to flourish amidst the remnants of chaos. Children darted between tables, their giggles like tinkling bells, while adults reveled in the joy of togetherness, exchanging stories and dreams like precious gifts. I couldn't help but smile, basking in the glow of our collective triumph. The chaotic energy of the storm had forged connections, and tonight, we celebrated those bonds.

"Lila! You've outdone yourself," exclaimed Maeve, a local painter whose canvases practically sang with life. Her hair was an explosion of curls, a whirl of color that mirrored her art. She embraced me tightly, her paint-splattered apron leaving a mark on my crisp white shirt.

"Only because you all came together," I replied, pulling back to admire her latest piece—a large canvas depicting the town's skyline, the colors of sunset bleeding into one another. "This is stunning! You've captured the spirit of our little town beautifully."

"It's nothing without your chocolate," she quipped, her blue eyes sparkling. "You know, I considered using chocolate as paint."

"Please don't! I'm not sure my shop can handle the calories of your artistic ambitions," I laughed, my eyes twinkling back at her. But beneath the laughter, a twinge of anxiety lurked. I had put everything into this event, and as much as I enjoyed the festivities, I couldn't shake the feeling that something—someone—was waiting to disrupt this fragile peace.

The night unfolded in a symphony of flavors and sounds, the chocolaty decadence drawing the crowd in like moths to a flame. I took a moment to step back and soak it all in, the sheer vibrancy around me. However, just as I began to truly relax, my heart sank as I caught sight of Oliver, his tailored suit stark against the whimsical chaos of the evening.

He approached with the practiced ease of someone who thrived on charm, his smile both inviting and disarming. I could almost hear the proverbial record scratch as the atmosphere shifted. My stomach twisted as I watched him weave through the crowd, his presence slicing through the joyous murmurings like a knife. It was infuriating how someone could carry such polished perfection yet radiate an unsettling undercurrent of danger.

"Lila," he greeted, his voice smooth as velvet. "You've turned this place into quite the spectacle."

"Oliver," I replied, attempting to keep my voice steady. "What a surprise to see you here." My mind raced, recalling our last conversation, which had felt like a game of chess where I'd been cornered, the stakes far too high for comfort.

"Surprised?" He arched an eyebrow, a smirk playing on his lips. "After the storm, I'd say your shop is the pulse of this community now. I couldn't miss it." His gaze swept the room, lingering just a moment too long on the vibrant artwork before settling back on me, scrutinizing.

"Glad you could join us," I said, forcing a smile, though my insides were churning. "I didn't expect to see you so soon after everything that happened."

"Ah, you know me," he replied with a feigned nonchalance. "Always one to keep my finger on the pulse of the market." He leaned closer, lowering his voice to a conspiratorial whisper. "But it's not just business that interests me tonight. You've been making quite the impression, Lila. I think it's time we had a real conversation."

The way he spoke sent chills down my spine, like I was being drawn into a web I couldn't see. I glanced around, searching for a distraction, anything to break the moment's tension. The air felt charged, as if the laughter and chatter faded into the background, leaving only the two of us suspended in this dizzying exchange.

"I'm busy, Oliver," I replied, trying to shake off the unease that clung to me like a shadow. "Tonight is about celebrating the community. I really should—"

"Celebrate?" he interrupted, his tone sharp as a blade. "Is that what you think this is? Just a celebration?" He leaned back, crossing his arms, the façade of charm dropping slightly to reveal something more calculating beneath. "I think you know this is about more than just chocolate."

I swallowed hard, feeling the weight of his gaze. His words hung in the air, thick with implication. Suddenly, the laughter around us felt distant, like an echo of a world I desperately wanted to remain in. But the reality Oliver presented was inescapable. He wasn't here for small talk or community spirit; he had come to stake his claim, to unravel the progress we had made.

"Oliver, if you're here to discuss business—"

"Ah, business," he interrupted again, shaking his head in mock pity. "Always with the business. Lila, you're missing the bigger picture. This isn't just about the chocolatier; it's about your future—and mine. You wouldn't want to jeopardize that, would you?"

The weight of his words pressed down on me, suffocating. I forced myself to breathe, to steady the trembling in my hands. The night was supposed to be a turning point, a symbol of new beginnings, but his presence threatened to turn it into something far less sweet.

"I'll think about it," I replied, the words slipping out, unsure if they were even true. I turned away, desperate to escape, to lose myself in the vibrant laughter of my friends, but Oliver's voice followed me like a dark cloud.

"Just remember, Lila, every sweet ending has its sour beginnings."

And with that, the festival of color and joy dimmed slightly, the shadows of his words clinging to me, as I pushed through the crowd, feeling more alone than ever, even amidst the warmth of our newfound community.

The crowd buzzed with the electric energy of creativity, and as I moved deeper into the heart of the event, I tried to shake off the ominous chill that Oliver had left in his wake. My gaze wandered over the throngs of joyful patrons, their laughter filling the air like the sweet notes of a symphony, yet the taste of uncertainty lingered on my tongue. I found solace in the little details—the glittering glass beads on Maeve's jewelry, the earthy aroma of herbal soaps crafted by Charlotte, and the hand-painted mugs that somehow made coffee seem like a luxury experience. Each artisan was a testament to the community's resilience, yet Oliver's words rattled in my mind, casting a shadow over the vibrant tapestry of the night.

Just then, the clinking of glasses caught my attention. I turned to see Ben, the local musician, strumming his guitar near the makeshift stage, his fingers dancing over the strings with a confidence that made my heart flutter. He had a knack for weaving melodies that felt like sunlight on a warm afternoon, brightening even the darkest of moods. His voice, smooth and soothing, floated through the air as he began to sing an upbeat tune that perfectly encapsulated the spirit of the night.

"Come on, everyone! Join me!" he called, his infectious smile beckoning the crowd. Without a second thought, I was swept up in the wave of revelers, laughter spilling from my lips as I joined in the fun, momentarily forgetting the unease that lingered. The collective joy felt like a buoy in a turbulent sea, pulling me back from the edge of my worries.

"Is this a concert or a dance-off?" Maeve teased as she twirled, her paint-stained apron flaring out like a cape. I laughed, letting the music drown out the remnants of Oliver's threat.

"Let's make it both! What do you say?" I shouted back, my spirits lifting with every strum of Ben's guitar. The world outside the shop felt far away, the problems of life dissolving into the air like the delicate chocolate truffles I'd prepared for the event. The more I danced, the more I realized that even the most tumultuous storms could give way to nights like these, filled with laughter and connection.

The rhythm of the music entwined with the clamor of voices, creating a cacophony that wrapped around us like a comforting embrace. I closed my eyes for a moment, letting the melody wash over me, each note stirring memories of laughter and warmth. But just as I was beginning to feel safe, a familiar figure caught my eye, his polished demeanor slicing through the joyous atmosphere.

Oliver had taken a seat at the back of the room, his gaze fixed on me, a predator observing its prey. The fleeting moments of happiness began to fade, the laughter around me dulled as I caught sight of the man whose presence felt like a storm cloud looming over my brightest day. A knot formed in my stomach, a reminder that I couldn't escape the reality he represented.

"Hey, you okay?" Maeve asked, her voice laced with concern as she caught my eye, noticing the change in my expression.

"Yeah, just... thinking about the chocolate fountain," I replied, forcing a smile. "We really should set one up next time. Imagine the chaos!"

Her laughter bubbled up, cutting through my worries like a warm knife through chocolate. "Chaos is my specialty! But I have to say, I'm more of a caramel girl myself."

"Caramel, huh? I can work with that. We'll have a caramel fountain next time, and I'll watch you swim in it," I joked, the warmth of her presence igniting a flicker of hope in my chest.

As the evening continued, I found myself leaning into the joy around me, the tension between Oliver and me ebbing momentarily. I moved from stall to stall, engaging with each artisan, their passion infectious. A painter demonstrated her techniques, and I marveled at how colors transformed canvas, much like our community had transformed in the wake of disaster. I felt proud, buoyed by a sense of belonging I hadn't fully realized I craved.

Then, just as I was beginning to forget my worries, I turned to find Oliver standing directly in front of me. "You really should take a break from the festivities," he said, his tone smooth yet laden with something more sinister. "There's something important we need to discuss."

I crossed my arms, my body tensing. "I'm busy, Oliver. I have a shop to run and a community to celebrate. Whatever you think we need to discuss can wait."

His smile remained, though it didn't reach his eyes. "Can it really? I think you know better than that. You're building something beautiful here, and I'd hate for you to jeopardize it."

"Jeopardize? You're the one who wants to turn my passion into a transaction. That's not what this is about." I felt my heart race, the adrenaline pulsing through me like hot chocolate poured too quickly.

"Isn't it? The chocolatier is a business, Lila. A beautiful one, yes, but a business nonetheless. And I know you're smart enough to understand the implications of losing your foothold in this community."

I took a deep breath, trying to keep my composure. "The only implication I see is that you're trying to bully me into something I don't want. This is about more than just money."

"Is it?" he challenged, tilting his head slightly, his expression a mask of calculated charm. "Because it seems to me you've built your dream on shifting sands. I can offer you stability, a chance to thrive in a way you've only imagined."

My pulse quickened as the reality of his offer sunk in, a swirling mix of temptation and fear. "And what's the catch, Oliver? What do you want in return?"

He stepped closer, lowering his voice. "Just a partnership, Lila. Your talents combined with my resources—think of what we could achieve. This town could be a culinary hotspot."

I scoffed, my irritation bubbling to the surface. "You mean your culinary hotspot, with me as the figurehead while you pull the strings behind the scenes?"

"Smart girl," he replied, a hint of admiration flickering in his gaze. "But you have to ask yourself, what's more important—pride or progress?"

I opened my mouth to respond, but the sound of laughter broke through, a wave of people swirling around us, blissfully unaware of the tension that crackled like static electricity in the air. I took a step back, breaking his gaze. "This isn't the time or place for this conversation. I'm not interested in your proposition."

With that, I turned, weaving back into the crowd, the laughter and music wrapping around me like a protective shield. Each step away from Oliver felt like shedding a layer of doubt, even as his voice echoed in the back of my mind. I could almost hear the gears turning, the machinations behind his charming smile. He might have his sights set on me, but I wasn't ready to be another pawn in his game.

The night pulsed around me with warmth and laughter, and I clung to it like a lifeline. I moved to Ben, who had switched to a slower tune, the sweet sound wrapping around me like a soft blanket. I felt lighter, even as the darkness of Oliver's offer loomed, threatening to cast a shadow over everything I had built. But for now, I allowed myself to be swept away, trusting that the light would return.

The pulsating energy of the night enveloped me as I made my way back to the makeshift stage where Ben was still strumming away, his fingers deftly plucking notes that seemed to weave through the very fabric of the gathering. I let the rhythm wash over me, trying to drown out the remnants of my conversation with Oliver. The lighthearted banter of friends wrapped around me like a warm shawl, soothing the frayed edges of my anxiety.

"Care for a dance?" Ben asked, his gaze warm and inviting as he caught my eye. There was something in his expression that seemed to promise a reprieve from the darkness Oliver had brought into my world. I didn't hesitate; the music was too enticing, too alive, to resist.

"Only if you promise not to step on my toes," I shot back with a playful grin, letting the music guide my movements as I twirled into the moment. The world around us faded, the shadows from earlier slipping further away as we lost ourselves in the notes and rhythms, our laughter mingling with the melodies.

"Who, me? I would never!" Ben laughed, though there was a glint of mischief in his eyes that suggested otherwise. He pulled me closer, his hands steadying me as we danced. I found comfort in his presence, a grounding force against the backdrop of swirling colors and lively chatter.

"Right, because that would definitely ruin your reputation as the town's most talented musician," I teased, my heart lifting with each beat of the song.

As we swayed, I noticed how he made every movement seem effortless, his confidence infectious. "I've always said it's the dancer's fault if they get stepped on," he quipped, a cheeky grin on his face. "Besides, I've been practicing my 'avoidance technique' just for you."

"Oh really? That sounds very scientific." I laughed, feeling lighter than I had all evening. Yet, beneath the surface of the joy, a flicker of doubt flickered. Oliver's words echoed in my mind—would I really risk it all for the sake of pride?

The song faded into a gentle conclusion, leaving us breathless. I stepped back, and the spell of the moment shattered as reality seeped back in. I could see Oliver lurking at the periphery of the crowd, his gaze unwavering. I glanced away, unwilling to let him cast a shadow on my hard-won happiness.

"Everything okay?" Ben asked, his brow furrowed with concern as he followed my gaze. "You seem a bit... distracted."

"Just a little pesky reminder that life isn't always as sweet as chocolate," I replied, forcing a smile, though the corners of my mouth felt heavy.

"Want to talk about it?" His sincerity cut through the noise, and for a moment, I considered confiding in him. But before I could speak, Maeve danced over, her hair bouncing with every step.

"Lila! You have to see this!" she exclaimed, practically dragging me toward a corner where a crowd had gathered. Intrigued, I followed, the tension of my earlier conversation forgotten, if only temporarily.

We squeezed through the throng, finally arriving at a table displaying an elaborate cake, its layers swathed in chocolate ganache and adorned with edible flowers. "It's a masterpiece!" I gasped, taking in the artistry.

"It gets better," Maeve said, her eyes wide with excitement. "The baker is about to unveil something even more amazing."

The baker, a cheerful woman named Clara, stood proudly next to her creation, beaming at the gathered crowd. "I present to you my pièce de résistance: a chocolate fountain that flows with molten caramel!"

A collective gasp erupted from the crowd as she unveiled the fountain, its warm caramel cascading down in a mesmerizing flow. The golden liquid shimmered under the lights, and the aroma wafted through the air like a sweet promise.

"Who wants to dip something?" Clara called, handing out skewers to the eager crowd. Laughter bubbled up, and I could feel my spirits lift once more as people scrambled to get their fair share of the confectionery wonder.

"Okay, that's it. I'm diving in," I declared, grabbing a skewer and diving toward the fountain. "If I'm going to face Oliver later, I need all the sugar I can get."

"You have to dip an entire strawberry!" Maeve challenged, her eyes gleaming with mischief.

"Challenge accepted!" I replied, my competitive spirit igniting. I plunged the skewer into the warm caramel, pulling it out triumphantly, the strawberry glistening with a thick coating of sweet liquid. I took a bite, the flavors exploding in my mouth, the sweetness enveloping me like a cozy hug.

"Now that's a strategy I can get behind," Ben said, joining me with his own skewer of pineapple. "If Oliver tries to corner you again, just throw chocolate at him. Works every time."

"Right? Nothing says 'stay away' like a face full of melted chocolate," I laughed, but as I turned to respond, I spotted Oliver making his way through the crowd, his sharp gaze locked onto me.

My heart raced as the atmosphere shifted again, the warmth of the caramel fountain suddenly feeling cold. I wasn't prepared for another confrontation, not with the sweet taste of victory still lingering on my tongue.

"Hey, I think I need a refill on caramel," I said, stepping back from the group, feigning a casualness I didn't feel. "I'll be right back."

"Lila!" Ben called after me, but I waved him off, my mind swirling with uncertainty. I needed space, needed to gather my thoughts before facing the reality that Oliver represented. I pushed my way to the fountain, trying to keep my breathing steady, but it felt like a weight bore down on me, pressing me into the ground.

I filled my skewer again, watching the golden caramel drip, trying to gather my thoughts. The cacophony of voices faded into a dull roar as I focused on the warmth of the fountain, the heat radiating through my fingertips. It was a small comfort against the storm brewing behind me.

"Lila," came Oliver's voice, smooth and low, drawing me back into reality. I turned to face him, clutching my skewer like a shield. "We need to talk. This can't wait."

"Do you always corner people when they're enjoying themselves?" I shot back, my nerves frayed. "I'm really not in the mood for your business proposals."

"It's not just business," he insisted, stepping closer, the confidence radiating from him like an imposing force. "It's about your future. My offer still stands, and I think it's time you seriously consider it."

I opened my mouth to respond, but before I could articulate the sharp retort forming in my mind, a commotion erupted nearby. Heads turned, laughter faded, and the jubilant atmosphere shifted dramatically.

"Did you see that?" someone shouted, pointing towards the entrance. "There's a problem outside!"

My heart raced again, adrenaline kicking in as I turned to see a figure standing in the doorway. The lights behind them illuminated a silhouette that felt familiar, yet unsettling.

The crowd began to murmur, and I could feel a chill in the air, the night's warmth evaporating as tension gripped us. As the figure stepped into the light, my breath caught in my throat.

It was Jake, my old friend, his face drawn and serious, and he didn't look like he had good news.

"I need to talk to you, Lila. It's urgent."

The laughter and music faded entirely, replaced by an overwhelming sense of dread that settled over me like a heavy shroud. Whatever he was about to say would change everything.

Chapter 19: Crossroads of the Heart

The event buzzed with energy, a swirling blend of laughter and clinking glasses, punctuated by the rich aroma of dark chocolate wafting through the air. The venue, a chic loft with exposed brick walls and string lights twinkling overhead, exuded an air of casual sophistication. It was the perfect backdrop for the launch of our new artisanal chocolates, the culmination of months of hard work and late-night brainstorming sessions. But amidst the jubilant atmosphere, an undercurrent of tension thrummed, tethered tightly to the presence of Oliver.

He appeared like a finely-tuned instrument, ready to play my heartstrings with the skill of a master conductor. As he approached, I could feel my breath hitch in my throat, caught somewhere between anxiety and anticipation. He was everything I had ever admired and loathed—a magnetic force wrapped in tailored suits and charming smiles. It was infuriating how easily he navigated the space, a silver-tongued diplomat weaving his way through the crowd, each word draping itself over listeners like velvet. I gripped my own glass tightly, the stem cool against my palm, a small comfort in the whirlwind of emotions that swirled within me.

"Jessica!" he called out, his voice smooth as the silk of our finest chocolates. I turned to face him, forcing a smile that felt more like a grimace. He flashed that trademark grin, the one that had once made my heart skip a beat but now felt like a prelude to a storm. "I was hoping to catch you before you got lost in all this madness. The event is spectacular, don't you think?"

"It certainly has its charm," I replied, my voice steady but laced with a hint of frost. The truth was, I wasn't interested in small talk. Not when my mind was racing with thoughts of Max, who was somewhere in the crowd, probably trying to charm the socks off a potential client. He had a knack for that, drawing people in like moths to a flame while I stood on the periphery, balancing my dreams and fears like a tightrope walker.

Oliver leaned in, his gaze piercing. "I wanted to talk about the franchise opportunity. I believe it could be a game-changer for you and the chocolatier. Picture it: locations popping up in every major city, a brand that becomes synonymous with quality. You could be the face of it all."

A game-changer. The words danced in my mind like a sugar rush, intoxicating yet alarming. Part of me longed for that kind of success—the kind that promised to elevate our little shop into something grand. I could see it clearly: glossy storefronts, smiling customers, the scent of chocolate enveloping each location. But with that vision came a darker shadow, a fear that crept in quietly. What would happen to the soul of our beloved shop? The very heart that pulsed in the small kitchen where Max and I had poured our souls into every truffle and bar.

"Franchising sounds great, Oliver, but it's not just about expansion for me. It's about preserving what we've built. This place isn't just a business; it's our dream." My words hung between us, the weight of them palpable.

He raised an eyebrow, an amused smirk playing at the corners of his mouth. "Dreams can evolve, Jess. Isn't it time to think bigger? You've spent so long nurturing this, but what if there's a way to reach even more people? Isn't that what we all want? To be seen? To be tasted?"

"Or to be consumed until there's nothing left?" I shot back, the sarcasm slipping from my tongue before I could catch it. Oliver's smirk faltered for just a second, and I seized the moment, diving deeper. "You're right; I want to be seen, but I don't want to lose what makes us special in the process. What's the point of success if it comes at the cost of our identity?"

He regarded me for a moment, his expression shifting from playful to contemplative. "I admire your passion, truly. But you're thinking about this all wrong. This could be your legacy, a chance to share your chocolates with the world. Isn't that worth some risk?"

Risk. The word buzzed in my ears, wrapping itself around my thoughts like a vine choking a delicate flower. I glanced around the room, searching for a glimpse of Max, hoping he would swoop in and remind me of the joy we shared in our little bubble, the sweetness of our concoctions made with laughter and late-night chats. But he was nowhere in sight, lost in the throng of attendees, and the absence gnawed at me.

"Oliver, it's not just about the chocolates. It's about the late nights spent experimenting, the laughter over burnt batches, and the sense of community we've built. Those memories aren't just fodder for a corporate boardroom." My voice wavered slightly, vulnerability creeping into my tone. "I can't just hand that over to someone else. It feels... wrong."

"Sometimes you have to take a leap of faith," he replied, and the earnestness in his eyes made my pulse quicken. "Imagine what you could accomplish, what we could accomplish together. You and I, we could be unstoppable."

The implication hung between us, heavy and charged. "You mean, you and I in business together?" I questioned, unable to hide the incredulity in my voice. "That's quite the proposal."

He chuckled, a sound that was almost musical. "Well, I have always believed in a strong partnership, but I guess we'd have to define what that looks like, huh?"

The way he looked at me sent a familiar warmth cascading through my veins, but I smothered it quickly. There was an undeniable chemistry, a spark that had once ignited something in me, but the stakes were too high now. I needed to think of Max, of us.

"Look," I began, forcing the words out with a firmness I didn't quite feel. "I appreciate your offer, but I need time to think. It's not just my decision; it's Max's too, and I won't make a move without discussing it with him first."

Oliver's eyes narrowed slightly, the warmth retreating like a tide. "You really think he'll see the bigger picture? That he'll want to expand beyond what you have?"

The challenge in his tone ignited something fierce within me. "Max is my partner, both in business and in life. He deserves the same consideration I'm giving you."

"Very noble of you," Oliver replied, his voice dripping with sarcasm. "But just remember, sometimes the people we trust the most can hold us back."

As the words hung in the air, I felt a shift within me, a storm brewing at the crossroads of ambition and loyalty. What would it mean to chase this dream? Would it come at the expense of my heart? My resolve trembled, but I held firm. I would fight for my vision, for my partnership with Max, and against any force that threatened to tear us apart. The night stretched on, the vibrant world around me fading into a blur as I braced myself for the tumultuous journey ahead.

The air around me thickened, the sweet scent of chocolate mingling with the subtle tension crackling between Oliver and me. As he stepped back, clearly taken aback by my refusal, I felt an unexpected surge of defiance. This was my moment—not just to defend my choices but to reaffirm the bond I shared with Max, a bond forged in countless hours of laughter, frustration, and the occasional, chaotic explosion of chocolate batter.

I scanned the room again, desperately searching for Max. There he was, standing at the edge of a conversation, animatedly gesturing with his hands as if each word he spoke was a morsel of our shared dreams. My heart fluttered at the sight of him, his dark hair tousled in that charmingly reckless way that I found utterly irresistible. The way he lit up when talking about chocolate was a reminder of everything I loved about our partnership. And it was all the more reason I couldn't let Oliver's enticing vision cloud our reality.

"Jess!" Max's voice cut through the noise, pulling me from the magnetic pull of Oliver's presence. He wove through the crowd toward me, his eyes sparkling with enthusiasm. "You won't believe the feedback we've gotten on the dark sea salt truffles! People are raving, and I think we might have actually cracked the secret to the perfect ganache."

I felt a wave of relief wash over me as he reached me, the warmth of his presence dispelling the chill Oliver had left in his wake. "That's amazing!" I said, my smile genuine now, driven by Max's infectious energy. "We should celebrate later, maybe grab a late-night slice of that ridiculous cake from Baker's Delight?"

"Only if we can eat it in the back, away from the prying eyes of the world," he quipped, his face lighting up. "You know, the place where we can plot our world domination over chocolate. I've always dreamed of being a chocolate overlord."

His playful spirit lightened the air, and I felt the tension ease from my shoulders. "Only if you promise to wear a crown made of chocolate," I teased back, nudging him with my elbow.

Before Max could respond, Oliver's voice interjected, smooth and confident. "Max, great to see you. Jess and I were just discussing some exciting possibilities for the chocolatier. You should join in on the conversation."

The sharp edge in Oliver's tone ignited a spark of defensiveness in me. "We were discussing it, yes, but I'm not sure it's the kind of conversation you'd want to join," I replied, meeting Oliver's gaze with a mix of determination and protectiveness.

Max's eyebrows shot up, an unspoken question hanging in the air between us. "What kind of possibilities?"

I took a breath, choosing my words carefully. "Just some ideas Oliver had about expanding the shop into a franchise. You know, making it a big brand, potentially losing the charm that makes us who we are."

Max's expression shifted, a cocktail of curiosity and concern. "Franchising? Jess, that's... huge."

I nodded, feeling a rush of solidarity with him, grateful that he understood the weight of the decision looming over us. "Exactly. But what's the point if it sacrifices our identity?"

Oliver leaned back slightly, a calculating glint in his eye. "It wouldn't have to. You both are incredibly talented, and your chocolates deserve to be savored by more people. Imagine a world where your creations aren't confined to this quaint little shop." He paused, letting the idea settle like fine cocoa powder. "You could make history."

Max's brow furrowed, and I could see his wheels turning, wrestling with the allure of the proposal. "But what about the small-batch feel? The unique flavors that set us apart?"

"Unique flavors can be replicated," Oliver interjected, his tone almost coaxing. "What you can't replicate is the story behind them, the heart that goes into each piece. And that story can be told across multiple locations, creating a legacy that's much larger than this single shop."

I clenched my jaw, fighting the urge to launch into another impassioned defense of our shop's roots. I glanced at Max, hoping he would see my resolve reflected in my eyes. "We have something special here," I insisted, my voice steady. "We've built this from the ground up, and every customer who walks through that door feels it. It's about more than just chocolate."

Max nodded slowly, his gaze shifting between me and Oliver, weighing each word like the finest ingredients. "I think I agree with Jess. We're not just a brand; we're a community, a family."

Oliver's expression darkened slightly, but his charm never faltered. "Family is great, but family can also limit growth. Look at it this way: a tree can only grow so much in a small pot. What if you repotted it and let it stretch its roots?"

"Then you risk uprooting everything," I shot back, my voice rising slightly. "What if it doesn't survive the transplant?"

Max placed a reassuring hand on my shoulder, grounding me in the moment. "It's true, Jess. Growth can be painful. We've both seen it in our work. But maybe... maybe it's worth considering."

His words hit me like a sudden rainstorm. Hadn't we talked about the dreams we shared? Wasn't this the very reason we opened our shop—to share something we loved with the world? But as I looked into his eyes, I could see the confusion swirling there. I didn't want to pull him into a decision that could reshape everything we had built together.

"Max, think about it," I said softly, my tone pleading. "This is our home. I can't lose sight of that in pursuit of something bigger. I'm not ready to hand over our story to someone else."

Oliver's presence loomed over us, his demeanor shifting as if he sensed the tide turning against him. "I understand your concerns, but let's not forget that opportunities like this don't come knocking every day. You have to be willing to take risks if you want to truly achieve your dreams."

"Or we could just keep making our chocolates, perfecting our craft, and letting our story unfold naturally," I countered, feeling a surge of defiance wash over me. "We have time to grow, and we're doing it at our own pace. No one is rushing us."

Max's gaze locked onto mine, and I could see the battle raging within him, the tension building as he processed everything. "What if there's a way to do both?" he proposed, his voice a low murmur. "What if we could expand without losing what makes us us?"

The air shifted again, a new idea blossoming in the space between us. Oliver's eyes glimmered with interest, but I could feel the walls closing in around me. "You can't seriously be considering this," I said, my heart racing. "You know how much we care about our identity."

"I know," Max replied, stepping closer. "But we could explore our options, maybe find a middle ground. I trust you, Jess. I trust us."

As I looked at him, I felt the weight of that trust settle on my shoulders. It was a fierce, formidable thing, tethering us together in a world that felt increasingly chaotic. I wanted to believe there was a way forward that wouldn't tear us apart, a way to grow without losing ourselves in the process. But in that moment, standing between Oliver's tantalizing vision and the solidity of my partnership with Max, I couldn't shake the feeling that this crossroads held more than just our future—it held the essence of who we were.

The moment lingered, taut as a chocolate tempering at just the right heat, waiting for someone to tip the balance. Max's eyes flickered with an intensity that both soothed and unsettled me. I could feel the pulse of the party around us, laughter and music intertwining in a sweet symphony, but our bubble felt fragile, a delicate truffle waiting to be dropped. The implications of Oliver's proposal loomed like an uninvited guest, and every breath felt heavy with unspoken words.

"Jess, if you think we can find a way to scale without losing our identity, then maybe we should consider it," Max suggested, his voice softer than I expected. "What if we set clear boundaries and guidelines? We can keep the heart of the chocolatier while reaching more people."

I opened my mouth to protest, to insist that he was overlooking the core of what we had built, but the way he looked at me—earnest and hopeful—stopped me. It felt like staring into a recipe I'd never dared to try, uncertain but tantalizingly fragrant. What if he was right? What if we could find a way to share our creations with the world while keeping our unique touch?

"Max, I just don't want to end up as a factory," I replied, feeling the desperation creep into my voice. "This place, our chocolates—they mean everything to us. What if a franchise dilutes the magic? What if we lose the very essence of why we started this?"

Oliver chuckled, leaning back as if he were watching a tennis match, enjoying the back-and-forth of our burgeoning conflict. "You see, Jess, this is why I'm here. I'm not just some investor looking to cash in; I want to help you scale without losing that essence. I understand the heart behind the chocolate, but I also know that passion can't pay the bills forever. The world is changing; you have to adapt or risk being left behind."

The weight of his words hung in the air, and I could feel the crowd shifting around us, a tide pulling us further into a dilemma. I turned to Max, searching his eyes for the spark of certainty that had ignited my own ambitions. "What do you really want?" I asked, my voice barely above a whisper. "Are you excited about this idea? Or are you just trying to please me?"

He hesitated, and in that pause, I felt a crack in the foundation we had built. "I'm excited about what we could create together, Jess. But I don't want to do it if it means losing you in the process."

Oliver cleared his throat, breaking the fragile silence. "There's no reason you have to lose each other. You could be partners with a vision, expanding the chocolatier into something incredible. Just think about it: more flavors, more fans, and all those new memories waiting to be made."

"But what about the memories we've already made?" I shot back, frustration bubbling beneath my carefully curated composure. "The laughter in the kitchen, the messy experiments, the way our shop feels like home. How do you franchise that?"

Max's hand found mine, fingers intertwining in a gesture that felt both grounding and electrifying. "We create the essence of home in every new shop. It doesn't have to be just a copy; it can be an extension of us."

I looked into his eyes, seeking the reassurance I so desperately needed. My heart thudded as I considered the possibility, the adventure that lay ahead, but it felt wrapped in uncertainty. The future stretched out like a ribbon of melting chocolate, decadent yet daunting.

"I just don't want to wake up one day and realize we've lost ourselves along the way," I murmured, the weight of our dreams pressing against my chest.

Max nodded, his gaze unwavering. "We won't. We'll keep our core, our values. This isn't just about chocolate; it's about our journey together. I'm with you, no matter what you choose."

Oliver leaned closer, a predator sensing vulnerability. "Then let's set up a meeting to explore this in detail. I want to help you build your dream, but we need to act quickly. Opportunities like this can slip away faster than a batch of ganache if you're not careful."

The tension in the air was electric, crackling with possibilities. Yet I felt an unsettling twist in my gut. Was I really ready to leap into the unknown? The enticing images Oliver painted danced before me like mirages, beautiful yet fragile.

"I'll think about it," I replied, trying to keep my voice steady, but the truth felt like a marzipan layer hiding the bittersweet chocolate beneath. "But we need to do this together, all three of us. If we're going to consider expansion, it has to be a joint decision."

Oliver's smile was enigmatic, a glint of victory flashing behind his eyes. "That's the spirit! A true partnership is essential. Why don't we sit down tomorrow, you, Max, and I, to flesh this out? I can show you my plans, and then you can really understand the possibilities."

"Tomorrow sounds good," Max replied, squeezing my hand gently. "We'll work through the details, and we can make sure this is the right fit for us."

I could sense Oliver's victory, but it felt like a bittersweet promise—a chance to explore what could be while risking everything we had. "We'll meet," I said, though unease settled like a dark cloud overhead.

As the night wore on, the celebration continued around us, laughter ringing like the delicate chime of sugar bells. Max and I drifted back into the crowd, the hum of conversation enveloping us like a warm blanket, but the excitement of the evening was dulled by the heavy weight of uncertainty.

"Let's celebrate," Max suggested, trying to lift the mood. "A toast to our future, whatever it may hold!"

I nodded, a smile breaking through the haze of worry. "To our future," I echoed, raising my glass. "And to chocolate, the only thing that should never change."

We clinked glasses, and for a moment, I felt a flicker of hope. Perhaps we could navigate this path together. But as I glanced across the room, I caught a glimpse of Oliver speaking to someone—his demeanor confident, almost conspiratorial. My stomach twisted, the knot of unease tightening.

Before I could dwell on it further, I felt a hand on my shoulder. Turning, I came face to face with a woman whose presence radiated a magnetic energy. Her eyes, sharp and penetrating, narrowed slightly as she took in the scene. "I think we need to talk," she said, her tone suggesting she had far more than small talk in mind.

The world around me faded into a blur, the laughter and music turning into a distant hum. I felt the air grow heavy, anticipation crackling like static electricity as her gaze bore into mine. I could sense that whatever she had to say would alter the course of the night—and perhaps our future.

"What do you mean?" I managed, my voice steady, but a thousand questions raced through my mind, each one more urgent than the last.

"Oliver isn't the only one with plans for your chocolatier," she said, her lips curving into a knowing smile. "And trust me, you might want to hear what I have to say before you make any decisions."

The weight of her words crashed down on me like a wave, and the world shifted beneath my feet. Everything was about to change, and I had no idea if it would be for better or worse.

Chapter 20: Tempests and Tensions

The coffee shop was alive with the rich aroma of freshly ground beans mingling with the faint sweetness of cinnamon wafting from the pastry case. I inhaled deeply, letting the warmth of the scent settle in my chest as I frothed milk for the lattes that would soon grace our counter. The soft clink of ceramic cups was comforting, grounding me as I maneuvered through the morning rituals. Sunlight streamed through the window, casting a golden hue over the polished wooden tables, yet the warmth outside failed to penetrate the chill that had settled into my bones. I couldn't shake the feeling that something was brewing—not just the coffee but in the air, thick with the remnants of last night's storm.

Max was late, and with each tick of the clock, my heart quickened in time with the fleeting moments. He had promised to be here early to help set up for the community tasting event, but as I wiped down the counter for the umpteenth time, my thoughts spiraled. The storm had wreaked havoc not just on the weather but on our fragile truce. He had stormed out after our last conversation, leaving me standing amidst a flurry of emotions, unsaid words swirling around us like the debris that had littered the streets after the tempest.

I busied myself with arranging colorful spreads of artisanal cheeses, fresh fruits, and delicate pastries, the bright hues contrasting against the deep, rustic tones of the café. Each piece was a distraction, a way to keep my mind occupied while I waited for Max's arrival. The chatter of regulars filled the space, laughter punctuating the air like little bursts of sunshine, yet I felt like an outsider in my own world, yearning for the spark of conversation that only Max could ignite.

Finally, the bell above the door jingled, slicing through my thoughts like a sharp blade. I turned, and there he stood, drenched from head to toe, the rain clinging to him as if the storm hadn't entirely released its grip. His hair was disheveled, a few errant strands falling over his forehead, and his expression was a storm of its own—frustration mixing with something deeper, something raw.

"Hey," I said, attempting to mask my concern with a lightness I didn't quite feel.

"Sorry," he replied, shaking off his umbrella like a dog emerging from a bath, droplets scattering across the floor. "The roads were a mess. I thought I'd never get here."

His eyes darted around the café, lingering on the preparations I had made, a flicker of appreciation breaking through his tense demeanor. It was a small victory, yet it filled me with a warmth that momentarily eclipsed the knot of anxiety tightening in my stomach. "You could've called," I suggested lightly, trying to crack through the ice that had formed between us.

"Wouldn't have changed anything," he replied, a hint of sharpness in his tone that caught me off guard.

I nodded, feeling the weight of the unspoken hang between us. It was hard to ignore the way he seemed to pull away, the distance between us palpable, as if we were both trying to navigate an invisible minefield of our own making. I wanted to reach out, to bridge the gap, but every attempt felt clumsy, like I was reaching for something just out of grasp.

As we began to set up the tasting stations, the silence stretched uncomfortably. My heart raced each time our fingers brushed against one another, electric and jarring in the thick air. I could feel the emotions simmering just beneath the surface, both of us tiptoeing around the conversation we desperately needed to have. Every lingering glance felt like a challenge, a dare to break the silence that hung heavily between us.

"Did you see the damage on Maple Street?" I ventured, desperate for some form of connection.

He looked up, surprise flashing across his features. "Yeah, it was bad. People lost a lot. It's going to take time to fix everything."

"Time and effort," I replied, gesturing towards the stack of brochures I had printed for the community clean-up initiative. "We're going to need everyone to pitch in. I thought it might help us come together, you know? After everything."

Max studied me for a moment, his expression softening. "You always know how to rally people. It's one of the things I admire about you."

The compliment hung in the air, buoying my spirits for a fleeting moment before reality crashed back in. I busied myself with arranging glasses, avoiding his gaze, my heart racing with an array of emotions I couldn't quite categorize. The unspoken words sat like stones in my throat, heavy and uncomfortable, and I wished for nothing more than to shatter the glass wall that separated us.

"Why did you really leave last night?" I finally blurted out, the words escaping before I could stop them.

Max froze, the tension thickening as he processed my question. "Because I didn't want to fight. Not again."

"Not again?" I repeated, incredulity lacing my voice. "So we're just supposed to pretend everything's fine? That nothing happened?"

"Maybe it's better if we do," he shot back, his frustration bubbling to the surface. "You don't get it, do you? I care about you, and I don't want to ruin what we have."

A silence enveloped us, and I could feel my heart pounding as I met his gaze. The truth of his words resonated within me, yet the weight of unspoken fears loomed large. "But not addressing it could ruin us, Max. Can't you see that?"

His expression shifted, and for a brief moment, the storm within him calmed. "Maybe," he admitted, his voice barely above a whisper. "But it's terrifying to think about what that might mean."

I took a deep breath, feeling the intensity of the moment coalesce around us. The aroma of coffee and pastries filled the air, grounding me even as my heart raced. The storm outside had faded, but the one brewing between us felt electric, a mix of vulnerability and the spark of something greater. Each word we exchanged felt like a step closer to the edge, a leap of faith that might either bind us together or tear us apart.

The tension between us hung like a thick fog, palpable and suffocating. I busied myself with the remaining preparations, darting around the café as though the bustle could shield me from the reality of our conversation. With every soft clang of a dish and the low hum of chatter from the regulars, I felt the weight of our silence deepen. Max was flipping through the brochures I'd printed, his brow furrowed, the light catching the curve of his jaw in a way that reminded me of summer evenings spent debating everything from pizza toppings to the best superhero.

"Are we really doing this?" he finally asked, breaking the silence like a sharp crack of thunder.

"Doing what?" I replied, feigning ignorance, though I knew exactly what he meant. The unsteady foundation of our friendship felt fragile, and I wasn't sure if this community event was meant to solidify it or just highlight the cracks.

"Pretending this is just about the tasting event," he said, setting the brochures down with an audible thud. "I'm tired of dancing around what happened. Aren't you?"

His honesty struck me, piercing through the heaviness of my heart. I took a moment to collect my thoughts, watching as a couple of kids burst through the door, giggling and throwing off droplets of water like confetti. They were the kind of chaos that made everything else fade, and I envied their carefree spirits, the way they seemed unburdened by the world.

"Okay," I said finally, meeting his gaze head-on. "Let's not pretend anymore. What do you want to say?"

He took a step closer, and I could see the storm of emotions swirling in his eyes—fear, desire, uncertainty. "I want to say that this... whatever this is between us, it matters. But I'm scared, and I don't want to ruin it. Not with all the baggage we both carry."

The honesty in his voice sent a shiver down my spine. "Baggage?" I echoed, folding my arms defensively. "You think I'm just a suitcase away from being closed forever?"

"I didn't mean it like that," he protested, running a hand through his tousled hair, a gesture I found both endearing and infuriating. "But we both have our issues, and jumping into something more could just complicate things."

"Complicate? Or enrich?" I shot back, my voice rising slightly. "Isn't that what life is about—taking risks? You can't just stand still, Max. You know what happens when you do."

He opened his mouth, ready to retort, but then paused. "I know. I just wish it didn't feel like we're walking a tightrope above a pit of alligators."

"Better than a pit of snakes," I quipped, trying to lighten the mood even as my heart raced. "Those things give me the creeps. At least alligators are straightforward. You know they're coming for you."

A hint of a smile broke through his serious facade, and I felt a flicker of hope ignite between us. Maybe humor was the lifeline we needed to navigate this storm. "So you're saying you'd rather take your chances with an alligator than confront your feelings?"

"Exactly!" I exclaimed, my heart warming at the shared laughter. "I mean, who wouldn't?"

"Clearly, you're not the type to back down from a challenge," he said, the amusement in his eyes deepening. "But are you really ready to dive into this? Because I'm not sure I am."

"Why not?" I pressed, curiosity intertwining with my anxiety. "What's holding you back?"

Max hesitated, a myriad of thoughts flashing across his face. "I guess... I've never been good at vulnerability. It feels like opening a door to a room full of ghosts, and I'm not sure if I'm ready for that."

"Every room has ghosts," I said, my tone softer now, laced with understanding. "But they don't have to haunt us. They can just be reminders of where we've been. What if we opened the door together?"

His expression softened, and for a moment, I could see the flicker of hope mirrored in his gaze. "You make it sound so easy," he said, the tension easing slightly between us.

"Because it should be," I replied, taking a small step closer. "You and I... we've already built something here, even amidst the chaos. Why not take the next step?"

"Maybe we could," he said slowly, weighing his words as if they held the key to a treasure chest. "But what if it doesn't work? What if we mess this up?"

"Then we'll just laugh about it over coffee, like we always do," I countered, an uncharacteristic boldness rising within me. "Maybe we could even put it on the menu: 'Two Hearts, One Coffee Disaster.'"

"Just like you to make a joke out of it," he chuckled, but the laughter didn't reach his eyes fully. There was still hesitation lingering in the air.

"Because humor is my coping mechanism," I admitted, a hint of vulnerability creeping in. "But I'm serious, Max. I care about you. We've been through too much for this to slip through our fingers."

He looked at me, really looked, as if he were searching for something deeper within my gaze. "I care about you too. More than I probably should."

"Then stop overthinking it," I urged, feeling a sense of urgency building within me. "Let's be brave for once. Just jump."

Max took a deep breath, his shoulders relaxing just slightly. "Okay," he said, the hint of a smile returning to his lips. "But if we're doing this, we're doing it right. No half-measures. Promise?"

"Promise," I replied, a rush of warmth flooding my chest as the weight of our shared tension began to lift.

Just then, the door swung open again, and a gust of wind swept through the café, rattling the loose napkins on the tables. The bell chimed cheerily, a reminder that life was still happening outside our little world. In walked Mrs. Henderson, the town's unofficial gossip and a relentless cheerleader for our café. Her entrance brought with it an energy that felt almost electric, disrupting the bubble we had built around ourselves.

"Good morning, you two!" she called out, her eyes sparkling with mischief. "What's this I hear about a community event? Have you finally decided to make your relationship public?"

I felt my face flush, and I shot a panicked look at Max, who looked equally flustered.

"Mrs. Henderson, we—"

"Oh, don't even try to deny it!" she laughed, waving a hand dismissively. "You two are practically glowing. It's like I've walked into a rom-com."

Max and I exchanged a glance, the weight of our earlier conversation returning with a new urgency. "What if she's right?" I wondered silently. "What if this was meant to be?"

With a grin, I leaned over the counter, playing along with Mrs. Henderson's teasing. "Well, we can always name the coffee blend after our future relationship status, can't we? 'Caffeine and Confessions.'"

"Or maybe just 'Turbulent Brews,'" Max added, a spark of humor igniting between us again.

"Now that's the spirit!" Mrs. Henderson clapped her hands, delighting in our banter. "I can already see the headlines: 'Local Café Love Blooms Amidst the Coffee Chaos.'"

As she continued to chatter, my heart raced not just from the embarrassment of being thrust into the spotlight, but from the realization that the very chaos I feared could also be our greatest strength. Max and I were on the brink of something—something raw and real—and in that moment, surrounded by laughter and love, I felt ready to embrace whatever came next.

The laughter from Mrs. Henderson faded into the background, leaving a charged silence in its wake. Max's eyes, usually so expressive, now seemed a swirl of uncertainty as he turned back to face me. The moment felt fragile, suspended in time, a fragile thread holding together all our hopes and fears.

"Right," I said, trying to shake off the weight of the gossip that had just landed between us. "So, we'll call the blend 'Turbulent Brews' and market it as a celebration of our impending drama."

Max chuckled, but the laughter didn't quite reach his eyes. "Not sure I'm ready for that level of commitment."

"Just think of it as a tasting adventure! I mean, if we can survive this community event together, we can survive anything." My attempt at lightness felt tenuous, but I was desperate to keep the momentum going, desperate to prevent the atmosphere from collapsing back into that awkward tension.

Mrs. Henderson leaned over the counter, her eyes sparkling with mischief. "You two should really consider taking your act on the road. The 'Coffee and Chaos' tour would sell out in a heartbeat!"

I shot her a grin, but internally I was grappling with the very real chaos of my feelings for Max. Would this tasting event serve as our battleground, or could it be the launchpad for something beautiful?

Just then, a gust of wind whipped through the door again, rattling the windows, bringing with it the scent of rain-soaked earth and impending storm clouds. The patrons who had once filled the café now murmured in low tones, stealing glances toward the window as dark clouds rolled in like an army ready to lay siege.

"Looks like we might get another round of bad weather," Max noted, his voice low. "We should probably check on the tents outside before everyone arrives."

"Good idea," I replied, feeling a rush of anxiety return. The community tasting event was important; it was meant to bring us all together, but with the unpredictability of nature and emotions swirling, I couldn't shake the feeling that something was about to go awry.

We slipped out the back door, the air outside thick and humid, the storm brewing above us casting an ominous shadow over the vibrant colors of the flowers lining the café's entrance. I felt the first drops of rain patter against my skin, a stark contrast to the warmth that had enveloped me inside. The tension between us was still palpable, charged like the air before a lightning strike, and I could sense that whatever was left unsaid hung heavily between us.

"We need to secure the tents," I said, trying to focus on the task at hand. I could feel Max's presence next to me, each shared breath amplifying the weight of our unspoken connection. "Grab that side and let's pull it down tight."

As we wrestled with the fabric, laughter spilled between us, lightening the mood momentarily. "You know, if we both end up soaked, we can start our own version of 'Splash Zone Coffee,'" I joked, a grin breaking through the nervous energy.

He grinned back, but his gaze shifted, lingering on my face a moment too long, as if trying to decipher something hidden behind my bravado. "You're really good at this, you know," he said softly, pulling the tent down securely. "Joking around, making it seem like everything is fine when it's not."

"Isn't that the definition of being human?" I replied, a hint of sincerity creeping into my voice. "We all wear masks, Max. I just happen to wear mine over a steaming cup of coffee."

"Maybe," he replied, his voice thoughtful. "But it doesn't mean we should avoid the hard conversations forever."

I met his gaze, feeling the charge of honesty electrifying the space between us. "You're right. So let's not avoid it. Let's talk."

Just as I thought we might finally break through that wall, a loud crash echoed in the distance, followed by the sound of splintering wood. My heart raced. "What was that?"

Max looked toward the source of the noise, his eyes widening in concern. "I don't know, but it sounded like it came from the market square. Let's check it out."

We raced toward the sound, the rain now coming down in earnest, drenching us as we sprinted through puddles that had formed on the cobblestone street. The square was already beginning to fill with our neighbors, all eyes drawn toward a toppled stall that had once housed an array of handmade goods. The scene was chaotic; a table of fresh produce lay scattered, tomatoes rolling away like little red balls of panic.

"Is everyone okay?" I shouted over the din, my heart pounding as I scanned the crowd.

A few people were tending to a woman who had tripped over the debris, her ankle twisted at an awkward angle. My instincts kicked in. "I can help!" I yelled, racing toward her.

As I knelt beside the woman, I could feel Max's presence hovering nearby, his concern radiating like heat. "Stay still," I instructed the woman, assessing the situation. "We'll get you some help."

In the midst of the commotion, the air suddenly thickened with a different kind of tension, something I couldn't quite place. I felt a sudden chill, the kind that creeps up your spine when someone is watching you. I glanced up and locked eyes with a stranger standing at the edge of the crowd. His dark hair fell over his forehead, shadowing his intense gaze, but there was something about the way he was watching me that sent a jolt of unease through my chest.

"Who's that?" I murmured to Max, trying to keep my voice steady as I focused on the woman's pain.

"Not sure," he replied, frowning slightly. "I've never seen him around before."

I tore my gaze away, returning to the woman. "Can you wiggle your toes for me?" I asked, keeping my voice calm as I reached for her ankle.

A rumble of thunder rolled overhead, punctuating my thoughts with an unsettling finality. As I focused on tending to the woman, I could feel the stranger's gaze bore into me, heavy and unyielding. Just when I thought I could shake off the sensation, a loud shout broke through the rain-soaked chaos.

"Everyone, stay back!"

I turned my head to see the man stepping forward, his voice cutting through the murmurs. "We've got a situation here. No one should leave the square!"

Panic flared, and the crowd shifted, uncertainty spreading like wildfire. I exchanged a glance with Max, whose eyes reflected a mix of concern and curiosity.

"What's happening?" I whispered, dread pooling in my stomach.

"I don't know," he said, his voice tight. "But we should stay close. Something feels off."

Before I could respond, the stranger took another step forward, his presence dominating the space. "Listen to me," he continued, the authority in his voice silencing the crowd. "There's been a disturbance nearby, and I need you all to remain calm."

My heart raced as I glanced between him and Max, unsure of what lay ahead. The air was thick with tension, both from the storm brewing above and the uncertainty of the situation unfolding around us.

"Stay calm?" I whispered to Max, my voice trembling slightly. "That's easier said than done."

As thunder roared overhead, the stranger raised his hand, a shadow passing over his face. "I need to speak to the owner of this café. Now."

Every instinct within me screamed that this was no ordinary situation, and as I glanced back at Max, the gravity of the moment settled in. The crowd parted like the Red Sea, and I felt every pair of eyes shift toward me, the weight of their expectation heavy on my shoulders.

I took a deep breath, realizing that I was about to step into uncharted territory, where coffee and chaos would soon collide in a way I had never anticipated. The moment felt suspended, and I could only wonder what awaited me beyond the stranger's piercing gaze.

Chapter 21: Bitter Rivalries

The sweet, intoxicating aroma of melted chocolate filled the air, wrapping around us like a warm embrace. The shop was a haven of rich browns and vibrant hues, each display a meticulously arranged work of art. My heart raced as the clock crept closer to six, the hour our little chocolatier would transform from a quiet afternoon sanctuary into a bustling marketplace of indulgence. I stood behind the counter, my apron tied snugly around my waist, feeling the familiar thrill of anticipation mixed with the unease that danced just beneath my skin.

Max leaned against the display case, his easy smile a stark contrast to the tight knot in my stomach. "You ready for this?" he asked, adjusting his glasses and pretending to inspect a tray of truffles. His casual demeanor was always a source of comfort, yet tonight, it felt like a thin veil over the tension that had settled in the shop.

"Ready as I'll ever be," I replied, trying to keep my voice steady. But as the door swung open, allowing a gust of evening air to swirl inside, my confidence wavered. Oliver strolled in like a celebrity making a grand entrance, the soft jingle of the door chime drowned out by the murmur of awe that followed him. His tailored suit clung perfectly to his athletic frame, the sharp lines of his jaw accentuating that devil-may-care grin. I could practically hear the collective sigh of admiration from the crowd, and I hated him for it.

"Ah, the enchanting chocolatier and her loyal sidekick," he announced, his voice dripping with feigned sweetness as he approached us. "What a delightful little soirée you've planned. I must say, it pales in comparison to what I could offer."

Max stiffened slightly beside me, a flicker of conflict passing through his expression. I shot him a glance, silently urging him to remember our mission—to protect what we had built together. "We appreciate the compliment, Oliver," I managed, forcing a smile that felt more like a grimace. "But we're happy with how things are."

"Of course you are," he retorted, his charm slipping ever so slightly. "You wouldn't want to shake things up, would you? Change can be scary, especially for someone as... grounded as you."

The way he emphasized "grounded" felt like a veiled insult, a reminder of all the ways he believed I fell short. My fingers twitched at my sides, itching to grab a handful of chocolate and throw it at his impeccably styled hair. Instead, I plastered a smile on my face and turned to the customers gathered nearby, ready to distract myself with the task at hand.

The first batch of chocolate samples melted smoothly on eager tongues, and I reveled in the way people closed their eyes, savoring the rich flavors. It was a momentary escape, the chaos of the world fading away in the face of chocolate's sweet embrace. Yet, every time I glanced back at Oliver, my heart sank. He was captivating the crowd with his charisma, every word laced with an allure I couldn't compete against.

Max had begun serving samples on his own, casting nervous glances my way, torn between his loyalty to our shared dream and the magnetic pull of Oliver's world. It was infuriating. "You know, Oliver," I called out, forcing myself to sound upbeat despite the tightening knot in my chest. "This isn't just about the chocolate. It's about the experience. The heart behind it."

"Oh, darling," he purred, strolling closer, "you're so naive. Experience is only as good as the spectacle that surrounds it. I could help you—"

"Help us?" I interrupted, my voice sharper than intended. "We're not in need of help, Oliver. We built this place ourselves, and it's ours."

His smile faltered, the faintest flicker of surprise crossing his features. "How quaint," he replied, his tone dripping with condescension. "You think this little corner of the world is enough to hold your dreams? You could have so much more."

The tension in the air thickened, a heavy weight pressing down on me. I could see it reflected in Max's eyes, the way he hesitated as he offered samples, caught between two worlds. I wanted to scream, to shake him out of this illusion Oliver was weaving, but instead, I gritted my teeth and focused on the next customer.

The night wore on, the sweet cacophony of laughter and conversation echoing in the air. The gallery walls adorned with local art, each piece a testament to creativity, began to blur in my vision as I felt my determination waning. With every charming smile Oliver flashed, it became clearer that he was not just another competitor; he was a predator circling his prey.

"Can you believe this place?" he called out to a group of captivated patrons, waving a hand in my direction. "It's quaint, really. Almost charming in a nostalgic way. But imagine—"

I cut him off, the desperation creeping into my voice. "We're not a nostalgia project, Oliver. We're building a legacy here, brick by chocolate brick."

He raised an eyebrow, clearly entertained. "A legacy? You think a handful of truffles and a few local art pieces will carve your name into history? Sweetheart, I hate to break it to you, but legacy is built on ambition and influence. Not just... chocolate."

My heart raced, a fire igniting within me. "And here I thought passion was what fueled ambition," I shot back, feeling the warmth of my words ignite a spark in the atmosphere.

"Passion is lovely, but it won't pay the bills, will it?" he replied, his voice smooth but cutting.

I felt the air shift, the crowd around us quieting, hanging onto our exchange like it was the finale of a fireworks show. It was infuriating to see them caught in his web of charm, but I would not back down. "We'll see which is more powerful, Oliver. Passion or your shallow offers."

The moment hung suspended, like the delicate balance of flavors in my finest truffle. A hush enveloped us, and I could sense Max's internal struggle; it hung between us, a silent war of loyalties.

Just then, a sharp laugh broke through the tension, a familiar voice cutting through the thick air like a knife. "Well, well, well! If it isn't our favorite chocolate warrior and her dark knight!" My best friend, Clara, burst through the door, her presence a welcome wave of exuberance. She always had a knack for timing, and right now, I needed her.

"Clara!" I exclaimed, relief flooding my senses as she swept past Oliver, completely ignoring him. "You made it!"

"Of course! You think I'd miss this circus?" she grinned, her dark hair bouncing around her shoulders. Her eyes sparkled as she took in the scene, the tension dissipating like steam from a freshly poured cup of cocoa. "What's going on? I felt the drama from two blocks away."

"Just the usual," I replied, allowing a wry smile to cross my lips. "Oliver trying to convince me to sell out."

"Sell out?" Clara scoffed, her brows knitting together in feigned outrage. "As if. I'd rather eat cardboard than give in to his schtick."

"Welcome to the chocolate revolution, my friend," I said, and as Clara chimed in with witty banter, I felt the tension dissolve into laughter, the warmth of camaraderie wrapping around us like a well-worn blanket.

But the night was far from over, and the game had only just begun. As Clara and I exchanged playful jabs, I felt a renewed sense of purpose rising within me. Oliver may have waltzed in with his charm, but I had something far more potent—an unwavering spirit fueled by friendship and passion.

The evening swirled around me, a chaotic blend of laughter and clinking glasses, punctuated by the rich, decadent scent of chocolate wafting through the air. Clara had settled beside me, a buoyant force in the sea of uncertainty that threatened to engulf me. As she expertly navigated her way through our loyal customers, her energy seemed to disarm Oliver's pervasive influence, if only momentarily.

"Do you see him?" Clara whispered, nudging me with her elbow, her eyes wide with mock horror as she gestured toward Oliver, who was now animatedly engaging a couple at the far end of the shop. "What's his game? He looks like he's auditioning for a rom-com where the villain pretends to be the hero."

"Right? As if charm alone will buy you a ticket to the chocolate kingdom," I replied, rolling my eyes. The sight of him leaning casually against the display case, flashing that disarming grin, sent a shiver of annoyance down my spine. He was good, too good, and he knew it. It was like watching a cat play with a mouse, and I wasn't sure how much longer I could keep my composure.

"You know, I think he might have a point," Clara said, biting into a dark chocolate sea salt caramel. Her expression shifted to one of contemplation, the corners of her mouth quirking upward. "I mean, you do have that whole 'starving artist' vibe going on."

I feigned a gasp, clutching my chest in mock despair. "Excuse me! I am a successful chocolatier who has worked tirelessly to build this place from the ground up, thank you very much!"

"Oh, I know! But imagine if you threw in some sparkles or a little more drama. Maybe a live tiger or two?" she mused, her eyes alight with mischief.

"Right, because nothing says 'high-end chocolate' like a tiger leaping through a flaming hoop," I shot back, stifling a laugh. But deep down, I knew there was an edge of truth to her words. The thought of Oliver turning our heartfelt creation into a spectacle made my stomach churn.

Our banter was interrupted when a group of regulars approached, their eager faces lighting up at the sight of Clara. "Hey, Clara! Are you here to save us from Oliver's sales pitch?" one of them joked, a playful smirk dancing across her lips.

Clara winked, leaning conspiratorially towards them. "I'm here to make sure our beloved chocolatier doesn't go rogue. The last thing we need is a reality show featuring dramatic chocolate meltdowns."

"Or a villain plotting to take over the chocolate world," I added, my voice dripping with mock seriousness. "I can see the title now: 'Cocoa Conquests: Battle for the Bonbons!'"

Laughter erupted around us, but as the lighthearted moments danced through the air, my gaze drifted back to Oliver, who had successfully captured a small audience. I could almost see the threads of his charm weaving through the crowd, ensnaring them with his carefully crafted words. Each smile he flashed seemed to dim the light in our cozy sanctuary.

"Do you think he actually believes all this?" I asked Clara, my voice quieter, laced with genuine concern. "Or is he just that good at pretending?"

"Probably a bit of both," she replied, her brow furrowing. "But you know what? You've got something he doesn't—heart. And while he might have the glitz, you have the soul of this place. That's what will keep people coming back."

I took a deep breath, letting her words anchor me amidst the chaos. It was true; every truffle I crafted, every chocolate bar I shaped, was imbued with my passion, my love for the art. It was a piece of my heart, and I wasn't about to let Oliver's smirk diminish that.

Suddenly, Oliver approached, eyes sparkling with mischief. "Looks like the party is hopping, huh? Maybe I should show everyone how to truly enjoy chocolate," he said, an eyebrow raised, a challenge lingering in his tone.

"Good luck with that," Clara shot back, crossing her arms defiantly. "You know, chocolate isn't just about the taste. It's about the experience. You can't sell a memory if you're just a pretty face."

"Touché," he replied, an amused grin creeping across his features. "But isn't a pretty face the first step to creating an unforgettable memory?" He turned his gaze to me, and for a moment, I felt the weight of his scrutiny, the challenge implicit in his smirk.

"Ah, yes, the age-old debate of substance versus style," I replied, my voice steady despite the heat rising in my cheeks. "But perhaps you'll find that substance has a way of sticking around longer than a pretty face."

"Are you challenging me to a chocolate-off?" he teased, leaning closer. "I like a good competition."

"Only if you can handle losing," I shot back, daring to meet his gaze. The tension hung in the air like the sweet scent of chocolate, thick and palpable, as our eyes locked in an unspoken challenge. The customers nearby paused, clearly entertained by the banter that danced between us, unaware of the storm brewing just beneath the surface.

"Don't underestimate my skills," he replied, voice low and teasing. "I've conquered far more complex challenges than a little chocolate."

"Complex?" I echoed, incredulous. "Please. It's chocolate, not a game of chess. If you can't appreciate the artistry, you might as well be playing with cardboard."

"I'll have you know I've seen more than my fair share of chocolatiers who think they're Picasso in a pastry shop," he replied, his tone light but the spark of rivalry flickering between us. "I'm simply here to elevate the experience. And trust me, it's not as easy as it looks."

"I'll take your word for it," I said, forcing a smile, knowing the battle was far from over. "But I'd rather let my chocolate speak for itself than rely on flashy tactics."

Oliver chuckled, the sound smooth like molten chocolate, and I felt a flicker of warmth in my chest, quickly smothered by the realization of who I was dealing with. He might have been charming, but I was determined to hold onto the authenticity that had always been the backbone of my work.

As the evening progressed, I lost myself in the rhythm of the night, focusing on the sweet reactions from our customers, the way their faces lit up with each sample. Clara remained by my side, her laughter and teasing comments a balm against the prickly tension Oliver had brought with him.

But as I prepared another batch of chocolates, I couldn't shake the feeling that this wasn't just a simple rivalry over confections; it was a battle for the soul of our shop. With every smile Oliver flashed and every compliment he handed out, I felt him eroding the foundation I had built so painstakingly.

The clamor of the evening began to dim, the energy shifting as the crowd meandered toward the back of the shop, drawn by the sweet siren call of our final creations. I caught Oliver's eye once more, and the challenge was clear—tonight was not just about chocolate; it was about proving that passion could outshine the most polished façade.

And I was determined to show him that my heart had crafted something far more powerful than a mere illusion.

The crowd thinned as the clock approached eight, the buzz of laughter and the clinking of glasses fading into a gentle hum, leaving the air charged with an electric tension. I busied myself behind the counter, preparing the final batch of assorted chocolates, each piece a small, sweet rebellion against Oliver's insidious charm. Clara had ventured out to engage with our customers, her laughter punctuating the night as she shared stories about our chocolate-making adventures. I admired her ease, a vibrant presence that lit up the shop like the flicker of a candle against encroaching darkness.

Oliver, however, was a different story. He had commandeered a small group of patrons, his voice rising above the chatter, smooth and enticing like molten chocolate. My skin prickled as I caught snippets of his pitch—how he could elevate our chocolate shop to new heights, turn it into a brand that could compete on a national scale. It was a tempting offer, the kind that could make anyone pause and reconsider, but it was underlined by a sense of predation that made my stomach churn.

"Look at him," I murmured to Clara, gesturing subtly toward Oliver, who was animatedly showcasing his ideas. "He's got them wrapped around his finger. It's like watching a magician at work, only I'm terrified of what he'll pull out of his hat next."

Clara leaned closer, her eyes narrowing with mock seriousness. "Should I alert the authorities? Or at least get you a tinfoil hat? Maybe we can keep his evil charm from infiltrating your mind."

"Very funny," I shot back, but a smile crept onto my face. "If I'm not careful, I might just end up with a lifetime supply of generic chocolate and a glittery business card."

"You mean a glitzy one, right? Because he's all about that sparkle." Clara winked, and just then, a commotion broke out at the other end of the shop. A couple of customers had spotted one of our new confections—dark chocolate infused with sea salt and a hint of chili—and the excitement spread like wildfire.

"Perfect distraction!" I said, relieved, and we both turned to watch the frenzy of eager tasters.

Yet as I focused on the crowd's delighted expressions, I felt Oliver's gaze shift to me, his smirk unmistakable even from across the room. It was a challenge, a silent dare, and my heart raced in response. I took a steadying breath, reminding myself of the commitment I had made to this place, the love I poured into every recipe, every interaction.

"Just keep your chin up," Clara said, sensing my moment of vulnerability. "You're not just a chocolatier; you're the chocolatier. Remember that. The only magic he has is smoke and mirrors."

As the evening wore on, I found myself retreating to the back of the shop, a sanctuary where I could gather my thoughts. The walls were lined with shelves of jars filled with various chocolate ingredients—cocoa powder, vanilla beans, and an array of spices. The comforting smell enveloped me, grounding me in the midst of the swirling chaos outside.

"Hey," Max said softly as he stepped into the back room, his expression earnest. "Are you okay?"

"I'm fine," I replied, trying to sound convincing. "Just... processing everything."

He took a seat on a stool nearby, running a hand through his hair. "You don't have to pretend with me, you know. I can see the worry in your eyes."

I sighed, allowing the weight of the day to seep into my words. "It's just frustrating. He's so confident, so polished, and I'm afraid that's all people will see."

Max leaned forward, concern etched into his features. "But what about the heart behind this place? People come here for the experience, the love you put into everything. They won't be swayed by shiny packaging."

"You really believe that?" I asked, my heart fluttering at the thought.

"I know it," he replied, his voice steady. "And you know it too. You just have to remind yourself. Oliver may have the glitz, but you have the grit."

A sudden clattering noise interrupted our moment, followed by an excited shout from the front of the shop. Clara burst through the door, her cheeks flushed with exhilaration. "You won't believe what just happened! Oliver was just offering a tasting event for the local newspaper, and he wants us to join!"

"What?" I exclaimed, my heart dropping. "He wants us to team up? Is he out of his mind?"

"Actually," Clara said, her eyes gleaming with mischief, "he said you're the best chocolatier in town and it would be a 'travesty' not to have you involved. He thinks it will generate more buzz."

"Or he thinks he can win me over by pretending to respect me," I said, frustration bubbling to the surface. "This is just a ploy to steal my spotlight, and it might work."

"Maybe it's an opportunity?" Max suggested, though I could see uncertainty flickering in his eyes.

"It's a trap, plain and simple." My voice rose with conviction, each word infused with the urgency of my fears. "If I agree to this, he'll use it to bolster his image, and we'll just be background noise in his grand performance."

"Or," Clara countered, "you could use it as a chance to showcase your skills, stand your ground, and show everyone that your chocolate speaks louder than his flashy ideas. If you hold your own, you'll come out even stronger."

I opened my mouth to argue but found myself at a loss. Clara's fiery spirit always ignited something within me, yet the thought of sharing the spotlight made my stomach twist. The battle was no longer just about chocolate; it was about identity, reputation, and the soul of my craft.

"Are you seriously considering it?" I asked, uncertainty flooding my voice.

"Maybe. I mean, if it's an opportunity to shine, then it could work in our favor. But I won't do it unless you're on board," he replied, his sincerity disarming me.

Before I could respond, a sudden loud crash echoed from the front, followed by an unmistakable shout of panic. The three of us exchanged alarmed glances, hearts racing as we rushed back to the shop.

What we found froze me in place. A throng of customers stood clustered around Oliver, who had stumbled backward, his foot caught in a decorative wire basket. It tipped over, sending an avalanche of chocolates cascading across the floor like a sweet avalanche, coating the tiles in a chaotic chocolate chaos.

"Is everyone okay?" I called out, my heart racing as I moved closer, desperate to assess the situation. But my focus quickly shifted back to Oliver, who was attempting to regain his composure, his face a mix of surprise and embarrassment.

"Just a little mishap," he said, laughing nervously, but I could see the annoyance brewing beneath the surface. He shot a glance my way, eyes narrowing slightly as if to say this was my fault, my shop.

"Why don't we help him clean up?" Clara suggested, her voice laced with an edge of amusement. "After all, chocolate doesn't clean itself, and we wouldn't want to be accused of leaving our rivals in a sticky situation."

I couldn't help but smile at her wit, even as the tension in the air thickened. We stepped forward to help, but the moment I reached out to offer my hand, Oliver shot me a look, his smile tight and his eyes stormy. "No need," he said, voice steely. "I've got it."

But just as he turned back to the floor, a loud crash erupted from the back room. The sudden noise sent the crowd jumping, and my heart dropped as I realized what it could mean. The shelves! The jars of ingredients! My stomach sank, a wave of panic crashing over me.

"Max! Clara! Stay close," I shouted, urgency fueling my voice. We pushed through the crowd, rushing toward the source of the sound, but as I approached the door, I froze, the sight before me taking my breath away.

The back room was in chaos, ingredients scattered like confetti, but more alarming was the faint trail of crimson seeping from the corner, pooling on the floor. My breath caught in my throat as dread unfurled within me.

"Call an ambulance!" I shouted, my heart racing, and as I rushed forward, the world around me began to blur, reality slipping into a haze of fear.

In that moment, everything I thought I knew about rivalry, loyalty, and ambition shattered like glass around me, leaving only the raw edges of uncertainty and a cliffhanger I never saw coming.

Chapter 22: Secrets Unveiled

The vibrant hum of the crowd began to fade, leaving behind echoes of laughter and the clinking of glasses that had once filled the air with warmth. The tasting event had started as a celebration, a showcase of culinary artistry and ambitious dreams. But now, as the last guests trickled out, their satisfied smiles morphing into the evening shadows, I felt the weight of unspoken words pressing down on me like the heavy, oppressive humidity of a summer night.

Max stood just a few feet away, his expression caught between frustration and concern. His dark hair, tousled from the chaos of the evening, fell across his forehead in a way that had always struck me as charming, even now when the moment felt anything but. "We need to talk about Oliver," I finally managed, my voice a whisper, strained yet urgent. It was strange how those words, so simple, held the power to shatter the fragile bubble we had been floating in, a bubble filled with camaraderie and unacknowledged tension.

He hesitated, eyes searching mine, as if he were searching for a hidden door to escape through. I could see the gears turning in his mind, wrestling with the reality I had just unleashed. It was a dangerous game, and the stakes were high. The twinkle lights strung around the room flickered, casting playful shadows on the walls, but the glow felt dimmer now. The realization of the emotional tempest ahead loomed between us.

"Clara," he said, his voice low, almost a plea. "What about Oliver?"

A knot twisted in my stomach, hot and uncomfortable, threatening to spill over. I took a step closer, the familiar scent of his cologne mixing with the lingering aroma of spiced wine from the tasting tables. "He's pushing too hard, Max. He's always been about the numbers, the growth, the 'next big thing.' But what about us? What about the heart of this place?" I gestured around, my frustration spilling out. This shop had been our sanctuary, a dream sculpted by our shared hopes and late-night conversations. "You know we can't sacrifice our vision for some corporate plan that doesn't consider the soul of our business."

Max sighed, his brow furrowing. "I get that. I do. But Oliver sees something in the market we might be missing. This could elevate our brand." He ran a hand through his hair, an anxious gesture I had come to recognize. "But that doesn't mean we have to lose everything we built."

My heart sank. His words danced precariously on the edge of reason, and I felt a rush of panic. "But do you trust him?" I blurted out, and immediately regretted the urgency in my tone. I was asking for a loyalty that felt like it was about to unravel.

Just as the air thickened with uncertainty, Oliver's smooth voice sliced through our tension. "Clara, you can't deny this opportunity. The future of the shop depends on growth." He emerged from the shadows, a predator drawn to the scent of conflict. He had a way of commanding a room, all polished charm and sharp wit, but tonight his presence felt like a dark cloud looming over our fragile moment.

"Oliver, this isn't just about numbers," I shot back, my frustration morphing into anger, simmering just beneath the surface. "It's about the essence of what we're creating here, about the community that's grown around us."

He chuckled softly, a sound that sent a shiver down my spine. "Community doesn't pay the bills, Clara. You know that. This isn't a charity; it's a business. We have to be pragmatic."

I glanced at Max, desperately seeking his support, but he remained silent, a statue caught in the crossfire of our ideological war. My heart raced, blood pounding in my ears. The once sweet aroma of fresh pastries and roasted coffee that filled the shop now felt tainted, suffocating.

"Max," I implored, my voice softening, pleading for a lifeline, "you see what he's doing, right?"

He shifted uncomfortably, the tension radiating from him like heat from a furnace. "I think he has a point, Clara. We can't just cling to nostalgia."

The words hit me like a slap. I couldn't believe what I was hearing. Nostalgia? Was that what we had built—just a fleeting moment in time, a memory waiting to fade? I felt a storm brewing inside me, a whirlpool of emotion that threatened to pull us all under. "Max, please. Don't let him do this to us. Don't let him take away what we've fought so hard to build."

Just then, a sudden noise interrupted our standoff—the crash of glass breaking, sharp and jarring. All eyes turned toward the source, where a waiter stood frozen, wide-eyed, looking down at the shards of crystal scattered across the floor.

The tension hung thick, a tapestry woven from our unsaid fears and raw emotions. I caught Oliver's smirk as he leaned against the counter, his confidence unshaken, while my heart raced. "See? Even the staff is nervous," he taunted, his eyes glinting with mischief.

I felt Max shift, a brief moment of solidarity igniting between us. "We're not backing down," he finally said, his voice steady and resolute. It felt like a small victory, but one I clung to fiercely, a fragile thread connecting us amidst the chaos.

As the reality of our conversation crashed like waves against the shore, I understood that this confrontation was merely the beginning. Choices lay ahead, forks in the road that could lead us to wildly different destinations. Would we fight for our vision or let it be swept away in the tides of ambition? My heart raced at the thought of what was to come, every twist and turn looming like the dark clouds gathering on the horizon.

The awkward silence settled over us like a heavy fog, the kind that rolls in off the coast and blankets everything in an uncomfortable chill. I could feel the prickle of Oliver's gaze as it darted between Max and me, a hawk assessing its prey. The scattered shards of glass from the floor shimmered under the dim lights, a grim reminder that chaos had an uncanny way of finding its way into our neatly arranged lives.

"Clara," Oliver said, his tone almost patronizing, "you're not really considering going against this, are you? Your vision is important, but we're not living in a bubble."

I shot him a glare, a mixture of defiance and disbelief. "Living in a bubble? That's rich coming from you. The only thing you seem to care about is the bottom line."

Max shifted beside me, his body language tight and defensive. "It's not just about numbers, Oliver. We want to build something sustainable, something real."

Oliver crossed his arms, a smug grin playing at the corners of his mouth. "Real? That's cute. But you know what's real? Bills. Rent. Salaries. This isn't a fairy tale; it's business."

The heat of anger swelled within me again, and I felt the urge to defend our dream rise up like a tidal wave. "And what about our values? Our integrity? What good is success if it comes at the cost of what we believe in?"

"Values don't pay for ingredients," he retorted, a flash of irritation sparking in his eyes. "You both seem to forget that."

In that moment, I felt a crack in the foundation of everything we had built. How had we arrived here, in this tension-filled standoff, where ambition threatened to drown out our passion? My heart raced, but beneath the surface, I could feel the steely resolve forming.

"Let's not pretend that you care about this place, Oliver. It's just a stepping stone for you," I shot back, feeling empowered by the truth of my words.

He raised an eyebrow, unimpressed. "That's rich, coming from someone who's been dreaming of a quaint little shop since she was ten."

"Better to dream than to scheme," I countered, my voice gaining strength.

"Okay, you two, enough," Max interjected, stepping between us, his hands raised in a gesture of peace. "We need to find a middle ground. Clara, you're right about wanting to keep the heart of this place intact. But Oliver's also correct; we can't ignore the financial realities."

I looked at Max, searching for that glimmer of hope, the reassurance I desperately needed. "But what does that middle ground look like? Turning this place into a soulless franchise?"

"Not at all," he said, his tone calming, though the tension in his shoulders remained. "What if we brainstorm some ideas? Find ways to grow that align with our vision?"

As the suggestion hung in the air, the crowd outside began to thin out, laughter and chatter fading into the night. I could hear the rustle of leaves outside, a gentle reminder that life continued beyond these walls.

"What kind of ideas?" Oliver asked, an eyebrow raised, skepticism etched across his features.

"Collaborations, local pop-ups, maybe even seasonal themes," Max suggested, glancing at me for support. "If we can create an experience that keeps our integrity intact, we could expand our reach without compromising our soul."

Oliver leaned back against the counter, arms crossed, the light from the overhead fixtures glinting off his watch. "You really think you can turn this into a marketing campaign? Some feel-good story that'll get people through the door?"

I opened my mouth to protest, but Max spoke first, his voice steady. "If we can tell our story right, then yes. But it's not just about marketing; it's about connection."

I felt a flicker of hope. There was something beautiful in what Max was proposing—a bridge between our ideals and the reality we faced. "It's about bringing the community in, making them part of the experience," I added, encouraged by Max's conviction.

Oliver remained silent for a moment, his expression inscrutable. Finally, he shrugged, the tension easing slightly in his posture. "Alright, I'll play along. But we're going to need a solid plan, something tangible."

"Then let's start brainstorming," I replied, determination filling me.

As we settled into a huddle, the air shifted, each of us drawing closer to a collective goal. I could feel the spark of creativity igniting within me, ideas swirling like leaves in a brisk autumn breeze. "What if we host a 'Taste the Season' event? Each month could highlight local producers, showcasing what's fresh and available. We could create a community vibe and strengthen local ties."

Max nodded enthusiastically, his eyes lighting up. "That's a fantastic idea! We could invite local farms and artisans, share their stories alongside our food. Make it an experience, not just a meal."

Oliver, surprisingly, seemed engaged, his brow furrowing in thought. "We'd need a strong marketing push to get the word out. Social media, partnerships with influencers... something to give it momentum."

The conversation flowed like a well-crafted wine, the ideas bubbling and mingling until they formed something truly exciting. I could feel the earlier tension dissipate, replaced by a vibrant energy that surged through me.

Suddenly, the door swung open, and a gust of chilly air swept in, carrying the faint sound of music from a nearby street fair. A woman entered, her cheeks flushed from the cold, and she paused at the sight of us. "Am I interrupting something?"

Her presence was a jolt of fresh energy, the kind that could shift the atmosphere entirely. She wore a bright yellow scarf that popped against the backdrop of muted tones in the shop, and her eyes sparkled with curiosity.

"Not at all," Max replied, stepping forward, his demeanor shifting to a welcoming warmth. "We're just brainstorming some ideas. Come on in!"

The woman smiled, her confidence radiating as she approached us. "I heard there was an event, and I couldn't resist checking it out. I'm Zoe, by the way."

As we introduced ourselves, I felt the dynamic shift once more. Zoe's enthusiasm was infectious, her presence like a splash of bright paint on a canvas. "What kind of ideas are you brewing? I love a good collaboration."

I couldn't help but smile, feeling the potential for new beginnings ignite within me. Maybe, just maybe, this shop could grow in ways I hadn't yet imagined—ways that could honor our roots while reaching for the stars. In that moment, the weight of uncertainty lifted just enough to let a ray of hope shine through, illuminating the path ahead.

Zoe settled into the cozy corner of our shop as if she'd belonged there all along. With an exuberance that felt almost infectious, she leaned forward, resting her elbows on the polished wooden table, her eyes sparkling with mischief. "So, what are we scheming about? Let me guess—how to make this place the hottest spot in town?"

I chuckled, the tension from before beginning to wane. "We were just brainstorming a series of events that could draw in more customers while highlighting local producers. You know, keep the heart of our shop beating strong."

"Ooh, I love a heart-thumping plan!" Zoe exclaimed, her enthusiasm radiating warmth. "What about a monthly 'Taste the Neighborhood' night? Each month could focus on a different local farm or artisan. It could be a culinary tour without leaving your seat!"

Max's eyes lit up at the idea, and I felt a renewed sense of hope. "Exactly! We could do a pairing menu with dishes inspired by each producer's offerings. It would create a deeper connection with our community."

"Plus, we can bring in local musicians to liven up the atmosphere. People love a good ambiance," Zoe added, bouncing slightly in her seat, clearly invested. "Imagine it—a cozy evening with wine, local bites, and live music. You'd have folks lining up at the door."

Just as I was about to dive deeper into our planning, Oliver's voice sliced through the excitement, dripping with skepticism. "I can already see the marketing pitch: 'Enjoy a night of mediocre food under the guise of local charm.'"

Zoe whipped around, unphased by his dismissive tone. "Mediocre? If you put your mind to it, Oliver, this could be anything but. It's about passion! If you don't have passion, what do you have?"

"An effective business model?" he shot back, his smirk infuriatingly nonchalant.

"Right, because passion is such a bad thing," I countered, feeling my blood pressure rise. "This place started because we loved what we do, not because we wanted to cash in on the latest trend."

"Passion doesn't pay the bills," he said, folding his arms as he leaned back, a permanent look of indifference etched across his features.

Zoe rolled her eyes, clearly not one to back down from a challenge. "And yet, here you are, in a shop with a unique vibe and community spirit. If that's not worth investing in, I don't know what is."

I couldn't help but smile at her bravado. She had a way of sparking fire in the air, making Oliver seem a bit less formidable. "Exactly! We can infuse our personality into the events, showcase the stories behind the food and those who make it. That's where the magic happens."

Max nodded along, and I felt an unspoken agreement forming between us. "How about we plan a pilot event for next month? We can set a date and get the word out through social media and local influencers. Let's make it a launch to remember."

Oliver shifted in his seat, contemplating our enthusiasm. "You really think people will turn out for that? The local crowd can be fickle."

Zoe leaned in, confidence radiating from her. "If you make it special enough, they will come. Besides, what's more appealing than a gathering that celebrates local talent? We'll create an event that resonates with people."

The room buzzed with possibilities as we bounced ideas off one another, weaving together a tapestry of flavors, sounds, and connections. I could envision vibrant scenes—the clink of glasses, laughter spilling into the streets, and the rich aroma of seasonal dishes wafting through the air. For the first time in weeks, I felt the lightness of hope returning.

But just as the energy reached a fever pitch, the atmosphere shifted again, heavy with an unexpected tension. The door swung open, letting in a gust of wind that tousled Zoe's hair and sent a shiver through me. I turned to see a figure standing in the doorway, silhouetted against the streetlights outside.

"Hey, is this a private party, or can anyone join?" The voice belonged to Jake, a mutual friend from the neighborhood, known for his easy smile and penchant for drama. He strode in, shaking off the chill from the evening air, his eyes gleaming with mischief.

"Just a little planning session," I said, smiling back at him. "What brings you here?"

Jake leaned casually against the counter, a glint of curiosity in his eyes. "I heard there was some serious brainstorming happening. Thought I'd crash the party. You all look like you're cooking up something spicy."

I could sense Oliver's irritation bubbling beneath the surface, but before he could comment, Zoe jumped in. "Spicy is exactly what we're going for! We're planning a 'Taste the Neighborhood' event to showcase local flavors and talent."

"Count me in!" Jake exclaimed, his enthusiasm infectious. "I know some great local musicians who'd love to play at something like that. You're going to need good vibes, after all."

Max looked at me, his excitement palpable. "See? Everyone wants to be a part of this. It's a sign!"

As the conversation spiraled into more possibilities, I felt the weight of uncertainty start to lift. The synergy of our ideas blended together into something beautiful, like a complex dish that required just the right ingredients to come alive.

But then, Oliver's phone buzzed, cutting through the laughter and chatter like a knife. He glanced at the screen, and his expression shifted instantly from casual interest to something more serious.

"What's wrong?" I asked, my heart skipping a beat as I caught the change in his demeanor.

He frowned, his fingers tapping against the screen as he read whatever had just come through. "I... I have to take this."

"Now?" I questioned, irritation creeping back into my voice. "We're in the middle of—"

"Just a second!" he snapped, already stepping away from the table. The air around us grew taut, as if we were waiting for a storm to break.

The laughter faded, and a heavy silence settled in, punctuated only by Oliver's hurried footsteps toward the back of the shop. I exchanged glances with Max and Zoe, confusion etched across our faces.

"What was that about?" Zoe murmured, tilting her head as she watched him disappear.

"I have no idea," I replied, anxiety creeping back in. "But it can't be good. Not when we're finally making progress."

Just then, my phone buzzed in my pocket, a sharp reminder of reality that pulled me from my thoughts. I pulled it out, heart racing, but it was just a notification from the shop's social media account—nothing urgent.

When I looked back up, Oliver had returned, his face pale, as if the very weight of the world had just crashed down on his shoulders. "We need to talk," he said, his voice low and urgent.

A chill ran through me, and I felt the tension coil tightly in my stomach. "About what?"

He glanced at us, hesitating for just a moment, and that tiny pause felt like a lifetime. "About the shop. And... some things you might not know."

The words hung in the air, heavy and foreboding, the vibrant energy we had just built slipping away like sand through our fingers. I could see the worry in Max's eyes, mirrored by the apprehension on Zoe's face.

Just as I opened my mouth to press for answers, the lights flickered ominously, plunging us momentarily into darkness. The sound of glass shattering echoed from the back, a prelude to the unease swirling around us.

"Oliver?" I asked, my heart racing. "What's happening?"

His eyes darted around the room, and I could see a storm brewing behind them, dark and unpredictable. "I... I don't think we're safe."

And with that, the ground beneath us shifted, propelling us into the unknown, where secrets long buried began to claw their way to the surface, threatening to unravel everything we had built.

Chapter 23: The Fractured Heart

The days slid past like melted chocolate left out in the sun, slowly pooling into a sticky mess of regret and missed opportunities. The once-vibrant atmosphere of the shop felt suffocating, every corner heavy with unsaid words and unresolved feelings. I had always believed that creating chocolate was like breathing; it was a rhythm I could dance to, the cadence of cocoa and sugar a familiar melody in my life. But now, as I stared at the sleek rows of confections, their glossy exteriors reflecting the muted light of the shop, I felt as though I was crafting tiny reminders of a happiness I could no longer touch.

Max and I used to share laughter that echoed through the shop like the bubbling of a ganache left on the stove, spontaneous and delightful. Now, we moved around each other like two cautious dancers, each step careful to avoid the other's gaze. His silences were punctuated by the clinking of tools, the scraping of spoons against mixing bowls, and the gentle hum of the refrigerator, each sound a reminder of the gap that had formed between us. The days of bantering over the perfect ratio of cream to chocolate were long gone, replaced by a tension thick enough to slice through.

I found myself retreating into my work, pouring my heart into each recipe as if I could coax our laughter back to life through the rich, dark layers of cocoa. On particularly quiet afternoons, I became a mad chocolatier in a kitchen filled with bittersweet memories, using every ounce of creativity to drown out the ache of our estrangement. Raspberry ganache had become my solace, its vibrant color a stark contrast to the gray clouds of uncertainty hovering over us. Each truffle I crafted felt like a small rebellion, a desperate attempt to reclaim the passion that had once defined us.

As I rolled the ganache into perfect spheres, I closed my eyes, imagining the flavor blooming on my tongue, the way it would have when we shared it together. The tartness of the raspberries mingled with the deep, dark chocolate, creating a dance of flavors that mirrored the complexity of our relationship. Yet, with every bite, a hollow sensation crept in, reminding me of the laughter that had faded into silence. The kitchen, once a symphony of clanging pots and teasing jests, now felt like a mausoleum of our shared dreams.

The afternoon sun cast a soft glow through the shop's front window, illuminating the dust motes swirling in the air, a gentle reminder that life continued outside, indifferent to the turmoil brewing within. I glanced up, catching a fleeting glimpse of Max as he stepped into the shop, his brow furrowed, his eyes clouded with thoughts I longed to unravel. The sight of him sent a flutter through my chest, a mixture of warmth and ache. In that moment, he was both my muse and my tormentor, the embodiment of everything I craved yet couldn't grasp.

"Are you planning to drown in chocolate, or is there a plan for lunch?" His voice cut through the silence, tinged with a teasing lilt that felt both familiar and foreign. It was a challenge wrapped in a question, one that suggested he was still there, lurking beneath the surface, waiting for a crack in the wall I had built around myself.

I shrugged, forcing a lightness into my voice that I didn't quite feel. "Well, if I could survive on ganache alone, I'd be in heaven. But alas, I do have to eat real food eventually." I punctuated the sentence with a playful roll of my eyes, hoping to coax a smile from him. Instead, I was met with a noncommittal grunt, the hint of a smile fading before it could fully form.

Silence settled again, thick and uncomfortable. I busied myself with decorating a tray of chocolates, each swirl of the icing a frantic attempt to distract myself from the tension hanging in the air. The chocolate melted under the heat of my fingers, but I barely noticed, my thoughts racing faster than I could manage. I wanted to scream, to demand answers to the questions swirling in my mind. Why had things unraveled so quickly? What had changed between us, and could we ever find our way back to that easy laughter?

"Are you mad at me?" Max's question sliced through my thoughts, the directness of it surprising me. He leaned against the counter, arms crossed, a defensive posture that hinted at vulnerability. I could see the way he fought to hold onto his composure, yet the slight tremor in his voice betrayed him.

I paused, the chocolate I was working with forgotten as the weight of his question settled heavily on my shoulders. "Mad? No, just... frustrated," I admitted, my voice barely above a whisper. "Frustrated that we can't seem to talk about this."

He nodded, a flicker of understanding passing between us. "I don't want to lose you," he said, his voice earnest, the words hanging in the air like the rich aroma of melted chocolate. "But I also don't know how to fix this. It feels like we're both walking on eggshells."

I took a deep breath, letting the warmth of his words wash over me. "Then let's stop walking on eggshells," I said, finally meeting his gaze. "Let's talk. Really talk." The challenge was there, unspoken but palpable, echoing in the charged space between us.

His eyes brightened at my words, hope flickering in the depths. "Okay, then let's figure it out." The resolve in his voice ignited something within me—a spark that promised to illuminate the shadows that had settled between us. Perhaps, just perhaps, we could find our way back to the joy we had once shared, one truffle at a time.

The conversation lingered in the air, a fragile thread between us, and for the first time in what felt like an eternity, I sensed a shift. The weight of unspoken words was still there, but now, perhaps for the first time, we were standing on the precipice of vulnerability. Max leaned closer, a glimmer of determination lighting up his eyes. "Let's start with the basics. What do you need from me right now?"

The question hung there, loaded and beautiful, like the perfect truffle waiting to be unwrapped. My heart raced as I pondered the answer. What did I need? I'd spent so long drowning in my thoughts, tangled in my own feelings, that the answer felt like a slippery fish in a pond. But as I watched Max, his earnest expression inviting me to share, I realized it was time to unearth the truth buried deep within me.

"I need you to listen," I said, my voice steadier than I felt. "To really listen. We've been dodging around the issue, trying to maintain this façade of everything being fine while we're slowly sinking." The words flowed out like a velvety ganache, smooth yet rich with unprocessed emotions.

Max nodded, his features softening as he leaned in, a sign that he was ready to absorb whatever I had to say. "I'm all ears," he replied, a hint of a smile breaking through the somberness, reminding me of how easily we had once laughed together. "Give me the raw version."

I took a breath, feeling the tension release slightly, like the first bubble of air escaping a chocolate mousse. "I've been feeling lost," I admitted, the truth escaping my lips as if it had been waiting for this moment. "When we started this shop, it felt like a dream we were building together, but lately, it's felt like I'm just going through the motions. And it's killing me."

Max's expression shifted, his gaze intense. "I can see that. I thought maybe it was just me who felt like we were wandering in circles, like the flavors we used to create were fading into blandness."

The honesty between us was electric, a current I hadn't realized we'd both needed to feel again. "Exactly! It's as if we've forgotten how to be us," I confessed, my voice cracking slightly. "I miss the way we would brainstorm wild ideas at two in the morning, how every creation was an adventure. Now, it feels more like a chore."

"I miss that too." Max leaned back against the counter, the tension in his shoulders easing. "Somewhere along the way, we got too caught up in the business part of it all. We let the stress overshadow the passion."

"Yes!" I nearly shouted, a burst of excitement flooding me. "It's like we've been wearing blinders, focused only on the numbers and the next order, forgetting the joy we once found in experimentation."

Max's eyes sparkled with the hint of a playful smile. "So, what do you say we change that? Let's throw caution to the wind—well, at least to the chocolate—and have a brainstorming session like the good old days. I'm thinking of something wild, like chocolate-infused chili or lavender truffles."

The idea of a brainstorming session sent a thrill through me. "Lavender truffles? Are you trying to turn our shop into a botanical garden?" I teased, leaning against the counter, feeling more at ease.

"Hey, if it can be delicious, why not?" he shot back, his playful demeanor lifting the heaviness that had weighed us down for weeks. "Besides, remember that one time we combined salted caramel with chili? That was a disaster, but at least it was memorable!"

We both burst into laughter, the sound echoing off the walls, chasing away the shadows that had lingered for too long. It felt like the sun had finally peeked through the clouds, and the warmth enveloped us. "Okay, maybe a few experiments are in order," I conceded, my heart racing with newfound excitement. "But I draw the line at anything that might taste like a garden."

"Deal." Max raised an eyebrow, a mischievous glint in his eyes. "Let's meet here after hours, just like we used to. No customers, no pressure—just us and our crazy ideas."

As the day turned to dusk, the shop transformed under the warm glow of the hanging lights, the ambiance shifting into something almost magical. We closed up earlier than usual, leaving behind the clutter of orders and paperwork. Instead, we set out ingredients as if we were preparing for a culinary revolution—chocolate, cream, spices, and an assortment of unexpected additions.

"Are we really doing this?" I asked, a nervous laugh escaping my lips as I surveyed the eclectic array of ingredients spread before us. "It feels like we're planning a heist, not a truffle-making session."

Max flashed a grin, one that sent a ripple of warmth through me. "Well, we are stealing our joy back, aren't we? Let's make this fun."

With that, the first truffle we attempted was a wild concoction of dark chocolate mixed with a hint of rosemary and a sprinkle of sea salt. The combination felt audacious, daring. As I melted the chocolate, the rich aroma wafted through the air, blending with the earthy scent of the rosemary, igniting memories of our late-night escapades.

"Now that's a smell I can get behind," Max said, leaning in to inhale deeply. "If we could bottle this, we'd have the best perfume on the market."

I chuckled, pouring the warm chocolate over the chopped rosemary. "Just don't go wearing it. I can't have customers mistaking you for a chocolate-scented candle."

"Why not? It could be a new marketing strategy," he quipped, grinning as he expertly stirred the mixture. "I'll be the candle that brings all the customers to the yard."

I rolled my eyes playfully, the familiar banter igniting a spark I had almost forgotten. We moved in sync, as if the rhythm of our past was drawing us closer. Each truffle we crafted together was a step toward reclaiming what we had almost lost—a piece of our connection, a glimmer of hope for what could be.

As the evening wore on, the laughter echoed louder, intermingling with the clinking of bowls and the rustle of chocolate wrappers, creating a symphony of camaraderie. With each creation, we tasted, evaluated, and laughed, the tension from earlier dissipating like sugar melting into warm cream. By the time we had concocted our latest batch of daring flavors, I felt a warmth blossoming in my chest, a flicker of the joy we had once taken for granted.

"Alright, last round," I declared, eyeing a jar filled with unexpected chili flakes. "Let's go bold."

Max raised an eyebrow, his expression a mix of intrigue and concern. "Chili? You're really going to test my taste buds tonight, aren't you?"

"Only if you promise to keep an open mind," I challenged, our eyes locking in a playful standoff.

With a flick of my wrist, I tossed a pinch of chili flakes into the warm chocolate, and we watched in awe as it swirled, transforming into something both beautiful and terrifying. "To the bold and the brave!" I proclaimed, raising an imaginary glass.

"To the bold and the brave," he echoed, and as our laughter filled the shop once more, I felt the fractures in my heart beginning to mend, one truffle at a time.

As the evening wore on, we danced through the chaos of melted chocolate and scattered ingredients like two artists caught in a playful frenzy, each flavor a brushstroke on our shared canvas. Max and I crafted wild combinations that should have never worked together—lavender infused with chili, dark chocolate kissed with hints of orange zest, and one particularly disastrous experiment involving almond butter that somehow ended up with a splash of pickle juice. With each new truffle, we tossed our heads back in laughter, the sound cascading through the shop and drowning out the ghosts of our earlier hesitations.

"Okay, I have to say, pickle juice is not the secret ingredient I envisioned for our triumphant return," I said, grimacing as I fished one of the disastrous truffles from the bowl. "I think this one might need a sacrificial taste tester."

Max leaned in, a conspiratorial grin dancing on his lips. "You know what they say: behind every successful chocolatier is a brave soul willing to suffer for the art."

With a theatrical flair, he popped the rogue truffle into his mouth, his face transforming from cheeky confidence to bewildered surprise. I could hardly contain my laughter as he fought through the mingled flavors, trying to mask his shock. "You know," he said, voice muffled, "it's not awful, just... uniquely challenging."

"Uniquely challenging? Is that what they're calling culinary disasters these days?" I teased, folding my arms and raising an eyebrow. "I think we might need to rethink our marketing strategy."

"Rethink? No, no, I'm more of a 'embrace the chaos' kind of guy," he replied, still chewing as if to prove his point. "I think we could call it 'Adventurous Delight.'"

"More like 'Mystery Box of Regret,'" I countered, snorting with laughter. The warmth between us felt almost palpable, a thread of connection pulling us closer with each shared moment, each playful jab at one another.

Eventually, we decided to revisit our culinary roots, crafting a classic dark chocolate truffle with just a hint of sea salt. The familiar rhythm returned as we worked side by side, our movements fluid, each action imbued with the easy companionship we had nearly lost. I watched as Max melted the chocolate, the glossy surface shimmering like polished obsidian, while I prepared the ganache with a delicate hand.

"It's funny, isn't it?" I mused, trying to keep my tone light, even as the underlying seriousness threatened to bubble up. "How something as simple as chocolate can pull us back together?"

Max paused, his brow furrowing slightly as he considered my words. "It's not just the chocolate. It's the memories we've tied to it. All those late nights, the laughter, the way we challenged each other. That's what makes it special."

His voice was low, almost reverent, and for a moment, the air thickened with a shared understanding. I nodded, feeling the flutter in my stomach return, a blend of nostalgia and yearning. "I remember when we first opened the shop. I was terrified. I thought I'd fail. But you..."

"I believed in you," he interjected, a gentle smile playing on his lips. "You were the heart of this place. Your passion was infectious."

A silence fell between us, the kind that felt heavy with potential. I was struck by the realization that beneath the laughter and the shared recipes, there was still an undercurrent of tension lingering, a question that loomed over us like a dark cloud threatening to burst. I could sense it in the way Max's gaze lingered on me, the unspoken words teetering on the edge of his tongue.

As if sensing my thoughts, he shifted the conversation, his tone suddenly more serious. "What if we used this opportunity to not only experiment but to really explore what we want for the shop? To reimagine it completely?"

The thought sent a jolt through me. "You mean, like a complete overhaul? New recipes, new branding?"

"Exactly! A fresh start, but with the heart of what we've always been. It could be exciting!" He leaned closer, his enthusiasm infectious. "We could tap into flavors that reflect who we are now, not just who we were."

The idea danced in my mind, igniting a spark of inspiration. "That could be amazing! I've always wanted to create a line of chocolates that represent different emotions. Each flavor could tell a story—happiness, nostalgia, even heartbreak."

"Heartbreak? Now that's intriguing," he said, tilting his head thoughtfully. "What would that taste like? A bitter chocolate with a hint of salt, maybe?"

I chuckled, my heart racing at the idea of exploring such depths. "Or perhaps a combination of dark chocolate and tart cherries—a beautiful representation of something bittersweet."

"Okay, I'm on board," he said, his eyes brightening. "But I get dibs on the 'joy' flavor. I'm thinking something rich and creamy, like a perfect salted caramel."

The lightness in the air was electric as we tossed around ideas, the brainstorming session turning into a playful battle of wits. We discussed flavors, textures, and names, our creativity flowing like melted chocolate, unrestrained and bold. Every suggestion felt like a step further away from the shadows that had loomed over us.

But as we immersed ourselves in this newfound energy, a sudden noise shattered our bubble—a loud crash from the back of the shop. My heart lurched as I turned toward the sound, dread settling in the pit of my stomach. "What was that?" I asked, the lightness of our earlier conversation slipping away.

"I don't know, but it didn't sound good," Max said, his brows furrowing in concern. We both exchanged anxious glances before instinct kicked in.

"Let's check it out," I urged, stepping cautiously toward the back room, my heart racing as the shadows danced along the walls. The shop, once a sanctuary filled with laughter and creativity, suddenly felt ominous, as if the walls themselves held secrets we had yet to uncover.

As we pushed through the door, the sight before us sent a chill racing down my spine. The shelves were overturned, ingredients strewn about like confetti after a wild party, but there was no sign of a celebration—only chaos. A figure loomed in the corner, their back to us, seemingly rummaging through our supplies.

"Who's there?" Max's voice was steady, but I could hear the tension underneath, a protective instinct kicking in.

The figure turned slowly, and my breath caught in my throat as recognition washed over me. "What are you doing here?" I gasped, the reality of the moment crashing down like the shelves that had fallen.

The face that met mine was familiar yet foreign, a specter from the past I had hoped to never see again. The air thickened, the warmth of our earlier camaraderie dissipating as I stood frozen, caught between the safety of my present and the turmoil of my past.

"Surprise," the figure said with a smirk, their eyes glinting with mischief. "I thought it was time for a little reunion."

Chapter 24: A Leap of Faith

After a week filled with heavy silence, I decided to take a leap of faith. It felt like jumping off the edge of a precipice, the kind where you're not quite sure if you'll soar or plummet. But after countless nights spent tossing and turning, haunted by the unspoken words and the cold, hollow space between us, I knew I had to act. The shop, our haven, had turned into a mausoleum of unshared thoughts and unresolved tension. I couldn't let it remain like that. So, I set about crafting a surprise for Max, a way to coax him back into the warmth of our shared world.

As twilight draped its purple cloak over the city, I transformed the bakery into a realm of enchantment. Fairy lights twinkled overhead, their soft glow casting playful shadows on the flour-dusted counters. The aroma of freshly baked bread mingled with the rich scent of chocolate, wrapping around me like a comforting embrace. I draped gauzy fabric over the tables, letting it billow gently in the evening breeze that slipped through the slightly ajar door. I felt a flutter of hope each time I stepped back to admire my handiwork, the space gradually morphing from a mundane bakery into an intimate sanctuary.

I carefully placed a rich chocolate tart—our latest creation—on a small pedestal at the center of the shop. The tart glistened, dark and luscious, topped with a light dusting of cocoa powder and garnished with fresh raspberries. It was an edible ode to everything we had built together, a celebration of flavors that echoed our partnership. I took a moment to breathe it all in, the heady mix of chocolate and sugar combined with the lingering anxiety that simmered beneath my excitement.

When Max finally walked through the door, I could hardly breathe. He paused, his silhouette framed by the soft light spilling from inside. The world outside melted away, leaving just the two of us suspended in this moment. His eyes widened slightly, reflecting surprise that quickly morphed into something softer, more tender. As he stepped further into the shop, the tension that had woven its way into our lives began to dissipate, unraveling like the threads of an old sweater.

"Wow," he said, his voice thick with disbelief. "This looks incredible."

"Thanks," I replied, my heart fluttering in my chest. "I thought we could have a little celebration—just the two of us."

His gaze swept over the decorations, lingering on the tart as if he could sense all the words I hadn't yet spoken infused in the rich chocolate. "You really went all out, didn't you?"

"Only the best for you," I said, trying to keep my tone light even as a weight pressed down on my chest. I could feel the unspoken questions lingering between us, thick and heavy in the air. But for now, I wanted to focus on the moment we shared.

As we settled at the table, I watched him take a bite of the tart, his eyes lighting up with delight. The sound of his laughter, rich and genuine, filled the air and chased away the shadows that had been lurking in the corners of the shop. "This is amazing," he said, his voice muffled by chocolatey goodness. "You've outdone yourself."

We slipped into familiar banter, our words flowing with the ease of well-worn paths. Each shared joke felt like a balm on the scars that had begun to form between us. We recounted our favorite moments from the shop—like the time we accidentally created a pastry so disastrous it became a running joke among our regulars, or the laughter that erupted when we tried to bake a cake for a customer's wedding but forgot the flour.

With each story, the air grew lighter, and I felt the cracks in my heart begin to mend, if only for a moment. "Do you remember the first time we worked together?" I asked, leaning in slightly, my elbows resting on the table.

He chuckled, a low, rich sound that made my heart flutter. "How could I forget? You had flour everywhere—on your face, in your hair. I thought you were trying to sabotage me."

"Oh, please. You were the one who accidentally turned on the mixer with no lid. Flour went everywhere. It looked like a snowstorm hit the bakery!"

We laughed, and in that moment, I could almost believe that the weight between us had lifted entirely. But as the laughter faded, reality seeped back in, bringing with it the uncertainty I had tried so hard to keep at bay.

Taking a deep breath, I steadied myself, the flickering light casting shadows across my face. "Max," I began, my voice trembling slightly, "there's something I need to tell you."

His gaze locked onto mine, a mix of curiosity and apprehension reflected in his eyes. I could feel my heart racing, each beat echoing in the silence that had fallen between us. "I can't lose you," I confessed, vulnerability spilling out in a torrent. "I can't lose this shop. You mean too much to me."

The words hung in the air, raw and unrefined, like the freshly rolled dough we often worked with. I watched as a myriad of emotions played across his face—confusion, realization, hope. "You won't lose me," he finally said, his voice steady but soft. "But we need to talk about everything. About us."

A wave of relief washed over me, but with it came a tremor of anxiety. I had taken the leap, but the ground still felt shaky beneath my feet. As we sat there, surrounded by twinkling lights and the comforting scent of chocolate, I couldn't help but wonder if this was the beginning of something new or the final act of a beautiful story that was slipping through my fingers.

The moment hung between us, suspended in the sweet fragrance of chocolate and the warm glow of twinkling lights. Max's eyes held a mixture of surprise and something deeper, something I had been desperate to see. Yet, as I leaned closer, the flicker of hope in his gaze wavered slightly. The weight of what I had just confessed settled around us like a thick fog, and for a brief moment, I was afraid he might retreat, just as he had during our recent silence.

He swallowed hard, the tension in the air palpable. "You won't lose me," he said, and his voice, though steady, betrayed an undercurrent of uncertainty. "But we need to figure this out. I can't ignore what's been happening between us."

My heart sank. I had feared this moment, the reality of dissecting our relationship after the fragile reprieve of laughter and dessert. "What do you mean?" I asked, desperately trying to keep my tone light, as if we were discussing a recipe rather than the state of our hearts. "Isn't that what we're doing right now? Figuring it out?"

Max leaned back in his chair, arms crossing as he contemplated my words. "It's more complicated than that. We can't pretend everything is fine just because we shared a chocolate tart and some laughs. I've been thinking a lot about... us."

I felt my chest tighten, a familiar dance of anxiety and anticipation sparking to life within me. "Thinking is good, right?" I tried for a smile, but it faltered under the weight of his expression. "I mean, I hope you were thinking about all the ways we can dominate the pastry scene together. Our next big hit—'Max and Mia's Flour Power.' We can conquer the world one croissant at a time!"

Max's lips twitched, caught between a smile and a sigh. "I was thinking more along the lines of how we navigate the feelings that have been brewing. This shop—it's become our everything, but that makes things tricky."

He had a point, and it stung to admit it. The bakery was our refuge, but it also felt like a delicate balancing act. "You mean we're going to have to talk about... feelings?" I cringed, trying to inject some levity into the moment. "I thought we were avoiding that. I didn't bring tissues for a reason."

He chuckled softly, the tension easing just a bit. "It's a necessary evil, I'm afraid. We've been so focused on the shop and making things work here that we've let everything else hang in the balance. But I don't want to lose what we have. I just—"

"Just what?" I pressed, leaning forward, intrigued and terrified in equal measure. "Just want to go back to pretending we're only business partners?"

"Honestly? Yes." He sighed, running a hand through his hair, tousling it into delightful disarray. "But I also know that's impossible. It's a tangled web we've woven, and I'm not sure how to untangle it without losing some threads along the way."

I blinked at him, trying to comprehend the magnitude of what he was saying. "You think we're too tangled to work this out?" The words felt heavier than the flour bags I lifted every day.

Max's gaze locked onto mine, piercing yet soft. "No, I think we're more than capable of figuring it out. But I'm scared. Scared of losing you, scared of losing the shop. You know, just the typical existential crisis." He offered a wry smile, and for a heartbeat, it felt like we had stepped back into the comfort of our routine.

"Ah, the good old existential crisis. Can't have a bakery without one," I teased, but my voice was laced with a sincerity that seemed to resonate in the space between us. "You know I'm here for the ride. It's not just the pastries we're making; it's our lives, right?"

"Exactly." His eyes softened, and I saw a flicker of hope. "But we need to be honest with each other. I've been thinking—maybe we should take a step back from everything. A little space might give us clarity."

The suggestion struck me like a bolt from the blue, unraveling the warmth that had built between us. "Space? You want to put distance between us?" My voice trembled, and I couldn't mask the fear creeping into my chest.

"No, no, not in a 'let's break up' way," he rushed to clarify. "More like a chance to figure out what we really want. We've been so enmeshed in this shop, in each other, that it's hard to see the bigger picture. I think we need to rediscover who we are, separately, before we can figure out how to be together."

The idea felt foreign, like offering a lifeboat to someone who feared drowning. "I'm not sure I like the sound of that. What if space means we drift apart? What if you realize you don't need me?" The thought hung there, heavy and raw.

He reached across the table, his fingers brushing against mine, sending a spark up my arm. "That's just it, Mia. I don't want to lose you. But I also don't want to pretend everything is perfect when we both know it isn't. We need to be sure about what we want, and that means looking at this from all angles. I can't make decisions for you, and you can't make them for me. We have to decide together."

The weight of his words settled in my chest, a blend of dread and hope swirling within me. "So, what are we doing? Do we put the shop on hold? Close the doors while we find ourselves?"

He shook his head, a small, determined smile playing on his lips. "No, I think we keep going. But we set some boundaries. We'll still work together, but we take time for ourselves, too. Maybe a night or two a week where we don't talk about the shop or each other. Just... live."

"Live?" I echoed, the concept both exhilarating and terrifying. "What does that even look like? I haven't just 'lived' in years."

"It looks like rediscovering what makes you, well, you. We both need to remember what we love outside these walls. It could be anything—hobbies, friends, even just some quiet time alone. We're not just bakers, Mia; we're people."

I watched him, the soft light playing across his features, revealing a depth I hadn't fully appreciated before. This was Max—my partner, my friend, and possibly something more. And in that moment, I realized that perhaps this leap of faith was about more than just saving our relationship. It was about embracing the uncertainty and finding strength in the unknown, together and apart.

"Okay," I said slowly, a sense of resolve building within me. "Let's do it. But we're not closing the shop completely. I'm not giving up on my pastries or my favorite person."

Max's smile broadened, illuminating the dimness of our previous discussions. "Deal. We'll find a way to balance it all."

As we sat there, fingers entwined across the table, the flickering lights casting a gentle glow around us, I felt the heavy weight of uncertainty transform into a lightness that set my heart free. It was a beginning of sorts—neither of us knew where this path would lead, but it felt right, like the perfect recipe still waiting to be perfected.

A glimmer of understanding flickered in Max's eyes, and I could sense the enormity of what we were attempting to navigate. The atmosphere shifted, lightening as we leaned into our new reality, both thrilled and terrified by the prospect of redefining our relationship. "So, we're really doing this? Setting boundaries?" I asked, half-joking, half-hopeful. "Because I'm not great with rules unless it involves baking."

"Right," he said, laughter spilling from his lips. "No rule-breaking. Only cookie-baking." His gaze locked onto mine, a warmth radiating between us that melted the lingering tension. "But seriously, I think we'll both feel better if we have a little space. Plus, we can find out what sparks joy for us outside of this place."

"Joy," I mused. "Isn't that what they say we should chase? What about you? What brings you joy?"

"Honestly?" He paused, his brow furrowed slightly as he pondered. "It's the little things. Like watching the sunrise while sipping on an overly sweet coffee or catching up on the latest mystery series. You'd be surprised how much I enjoy just curling up with a book and losing track of time."

I grinned, picturing him bundled up with a cozy blanket, a book resting on his lap while the world outside turned into a blur. "You're such a softie," I teased, nudging him playfully. "I never would've guessed. But I guess I should've known the guy who gets excited over perfectly baked goods would have a soft spot for mysteries."

"And what about you?" he countered, leaning in closer, his interest genuine. "What lights that fire in your soul, other than baking, of course?"

"Definitely the thrill of creating something new," I replied, my heart fluttering as I shared this piece of myself. "There's nothing like the feeling of taking a risk, like when we created that lavender-infused macaroon that somehow became a hit. I love experimenting, and that little rush of excitement? It makes my heart race."

"Lavender macaroons?" He raised an eyebrow, the corner of his mouth quirking up. "You should know better than to mention that when we're trying to steer clear of pastries."

"Hey, I'm just saying! It was a risk worth taking," I shot back, laughter dancing between us like the lights overhead. "And there's always room for a little fun, right?"

The conversation flowed effortlessly, our connection gradually unearthing layers of vulnerability and understanding. We talked about everything and nothing, weaving a tapestry of light-hearted anecdotes and serious discussions. Yet, amidst the playful banter, I couldn't shake the nagging feeling that beneath this newfound clarity lay deeper issues waiting to be addressed.

As the night wore on, the bakery took on a surreal quality, like a warm cocoon wrapping around us. The soft glow of the fairy lights painted our faces in a golden hue, illuminating the path we were starting to navigate. Yet, just as I felt the embrace of optimism, a shadow flickered in the corner of my mind—doubt.

"What if this space doesn't change anything?" I asked, my voice barely above a whisper. "What if we still end up lost?"

Max's expression shifted, the mirth fading momentarily. "Mia, we can't control everything. That's part of the uncertainty. But I believe in us. We've weathered storms before. This is just a different kind."

"But what if one of those storms is too big?" I questioned, the fear creeping back into my tone. "What if it washes everything away?"

He reached across the table, his hand warm against mine. "Then we rebuild. Together. But first, we have to give ourselves a chance to breathe."

His grip was steady, anchoring me as I wrestled with the waves of anxiety that threatened to overwhelm my resolve. But even as I clung to his words, uncertainty nagged at me. Could we really navigate this uncharted territory without losing sight of one another?

We lingered in the moment, savoring the intimacy of our shared silence, until the sudden ringing of my phone shattered the tranquility like a glass dropped on a tiled floor. I fished it out of my pocket, a frown creasing my forehead as I saw the caller ID flash across the screen. It was my sister, Claire, and the urgency in her voice when I answered sent a chill down my spine.

"Mia, I need you to come home. It's about Mom," she said, her tone a mix of panic and determination.

"What's wrong?" I asked, my heart racing, the warm bubble of the evening suddenly bursting.

"It's serious. Just come home, please." The line went dead before I could even respond, leaving me staring at the screen, confusion spiraling into dread.

"Is everything okay?" Max asked, concern etched across his face as he noticed my sudden change in demeanor.

"I... I don't know," I stammered, the panic from my sister's words clashing with the serenity of our evening. "My sister just called. She said it's about Mom. She sounded upset."

Max's expression shifted, shifting from concern to immediate understanding. "Then you should go. You don't have to explain. Just... go."

"But what about..." I faltered, my heart torn between my obligations at home and the fragile moment I had built here with him.

"We'll figure it out later," he insisted, his voice steady despite the uncertainty crackling in the air. "You need to be there for your family. We can talk more once things settle down."

I nodded, fear bubbling beneath the surface as I grabbed my jacket and phone. "I'll call you when I know more," I promised, but as I stepped toward the door, I felt an unease settle over me like a shadow. The warmth of our connection felt miles away, replaced by the icy grip of the unknown.

As I stepped into the cool night air, the weight of the world bore down on my shoulders. I cast one last glance back at the shop, its glowing lights a beacon of comfort, and my heart twisted with a sense of loss. Could I really face what awaited me at home without losing everything I had just begun to reclaim?

The car ride felt surreal, the streets blurring past in a wash of colors and lights. Anxiety coiled tighter within me, every bump in the road amplifying my dread. As I reached the familiar threshold of my family's home, a pit of worry formed in my stomach.

I opened the door, the usual scents of home—baking spices and the lingering aroma of coffee—greeted me, but something felt off. The air was thick with an unspoken tension, the kind that seemed to vibrate with fear.

"Claire?" I called out, my voice echoing in the stillness. The silence that followed sent a shiver down my spine, a sense of foreboding creeping in.

Just as I stepped further into the house, I caught sight of Claire in the living room, her face pale, eyes wide with unshed tears. "Mia, thank God you're here," she said, her voice trembling.

"What's going on?" I pressed, my heart racing as she stepped closer, anxiety radiating from her like an electric current.

"It's Mom. She... she's been taken to the hospital," Claire said, the words falling from her lips like a heavy stone.

The world tilted, the ground beneath me seeming to give way as shock washed over me. "Taken to the hospital? Why? What happened?"

"It's serious, Mia. They think she might—"

Before she could finish, my phone buzzed in my pocket. I pulled it out, my heart racing, and saw a text from Max that sent ice flooding through my veins. "I need to talk to you. It's about the shop. Something's come up."

In that instant, the two worlds I had tried to keep separate collided, a fierce storm brewing within me. My heart was torn between family and the fragile connection I had built with Max, both now hanging in the balance, each moment pressing heavier than the last.

Chapter 25: Shadows of the Past

The bell above the door jingled with a cheery tinkle, announcing Lily's arrival like a misguided alarm. I straightened up behind the counter, instinctively brushing a loose strand of hair behind my ear, a nervous habit that had resurfaced with the sudden reappearance of someone who knew too much about me, and far too little of what I had become. The scent of freshly brewed coffee mingled with the buttery notes of pastries cooling on the rack behind me, filling the small shop with warmth, but all I felt was a chill creeping in.

Lily was a whirlwind in a designer coat, her presence cutting through the cozy ambiance like a knife through warm bread. Her hair fell in perfect waves, the kind that could only be achieved through both skill and a small fortune in hair products. She glided across the floor with the confidence of someone who believed every step they took was an entrance, a spotlight finding them in the mundane. When her eyes landed on me, they sparkled like diamonds—sharp and unyielding.

"Look who it is!" she exclaimed, her voice laced with a sugary sweetness that felt overly familiar, almost too much like a candy-coated invitation to a trap. "I can't believe you're still here, in this adorable little shop." Her gaze swept around the quaint interior, pausing momentarily on the chalkboard sign advertising today's special. "It's so... quaint."

I bit back a smirk, knowing full well that 'quaint' was code for 'not what I expected.' My little shop, a sanctuary I had built from scratch, was anything but quaint to me. It was a tapestry of sweat and passion, every corner filled with the love of artisanal coffee and the aroma of baked goods, but I could feel her insincerity lingering like smoke in the air.

"Thanks," I managed, forcing a smile that felt more like a grimace. "It's... working out."

"Of course it is," she replied, leaning against the counter as if it were a bar in some posh Manhattan lounge. "I knew you'd make it. You always had that spark." The flattery was thick enough to slice, but I didn't trust it. I could practically see the gears turning in her mind, each compliment a carefully calculated move in a game of chess I didn't even know I was playing.

Her eyes darted around, taking in the mismatched chairs, the vintage mugs lining the shelves, and the patrons curled up in corners, sipping lattes and flipping through books. The more she admired, the more I felt the urge to defend my choices. But who was I defending them from? Her or myself?

"Have you met Max?" I gestured toward the back, where he was meticulously arranging freshly baked croissants, his brow furrowed in concentration. The sunlight poured through the window, catching in his dark hair, and for a moment, he looked almost ethereal, a stark contrast to the whirlwind standing next to me.

Lily's interest piqued, her eyes lighting up as she turned to watch him. "Oh, he's cute," she chirped, her tone shifting effortlessly into one of flirtation. It twisted something deep within me, a primal instinct to defend what I had slowly cultivated over these past months. I didn't want to be the girl from the past; I wanted to be someone worthy of him, someone who didn't flinch at a flirtation that danced dangerously close to my own insecurities.

I watched her saunter toward him, her hips swaying with that irritating confidence that felt like a challenge. "Max!" she called, her voice saccharine and sweet. "I can't believe you've been hiding in this gem of a shop!"

His head turned, surprise crossing his features before a smile broke free. "Lily! What a surprise." He stepped away from his task, wiping his hands on his apron, completely unaware of the tempest brewing within me.

"Can I get you a coffee?" I offered, injecting a bit of bravado into my words, but it came out more like a plea for distraction. I busied myself with the espresso machine, forcing my mind to focus on the rhythmic hum and the rich, dark brew that bubbled forth, as if I could drown out the sound of my insecurities rattling around like marbles in a jar.

"Espresso, please. I have a feeling I'll need it," Lily chimed, her eyes sparkling with mischief. I couldn't help but wonder what secrets she carried from our past, what stories she might unravel, and whether any of them would put me at risk. As I poured the steaming shot into a delicate cup, the steam clouding my vision, I realized I had been holding my breath.

"You're back in town for long?" Max asked, his voice cutting through the fog of my thoughts.

"Oh, just for a few days. I have some business meetings, but I couldn't resist popping in to see my favorite little barista." The way she looked at him made my stomach twist, a mixture of irritation and a sting of envy.

"Lucky for you, she's one of the best," he said, tossing me a smile that was meant for me, but somehow felt like it was being shared. "You should try the blueberry scones. They're amazing."

I handed Lily her coffee, watching as she took a long, dramatic sip, her eyes widening as if the taste was some life-altering revelation. "Mmm! This is divine. You're such a genius, really."

"Thanks," I muttered, forcing a smile that felt more like a grimace. Each word of praise dripped with a sticky sweetness that made me want to roll my eyes. "I try."

"Lily's always been good at flattering people," I added, trying to keep my tone light, but the edge crept in. Max caught it, glancing at me with that familiar furrow of concern in his brow.

"Oh, I don't need to flatter anyone," she laughed, tossing her hair back. "I just tell it like it is."

"Or how you want it to be," I shot back, a little too sharply.

The smile on her face faltered for just a second, a glimmer of surprise flickering in her eyes before she recovered, her demeanor shifting like the wind changing direction. "Touché, my dear. Touché."

As the tension hung between us like a thick fog, I couldn't shake the feeling that I was caught in a game I didn't even know I was playing, where the stakes felt higher than they ever had before. In that moment, the warmth of the shop felt distant, as if the walls were closing in, leaving me standing on the precipice of something I didn't understand—a past rearing its head and a future I feared would slip through my fingers.

I was trapped in a peculiar kind of limbo, one that blended the sweet smell of coffee with an acrid tinge of anxiety. Lily had commandeered the space, her laughter echoing off the walls like an unwanted echo, demanding attention. She leaned in closer to Max, her tone conspiratorial, as if they were sharing secrets that should never have crossed my threshold. I busied myself with a fresh batch of blueberry scones, the oven's warmth wrapping around me like a protective cloak, but it did little to stave off the gnawing unease that crept along my spine.

"Tell me, Max, how do you get the croissants to be so perfectly flaky? It's an art, isn't it?" Lily leaned on the counter, her fingers tracing the wooden surface with a deliberation that felt far too intimate. I could feel my heart thumping in my chest, a drumbeat of worry. Would he be charmed by her soft-spoken compliments? Would he get lost in the theatrics of her stories about New York's elite? I swallowed hard, the taste of panic almost as bitter as the espresso brewing nearby.

"Honestly?" he replied, a hint of mischief lighting up his eyes. "It's all in the butter. I use a ridiculous amount. My cholesterol probably hates me, but the croissants don't lie." He grinned, the warmth of his smile radiating toward me, grounding me, even as I felt my breath hitch.

Lily laughed, a sound that sparkled and danced, but beneath it, I sensed an undercurrent of competition. "Well, it's working. You might have a future as a culinary star, Max. You could be in New York, mingling with the best." The way she said "New York" rolled off her tongue like a secret ingredient, full of allure, and I bristled.

"Thanks, but I think I'm pretty happy right here," he replied, glancing my way as if to catch my eye, as if we were bound by an invisible thread. My heart swelled with gratitude, yet the knot in my stomach tightened. Did he mean it? Or was he simply being polite? I wanted to believe he wasn't captivated by the glimmer of someone like Lily, who moved through life like a comet—brilliant, fiery, and destined to leave a trail of ashes.

I leaned against the counter, arms crossed tightly as I tried to maintain an air of casual indifference, but every laugh from Lily felt like a jab, each innocent comment a reminder of what I lacked. She was the picture of confidence, effortlessly floating from one charming remark to the next, while I was rooted in my own insecurities, clinging to the familiarity of the café like a lifebuoy in turbulent seas.

"So, what brings you back to this little slice of heaven?" I asked, forcing a smile that felt like it was etched into my face. "Surely, there's more to your trip than just dropping by a random coffee shop."

"Oh, you know," she said, waving her hand dismissively. "Just some meetings with investors, trying to launch my next big thing." Her eyes sparkled with the thrill of ambition, and I felt my insides twist again. "But I just had to see how you were doing. I mean, you always were the most talented one in our circle."

Her flattery was a double-edged sword, and I could almost see the glint of the blade. "Right, because we all know the true measure of success is how many scones you can whip up in a morning," I replied, my voice dripping with a sarcasm I hoped would veil my discomfort.

"Oh, please," she laughed, the sound as light as the foam on her cappuccino. "You know I've always admired you. You've got this... homey vibe going on. People come in here and feel all warm and fuzzy. I mean, who wouldn't want to sit here for hours?"

I couldn't tell if she genuinely meant it or if it was all part of her grand strategy. It made my stomach flip, that combination of admiration and jealousy swirling inside me like the steam rising from the espresso machine. I needed to steer this conversation away from whatever game she was playing, but before I could formulate a thought, Max interjected.

"Honestly, I think it's more about the coffee and the scones," he said with a charming grin that made my heart flutter just a bit. "And of course, it helps to have a good barista." He flashed me a wink that sent a rush of warmth through me, reminding me of the connection we had built over the months, the laughter shared, and the quiet moments of understanding.

Lily seemed undeterred. "Maybe we should do a collaboration sometime, Max! I could introduce you to some fabulous chefs in the city. You'd be a hit!" She leaned closer, her enthusiasm palpable, as if she were trying to ensnare him with her ambitious vision.

I felt a knot of frustration tighten in my chest. "And what would that entail, exactly?" I couldn't help but interject, my voice edged with the sharpness of protectiveness. "I mean, do you even know how many mornings Max has spent perfecting his recipes? This isn't just a side gig for him."

Lily turned to me, a mixture of surprise and amusement crossing her features. "Oh, darling, it's just a suggestion! It's not like I was asking him to abandon his little café."

"Yeah, no offense, but I think I'll pass," Max said, his tone light but firm. The way he stood his ground sent a thrill of pride coursing through me, even as my heart raced with the uncertainty of the moment.

The atmosphere shifted, a palpable tension hanging in the air as we navigated this delicate dance of old friendships and new rivalries. It was like watching a game unfold, where everyone held cards they weren't ready to reveal. Lily's smile faltered, and for the first time, I saw a crack in her polished facade.

"Suit yourself," she said, her voice cool, as if she had simply brushed aside an insignificant detail. But her eyes were sharp, calculating. "Just remember, the city has a lot to offer."

"And so does this little shop," I retorted, meeting her gaze, my confidence flaring. "We're good here. Really good."

Max nodded in agreement, and I felt a surge of gratitude toward him. Maybe it was the warmth of the coffee shop, or perhaps it was something deeper—a connection that grew stronger with every shared smile, every playful jab. But as I looked at Lily, I realized this wasn't just about her; it was about me, my fears, and the life I was trying to build.

"Can I get a croissant to go with that coffee?" I asked, breaking the tension, desperate to find humor in the situation. "Or do I need to schedule that?"

Lily's laughter rang out, a rich, full sound that startled me. "You're cheeky! I like that!"

"Yeah, well, it's a defense mechanism," I shot back, unable to keep the playful banter at bay.

As the laughter wove around us, it felt like a fragile peace had settled over the moment. But deep down, I knew that beneath the surface, the currents were still swirling. And while I had managed to hold my own for now, I couldn't shake the feeling that the real battle was just beginning, one that would force me to confront the shadows of my past and the uncertainty of my future.

The air in the café was thick with an unspoken tension, a lingering unease as we navigated our interactions like ships passing in a stormy sea. The laughter that had bubbled up so easily moments ago faded into a fragile silence, punctuated only by the soft clinking of cups and the distant sound of the coffee grinder. Lily stood there, a shining star in a constellation I didn't recognize, and I felt increasingly like a shadow cast by her light.

"Let me help you with those scones," Lily offered, a sharp glimmer of competitiveness in her voice. She stepped behind the counter, slipping into my space as if she belonged there. Her fingers moved deftly, but her presence felt invasive, like a storm cloud threatening to unleash rain over my carefully cultivated garden. I watched, half-heartedly, as she arranged the pastries on a plate, her movements graceful, precise—a dancer in a show I had not auditioned for.

"Actually, I've got it covered," I replied, my tone light, but the firmness in my voice held a hint of desperation. It was my domain, my little sanctuary, and yet here she was, charming everyone in sight, her laughter ringing like wind chimes. The patrons had started to turn their attention to her, and with every smile she flashed, I felt the warmth of my own confidence flicker.

"Oh, come on! It's all about collaboration, right?" Lily said, her voice a playful lilt that seemed to dance around the edges of insincerity. "Besides, if I can help you, think of the exposure! You could be the next big thing in culinary delights."

Her suggestion stung like a bee; it was simultaneously flattering and dismissive, as if she were offering me a lifeline while holding me at arm's length. I took a deep breath, steeling myself against the mounting frustration. "I appreciate the offer, but I prefer to keep things a bit... personal."

"Personal, huh?" she shot back, a wry smile playing on her lips. "Sounds like a euphemism for 'I like to do everything myself.'"

"Maybe it is," I countered, refusing to back down. "But in this case, it's my business."

Max stepped in, sensing the rising tension. "You know, sometimes it helps to share the load, especially when it comes to creativity." He glanced at me, his eyes soft but firm, as if urging me to see the bigger picture, while also reminding Lily of my hard work.

"Creative collaboration can be inspiring, but sometimes it dilutes the message," I added, crossing my arms defiantly. "I mean, who wants a scone with too many cooks in the kitchen?"

Lily raised an eyebrow, amusement flickering in her eyes. "That's true, but sometimes a little chaos can spark something incredible."

"Like your chaotic life in New York?" I shot back before I could stop myself. "I mean, who wouldn't want to get tangled up in all that?"

Her expression momentarily faltered, revealing a flash of irritation before she masked it with her trademark charm. "Touché. But maybe I've learned a thing or two about thriving in chaos. You know, from the school of hard knocks."

Her words were loaded with unspoken challenges, and I felt the tension crackle between us, as sharp as a fresh brew of espresso. I could see Max watching the exchange, concern etched on his face, but there was also a spark of amusement, as if he found our banter entertaining.

"Why don't we just settle this over a taste test?" Max suggested, trying to break the tension with his signature easy-going attitude. "Let's see who can whip up the better scone. A friendly competition, perhaps?"

"Now you're talking!" Lily clapped her hands together, her excitement infectious. "I'm always up for a little challenge. What do you think, darling?"

I forced a smile, knowing I was about to step onto a battleground I had not prepared for. "Sure, why not? Let's see what you've got."

As we prepared for the impromptu bake-off, I tried to steady my nerves, reminding myself that this was my space. It was more than just pastries; it was my passion, my sanctuary, and I wouldn't let her make me feel small. I gathered the ingredients with precision, each item a lifeline to my own confidence. Flour dusted the counter, and the sweet scent of sugar filled the air as I whipped up my batter, trying to drown out the mounting sense of competition.

Lily, for all her flashiness, moved with the precision of someone who knew their way around the kitchen, and it unnerved me. As we both stirred and folded, the atmosphere simmered with an intensity that matched the heat of the oven.

"You're not really scared of a little competition, are you?" she teased, her voice a sultry whisper as she leaned closer, the scent of her perfume filling my senses.

"Not at all," I replied, forcing my tone to remain light even as my heart raced. "But then again, I'm not the one who's used to crowds. You might be all flash, but I've got substance."

Her laughter was rich, echoing in the small space as if she were unfazed by my jabs. "Substance, huh? Is that what you think you're serving? I mean, it's adorable, really, but I'm a little hungry for something more."

"Hungry for what, exactly? Validation from your old friends?" I shot back, my voice steady despite the tremors of insecurity that gripped me.

The challenge escalated as the oven timer ticked down, the anticipation growing thick and palpable. Max drifted between us, checking on our progress, his supportive demeanor somehow keeping the atmosphere buoyant.

Just then, the bell above the door jingled again, a sound that pulled our focus. I turned to see a familiar face standing in the doorway, someone I hadn't expected. It was Charlie, my old college roommate, her curly hair bouncing as she stepped in, a whirlwind of energy that could rival even Lily's.

"Hey, I heard the coffee here is amazing!" she called out, her eyes sparkling with excitement. "And what's this? A baking contest?"

"Welcome to the chaos!" I laughed, feeling a mixture of relief and dread. Charlie's unexpected arrival was like a fresh breath of air, but it also added another layer of complexity to the competition.

Lily flashed a bright smile, as if welcoming a potential ally into her corner. "You just might want to stick around, Charlie. This is about to get interesting."

As we resumed our baking, Charlie slipped behind the counter, instantly drawn into the banter. "Who's winning?" she asked, glancing from me to Lily, her brows raised in playful challenge.

"I am," Lily declared with all the confidence of a champion.

"Not if I can help it," I muttered under my breath, my determination solidifying with each passing moment.

The oven chimed, and we pulled our creations out, steam wafting into the air, the aroma intoxicating. As we presented our scones, I noticed the way Charlie's eyes flicked between our offerings, her excitement palpable.

"Let's taste!" she suggested, the thrill of competition lighting up her features.

Just as we were about to dig in, the door swung open again, this time with an urgency that sliced through the lighthearted atmosphere. A man in a suit strode in, his presence commanding and serious. He scanned the room, his gaze landing on Lily first, and I felt a jolt of unease.

"Lily," he said, his voice low and urgent, "we need to talk. Now."

The tension in the café shifted dramatically, the warmth replaced by a chilling apprehension. My heart raced as I glanced at Max, who seemed equally perplexed. Lily's smile faded, and the confident air that had surrounded her evaporated as the man stepped closer.

"What's going on?" she asked, her voice suddenly tight, as if the stakes had shifted in a game none of us were prepared to play.

I felt a surge of uncertainty course through me. Was this truly a friendly competition anymore, or had I unwittingly stepped into something far more complex? The scones, once a source of pride and camaraderie, now felt overshadowed by secrets and shadows creeping in from the past.

The man's words lingered in the air, heavy with implication, and I could hardly breathe, sensing the shift in the tide that would change everything in a heartbeat.

Chapter 26: Clashing Worlds

The days passed in a blur, the kind of hazy disorientation that only comes from being in love and utterly lost at the same time. Each sunrise brought with it a new sense of dread, a weight resting on my chest like a stubborn cloud refusing to dissipate. I wandered through my chocolatier, my sanctuary turned battleground, as doubts festered in the corners of my mind. The sweet scent of melting chocolate that once filled me with joy now felt like an ironic twist, mocking my insecurities as I watched Lily, her laughter chiming like wind chimes on a summer day, flirting with Max in ways that made my heart clench.

I had always prided myself on my resilience, but with Lily around, I felt like a house of cards caught in a draft. Each giggle she tossed his way sent a shiver down my spine, and I couldn't shake the feeling that my world was shifting beneath my feet. The chocolates I crafted, each one a small labor of love, seemed to mock me. They were meant to evoke happiness, to bring comfort, yet here I was, enveloped in jealousy and self-doubt, my artistry feeling as fragile as the delicate sugar flowers I painstakingly designed.

One evening, as we prepared for yet another community event, the air crackled with tension. I watched from the kitchen, my heart sinking as Max and Lily stood outside the front window, illuminated by the warm glow of streetlights. They shared some inside joke, and the way he leaned in, eyes sparkling with a joy I craved, was a dagger to my heart. It was as if the world had divided into two: on one side, the vibrant laughter and connection they shared; on the other, my spiraling insecurities threatening to consume me.

Unable to remain silent, I stormed out, the familiar smell of chocolate suddenly suffocating. "You seem to enjoy her company," I spat, my voice sharp and edged with an anger that surprised even me. I watched as Max's expression faltered, hurt flickering across his face, but I couldn't bring myself to back down. In that moment, it felt like the truth hung in the air, heavy and unyielding.

"Clara, you're reading this all wrong," he said, his voice a mixture of confusion and concern, but my heart had already hardened against him. The tension between us thickened like the molten chocolate I worked with, a bittersweet concoction of longing and resentment swirling together.

I crossed my arms, trying to appear unaffected while my insides twisted in knots. "Am I? Because it sure looks like you're enjoying her attention," I retorted, my words dripping with accusation. The words were like firecrackers, igniting the situation and shattering whatever delicate peace we had built. My mind raced with thoughts of inadequacy, of all the ways I didn't measure up. I could almost hear the invisible comparison meter ticking away as Lily effortlessly charmed her way into Max's world, leaving me to flounder in my own.

His gaze locked onto mine, the intensity of his eyes piercing through the haze of my anger. "I care about you, Clara. You know that," he said, each word heavy with sincerity, but it felt like a lifeline tossed into a stormy sea, and I wasn't sure I could grasp it. The storm roiled inside me, a tempest of fear that maybe I wasn't enough, that my chocolate creations, my late-night experiments with ganache and truffles, paled in comparison to Lily's effortless allure.

"Then why does it feel like I'm losing you?" I whispered, vulnerability creeping in around the edges of my bravado. I hated how raw and exposed I felt, but I couldn't stop the words from spilling out, an uninvited confession I had kept locked away for too long.

Max stepped closer, his presence warm and grounding. "You're not losing me, Clara. I promise. Lily is just...she's just someone I know, and we're getting along, but that doesn't change how I feel about you," he replied, the softness of his tone wrapping around me like a comforting embrace. Yet, I felt like a riddle even I couldn't solve, caught between two worlds that threatened to pull me apart.

But the distance between us felt insurmountable, and I couldn't shake the image of him and Lily laughing together, the carefree way they connected, as if they shared a language I had never learned. "You don't need to be nice about it, Max. Just say it. I'm not what you want," I snapped, the bitterness in my tone a mask for the desperation clawing at my heart.

"Clara, don't say that," he said, the urgency in his voice making me pause. "You are everything I want, but it's like you're standing on the edge, looking in, when you could just step forward. Why are you pushing me away?"

His words struck a chord within me, resonating with a truth I had tried to ignore. Maybe I had been so busy crafting my beautiful chocolates, pouring my heart into each creation, that I hadn't noticed the fragility of my own emotions. The walls I had built to protect myself had become a prison, and the taste of bitterness lingered in my mouth like overcooked sugar.

"Because it's easier to think you don't want me than to risk being vulnerable," I admitted, the confession spilling out before I could rein it in. There was a quiet power in the honesty, a recognition that I had been holding myself back out of fear.

He took a deep breath, the warmth of his hand brushing against mine, igniting a spark I thought I'd lost. "Then let's face this together," he said, his voice steady, unwavering in its resolve. "Don't let her shadow the light we have. You're the one I want by my side, Clara."

In that moment, as I looked into his eyes, I felt the weight of my fears start to lift, the tension easing just enough to allow a glimmer of hope to shine through the cracks. Maybe, just maybe, there was a way to navigate this complicated dance of emotions, to blend our worlds together without losing the sweetness that had first drawn us to each other.

The air crackled with an unspoken tension, a fragile thread woven between us that felt ready to snap. I took a deep breath, steadying myself as I grappled with the whirlwind of emotions swirling in my chest. The weight of my insecurities pressed down like a heavy blanket, stifling my thoughts and drowning out the laughter that had moments ago felt so joyous. I couldn't afford to let doubt creep in; I needed clarity. I needed to reclaim my voice.

"I'm sorry for snapping," I finally said, my tone softer but no less resolute. "It's just... it's hard to watch you be so comfortable with her when I feel like I'm constantly on edge." I caught a glimpse of vulnerability in Max's eyes, a flash of understanding that sparked something within me.

"Clara, listen," he urged, taking a step closer, the warmth radiating from him like the afternoon sun. "I appreciate you being honest. But I wish you could see how incredible you are. You've built this amazing place from scratch. You have a gift."

"Do I? Because sometimes it feels more like I'm just making fancy treats to distract myself from reality," I confessed, the weight of my words hanging in the air. It was unsettling to peel back the layers of my defenses, to let him see the messy truths I often concealed beneath my chocolate-coated facade.

"Maybe it's not just about the chocolates," Max said thoughtfully, his voice steady. "Maybe it's about what they represent: joy, comfort, a little magic in the world. You're not just a chocolatier; you're a creator of experiences."

His words wrapped around my heart, igniting a flicker of something I had buried deep—hope. It was maddening how easily he could make me feel like I was both the heroine and the damsel in distress in our little tale. And yet, as the warmth of his encouragement spread through me, I couldn't shake the gnawing feeling that Lily was a chapter I hadn't anticipated, a subplot that could unravel everything I had built.

As if reading my mind, he shifted the conversation. "So, what do you say we channel this energy into the event tomorrow? Let's make it something memorable. Show everyone what you can really do."

"Are you saying I should throw a chocolate party? You know I can't just whip up a chocolate fountain on a whim, right?" I raised an eyebrow, half-smirking, but the challenge was intriguing.

"Why not? If anyone can pull it off, it's you. Plus, who wouldn't want to dive into a chocolate fountain? It's practically an invitation to indulge," he said, his eyes sparkling with mischief.

I couldn't help but laugh, the tension between us easing as I imagined the scene. "You just want to take a dip in it, don't you?" I teased, playfully nudging his shoulder. "Let's be honest; you're really just after the chocolate-covered strawberries."

"Guilty as charged," he admitted, mock-innocence painting his features. "But seriously, Clara, you have a way of making everything feel special. Let's put on a show and remind everyone why they love coming to your shop."

I felt a surge of inspiration at his words, a bubbling excitement that sent butterflies dancing in my stomach. "Alright, then! A chocolate party it is. But you're on cleanup duty. I don't want to hear any whining about sticky fingers," I quipped, grinning up at him.

Max laughed, and it rang out like a clear bell, cutting through the remnants of my earlier jealousy. "Deal! Just promise you won't make me wear a giant chocolate suit or something equally ridiculous."

"Oh, but now that you mention it, I can't make any promises," I shot back, reveling in the lightness of our banter. It felt good to be back in this rhythm, to remember what drew us together in the first place.

As we set to work, gathering supplies and brainstorming ideas, I found myself lost in the thrill of creation. My mind whirled with possibilities—flavors to explore, decorations to craft, a scene bursting with color and sweetness. Each chocolate piece would be a reflection of my passion, a testament to the love I poured into my work, and I wanted Max by my side as we brought this vision to life.

The night wore on, our laughter echoing through the shop as we piled ingredients high and sketched out designs on napkins. The energy between us shifted, growing electric and charged, weaving a deeper connection that felt both thrilling and terrifying. I caught myself stealing glances at him, studying the way his hands moved, deft and confident, as he mixed together a chocolate ganache that made my heart race.

"Okay, but seriously, I have a question," I said, breaking the comfortable silence that had settled between us. "Why did you decide to help out with this event? I mean, it's a lot of work, and you could easily have said no."

He paused, glancing up at me, the vulnerability creeping back into his eyes. "Honestly? Because I want to be here with you. I want to support you and show you that you're not alone in this."

His sincerity caught me off guard, a rush of warmth flooding my cheeks. "But what about Lily? I thought you two were getting along?"

Max frowned slightly, a shadow crossing his features. "Lily's nice, and we click on some levels, but I'm not looking for another distraction. I want to build something real, and that's with you, Clara."

The words hung in the air, thick and potent, and for a moment, I let them wash over me like a gentle tide, pushing away the doubt that had lingered. "Real, huh?" I said, my voice light yet laden with seriousness. "Well, if we're doing this, I expect my very own chocolate crown. How else will the people know I'm the queen of the chocolate kingdom?"

He burst out laughing, the sound ringing like music in the quiet space. "I can arrange that. Just know it may end up being a little more 'crown of gooey chocolate' than 'glittering jewel encrusted,' but it'll be memorable."

"Perfect. I want something that'll make me stand out," I said, unable to hide the smile blooming on my lips. "If I'm going to rule this chocolate kingdom, I might as well do it in style."

Our banter filled the room, a sweet melody that wove through the air, and I felt my worries begin to dissipate like steam from a melting chocolate bar. In that moment, it didn't matter that Lily was around; what mattered was the bond forming between us, solid and real, built on laughter, trust, and shared dreams.

As we wrapped up for the night, I caught Max looking at me with a mix of admiration and something deeper, something that made my heart race. It was a gaze that stirred something within me, a quiet understanding that transcended words. Tomorrow would bring its own challenges, but for now, in the glow of our shared laughter, the world outside faded into a distant echo, leaving just the two of us in our little chocolate paradise, ready to create something extraordinary together.

The morning sun broke through the windows, spilling a golden hue over the chocolate-laden counters, illuminating the space where I often lost myself in the art of confectionery. Today, however, the light felt like a spotlight illuminating my insecurities, reminding me of the festering jealousy I had tried to suppress. I stirred the heavy ganache, watching the rich, dark liquid swirl, imagining it was capable of dissolving my doubts along with the bittersweet chocolate.

Max's laughter from the front of the shop rang through, a melody I had grown to adore, but today it grated on my nerves. As I poured the melted chocolate into molds, I couldn't help but overhear snippets of conversation drifting in from the front. "No,

I'm serious! Clara's creations are legendary," he said, and my heart fluttered, but it was quickly followed by a pang of unease. I leaned closer to the doorway, peering through the glass at the sight of him playfully tossing a chocolate truffle toward Lily, who caught it with a laugh that seemed to echo too loudly in the small space.

In that moment, the world outside my windows seemed brighter, as if mocking my internal storm. Wasn't it enough that I spent countless hours crafting these beautiful treats? Why did I feel like I was losing my ground, the very foundation of what made me unique slipping away like melted chocolate slipping through my fingers?

Lily's laughter turned into a low, conspiratorial whisper, and I felt a sharp twist in my gut. It was a sound that resonated with an intimacy I desperately wished to share with Max, but the barrier I had built around myself felt impenetrable. Taking a deep breath, I forced myself to re-enter the moment, clenching my jaw as I plastered on a smile.

"Good morning, lovebirds!" I announced, trying to inject a bit of levity into the air, though it came out more like a strained shout. I watched as they turned toward me, a momentary silence enveloping the room. Max's expression shifted, a hint of surprise mingling with concern.

"Hey! We were just—" he began, but I cut him off with a wave of my hand, stepping deeper into the shop, letting the familiar scents wrap around me like a comforting blanket.

"Making plans without me? I see how it is," I quipped, but my tone lacked the playful bite I intended. Instead, it sounded hollow, like the shell of a truffle without the rich filling.

"Actually, we were discussing the event and how to promote it," Lily chimed in, her voice sweet like the icing on a cake. It was infuriatingly charming, and I fought the urge to roll my eyes.

Max leaned against the counter, arms crossed, radiating a calm that only fueled the tempest in my chest. "Yeah, we thought we could create a few videos showcasing how you craft your chocolates," he said, his tone genuine. "You know, give people a taste of the magic that happens behind the scenes."

"Oh, perfect. Because nothing screams 'I'm a master chocolatier' like a shaky iPhone camera capturing me sweating over a hot stove," I replied, forcing a laugh. My sarcasm hung in the air, thick and palpable, but the tension danced around us, refusing to dissipate.

Lily tilted her head, studying me as if I were a puzzle she was eager to solve. "I think it could be fun, Clara! People love to see the process. It makes them feel connected."

"Right. Let's show them how to make a mess and burn their fingers on molten sugar. That'll really get the viewers in," I said, my voice dripping with irony. I watched as her smile faltered, but it was the way Max's brow furrowed that made me take a step back. I knew I was pushing it, spiraling further into my insecurities, and yet I couldn't stop.

"Come on, Clara. You're overthinking it," Max urged, moving closer. "People want authenticity. It doesn't have to be perfect; it just has to be you."

"Easy for you to say," I shot back, stepping away, creating a physical space that mirrored the emotional chasm between us. "You're not the one who has to deal with the aftermath if it all goes wrong. You have this effortless charm, and I'm just... me."

A tense silence enveloped us, filled with unspoken words and heavy breaths. I turned to walk away, desperate for some space to clear my head, when Max's voice cut through the air like a knife. "Clara, you are more than just 'you.' You're a force to be reckoned with. Why can't you see that?"

"Because it doesn't feel like it right now!" I snapped, spinning around to face him, my heart pounding with frustration. "With Lily here, it feels like I'm competing with some ideal that I can't live up to."

"Competing? Clara, that's not how it is," he said, his voice dropping into a gentler tone that softened the edges of my anger. "You're not in competition with anyone. You're amazing in your own right."

His sincerity sent my heart racing, and I caught a glimpse of vulnerability in his eyes—an honesty that disarmed me. "I just wish you could see yourself the way I see you," he added, taking a step closer, the warmth radiating from him like a beacon of hope.

Before I could respond, the front door swung open, and the bell chimed, shattering the moment. My heart sank as I saw Lily entering, her bright smile a stark contrast to the brewing storm within me. She carried a bouquet of colorful flowers, the kind that brightened a room but did nothing to lighten my mood.

"Look what I brought!" she exclaimed, her voice effervescent. "Thought we could use some cheer for the event!" She glanced between Max and me, her eyes sparkling with mischief, and I felt my chest tighten.

"Oh, perfect, flowers. Just what we need to distract from the fact that my entire life feels like it's falling apart," I muttered under my breath, irritation creeping back in.

Max shot me a warning look, but I couldn't help myself. "How about we do a floral arrangement video instead? You can show everyone how to hold a stem and pretend to be crafty."

"Or we could all work together and create something really special," Lily suggested, oblivious to the tension humming in the air. "I mean, chocolate and flowers? It's a classic combo!"

"Classic or cliché?" I quipped, feeling the walls I had built around my heart rising once more.

Max stepped between us, sensing the impending clash. "Let's focus on the event, yeah? We can incorporate flowers into the display." His voice was steady, but I could see the flicker of frustration in his eyes.

Lily clapped her hands, undeterred by my sarcasm. "Perfect! I can start arranging these while you two finish up the chocolates. Clara, why don't you show me your favorite techniques? I'd love to learn from you."

The suggestion felt like a double-edged sword, a thin veneer of camaraderie overlaying my tumultuous thoughts. I hesitated, knowing that every moment spent with her felt like a step further away from the ground I was trying to stand on.

But just as I opened my mouth to respond, the shop door swung open once more, the sound of hurried footsteps interrupting our gathering. A woman burst in, breathless and wide-eyed, her expression frantic as she scanned the room. "I'm so sorry to interrupt, but I need to speak to Clara immediately!"

All eyes turned to me, the tension shifting once again, a new layer of uncertainty creeping in. My heart raced, an unexpected thrill of anxiety mingling with curiosity. "What's going on?" I asked, my voice a mix of confusion and concern.

"There's been an incident at the community center," she said, her words tumbling out in a rush. "They need your chocolates for the event, but something went wrong, and they're short. Can you come help us?"

I felt my heart drop, an avalanche of chaos suddenly looming in front of me. "What do you mean, 'something went wrong'?" I demanded, adrenaline surging through my veins.

"I can explain on the way! They're in crisis mode and need your expertise," she insisted, urgency creeping into her tone.

Max looked at me, his brow furrowed with concern. "You should go. I'll hold down the fort here."

But as I grabbed my coat, glancing back at him and Lily, the storm within me surged once more. What awaited me at the community center? Could I handle whatever chaos lay ahead? With a quick nod, I dashed out, uncertainty swirling around me like a whirlwind, leaving behind the warm, comforting smell of chocolate and the tense undercurrents of our conversations, wondering if I was stepping into a solution or a catastrophe.

Chapter 27: Turning the Tide

The air inside the shop was thick with the intoxicating scent of dark chocolate, a heady aroma that enveloped me like a warm embrace. The soft glow of the overhead lights cast a golden hue over the counter, where rows of glossy truffles sat waiting, their surfaces shimmering like tiny black pearls. Each piece was a labor of love, a story encapsulated in rich ganache and unexpected flavors—lavender-infused dark chocolate, chili-spiced caramel, and a zesty citrus blend that danced on the palate. I had poured not just ingredients into these creations but fragments of my heart, desperately hoping they would resonate with our loyal customers.

As I meticulously arranged the truffles on a decorative slate, the door chimed, breaking the intimate solitude of the shop. I looked up, expecting to see a familiar face. Instead, it was a tall figure silhouetted against the bright light outside. My heart skipped a beat, half in dread, half in anticipation, as Max stepped inside. The moment hung in the air, thick with unspoken words, yet his presence pulled me like gravity. His dark hair was tousled, as if he'd just emerged from a storm, and his eyes searched the room, landing on me with a mixture of curiosity and concern.

"Working late again?" he asked, his voice deep and rich, tinged with a hint of teasing. I couldn't tell if he was genuinely worried or just taking the opportunity to poke fun at my obsessive tendencies.

"Someone has to keep this place afloat," I shot back, unable to resist a smile. "Besides, I've got a new line to unveil. You know, the one that'll save our chocolatier from certain doom." I gestured to the display, my pride blooming as I recounted the late nights and the countless chocolate-covered mishaps that had led to this moment.

Max stepped closer, his eyes narrowing as he scrutinized my creations. "You think these will turn the tide?"

301

"More like a chocolate tsunami," I quipped, feeling a surge of defiance. "I've infused each piece with the essence of Charleston itself. It's not just chocolate; it's a tribute."

He raised an eyebrow, clearly intrigued. "What's the 'essence of Charleston' taste like? Is there a truffle for sweet tea and biscuits?"

I laughed, the tension breaking. "Actually, it's more about capturing the spirit of the city—bold, surprising, and a little sweet with a dash of spice." I leaned against the counter, feeling more confident. "You've got to trust me, Max. This isn't just about saving the shop. It's about rediscovering who we are in the process."

Max crossed his arms, the corners of his mouth twitching in amusement. "So, what's the secret ingredient? Are you planning on magically incorporating the city's charm into the chocolate?"

"Absolutely!" I said, my tone playful yet earnest. "Each truffle is infused with a bit of our history, like the way the Spanish moss drapes lazily from the oak trees, or how the warmth of a summer night can make you feel alive."

He looked impressed for a moment, then grinned. "Okay, I'm intrigued. Let's see if they live up to the hype. Can I try one?"

"Only if you promise not to make a face if you don't like it," I countered, grabbing a truffle infused with ginger and dark chocolate, my own personal favorite.

He took a bite, chewing thoughtfully, and for a moment, the world narrowed to just us and that rich, complex flavor. "Wow, that's actually...really good. Like, I was expecting something gimmicky, but this has layers. It's like you're telling a story in chocolate."

"Exactly!" I beamed, feeling a swell of pride. "That's what I aimed for. Each flavor tells a story—like how the ginger represents the spice of life in Charleston. It's all about celebrating our roots."

Max nodded, seemingly impressed. "I get it. So, what's next? A chocolate launch party?"

"More like a chocolate revival," I corrected. "We'll invite our regulars, showcase these new flavors, and hopefully, reignite their passion for our shop. The last few months have been a bit dull."

"And by 'dull,' you mean practically on life support?" he quipped, eyes sparkling with mischief.

"Okay, maybe," I admitted with a laugh. "But this is it, Max. If we don't take this leap, we'll never know what could have been."

He considered me for a moment, his expression shifting to something more serious. "And what if it doesn't work? What if this doesn't save us?"

"Then at least we tried, right?" I countered, my voice steady despite the flicker of doubt that danced in my chest. "I refuse to let fear dictate my choices anymore."

Max leaned against the counter, a contemplative look on his face. "You really believe in this, don't you?"

"More than anything," I replied, the conviction in my voice solidifying. "I want to pour my heart into this shop, into these chocolates. I want to prove to everyone, especially myself, that I can do this."

He regarded me for a moment, a slow smile breaking across his face. "Then let's do it. Let's turn the tide."

With that, a surge of hope coursed through me, buoyed by the energy between us. I knew we were standing on the precipice of something extraordinary—both for the shop and for us. The night stretched out before us, filled with possibilities, and I was ready to dive in.

The morning sun streamed through the shop's windows, illuminating the chocolate display like a treasure trove of glistening secrets. I stood behind the counter, arranging the truffles with a practiced hand, each piece reflecting my late-night efforts and the spark of new life I had injected into the chocolatier. The once-familiar air felt different—charged with possibility, like the sweet anticipation that ripples through a crowd just before a performance begins.

Max was already at the coffee station, expertly crafting lattes with a flourish, his movements a dance of confidence. He caught me watching him and grinned, a hint of mischief in his eyes. "Don't just stand there like a deer in headlights. We're on the verge of a chocolate revolution here. Get ready to charm the pants off our customers."

I rolled my eyes but couldn't help the smile tugging at my lips. "You're one to talk about charm, Mr. 'I've-just-brewed-the-best-coffee-of-your-life'."

"Guilty as charged." He poured steaming milk into a cup, the froth forming a perfect heart atop the coffee. "But it's not just the coffee; it's the atmosphere. With your new truffles and my caffeinated concoctions, we'll have customers lining up down the block. It's time to reclaim our throne."

His enthusiasm was infectious, and I felt my resolve deepen. I watched him as he moved through the space, transforming the shop from a mere chocolatier into a vibrant hub of creativity and warmth. It was like witnessing a painter bring a canvas to life, and I wondered if he realized how much he inspired me.

"Okay, Mr. Coffee King," I said, stepping closer to him. "I think we need a strategy for our big reveal. Any ideas on how to draw a crowd?"

"Social media blitz," he said without hesitation. "Post some tantalizing photos, maybe a behind-the-scenes video of you making the truffles, all while I play the charming barista. It's a classic move."

"Good idea, but I'd rather not have the world witness my chocolate-covered disasters," I teased, recalling the chaos of last week's failed attempts. "How about we stick to the finished product?"

Max laughed, a sound that sent warmth flooding through me. "Fine, but you're missing an opportunity for some hilarious bloopers."

"I'll save those for the memoir," I shot back. "You know, 'My Life as a Chocolate Tragedy.'"

He chuckled, and I felt an undeniable bond forming, each joke weaving us closer together. As we bantered back and forth, the familiar bell above the door jingled, and our first customers of the day walked in—a couple, hand-in-hand, eyes sparkling with excitement.

"Welcome to our chocolate paradise!" I greeted them, my voice bright with enthusiasm. "What brings you to our corner of sweetness today?"

"We heard there's something new on the menu," the woman said, her eyes darting to the display as if it were a treasure map.

"New and exciting," Max chimed in, leaning against the counter with a roguish grin. "You're in for a treat."

As we shared samples and stories, I felt my heart swell with pride. The couple laughed at our playful exchanges, their laughter mingling with the rich scents of cocoa and coffee. Each positive reaction fed my confidence, and soon, more customers trickled in, drawn by the aromas wafting through the open door.

"Who knew chocolate could be such a magnet for people?" I marveled as the shop filled with chatter and laughter.

"It's not just the chocolate," Max said, glancing at me, his expression softening. "It's the experience. You've created something special here, and people can feel it."

His words lingered in the air, and I couldn't help but wonder if he realized how much I needed to hear that. But before I could respond, a familiar figure stepped inside—Katherine, my childhood friend and erstwhile rival, known for her cutthroat business strategies and a penchant for the dramatic.

"Ah, if it isn't the dynamic duo," she announced, her voice laced with mockery as she sauntered over, her designer heels clicking on the wooden floor. "I see you've taken up the mantle of 'Charleston's Sweethearts.'"

"Better than 'Charleston's Worst Nightmare,' don't you think?" I shot back, not missing a beat. "How's the competition treating you?"

"Charming, as always," she replied, eyeing our display with a mix of curiosity and skepticism. "I hope those truffles are as good as you claim. I'd hate to see my old friend fail."

"Why don't you try one?" I offered, my heart racing. "I promise it won't bite."

Katherine plucked a truffle from the tray with a raised eyebrow, popping it into her mouth. The silence that followed felt like an eternity, every second stretching into infinity as I waited for her reaction. Finally, her eyes widened, and a slow smile crept across her lips.

"Not bad, Walker. Not bad at all," she admitted, her voice a mix of surprise and grudging respect. "This could actually give my shop a run for its money."

"I'm glad you think so," I replied, a rush of triumph flooding through me. "We've got a lot more up our sleeves."

"Oh, I'm sure you do," she said, glancing at Max with an appraising look. "And I see you've brought in some talent. Handsome, isn't he?"

I felt a flicker of discomfort at her words, a rush of possessiveness igniting within me. "He's not just talent; he's a partner."

"Right," Katherine said, her tone teasing. "Partners are always a good way to navigate a failing business. How quaint."

Before I could retort, Max stepped forward, his expression shifting to one of playful defiance. "You might want to keep your friends close and your competitors closer, Katherine. We're not going anywhere."

The tension crackled between us, and Katherine regarded Max with a newfound interest, an eyebrow arched in challenge. "Interesting. Let's see how long that optimism lasts when the chocolate dust settles."

As she exited, the door chimed behind her, leaving a strange mix of exhilaration and anxiety in her wake. I looked at Max, whose face was a mask of confusion.

"Is she always that...charming?" he asked, clearly trying to decipher the encounter.

"Only when she's trying to rattle me," I admitted, shaking off the unease. "Don't let her get under your skin. We're building something special here."

Max nodded, determination flickering in his eyes. "And we'll keep it going. We've got a revolution to lead, remember?"

With renewed energy, I dove back into the rhythm of the day, the shop buzzing with excitement. Each customer who left with a smile felt like a small victory, each truffle handed over a tiny triumph. The world outside may have been uncertain, but in that moment, amidst laughter and chocolate, I felt invincible.

The hustle and bustle of the day began to wane as the afternoon sun dipped lower in the sky, casting golden beams through the shop windows. With the last of the customers happily departing, I leaned against the counter, catching my breath amidst the remnants of a successful launch. The air still hummed with energy, punctuated by the occasional clink of cups and the gentle whir of the espresso machine. I glanced over at Max, who was busy cleaning up, a focused expression on his face.

"Do you ever stop?" I asked, arching an eyebrow. "I swear, you're like a caffeinated squirrel with a cleaning obsession."

He looked up, feigning indignation. "This 'caffeinated squirrel' is trying to maintain a five-star establishment, thank you very much.

Besides, how else will we keep the chocolate dust from becoming its own eco-system?"

"Touché," I laughed, leaning forward, the lighthearted banter warming the air between us. "But let's be honest: our chocolate is the real star here."

"And don't you forget it!" he replied with a mock-seriousness, pointing a finger at me before tossing a damp cloth into the sink. "What's next for the illustrious chocolatier?"

"Well, I was thinking we could expand the line even further," I said, excitement bubbling within me. "I've got a few more flavor ideas swirling around in my head that could take us to the next level."

"Like what? Chocolate bacon?" he teased, crossing his arms and leaning against the counter, his expression playful.

"Actually, that's not a bad idea," I replied, pretending to consider it seriously. "But no, I was thinking of incorporating local ingredients—maybe even a collaboration with a local rum distillery."

Max's interest piqued. "Now you're talking. A dark chocolate rum truffle could be a game changer."

"Exactly! It's like a party in your mouth." I grinned, feeling more alive than I had in weeks. "And let's face it, what's Charleston without a little rum?"

"Or a lot of rum," he added, chuckling.

Our laughter echoed through the shop, but the light-hearted moment was abruptly interrupted by the chime of the doorbell. I turned to see a familiar face—Evelyn, our biggest critic and a food blogger with a sharp tongue and a sharper pen. Her presence was like a sudden chill, creeping through the warm, inviting atmosphere we'd worked so hard to cultivate.

"Ah, the chocolatier and her charming assistant," she said, her voice dripping with sarcasm. "I came to see if the buzz was warranted or just another sugar-coated fairy tale."

"Funny you should ask," I replied, stepping into the role of a gracious host. "Care for a sample? You might find it's more of a reality than you expect."

"I'm willing to give it a try," she said, eyeing me with a blend of skepticism and intrigue.

As I handed her a truffle, the entire shop seemed to hold its breath. I felt like a tightrope walker suspended above a pit of snapping crocodiles. Would she appreciate the craft, or would she tear it apart like a starving wolf?

With a slow, deliberate movement, Evelyn popped the truffle into her mouth. Her expression remained inscrutable as she chewed, but the seconds felt like hours. Max hovered nearby, his eyes darting between Evelyn and me, clearly as anxious as I was.

Finally, she swallowed, a flicker of surprise crossing her features. "This is... surprisingly good."

"Surprisingly?" I echoed, my voice laced with disbelief. "You mean to say it's not the disaster you were expecting?"

"Don't push your luck," she warned, smirking. "I haven't made up my mind yet. But I'll admit, there's depth here. Not what I expected from you two."

"Depth is our specialty," Max chimed in, his confidence blossoming as he leaned against the counter with an easy charm. "We aim to elevate chocolate from mere candy to an experience."

Evelyn regarded him with a hint of curiosity. "You're the barista, right? What's your angle in all this?"

"I'm just here to make the world a better place, one cup of coffee and one truffle at a time," he replied, his voice teasing yet earnest.

She nodded, intrigued, and for a moment, I could see the wheels turning in her mind. The tension shifted slightly, creating an opening for a more genuine interaction.

"I might just write about this after all," she said, her tone softening. "But don't get too comfortable. I'm still going to be honest."

"Honestly is what we live for," I replied, feeling a rush of relief. "But if it's a glowing review, we'll happily take it."

The exchange seemed to break the ice, and soon we were engaged in lively conversation. Evelyn asked about our inspiration, and I shared my vision of creating flavors that echoed the vibrant spirit of Charleston. I watched as she scribbled notes, her demeanor shifting from critical observer to genuine interest.

Just as I felt the momentum building, the door swung open once more, this time ushering in a figure from my past. My heart sank as I recognized the last person I wanted to see—David, my ex-boyfriend, standing there with a sheepish grin and an air of self-assuredness that sent an electric jolt of surprise through me.

"Well, well, well," he said, his voice smooth as silk. "If it isn't my favorite chocolatier."

"David," I said, my voice even, betraying none of the tumult swirling inside me. "What brings you here?"

"Just passing by and thought I'd check in on the local sweets scene. Heard there's a chocolate revolution happening," he replied, glancing around the shop with feigned nonchalance.

I glanced at Max, who had gone rigid, a flicker of uncertainty crossing his face. "Yeah, you could say that," I replied, forcing a smile. "We're making some exciting changes."

"Glad to see you're moving forward," he said, his gaze landing on me with an intensity that made me shiver. "I always knew you had it in you."

A wave of nostalgia washed over me, mixed with irritation. David had that ability to make me feel like I was standing on shifting sands, and just as I was about to respond, Evelyn interjected.

"Who's this?" she asked, her eyes narrowing with interest.

"Just someone who's taking a casual stroll down memory lane," I said, keeping my tone light but edged with sarcasm. "David and I used to be... close."

"Close?" Evelyn echoed, her voice dripping with intrigue. "Care to share more?"

Before I could answer, David stepped closer, his expression earnest. "I'm just here to support you, really. I know how hard you've worked to get this place off the ground."

The atmosphere shifted once more, tension coiling tightly in the air. Max stepped forward, arms crossed, his demeanor protective. "Support is great, but it's important to remember who's been here through thick and thin."

David's gaze flicked between us, a flicker of realization crossing his face. "Oh, I see. You've moved on."

"Maybe it's time you did too," I replied, feeling a surge of confidence.

Just then, the doorbell chimed again, but this time, it wasn't another customer. Instead, a man dressed in a crisp suit strode in, exuding an air of authority that immediately commanded attention. He scanned the shop with keen eyes before landing on me, a sharp smile breaking across his face.

"Is this the famous chocolatier I've heard so much about?" he asked, his voice smooth and confident. "I'm here to discuss a business opportunity."

The words hung in the air, charged with uncertainty. My heart raced as I exchanged glances with Max, the thrill of possibility mingling with the tension of unresolved feelings. David's presence, combined with the sudden appearance of this stranger, sent my thoughts spiraling into chaos.

"I'm sorry, who are you?" I asked, my voice steady but my pulse quickening.

"I'm Mark. I've been watching your journey, and I believe there's a partnership opportunity that could benefit us both."

Before I could respond, David stepped in front of me, a protective barrier formed between us. "I think you should leave her alone."

The room fell silent, and I could feel the weight of their unspoken rivalry thick in the air. My heart pounded as I realized I stood at a crossroads—facing not only my past but also an uncertain future. The sweet aroma of chocolate now mingled with a sharp undercurrent of tension, and I knew that the next few moments would determine everything.

Chapter 28: The Aftermath of Choice

The bell above the door chimed softly as I set down a stack of freshly bound journals, their leather covers warm from the late afternoon sun filtering through the shop window. Each journal felt like a piece of my soul, a testament to our shared dreams and late nights filled with laughter and the faint scent of espresso. I glanced around the shop, taking in the mismatched furniture that had become our hallmark—a collection of thrifted chairs and a worn mahogany table that had seen better days, yet somehow felt like home. I paused, letting the comforting chaos wash over me, but the sense of unease gnawing at my insides refused to dissipate.

Max was at the back of the shop, immersed in arranging a display of local artwork. He had a way of throwing himself into tasks with an infectious enthusiasm, his sandy hair tousled and a hint of a smile dancing on his lips as he examined a piece that depicted a sprawling ocean scene. Watching him, I felt the familiar tug of affection, yet that same feeling was undercut by the simmering tension between us, a restless current that threatened to pull us apart. I sighed, suppressing the knot of frustration tightening in my stomach.

"Hey," I called out, my voice light but trembling at the edges. "What do you think of this one?" I gestured toward the painting, a vibrant portrayal of waves crashing against jagged rocks, their foamy white caps a stark contrast to the deep blue hues swirling throughout the canvas. Max looked up, and for a moment, the flicker of his attention felt like a lifeline in a turbulent sea.

"It's... passionate," he replied, his brow furrowing in a way that made my heart ache. "But is it really us? I mean, it's beautiful, but it doesn't capture the spirit of the shop." His gaze drifted back to the painting, and I felt a jolt of irritation. It wasn't just about the artwork; it was about the vision we had painstakingly crafted together.

"What do you mean?" I asked, crossing my arms, feeling the heat of my frustration bubble to the surface. "It's a representation of struggle and beauty. Isn't that exactly what we've been through?"

Max straightened, running a hand through his hair, a nervous habit I recognized all too well. "Maybe. But right now, I can't help but think about Oliver's proposal. What if we—"

"We're not talking about Oliver," I interrupted, my voice sharper than I intended. "This is our shop, not a bargaining chip in someone else's game."

Max took a step closer, the air between us crackling with unresolved tension. "You think I don't want this place to thrive? But what if that means partnering with Oliver? What if we can't keep the doors open without his investment?"

"Then we figure it out together! I won't let this place turn into something that doesn't feel like us," I retorted, feeling the weight of my words resonate in the small space. I caught a glimpse of the uncertainty in his eyes, and for a fleeting moment, I saw the flash of fear that danced behind his usual bravado.

"Do you even know what you want?" he asked, his tone softer now, as if he were peeling away the layers to uncover the truth. "You're so quick to reject the idea, but are you afraid of change or afraid of failing?"

My heart pounded, a primal rhythm echoing in my ears. "I'm not afraid of failing; I'm afraid of losing what we have." I met his gaze, a fierce determination igniting within me. "This shop is our sanctuary. I don't want it to become just another business venture. I want it to stay a part of us."

The tension in the room shifted, palpable and electric. "And what if that means letting go of our dreams?" Max shot back, his voice rising slightly. "What if we're clinging to something that can't survive without change?"

"Then we change, but not at the cost of our identity!" I countered, my heart racing as I realized how deeply this issue ran between us. The stakes were higher than I had allowed myself to see.

Silence enveloped us, heavy and laden with unspoken words. I could see the internal struggle etched on his face, the way his jaw clenched as he fought to articulate his thoughts. The last light of day seeped through the window, casting long shadows that danced across the wooden floor, echoing the conflict swirling in my heart.

"Max, we've built something beautiful here. It's more than just a shop; it's our story," I urged, stepping closer. "We're not just selling books and art; we're creating a community. If we lose that, what do we have left?"

He paused, the tension thickening the air around us, and I could see him grappling with my words. "What if this is our chance to reach more people? To expand what we've started?"

"By sacrificing the essence of it all? That's not growth; that's selling out." My voice trembled, and I willed myself to stay steady. "I need you to understand that this place—this life we've built—it means everything to me."

Max's expression softened, a hint of recognition in his eyes, but the doubt lingered. "And what if we can't make it work as it is? What if we need Oliver to survive?"

I opened my mouth to respond, but the words stuck in my throat, caught in the whirlwind of our conflicting visions. The doubt crept in, an unwelcome companion whispering its insidious thoughts. What if he was right? What if we couldn't sustain our dream without compromise?

The thought was like ice water poured down my back, chilling me to the bone. I took a step back, breaking the fragile connection between us, feeling the weight of uncertainty settle heavily on my shoulders.

"Maybe we should take some time to think," I suggested, trying to inject a sense of calm into the storm brewing within me. "Figure out what we really want."

Max nodded, the flicker of acceptance crossing his features. "Yeah, maybe that's a good idea."

As we stood there, surrounded by the echo of our dreams and the ghosts of our choices, I couldn't shake the feeling that the walls of our sanctuary were beginning to close in. The choices we faced loomed large, casting long shadows over the bright future we had envisioned.

The next morning, the air in the shop felt different, charged with an unspoken tension that clung to the corners like dust. I arrived early, eager to wrap myself in the familiar scent of aged paper and fresh coffee. The early sunlight streamed through the windows, illuminating the rows of books that lined the walls, casting a warm glow that usually felt like a cozy embrace. But today, the atmosphere was taut, every creak of the wooden floor echoing in the silence.

As I prepared for the day, I could hear the faint sounds of the world waking up outside—a distant dog barking, the rhythmic thud of a passing truck, and the occasional chirp of a bird settling into its perch. Each sound, usually comforting, now heightened my awareness of the impending conversation with Max. I poured a cup of coffee, the steam swirling upward like the thoughts racing through my mind. It was just coffee, but in my hands, it felt like an anchor, grounding me in a moment where everything else felt unsettled.

When Max finally arrived, his footsteps were lighter than usual, but the heaviness in his eyes betrayed the buoyancy of his gait. I busied myself behind the counter, fiddling with the espresso machine, hoping to find solace in the familiar routine. He flashed a quick smile, but it didn't quite reach his eyes, and I felt a pang of regret for the sharpness of our last exchange.

"Morning," he said, his voice a blend of warmth and wariness. "Ready for another day of battling the forces of capitalism?"

I laughed, the sound feeling foreign against the backdrop of our recent conversation. "As long as the forces of capitalism don't come with a side of Oliver," I quipped, trying to lighten the mood.

Max chuckled softly, shaking his head. "I'm beginning to think he might be the actual villain in our story."

"Ah, but every good story needs a villain to make the hero shine," I replied, raising an eyebrow. "Just make sure I'm the hero, okay? I'd prefer to avoid any tragic endings."

He nodded, but the smile faded as he turned to face the back room. I could see him grappling with the weight of our conversation from the night before. "Speaking of stories," he said hesitantly, "I was thinking we should probably talk about Oliver again. We can't keep pretending he'll just vanish."

The playful banter was suddenly replaced by the suffocating weight of reality. I set down my coffee and took a deep breath, bracing myself. "Right. We can't ignore it."

I turned to him, meeting his gaze head-on, my heart racing with the thought of what was to come. "So, what do you want to do? Should we entertain the idea, or do we stand firm?"

Max rubbed the back of his neck, his brow furrowing as if the act would somehow massage the answer into clarity. "I want to explore our options, but at the same time, I don't want to lose what we have. This shop is everything to me. I just... I want it to thrive."

"It will thrive, Max. But we need to do it on our terms," I insisted, my voice steady but firm. "Maybe we can find a way to negotiate with Oliver. We don't have to accept his offer as is."

He leaned against the counter, his arms crossed over his chest as he considered my words. "What if he's not open to negotiation? What if it's an all-or-nothing deal?"

"Then we walk away," I replied, surprising myself with the certainty in my voice. "If it comes down to our dreams or some corporate vision, I choose us."

For a moment, a flicker of hope sparked in his eyes, and I felt a rush of exhilaration. But it was fleeting. "You make it sound so simple, but the reality is complicated. We've put everything into this place—our hearts, our sweat, our sanity. What if we fail without him?"

"Failure isn't the end of the world," I countered. "It's just a step in the journey. And you know what? We've already faced so many challenges. I refuse to believe we can't handle whatever comes next."

Max sighed, his shoulders drooping slightly as if the weight of the world rested on them. "You're right. But I can't shake this feeling that we're standing at a precipice. It's scary."

"Scary? Sure. But think about what we've built here. It's bigger than both of us, and it's worth fighting for," I urged, stepping closer, my heart racing with the fervor of my conviction. "Let's brainstorm. Maybe there's a way to make our case to him, to show him that we're not just a couple of kids running a shop. We're a community."

The spark of determination flickered to life in his eyes, and I felt the distance between us shrink. "A community," he echoed, the thought resonating with him. "You know, Oliver doesn't know us like that. Maybe we can leverage our relationships with the locals. If we show him how much we mean to them, maybe that'll sway his perspective."

"Yes! Exactly!" I exclaimed, my excitement bubbling over. "We can host a community event. Something that showcases what we've built. Invite Oliver and let him see how integral we are to the town."

Max's expression shifted, a hint of mischief lighting up his features. "So, we throw a party? I'm in. But only if you promise to dress up as a literary character."

I laughed, imagining the absurdity of donning a cape and glasses, channeling my inner Hermione Granger. "Deal, but only if you wear something equally embarrassing."

"Fine. I'll wear a giant book costume. That'll really draw the crowds," he replied, a grin breaking through the clouds of uncertainty.

We spent the rest of the morning brainstorming ideas, laughter echoing through the shop as we mapped out our plans. Each suggestion was met with playful banter, the weight of our previous conversation lifting like the morning fog, revealing a path forward.

As we jotted down ideas for activities, the thought of Oliver hung over us like a dark cloud, but for the first time, it felt manageable. The stakes were high, but so was our determination. In that moment, surrounded by the warmth of friendship and ambition, I knew we were more than capable of facing whatever challenges lay ahead. Together, we would stand firm against the tide of uncertainty, ready to defend the heart of what we had built.

The event arrived with an almost electric anticipation that crackled in the air, infusing every corner of the shop with an energy I hadn't felt in ages. We had spent the past week transforming our haven into a vibrant space, a celebration of community and creativity. Banners hung from the ceiling, colorful fabric draping down like confetti, while fairy lights twinkled cheerfully, casting a warm glow over our carefully arranged tables. The scent of baked goods wafted through the shop, courtesy of Mrs. Hargrove from across the street, her famous cookies making an appearance once again. I could practically hear the townspeople's stomachs rumble in unison.

Max and I had spent late nights planning every detail, our laughter mixing with the quiet rustle of paper as we brainstormed activities. The prospect of showcasing our shop to Oliver had turned the tension between us into something exciting, an unexpected bond forged in the fires of preparation. As we set up the last few decorations, I caught Max's eye, and in that fleeting moment, we shared a silent agreement: no matter the outcome, we were in this together.

"Are we really going to make him wear that ridiculous hat?" Max asked, holding up the oversized, comically large book hat I'd picked up at a local thrift shop.

I grinned, unable to resist the opportunity for some playful revenge. "Absolutely! If he thinks he can just waltz in and offer us a deal without getting a taste of our sense of humor, he's got another thing coming."

Max chuckled, shaking his head in disbelief. "I can't believe I let you talk me into this. If I get stuck wearing this in public, I'm blaming you entirely."

"Good! I'll gladly take the blame for any fashion faux pas, but only if you promise to wear it all night," I shot back, tucking the hat away with a laugh.

As the clock ticked closer to the event's start, our little shop began to fill with familiar faces. The excitement was palpable, voices rising in a joyful cacophony that enveloped us. I felt a surge of gratitude for our community, the friends and neighbors who had supported us through thick and thin. Each person who entered seemed to bring with them a piece of the warmth that made this place home.

"Look who it is! The main event!" Oliver's voice cut through the chatter, smooth and confident as he strode into the shop. He exuded an air of charm that could disarm anyone, but I couldn't help feeling a twinge of wariness as he scanned the room, his eyes landing on Max and me.

"Ah, the dynamic duo! I must say, I'm impressed. This looks amazing." He gestured around, his smile genuine but his gaze assessing. "A strong turnout. I love the energy."

"Thanks, Oliver! We're just trying to showcase what makes our little shop special," I replied, trying to sound more enthusiastic than I felt. "You know, community and all that jazz."

Max leaned against the counter, arms crossed, his expression an intriguing mix of confidence and tension. "Glad you could make it. We were just about to start some activities. Care to join?"

Oliver's eyes gleamed with interest, though I sensed an underlying calculation behind that smile. "I wouldn't miss it for the world."

As we moved through the afternoon, laughter and conversations melded into a delightful symphony, but I could feel Oliver's presence looming like a shadow. He mingled effortlessly, charm pouring from him as he spoke to our customers and friends, but I could see him watching Max and me closely, measuring our every interaction.

"Okay, everyone! Gather around!" I called, clapping my hands to get everyone's attention. "It's time for the first activity! A literary trivia contest, with prizes!" Cheers erupted from the crowd, and I felt the energy spike, boosting my confidence.

We split everyone into teams, and soon the shop was buzzing with friendly competition. Laughter filled the air as people vied for the title of trivia champion, the questions ranging from classic novels to contemporary bestsellers. As I moved through the crowd, I caught glimpses of Max, who was holding his own against Oliver's banter, exchanging playful jabs while keeping the mood light.

As the trivia contest wrapped up, I glanced at Oliver, who had managed to collect a small audience of admirers, weaving his charm around them like a warm blanket. "You know," I said to Max as we took a moment to regroup behind the counter, "I think he's genuinely enjoying himself."

Max's brows furrowed. "Or he's playing the long game, sizing us up. You know he's still interested in that partnership."

I nodded, biting my lip, unsure of how to feel about Oliver's charm. "True, but maybe we can use this to our advantage. He'll see how important this shop is to the community."

"Let's hope that works in our favor," Max replied, stealing a glance at Oliver as he held court. "But he's not going to make it easy for us."

The trivia contest ended with plenty of cheering and clapping, and as I began to gather the answer sheets, I felt a sudden tap on my shoulder. It was Oliver, his demeanor as casual as ever, but there was a sharpness to his gaze.

"Fantastic event, really. But you know, there's something I'd like to discuss with you both in private," he said, his voice smooth but edged with a note of urgency that sent a shiver down my spine.

"Uh, sure. Just give us a moment, will you?" I replied, forcing a smile, but dread coiled tightly in my stomach.

"Take your time," he said, stepping back slightly, but his gaze lingered, as if he were waiting for us to finish whatever private conversation we needed to have.

"What do you think he wants?" I asked, feeling the weight of his eyes on me, the atmosphere shifting as if the walls of our sanctuary were closing in.

"I don't know," Max replied, glancing around the bustling room filled with laughter and friends. "But I have a bad feeling about it. If he wants to talk privately, it can't be good."

I swallowed hard, the fun of the day morphing into a looming dread. "What if he's not impressed? What if he thinks we're not worth the investment?"

Max shook his head, his brow furrowing. "We can't think like that. We have to believe in what we're doing here. Remember, this is about more than just us now."

As I stood there, wrestling with my nerves, Oliver's eyes flicked toward us again, and I felt the pressure building. "Okay, let's do this," I said, attempting to sound braver than I felt.

We made our way over to him, the music of laughter fading into a hum in the background. Oliver's smile was all charm, but there was something predatory beneath the surface.

"Let's talk about the future, shall we?" he said, and in that moment, everything seemed to tilt on its axis, the excitement of the event giving way to an uncertain reality.

"What did you have in mind?" I asked, steeling myself for whatever was about to unfold.

Oliver leaned in slightly, lowering his voice as if sharing a secret, "You see, I think we need to reevaluate our approach. This partnership could benefit both of us, but..."

Before he could finish, the sound of the door swinging open startled us. A familiar figure burst through, breathless and wide-eyed. It was Laura, our dear friend and the town's unofficial news anchor. "You need to see this!" she shouted, the urgency in her tone cutting through the celebratory atmosphere like a knife.

"What's wrong?" I asked, the pit in my stomach deepening.

She hesitated, glancing at Oliver before locking eyes with me. "It's about the shop. There's something happening outside."

The words hung in the air, heavy and foreboding. I exchanged a worried glance with Max, his expression mirroring my growing dread. "What do you mean?" he asked, stepping closer.

Laura took a breath, her eyes wide with urgency. "There's a crowd outside. And they're not here to celebrate."

A knot of fear tightened in my chest. Whatever was happening, it felt monumental, like the ground beneath us was about to shift. My heart raced as I followed Laura out of the shop, the festive energy dissolving into a tense uncertainty that gripped my throat.

As we stepped outside, the scene that awaited us was far more chaotic than I could have imagined. A gathering of locals had formed, their faces a mix of anger and confusion. Signs waved in the air, some scrawled with phrases I couldn't quite make out, but the sentiment was clear—this was not a celebration; it was a protest.

"What is going on?" I whispered, my heart pounding as I surveyed the crowd.

Max stepped up beside me, his expression tense. "This can't be about us, can it?"

But just then, someone in the crowd shouted something I couldn't catch, and the murmurs grew louder, echoing back toward us, pulling me into the whirlwind of uncertainty.

I turned to Oliver, who stood rigid beside us, his earlier charm replaced with a calculating coolness. "What did you do?" I demanded, my voice barely above a whisper.

His gaze flickered to the crowd, then back to me, a hint of amusement playing at the corners of his mouth. "Let's just say the stakes have just gotten higher."

My breath caught in my throat as the realization hit me

Chapter 29: The Moment of Truth

The day dawned with a hesitant light, casting a golden hue across the cluttered workspace of our chocolatier, which seemed to mirror my tumultuous thoughts. As I stared at the shelves lined with glistening confections—each piece an explosion of color and flavor—anxiety curled around my insides like a viper. The scent of melted chocolate wafted through the air, rich and enticing, but today it felt heavy, almost oppressive, as if it too could sense the gravity of what was to come. I could hear the faint crackle of tempering chocolate in the back, a comforting sound I had grown to love, yet now it felt like a countdown clock, ticking away the seconds until our fate would be sealed.

Oliver, with his smooth confidence, was pacing in the back room, his hands gesticulating animatedly as he rehearsed his pitch. He was a master of charm, that much was clear; the way he could weave a story around every flavor, every technique, was captivating. I had always admired his ambition, but today it felt like a blade cutting through the fabric of what we had built. The thought made my chest ache. I turned to Max, who was meticulously arranging a display of our newest truffles, his brow furrowed in concentration. His eyes met mine, and in that instant, we shared an unspoken understanding—a pact, perhaps—of what was at stake.

"What if he sells out to someone else?" I whispered, a hint of desperation creeping into my voice. The idea of someone else taking our creation, our dream, and twisting it into something unrecognizable felt like a visceral blow.

Max sighed, his shoulders slumping slightly as he placed a hand on my arm. "We'll fight for it, Harper. We have to. Remember why we started this in the first place."

His words hung in the air, heavy yet filled with a flicker of hope. I nodded, taking a deep breath as I focused on the task ahead. The room we entered for the meeting was sleek and sterile, adorned with polished wood and minimalist décor. It felt so different from our cozy shop, where the walls were lined with the stories of our adventures and laughter. The table in the center felt imposing, a barrier between us and our dreams.

As Oliver launched into his presentation, detailing his grand vision for our chocolatier, I tried to tune into his words, but they slid past me like melted chocolate running off a mold—sweet yet ultimately ephemeral. His charisma filled the room, but underneath his smooth exterior, I could sense a current of something more ruthless, an eagerness to seize control that sent my heart racing.

"We have the opportunity to expand," he said, his voice dipping into that velvety tone that had always made my knees weak. "Imagine opening branches in every major city, our brand becoming synonymous with luxury chocolates."

The thought of losing our identity in a sea of commercialism made my stomach churn. "But what about our community?" I interjected, my voice unexpectedly firm. "We built this place on relationships, on the connections we foster with our customers. Isn't that worth protecting?"

Oliver's eyes flickered, but he quickly masked his surprise with a well-practiced smile. "Of course, but think of the exposure! We can reach so many more people, share our craft with the world."

I turned to Max, who sat beside me, a frown etched across his face. This was our moment. I could feel the pulse of the shop behind us, the customers who had come to love our creations, the joy we infused into every truffle, every bar.

"Oliver, what you're proposing is a betrayal of what we've built," I said, my voice shaking with emotion. "We're not just a product; we're a story, a feeling. Our customers don't just come here for chocolate; they come for the experience, for the love we pour into every piece. You can't just... strip that away for profit."

The silence that followed was palpable, each breath feeling like a small rebellion. Oliver's smile faltered, and for the first time, he looked uncertain. I pressed on, feeling the weight of our dreams pushing me forward.

"We have the chance to create something truly special. Let's not lose sight of what that is. We owe it to ourselves, to our community."

As I finished, I looked around the room, taking in the faces of those who had gathered. They were more than just investors; they were the heartbeat of our chocolatier. I saw nods of agreement, the subtle shifts in posture that indicated I wasn't alone in this fight. A flicker of hope ignited within me, illuminating the shadows of doubt.

In that moment, I realized I wasn't merely fighting for a business; I was fighting for a home, a family forged through flour and sugar, joy and sweat. The walls of our shop echoed with laughter, with memories of shared dreams and countless late nights spent perfecting recipes. I was determined not to let that slip away without a fight.

The atmosphere in the room shifted, a palpable tension replacing the initial excitement. It was no longer just Oliver's polished presentation; it had transformed into a battlefield for our dreams. I exchanged glances with Max, who squeezed my hand under the table, a silent vow of support. The stakes had never felt higher, but with each passing moment, I grew more resolute. This was it—the moment of truth where we would either redefine our future or let it slip away like sand through our fingers.

The air in the meeting room crackled with an intensity that felt almost electric. As Oliver's smooth pitch hung in the air like a heady aroma, I sensed the simmering discomfort beneath the surface, the tension coiling like a tightly wound spring. Max sat resolutely by my side, his presence a comforting anchor amidst the turbulence. I could practically hear the gears turning in the minds of our potential investors, their faces revealing nothing but a practiced neutrality. It was a game of poker, and I was determined to play my hand with conviction.

"Let's be honest, Oliver," I said, my voice steady yet laced with an underlying urgency. "Expansion sounds fantastic on paper, but it runs the risk of diluting what we've worked so hard to create. We're not just a business; we're part of a community. Our customers aren't simply numbers; they are the heartbeat of this place."

Oliver's brow furrowed slightly, the confident façade cracking ever so slightly. "I understand the sentiment, Harper, but can't you see the bigger picture? With the right funding, we could transform our little shop into something monumental. We could be the next big name in chocolate."

"Monumental is a lovely word," I retorted, fighting against the urge to roll my eyes, "but I'd rather be a cherished local secret than a soulless brand known for its mass-produced confections. Remember our first festival? The way we attracted families and made connections? That's what makes us special."

"I thought we were past the sentimentality phase," he countered, leaning forward, his eyes narrowing. "You're going to have to let go of that if you want to see growth."

Before I could respond, Max interjected, his tone as smooth as the tempered chocolate we worked with daily. "Growth doesn't have to mean losing our roots. It can mean reaching new heights while staying grounded in our community. We've spent years cultivating relationships that matter. We can't just toss them aside for a shiny new storefront."

A ripple of murmurs spread through the room, and I couldn't help but feel a surge of gratitude for Max's unwavering support. Our partnership had always been built on mutual respect and a shared vision, but today, as we faced Oliver's ambitious plans, it felt more vital than ever.

The investors exchanged glances, some nodding slowly as they considered Max's words. I felt a flicker of hope igniting within me, urging me to press on. "This isn't just about chocolate," I continued, my voice rising with passion. "It's about love, creativity, and the heart we pour into every truffle. It's about those families who come in to celebrate milestones, who return to relive memories forged over shared sweetness. Are we really willing to gamble that for a faceless corporation?"

Oliver's demeanor shifted slightly, the flash of irritation on his face giving way to something else—perhaps a glimmer of realization. "But think about the exposure," he argued, though his voice wavered slightly. "Imagine being featured in national publications, being known beyond this town. We could bring in artists, host workshops—create something truly unique."

"Yes, and we could also lose the essence of who we are in the process," I shot back, sensing the room's shifting dynamics. "Artistry isn't just about scale; it's about the story we tell, the community we foster. If we chase fame at the cost of our heart, what's left?"

Oliver opened his mouth to counter, but a soft voice from the back of the room interrupted. "Harper makes a valid point," said Jenna, one of the quieter investors who had always been supportive of our local efforts. "Authenticity matters. In a world driven by trends and fads, genuine connection is what stands out."

I felt a surge of adrenaline. Jenna's support felt like an unexpected lifeline, a sign that perhaps I wasn't alone in this fight. The room buzzed with murmurs of agreement, and for a moment, the atmosphere shifted from one of hostility to collaboration.

"That's all well and good," Oliver replied, but I could hear the strain in his voice. "But we have to be practical. This is a business."

"Exactly," Max chimed in, "and we have to be smart about how we navigate this. We can think outside the box without losing our identity. Let's explore partnerships that enhance our mission, not compromise it."

As the conversation flowed, I leaned back, allowing my thoughts to drift momentarily to our journey—the late nights spent perfecting recipes, the laughter that filled the kitchen as we experimented with flavors, and the warmth that enveloped us when our creations brought smiles to our customers' faces. Those memories felt like a foundation I could stand on, solid and unyielding against the winds of change.

"Maybe we could consider a compromise," I suggested, feeling emboldened. "What if we focus on local partnerships, collaborate with nearby artisans? We could expand our offerings without sacrificing our core values. The right collaborators could bring freshness without losing our essence."

The investors looked thoughtful, murmuring among themselves. I caught a glimpse of Oliver's expression, a mix of annoyance and intrigue. He had never considered that our expansion could be rooted in collaboration rather than outright takeover.

Max leaned in closer, his warmth radiating as he spoke. "Let's explore this together. There are plenty of ways to grow while still honoring our roots. A collaboration could bring us new audiences without overwhelming our current community."

The tension in the room gradually dissipated, the ice beginning to thaw as Oliver's frustration transformed into contemplation. "I suppose we could explore this angle," he said slowly, measuring his words. "But I want assurances that we're moving forward with a growth mindset."

"Then let's find a way to align our visions," I urged, a fresh wave of hope washing over me. "We can build something beautiful together, but we need to prioritize our values."

As we continued to discuss potential avenues for collaboration, I felt a shift within myself. It was more than just a meeting; it was a reckoning. Each idea exchanged felt like a brick laid in the foundation of a renewed dream. I glanced at Max, who wore a triumphant smile, and I couldn't help but mirror it. This was our moment—an opportunity to redefine what our chocolatier could be while staying true to the heart that beat within its walls.

Oliver's initial plans began to morph, reshaped by the rhythm of our passion and the voices of those who believed in the artistry of our craft. It felt as if the air around us was transforming, filled with possibility. I leaned back in my chair, feeling the tension ease, ready to embrace whatever twists awaited us ahead.

With each passing moment, the atmosphere in the meeting room felt increasingly charged, a mixture of trepidation and anticipation threading through the air like the delicate ribbons of melted chocolate we often used in our designs. Oliver leaned back, a hint of frustration flickering in his eyes, but it was clear he was re-evaluating his stance. The investors' murmurs faded into a soft hum, their gazes flitting between him and us, as if caught in a tug-of-war between ambition and authenticity.

"Okay," Oliver finally said, his voice steady but tinged with annoyance. "Let's say we entertain the idea of local collaborations. What does that look like practically? We can't just throw our hands in the air and hope for the best."

Max shifted slightly in his chair, a look of determination flickering across his face. "It starts with our existing connections. We can reach out to local farmers for fresh ingredients and partner with nearby artisans for cross-promotions. Imagine an event where we feature local wines paired with our truffles—celebrating community flavors while introducing new clientele."

I could see Oliver's expression soften slightly at the mention of an event, a glimmer of interest breaking through the stoic exterior. "Events could bring in a good crowd. But what's to stop them from just visiting for the wine and not returning for the chocolate?"

I leaned forward, adrenaline surging through me. "Because we won't just offer them chocolate; we'll offer an experience. A story behind each flavor that ties back to our community. Each truffle can represent a local farmer, each bar a memory shared with our customers."

The investors nodded, their interest piqued. Oliver crossed his arms, his mind clearly racing. "Fine, let's say we move forward with this. How do we ensure that the essence of our chocolatier doesn't get lost in the frenzy of expansion?"

Max caught my eye, a spark of camaraderie igniting between us. "By keeping the heart of our operations in the shop. We can implement a mentorship program for aspiring chocolatiers from the area. They'll learn from us, and we can inspire them to create unique flavors that tell their stories."

"Now we're getting somewhere," Oliver admitted, a slight smile breaking through. "But this requires commitment. You both need to be on board, ready to work double the hours to keep things afloat."

"I'm ready," I declared, adrenaline coursing through me. "But not if it means sacrificing our principles. We'll build something that honors our roots, not just profit margins."

The conversation flowed seamlessly, ideas bouncing back and forth like chocolate truffles tossed in a bowl, each one more delicious than the last. We discussed everything from sustainable sourcing to creative events that could draw in the local crowd while ensuring our shop remained a haven for those who had supported us from the start.

As the meeting progressed, I felt the initial tension melt away, replaced by a sense of collaboration that had seemed so elusive just moments before. I could sense the investors warming to our vision, their nods and murmurs of approval creating a melody of hope in the room. Oliver appeared to be letting go of some of his rigid ideas, engaging with our suggestions, his charisma shifting from a weapon to a tool.

Then, as we wrapped up the conversation, the mood shifted again. A knock at the door echoed sharply, slicing through the warm buzz of possibility. Everyone turned, surprised, and the door swung open to reveal Jenna, her expression a mixture of urgency and concern.

"Sorry to interrupt," she said, her voice tinged with anxiety. "But there's something you all need to know."

The room fell silent as she stepped inside, the weight of her presence heavy with unspoken tension. Oliver's brows furrowed, and I felt my heart drop. What could be so important that it warranted this interruption?

"What is it?" he asked, an edge creeping into his tone.

Jenna glanced around, her gaze landing on me and Max, before returning to Oliver. "I just received a call from the local health inspector. They've received an anonymous tip about potential health code violations in our shop."

My stomach dropped, a lead weight crashing to the bottom of my gut. "What? That's impossible!" I exclaimed, my voice tinged with disbelief. "We've passed inspections with flying colors!"

"True," Jenna replied, her voice steady but urgent. "But the inspector is required to follow up on every report, no matter how unfounded. They're coming for an inspection today."

The room buzzed with murmurs of concern, the warmth of collaboration evaporating like steam from a hot cup of cocoa. My mind raced as I recalled our recent shipments, the late nights in the kitchen, and the unexpected hiccups we had managed to navigate. Had we missed something?

Oliver's expression darkened, and for the first time, I saw genuine worry etched into his features. "We can't afford any negative press right now. If this gets out... it could ruin everything."

"Let's not jump to conclusions," I interjected, feeling the panic rise in my chest. "We need to gather the team and address this head-on. We can show them our processes, our cleanliness standards. We can prove there's nothing to worry about."

As I spoke, determination surged within me. We had fought too hard for this dream to let it slip away over a rumor.

Oliver nodded, his resolve returning. "You're right. Let's rally the team, make sure everything is in order. If we're diligent, we can turn this around."

Max leaned in, his hand brushing mine under the table, offering silent support. "We've handled everything thrown our way so far. This is just another challenge. We can do this."

Just as I began to feel a flicker of hope, Jenna's phone buzzed, and she glanced down, her expression shifting to one of disbelief. "Oh no... there's more," she whispered, her eyes widening. "They've received multiple reports. The inspector will be here shortly."

Panic rose in the room, tightening its grip around my throat. "Multiple reports?" I echoed, my voice trembling. "Who would do this? Why would someone try to sabotage us like this?"

Jenna shook her head, her brows knitting in concern. "I don't know, but we need to prepare for the worst. If this is intentional, we could be facing something much larger than a simple inspection."

My mind raced, an avalanche of possibilities tumbling through my thoughts. Was this truly an act of sabotage? Who would want to tear down the very heart of our chocolatier? The answer eluded me, but one thing was clear—this was no longer just about our dream; it was about survival.

As the door clicked shut behind Jenna, sealing off the outside world, I turned to Max, my heart pounding in my chest. The stakes had just risen, and with them, a sense of urgency coursed through me. We had fought to protect our creation, and now, it felt as though we were standing on the precipice of a new battle.

The inspector's footsteps echoed in the hall, a reminder that time was running out. As the tension coiled tighter around us, I knew we had to act fast. Failure wasn't an option—not when everything we had built was at stake. The questions gnawed at me, relentless and cold. Who was behind this? And more importantly, what would happen if we couldn't prove our worth in time?

Milton Keynes UK
Ingram Content Group UK Ltd.
UKHW041821201024
449814UK00001B/39

9 798227 127457